Tall Tales of the Devil's Apron

HERBERT MAYNOR SUTHERLAND

JOHNSON CITY, TENNESSEE

Original Copyright 1970
Reprinted with Index 1988
ISBN 0-932807-27-5
Copyright © 1988 by The Overmountain Press
All Rights Reserved
Printed in the United States of America

2 3 4 5 6 7 8 9 0

Table of Contents

Introduction 3
My First Visit to the Devil's Apron 5
Preacher Carries Samples With Him 11
Four and a Half and Four and a Half Makes Nine 14
Hosshead Bill 18
Who's Been Hyer Since I've Been Gone? 21
New Preacher Gets Bible Mixed Up 24
Taste of Iron and Leather 27
Pokey Joe Blowed First 30
Pointers and Setters 33
She Ain't Got No Mule 36
Fiesty Britches and Dirty-Butt 39
Toddy and the Pot 42
Taking A Drink At Gunpoint 45
Little Ike Picks Chickens 48
Whut Did Paul Say? 51
Dog Breaks Neck From Admiration 54
The Thawed Out Foxrace 57
Paw Traipsin' in Heaven in His Shirt-Tail 60
Business Bill's Cats Head for the Dirt 63
Maw Ate Wild Onions 66
Rosella and the Parsnips 69
Framing Grandma's Picture 72
Sin-Sockin' Sam's Coatail 75
Hungry Jim Sets Up In His Coffin 78
Thar Ain't No Hell 81
The Watch-Dog Rattlesnake 84
Too Poor To Keep A Cow 87
Scratching the Bull's Stomach 90
Business Bill Gives Lesson To the Bull at the Fair 93
That Makes Onct 96
Little 'Bijie Gets the Rabies 100
Good 'Lige Rescues Drowning Girl 103
Aunt Poll and the Sweet Potatoes 106
Little Toddy and George Washington 109
Persimmon Beer 113
Nine Forks and a Hand 116
Same Thing For Supper Last Night 119

Forgot To Hitch Mules To Plow	122
Good 'Lige Gets Religion	125
Couldn't Hold His Water	128
Lying Luke's Reputation	131
Uncle Hezzykiah and the Shotgun Wedding	134
Willie B.'s News	138
Brandy Bill and the Yeller Corn	141
Fresh Goose	144
Good 'Lige Hides From the Lawd	147
Heavenly Music from the Hounds	150
Didamey Jane Lights on Pile of Manure	153
The Teacher's Experiment	156
Snowdy Jane and the Skin Graft	160
The Fastest Hogs on the Apron	163
Mixed Medicines	166
The Original Lazy Man	169
Bad 'Lige and the First Automobile	172
Good 'Lige Suggests A Second Marriage	175
Good 'Lige Holds A Royal Flush	178
A Really Hot Summer	181
Aunt Serrepthy Gets Baptised	184
The Alcoholic Cure	187
Mule Eggs	190
The Prize Was A Groundhog	194
A Ten Dollar Mule	197
A Seated Horse Upon A Rock	201
Bad 'Lige Shoots A Ghost	204
Kissing the North End of a Mule	207
Little Toddy and the Constitution	210
Polly Ann Gets A Divorce	213
To Smell Like A Man	216
The Tornado	219
Brandy Bill Goes A'courtin	222
King Solomon's Diet	225
Was I Thar?	228
The Incense Pot	231
A Far Piece From Home	234
The Egg Beatin' Cyclone	237
Sophygene and Her Half-Brothers	240
Old Hide and Taller	243

The Reluctant Son-In-Law	246
The Hounds and the Fiddle	249
Little Sooner and the Ironing Board	252
Big Foot and the Rattler	255
Uncle Iry's Transmigration	259
The Hardworking Hen	262
More About Farming and Less About Preaching	265
Willie B. and the Cookoo Clock	268
Little 'Bijie Flavors the Gravy	271
Brandy Bill and the Churn	274
Getting the Crop Before the Fencing	277
Brandy Bill Tests 'Bijie's Special Brandy	280
Bad 'Lige Falls In A Grave	283
The Echo	286
A New Breed of Turkeys	289
Nailing the Roof on the Fog	292
The King of the Cold Trailers	296
The Peach Tree Deer	299
Pearls Before Swine	302
Constantinople	305
'Bijie's Path to Education	308
It Could Have Been Worse	311

Introduction

Dickenson County, Virginia, is the locale of these *Tales Of The Devil's Apron*. The county lies in the Appalachian Plateau in the extreme southwest area of Virginia. The Cumberland Mountains are on the northern border between Kentucky and Virginia. The entire county is hilly and rugged, broken by many streams in deep narrow valleys.

The first white people to come into the area were trappers and hunters, attracted by the plentiful game. One of the hunters is said to have been Daniel Boone. The pioneers who settled the Plateau were of hardy stock. Although game was plentiful, the forests were dense, the area isolated and living conditions difficult.

Because of their isolation, these pioneers had to be self-sufficient. They built themselves log cabins, cleared small "patches" of ground fit for tilling and little contact was made with the surrounding area. They raised their crops by digging the seeds into the hillsides. The grains produced were ground locally into flour and meal, with a portion always set aside to be made into "moonshine". It was commonplace for "stills" to be operated and the "gatherings" were enlivened by the home-made liquor resultant.

Grist mills were built along the streams and the settlers took their grain to these mills to be ground. The mills themselves became gathering places for the men folk, old and young. Here tales were swapped, the latest news and gossip exchanged, drinks enjoyed and a sense of community felt.

Religion played a big part in the lives of the early

settlers. "Meetins" were held in the homes until the neighbors could "raise a churchhouse". The preachers were usually settlers who were self ordained. Each interpreted the scripture in his own manner and there were many religious "sects". The same group who imbibed at the mills also attended the church "meetins".

As time went on, the descendants of the early pioneers continued many of the customs of their ancestors. They told their children the same folk tales, sang the same ballads and retained much of the dialect of the late Elizabethan era. They were independent, freedom loving, God-fearing and clannish. People from outside the mountains they considered "furriners".

Even today, men like those the author describes and quotes can still be found in the "Devil's Apron" and in other sections of the Dickenson County of which he writes. Their language is little different from that of their pioneer forebears and their outlook on life much the same.

My First Visit to the Devil's Apron

My first Visit to the Devil's Apron came at a time when I was working on a New York newspaper and had a chance to go back home on a vacation. All through my boyhood I had heard of the place but because of its inaccessibility I had never ventured over there despite the fascination of its strange name and the legend of its origin.

According to one of its denizens it had been named many generations ago when the Devil was moving Hell across the Cumberland mountains from Virginia into Kentucky. Satan was carrying the whole thing in a huge green leather apron but just before he reached Pound river he stubbed his toe, fell down, broke an apronstring and spilled hell all over the place. It had been called the Devil's Apron ever since.

Back in New York, a week before I left, some of the boys on the rewrite desk had asked me to bring them some of the famous "mountain dew" moonshine when I returned. They had heard of it often but never tasted it, Prohibition being still in force. So I had promised to try and find some.

Arriving in town soon afterward, I was told by some of my old boyhood friends that I might be able to get a quart or two from a certain Bad 'Lige Cantwell over on No-Business Creek up from Pound river on the Apron; and further, if I was lucky, might just be able to get some "backed and doubled" malt corn liquor or apple brandy, too.

It was June, and Pound River, over near the Devil's Apron, had long been one of my favorite fishing streams. So I got out an old rod and reel and drove over to Pound

River a day later and fished for an hour or so but with indifferent luck. Then I walked up the road on No-Business Creek where I had been told to locate Bad 'Lige.

Everything was serene and peaceful as I approached the Devil's Apron area and if there were any activities on the part of moonshiners or revenue agents I could see no indications of them. Soon, however, I came up to a small cabin in a clearing beside the road, and on the porch several bearded hillmen were sitting, staring silently in my direction with several gaunt hounds sleeping in the shade beside them.

A couple of high-powered rifles were leaning against the wall in back of them so I came to an abrupt halt. Apparently it was open season on suspicious characters who might be revenue officers and I was fearful that I might be placed in that category. Nevertheless I summoned up all my courage and walked boldly forward. The group sat motionless and silent and no one made a move for his gun. Just the same it made chills creep up my spine although I was perspiring freely at the same time. It was about two o'clock in the afternoon and I was hungry so I decided to call upon that as an excuse. However they gave no hint of a welcome as I entered the yard and it was not until several years later that I learned their names.

They were Good 'Lige and Bad 'Lige Cantwell — cousins, with little else in common — Brandy Bill Hopkins who operated the gristmill where the men of the Devil's Apron met regularly on Saturdays, Business Bill Mullins, Little 'Bijie Birdsong and among others a Willie B. Fuller once a brilliant trial lawyer across the line in Kentucky but at the moment a resident of the Apron where he was living in an uninterrupted alcoholic daze. Incidentally, as I found out later, Good 'Lige was the pastor of the Hard-Rock Firm Foundation Church and leader of the No-Heller faction of the old Hardshell Baptist Church in that neighborhood. He had been dubbed Good 'Lige to distinguish him from his moonshining cousin.

I drew near the steps.

"Howdy!" I greeted the group as affably as I could. "My name's Sutherland from over in town. I'm looking for a Mister 'Lige Cantwell."

"Yeah," growled one of them whom I rightly took for Bad 'Lige. "We know ye. Whut ye want?"

"I've been fishing," I told him, "but I didn't bring any lunch with me. I wondered might I get something to eat?"

"Hey, Maw!" Bad 'Lige bellowed at the top of his voice, looking out toward a field where a woman was plowing behind a small mule. "Ye've got compn'y," he shouted, and the woman obediently unhitched the mule and came to the house.

"Thus hyer feller wants somethin' to eat," he explained as she stepped up on the porch. "Fix him some vittels."

During the next twenty minutes I tried as best I could to start a conversation with the group but for the most part they were silent. Occasionally one of them would reply to a question with an affirmative or negative grunt of whose meaning I could only guess. In a little while the woman called me into the kitchen and I sat down at a table that was literally loaded with food, including a platter of the best country ham I ever tasted.

I tried to talk to her while I ate.

"This is a beautiful country," I declared. "I don't believe I ever saw a finer place. Timbered hills, rippling brooks and the rhododendron in full bloom. Must be a wonderful place to live."

"Wonnerful, huh!" she snorted. "It's shore fine fer men and dawgs but it's pyore hell on mules and wimmin."

Well, I got the moonshine and the apple brandy and an introduction to a group of men whose lasting friendship eventually provided me with an understanding of what life must have been like to our early pioneers and still is in parts of Appalachia.

In fact, of all the men I grew to know on the Devil's Apron only the alcoholic Kentucky lawyer remained a comparative stranger year after year, until one day after I had acquired the local county paper I received a letter from him addressed to my office. It said:

"Dear Editor;

"I notice from time to time that you seem to take a special delight in publishing articles in regard to the drinking habits and propensities of the inhabitants of this section, known to many as the "Devil's Apron". Judging by the tone of your writings, I gather that it is your considered opinion that the men over here spend practically all of their time imbibing the "mountain dew" for which these hills are justly famous.

"It is quite true that some of us, when we feel so inclined, do partake of a medicinal toddy made from the finest old apple brandy that ever soothed a man's palate, or from pure malted corn, backed and doubled in the manner our forefathers made and loved. We consider that modern "sugar-top" concoction that goes by the name of moonshine to be an abomination in our sight and we will not tolerate it.

"But to be perfectly honest with you, I have on my desk before me as I sit at my typewriter, a bottle of the finest appplejack that was ever distilled in the purpled shadows of the age-old Cumberlands. I can close my eyes and smell the sweet odor of the apple-blossoms, and even hear the songs of the little birds whose music went into the soul of this applejack. I can detect the smell of ripening mellow apples as they are carefully gathered and stored away for Thanksgiving pies and Christmas toddies and eggnog.

"In a moment I shall take a moderate drink of this ambrosia, and if it meets with my palpitant anticipations, I shall probably take another. It is my sincere and confirmed belief that for anyone to attempt to stop me would be an invasion of my personal liberties which I will deeply resent. I have tasted a few drops of this brandy, and I am convinced that by so doing I have not in any manner invaded the rights of any other person on earth.

"Just to show you that I don't give a hang how much you talk about us fellows over here in the Devil's Apron, I have taken another drink of this aforesaid highly medicinal brandy, and I will say to you that it is just about the smoothest concoction that ever trickled down a man's gullet. This second drink, or maybe it's the third, makes me feel that I don't give a whoop what you say or who you say it to.

"Now, Mr. Editor, I, and my buddies over hear, ain't bumn, and you can&t make us bums. I like a little drinl now and thwn as I said before, and as I will repeat if I want to anf when I want to. I have tajen a third drink, and maybe a fourth, and I am more than ever convimced that I have done nothing to whivh any man can take exception to whatever.

"If Me and the boys wan't to get togeser on satirday night to have us a little fun, and if we take a few drinls and don&t harm nobpdy but ourselfs then what I say is that it ain't noboy's bizness, no matter if he thinls it is his. That&s the way I feel abouy it.

"I wan&t to sa to yyiu that this likker is all rught. A lot of it wouldnT do on np harm. When we need stimulay we need it. My Granfyer wus broughr up on moobshine an' had it in the house al the time. He drunk it freelu, an even the Ministew dranj it when he coom to our housee. It&s a prettu kind of a cointry when a grabson is bettre than his gunfaher. I can drink this kind of brandu all day and nit be no worse a cicozen than I was befote. I could drink this hole quaet aud negger bat a etelashe.

"Bue whay I weant of yiou is to remund yio thqt you arw wronb obcr againain and agnian thqt you arw wronb ib comfsing evert bony whu drinkd as a bougm. We ain&t crimials.

Rexcevtfilly Yiotdx, O8Bd.srff.
wILLIE b. fULLER."

Once I had finished his letter I lost no time in seeking him out, and since then our relations have become very pleasant.

Preacher Carries Samples With Him

Perhaps you remember me mentioning that Little 'Bijie Birdsong was one of the original group I met on Bad 'Lige's porch those many years ago. Well, he's still around. He came to town the other day and dropped in at my office to kill an hour or so while he waited for a ride back to the Devil's Apron with Business Bill. And while he was here he told me another of his stories about Good 'Lige.

"Ever hear," he asked, "about the time ol' Sin-Sockin' Sam Tolliver and him rassled with the sperrits out thar in the Moonshine Flats?"

I acknowledged that I hadn't.

"Wall," said Little 'Bijie, "this hyer tuck place soon atter the ol' church was split both ways from the jack betwixt the Hellers and the NoHellers — musta been all of twenty five years ago. As ye know, Good 'Lige become the head of the No-Hellers but Sin-Sockin' Sam stayed on and was leader of the Heller believers. Ye see, in the beginnin' Good 'Lige he'd a been the reg'ler preacher at the Hard-Rock Firm-Founda-shun Church since it was fu'st built, and he hisself had allus preached Heller doctrun of e-tarnal punishment in a lake of fire an' brimstone forevermore. But about the time of the big bust-up he said he'd sorty got to thinkin' about it, an' changed sides. He figgered that a man ketched e-nuf hell in this worl' to pay fer all his sins, an' it was onlawful to try a man twict fer the same crime. Anyhow he soon diskivvered that the good brethern an' sistern liked that doctrinem an' it wasn't long ontel he'd done filled his meeting'-house 'til it was bu'stin' at the seams.

"On t'other han', ol' Sin-Sockin' Sam he rented the ol' Lost Meetin'-House thar at the forks of No-Bizz'ness Crick an he started out a-preachin' hellfire an' dam-mashun fer who laid the chunk. An' when he was in a big way, a-preachin' a-bout the awful sufferin' an' sizzlin' in hell fer all time to come, he shore could make the wimmin shout an' the men moan an' groan an' carry-on, an' he nigh a-bout skeered ever'body to death.

"It wasn't long ontel the Sin-Socker was a-takin' a-way some of Good 'Lige's flock, an' the longer it went on the fewer Good 'Lige was a-preachin' to. All of this kinda got Good 'Lige worried an' it looked like he was a-goin' to lose ever' member he had. It reached the p'int whar, when he got up in his pulpit to preach thar wasn't more'n a dozen folks on han' to hyer him, so he figgered it was high time to do somethin' a-bout it.

"So the next time ol' Sin-Sockin' Sam preached at his church, Good 'Lige was right thar a-settin' in the A-men corner, a-lissenin' fer all he was wu'th. When the Sin-Socker fu'st got up to preach, he tol' 'em he was a-goin' to give 'em four-hoss hell, an' that's egg-zackly whut he done. It was a-bout the skeeriest thing I ever heerd in all my life.

"When he'd finished an' the shoutin' an' carryin's-on had sorty died down, Good 'Lige tackled the Sin-Socker on his hellfire doctrine, an' in a few minnits they was in it hammer an' tongs, each one a-tryin' to prove by the Bible that he was right.

"It didn't take 'em long to diskivver that they wasn't a-gittin' no whar a-tall in their argy-ment. In fact, the longer they talked the wu'ss apart they got, an' they had the whole crowd a-standin' a-roun' not missin' none of it.

"'I'll tell ye whu le's do,' says Good 'Lige atter a while. 'Le's jest the two of us go back up thar in the woods, an' talk this hyer bizz'ness out. We can argy an' preach to each other, an' we can offer up our pra'rs, an' mebbe the sperrits'll tell us which is right. An' we won't leave them woods ontel we've got it settled onct an' fer all.'

"Ol' Sin-Sockin' Sam he tuck him up on that idee, an' they walked out thar in them Moonshine Flats an' locked horns. Thar wasn't nobody thar but them two, accordin' to whut Good 'Lige tol' me atterwards, an' it must a-been somethin' to see an' hyer. They didn't have no grub, an' they didn't have no shelter, an' it was a-gittin' late in the fall an' the nights was purty cold.

"Fer three days an' nights they preached an' they prayed, an' they argy-ed, but one was jest as stubborn as t'other'n, an' all they done was git madder an' madder. Good 'Lige said that he figgered he could a-stood the cold all right, but atter a couple of days he got so hongry he couldn't think of nothin' but vittels. They gnawed some sassy-fack, an' birch bark, but that didn't do no good, an' they was both jest a-bout starved out.

"Sin-Sockin' Sam he went out thar in the woods an' dug up a few Indian turnips, an' de-vided 'em with Good 'Lige. Now, ef'n ye've never tried to eat a Indian turnip, ye've shore missed somethin'. They're jest a-bout forty times hotter'n the hell they was a-preachin' about.

"Anyhow, Good 'Lige he bit into one of 'em, an' the tears come to his eyes, an' he plum lost his breath.

" 'Sam, he sputtered, 'I figger yore doctrine is a firm be-lief in everlastin' punishment in a lake of fire an' brimstone, ain't it?'

" 'That's kee-reck!' says Sam.

" 'Wall, I'll be durned,' says Good 'Lige, 'ef'n ye ain't the fu'st preacher I ever knowed who carried his samples a-roun' with him.' "

Four and a Half and Four and a Half Makes Nine

Between showers one Saturday afternoon last month Brandy Bill and Bad 'Lige dropped into my office, and both of them appeared to be in a rather gloomy state of mind. Neither had much to say, and for the most part sat and stared through the window at the steady drizzle.

"You fellows seem to be a bit under the weather," I said, offering them stogies which they accepted with nods of appreciation. "You look like you've lost your best friend."

"We durn nigh have," admitted Bad 'Lige. "It's Leetle 'Bijie an' Willie B."

"Why, what's wrong with them? Have they gone somewhere?"

"No, they're still a-roun', but the trubbel is their wives air a-keepin' their noses to the grindstone all the time, an' the funny part is that they 'peer to like it."

"Why, I thought the honeymoon was over with both of them," I observed. "They've both been married for several months now, haven't they? Let's see now! When did Little 'Bijie marry Snowdy Jane?"

"A-bout five months ago," replied Brandy Bill with a chuckle. "They've been a-gittin' a-long jest fine — er was ontel A'nt Hellfirey, Snowdy Jane's mother, come to stay with 'em fer a while—."

"Aunt what?" I demanded, sitting up in my reclining chair.

"A'nt Hellfirey," repeated Brandy Bill. "Her name's Elvirey, but be-kaze of her sharp tongue an' the fact that she's allus in a racket with somebody er t'other, she's knowed all over the Apern as 'A'nt Hellfirey', an I must say, it fits her to a tee-wighty.

"She's up thar now at 'Bijie's a-lookin' atter the baby—."

"Baby " I ejaculated. "But—but—but."

"Egg-zackly," grinned Brandy Bill. "It was borned last Satt'eday night, wasn't it?" he asked of Bad 'Lige, and the latter nodded in assent.

"Ye see, Leetle 'Bijie got him a job a-workin' at a sawmill over on Beefhide Crick in Kaintucky to sorty tide him over the winter months, an' he's been at home jest on Satte'day nights an' Sundays.

"Whilst he was a-way frum home thataway, A'nt Hellfirey has been a-stayin' with Snowdy Jane. Ever' time A'nt Hellfirey shows up at his place, Leetle 'Bijie he manages to take off some'rs er t'other. Ain't nobody but Snowdy Jane can git a-long with that woman nohow.

"Wall, it seems as though last Sunday Snowdy Jane she got to feelin' purty pyorely, an' Leetle 'Bijie stayed down at my place most of the day. Whut with Snowdy Jane a-complainin', an' A'nt Hellfirey a-raisin' cane, he jest couldn't take it. But atter supper he went on back up home bekaze he was worried some a-bout Snowdy Jane, an' said as how he'd sleep in the barn that night an' git him a early start back to work on Monday mornin'.

"I reckon A'nt Hellfirey seed him as he clum' up to the barn loft be-kaze a-long a-bout midnight, she come a-bustin' outta the house an' headed towarge the barn, a-yellin' fer Lettle 'Bijie at ever' jump. An' Lettle 'Bijie come mighty nigh a-fallin' outta the barn loft a-figgerin' Snowdy Jane was a-dyin'.

" 'Snowdy's time done come,' she yells. 'She's a-fixin' to have a baby,' she hollers. 'Git over thar to town, an' git that doctor as quick as the Lawd'll let ye.'

"Leetle 'Bijie he made a dive into thestall an' throwed a saddle on that leetle dun mule of his — the one he calls

Pokey Joe — an' he headed fer town, a-frailin' hell outta that mule at ever' jump.

"Now, Pokey Joe he wasn't ust to sich fast runnin' as that, but he tore down No-Bizz-ness Crick a mile a minnit. It had all happened so quick that Leetle 'Bijie he hadn't had no time to do any thinkin' a-bout it a-tall. It was all he could do to stick on Pokey Joe's back nohow.

"Purty soon they hit that ford acrost Poun' River all spraddled out, but a-bout the middle of the ford Pokey Joe de-cided that he wanted a drink, so he stopped dead in his tracks. 'Bijie let him drink, an' sorty got to thinkin' things over.

" 'Pokey Joe,' says he, 'le's sorty figger things out fer a minnit.' So he sot thar in the saddle, an', accordin' to whut he tol' me later, he got to figgerin' back a leetle.

" 'Le's see,' he says, 'it was in A-prile that me an' Snowdy Jane got married — A-prile the twenty-fu'st. An' this hyer's the twenty sixth day of August. Now, as best I can figger it out that makes it four an' a half months.

" 'But I want to be plum fair with Snowdy Jane an' give her the benefit of ever' doubt, so I'll have to ad-mit that she's been married to me fer four an' a half months, too. Now, four an' a half an' four an' a half makes nine months — right on the dot. Giddap, Pokey Joe!' "

Hosshead Bill

Last Sunday good 'Lige Cantwell sat in the Amen Corner all during the services at the Hard-Rock Firm-Foundation Church. He seemed to be interested in all three of the sermons that were preached by visiting ministers to whom he had been listening. It was the big "Association Meeting", and when the services were ended he appeared still engrossed with his thoughts. In fact, he almost forgot to invite me to the dinner at his home to which I had been eagerly looking forward for several days.

"I ain't never worried much a-bout the next worl'," he said as we walked along the winding, wooded path, "but this week — on an' off — I've been a-wonderin' whut is to be-come of some people I know when they die. By that I mean people who ain't never done nothin' whut ye might call downright sinful an' bad, but yit ain't done nothin' much to brag a-bout in the way of bein' Gawd-fearin' citizens."

I had no answer to that and the silence lengthened. The old preacher halted in his tracks and looked at his tarnished old silver watch.

"It'll be some time afore Marthy'll git that pot of chicken an' dumplin's done. Le's set an' talk a spell."

We sat down on a moss-covered log, and Good 'Lige stroked his patriarchial beard thoughtfully.

"I've been a-thinkin' some of pore ol' Hosshead Bill Maggard," he declared at last. "Ye never knowed Hosshead Bill, did ye?"

"No, but the name's familiar," I replied.

"Wall, a few weeks ago he died at his home over thar

on Beefhide Crick in Kaintucky, an' they sent fer me to come over thar an' preach his fun'ral. I saddled up an' rid over, a-gittin' thar on the evenin' afore the fun'ral. That same night they helt services over the body at the home, an' I said a few words.

"The next day they had the fun'ral proper at the meetin'-house, an' it was kinda sad-like to hyer that preacher over thar a-doin' his level best to say something comfortin' a-bout pore ol' Hosshead, but thar wasn't much ye could say a-bout him nohow.

"Now, ol' Hosshead he'd been a sorty wuthless feller. I reckon he come the clostest of livin' eighty years a-doin nothin of any man I ever knowed. He let his ol' woman an' the young'uns make the livin' outta that hillside rocky farm he had over thar, an' of cou'se he made a run of likker now an' then, but mostly he done nothin' but set in the shade — er afore the fire.

"It 'peered like he could git hisself into more trouble a-doin' nothin' much than anybody in these parts, er anywhar else fer that matter. Take the time he got that name 'Hosshead', fer instince. His face an' head was kinda long, like a hoss, an' he was the spittin' image of Black John Patton over thar in West Virginny — Mingo County.

"Black John was a powerful, big man, a-weighin' two an' forty er fifty poun's, an' ever' ounce of him was snakemean. Be-sides shootin' a few men, he made a reg-lar bizz'ness outta hoss-stealin'. One day Hosshead was a-visitin' some of his kinfolks over thar, an' somebody seed him an' tol' the law that he was Black John. They got 'em up a posse, an' they ketched Hosshead an' strung him up on a beech tree.

"In them days Hosshead was nigh a-bout as big as Black John an' he was as tough as they come. Anyhow, he bruk the rope when they run the hoss he was a-ridin' out frum onder him, an' he hit the groun' a-runnin'. He got clean a-way frum 'em, an' ever since then ever'body has called him Hosshead Bill, bekaze, like ye know, ye can't hang a hoss. His head jest slips outta the noose.

"An' a-thinkin' of them things at the fun'ral that thar preacher was hard put to say somethin' nice an' encouragin' a-bout the de-ceased. He hemmed an' he hawed, an' he sorty skippied a-roun' in the scriptoors, but not a-havin' much to say a-bout Hosshead Bill.

"Fine'ly he shet the Book, an' walked over an' stood be-side the coffin, a-lookin' sorrow-like down at the re-mains.

" 'Wall, I reckon ol' Bill has done de-parted frum this sinful worl',' he says solemlike. 'We air a-goin' to miss him down to the store an' the mill. We air a-goin' to feel sorty sad when we re-colleck how we allus hid our chawin' terbacker when we seed him a-comin' down the road.

" 'Yes, Brethern an' Sistern, pore ol' Hosshead Bill never done noboddy no harm. He went through this worl' in his slow easy-like way, an' he put no more into livin' amongst us than he tuck out. I'd say he jest a-bout bruk even when all is said an' done.

" 'The onliest thing I can think of to say a-bout him right now is that he was jest named atter the wrong eend of the hoss.' "

Who's Been Hyer Since I've Been Gone?

Brandy Bill dropped into my office alone one day last week, and we sat and small talked for a while. He was deeply interested, he said, in an old fiddlers contest that was being planned by some of the boys over on the Devil's Apron. I had been hearing rumors of this event for several weeks, but nothing definite.

"I come over hyer," he explained after his stogie was burning to suit him, "kinda hoping to see Bogue Robinson. We sorty figgered he might come over an' take a part in that fiddlin' con-test that's a-comin' up soon."

He paused and a faraway look came into his eyes as he watched the smoke from his cigar curl upward.

"Ye know," he continued softly, "we shore have been a-misin' pore ol' Sam Branham since he passed on. He was jest a-bout the finest fiddler we ever had over thar, an' the boys shore would like to hyer 'Ol' Joe Clark' an' 'Chicken in the Dough Tray ag'in. That's one reason why we air a-gittin' up that ol' fiddlers con-test."

"When did you say you were going to stage it?" I asked.

"We ain't rightly made up our minds yit, but I reckon it'll be in a-bout three weeks. We'll let ye know the time an' place."

We were silent for a few minutes, and then Brandy Bill stroked his drooping mustache thoughtfully.

"Did I ever tell ye a-bout Fiddlin' Fed Hill, an' how the Gov'ner got him outta the pen that time a good many years ago?"

"No." I leaned back in my chair and awaited the story.

"Wall, ol' Fiddlin' Fed was jest a-bout the best fiddler in his time, an' I don't keer whar they come frum. He could pyorely make that ol' fiddle of his set up an' talk, an' ye shore couldn't keep yore feet still when he struck up 'The Irishman's Trot', an' them t'other hoe-downs he ust to play. Jest give him a-bout three snorts of applejack an' he'd make the ha'r stand up on the back of yore neck.

"But Fiddlin' Fed wasn't whut ye might call a hard-workin' man, him a-givin' most of his time to fiddlin' that-away. But he did do a leetle moonshinin' on the side ever' onct in a while, an' that's whar trubbel stepped in. He ketched a feller a-foolin' a-roun' at his still one day, an' him an' that feller had a shootin' match. Fiddlin' Fed downed his man, but it happened that this feller was a revenooer.

"Fiddlin' Fed got a life sentence in the pen, a-leavin' his wife an' a youngster er two to shift fer themselves. They got a-long purty good, I reckon, an' in time I reckon we mostly fergot a-bout Fiddlin' Fed down thar in the Pen. But it seemed like Fiddlin' Fed didn't fergit to fiddle whilst he was down thar, an' he got him a job in the carpenters' shop atter a year er so.

"He got him a piece of hard maple fer the front an' some white pine fer the back, an' he spent weeks an' months on eend a-scrapin' an' a-shapin' that wood jest to suit him. An' when he got it all glued together he shore had him a humdinger of a fiddle. I've heerd ol' Fed play on that fiddle an' he could make it laugh like a happy child, er cry like a weepin' woman, an' he could jest play a toon on any man's heart-strings.

"Purty soon atter he got that fiddle finished an' was a-playin' it fer the men in the pen thar on rest days an' Sundays, a new Gov'ner got hisself e-lected, an' tuck over his office. He heerd a-bout Fiddlin' Fed an' he was crazy a-bout mountain music, 'speshully fiddlin'.

"One evenin' he went out thar to the pen, an' had the warden to fetch out Fiddlin' Fed an' play a few toons. Fed tol' us that he played Ol' Joe Clark, Hell up a Cold Holler, an' Hangin' John Hardy, an' it wasn't long ontel the Gov'ner was crying' like a baby. When Fed got through the Gov'ner got up an' put his arms around Fed's shoulder.

" 'I'm a-goin' to give ye a pardon,' says he, 'an' I'm a-goin' to give it to ye on one con-dishun. I'm astin' ye to go straight back to yore home in the hills, an' set down on yore doorstep, an' play 'Home Sweet Home' like ye've been a-playin' them toons fer me.'

"Fiddlin' Fed he promised him that he'd do it, an' a few days later he got out an' headed fer home. It was a-gittin' plum dusky-dark when he got up thar on the Devil's Apern an' there was a light a-shinin' through the winder of his house.

"Now, he'd been in the pen nigh onto eight years, an' hadn't been home in nine, countin' the time he was in the jail hyer an' on trial an' all. Anyhow, when he peeked through the winder he seed his wife an' three or four young'uns a-settin' afore the fire. Them young'uns ranged from a-bout twelve years ol' down to mebbe a two year-ol' boy.

"Fiddlin' Fed he scratched his head, an' then sad-like he sot down on the steps an' leaned back ag'inst the door-jam. He got his fiddle, an' poured out his heart in the toon that he played. It was:

" 'Who's Been Hyer Since I've Been Gone,
" 'A Sweet-tawkin' Preacher With a Derby On.' "

New Preacher Gets Bible Mixed Up

It was a sunny afternoon, and I could think of nothing better than a visit with the boys over on the Devil's Apron. As I had anticipated, I found most of them gathered in Brandy Bill's backyard near his springhouse.

"We was jest a-talkin' a-bout ye," said Brandy Bill, shaking hands with me as if he hadn't seen me for months. "We was a-hopin' that ye'd drap over fer a while."

"What's going on?" I queried.

"Somethin' tuck place at the Hard-Rock Firm-Found-a-shun meetin'-house," replied Brandy Bill, "an' we sorty wanted to tell ye a-bout it whilst it was fresh on our minds."

"Spill it," I said, finding a seat in the shade.

"We'll let Good 'Lige tell it," suggested Brandy Bill, nodding toward the old preacher.

"Wall, Good 'Lige acquiesed, " it was somethin' like this as best I re-colleck. Sometime back in the spring, I spent the night with ol' Hanse Maggard over in Kaintucky. Now, ef'n ye happen to know ol' Hanse, ye'll know that he raised ten er twelve boys, an' he named 'em all atter the prophets in the Ol' Testy-ment.

"Thar was Adam an' Moses an' Aaron, an' King Hiram an' E-li-gy, an' a whole passel of t'others. Whilst we was a-talkin' I ast him whut his boys was all a-doin' nowadays, an' he said as how they were mostly married an' moved a-way a-huntin' fer work.

" 'A few of 'em's turned out to be farmers an' moonshiners like me,' he explained, 'that is, exceptin' King Hiram, an' he was allus sorty strange-like. He thinks as how he's got a call frum the Lawd to preach the gospel, an' he's a-spendin' most of his time up thar in the field a-preachin' to them mules he's a-workin' with. He's up thar now, an' I reckon ye'll see him come suppertime.'

"Wall, purty soon a tall, ganglin' boy come in an' ol' Hanse says as how he was King Hiram. Atter supper we sot a-roun' a while, an' this young feller says as how he'd like to come over hyer an' preach in my pulpit sometime. Of cou'se thar wasn't nothin' I could say but to tell him to come ahead.

"But to tell the truth, I'd clean fergot all a-bout it, but yistiddy, whilst we was thar at the mill, this young King Hiram driv up. I tuck him up to my place to spend the night, an' atter supper we got to talkin', an' he tol' me as how it'd be the fu'st time he got up in a pulpit an' tried to preach afore a lot of people.

"He said as how he'd been a-studyin' on his sermon, an' that he figgered he'd done got it down pat, but he was worried be-kaze he was skeered he'd fer-git some of it. I tol' him I knowed jest how he felt, an' that mebbe we could think of somethin' to help him out afore the meetin' got started.

"Wall, this mornin' when he got up, he was still worried a-bout whar he could go through with that sermon er not, an' it shore did take a-way his appytite be-kaze he couldn't eat no breakfas'. When it got time to start out fer the meetin'-house, I went out to the barn an' I dug up a pint of Brandy Bill's best applejack that I'd been a-keepin' fer snake-bites an' sickness, an' I stuck it in my coat pocket.

"I got the water pitcher at the meetin'-house an' me an' young King Hiram we went down to the spring to fill it up with water. Then I give him that pint of applejack.

" 'I know egg-zackly how ye air a-feelin',' I tol' him, 'an' I figger that mebbe, afore ye git up to preach, ye'd better fill the glass with a lettle water an' the rest brandy, an' when ye hit a snag in yore sermon, jest take a leetle sip er two. It'll help ye to re-colleck whut ye was a-figgerin' on sayin', an' noboddy is a-goin' to notice the diff'rence.'

"Wall, he follered my ad-vice to the letter, an' wasn't long atter he started to talkin', he struck a knot an' stalled. He tuck him a couple of big gulps outta his glass, an' started out ag'in. He done that four er five times more afore he got through, an' he'd done drained his glass plum dry. When the meetin' was over he tuck me to one side.

" 'Wall, how'd I do?' he asts plum anx-shus-like.

" 'Ye done purty good,' I tol' him, 'ex-ceptin' fer two er three leetle things. In the fu'st place Joney didn't swaller that swale, an' in the secon' place when they throwed down Jezzy-bell off'n the wall, the re-mains wasn't twelve baskets-full, an' in the third place, it wasn't Solomon who jerked out the jawbone of a jackass an' beat the hind eend off'n ten thousan' Philly-del-fians.' "

Taste of Iron and Leather

I had a card from Willie B. Fuller last week in which he stated that he was having a little Christmas party at his home over on the Devil's Apron, and naturally I made a point of being there on time. I found several other convivial spirits there ahead of me, among them Bad 'Lige, Brandy Bill, Little 'Bijie and Good 'Lige.

Up to that time I had never been in Willie B's home, and I found it to be surprisingly comfortable and tastefully furnished. There were several wellfilled bookcases in the living room, and easy chairs were scattered about, together with an inviting corner divan. The boys were stretched out in indolent fashion staring into the open fire where a couple of hickory logs were blazing cheerfully.

They greeted me in such a manner that I knew that none of them felt any pains. For a while we sat and talked of this and that and admired the colorfully decorated Christmas tree standing in the corner of the room. And Willie B. seemed to be all set to enjoy the Yuletide — chiefly in liquid form.

Judging by the odor that permeated the room I knew that a pot of ginger-stew was simmering in the kitchen, and Brandy Bill got up and went in there to sample it. After tasting a couple of spoonfuls he nodded his head and smacked his lips in ecstacy.

Bad 'Lige had his eye on that kitchen, too.

"Is she a-bout done, Bill?" he called.

"I reckon so," drawled the latter, filling a cup for himself.

Then Willie B. became the perfect host. Apparently he had imbibed a few drinks before we arrived, for his dignity and decorum were above reproach.

"May I suggest," said he, "that we try the eggnog first of all?" He bowed gravely to me and Bad 'Lige. "It's made of pure cream, eggs, and the finest malted corn whiskey I ever tasted. I believe that you will find it palatable."

We trooped to the kitchen where he poured a full cup for each of us. It was delicious, exquisite — palatable was not the word for it. Willie B. insisted that we take a second cup, and none of us were averse to that idea. Even Brandy Bill, who was an expert in such matters, had a distinct look of reverence on his face.

"This hyer egg-nog is powerful good," he said with a deep sigh of contentment, "but ef'n a feller is a-goin' to water down his drinkin' likker, I'd say that ginger-stew has got 'em all skinned to a frazzle. That's whut I was a-tell-in' the boys afore ye got hyer." He nodded to me and then drained his cup.

"I put on a pot of stew," he continued, "an' I think I've got her jest a-bout whar she ort to be. All of ye warsh yore cups to take out the taste of the eggnog, an' fill her up with this ginger-stew an' tell me whut ye reely think of it."

We obeyed his suggestion with alacrity, and then relaxed in solid comfort as we sipped our steaming masterpiece. That stew *was* good — there was no denying that fact — just tangy enough with the ginger, and I was ready to agree with Brandy Bill that it was the final word in the Bacchanalian lexicon.

Brandy Bill slowly and thoughtfully consumed his potion, and then he turned to Willie B.

"Whar'd ye git that corn ye give me to put in this stew?" he demanded with a puzzled expression on his face.

"I'm not divulging the name of the man who made it," replied his host, "but I stood by at the time it was made, and I can assure you that it is as pure and unadulterated as the dew on the blushing rose at dawn. Why do you ask?"

"Was it made in a copper b'iler?"

"It was — and a brand new one at that."

"Wall, thar's a taste — jest a trace — of iron in it," he said sipping another swallow thoughtfully.

"Ye're wrong a-bout that, Bill," asserted Bad 'Lige, nodding sagely. "That is leather ye air a-tastin'."

"Both of you are in error," defended Willie B. with a soft hiccough. "I repeat that I saw that liquor backed and doubled from the beginning to the end, and I know that there was not any iron or leather near it at the time."

"But I'm a-tellin' ye that thar's jest the hint of the taste of iron in it," insisted Brandy Bill.

"It's leather." Bad 'Lige was equally positive.

"Wait a minute!" ejaculated Willie B. in a tone of surprise and something of awe. "Both of you boys just might be correct in your assumptions."

He left the room and returned a couple of minutes later carrying an empty five-gallon keg. He placed it on the hearthstone, and then pulled out the bung stopper. He peered owlishly at it for a full minute.

"Boys," he said with an elaborate bow, "we Kentuckians have always heard that Virginians were good judges of liquor, and I am forced to place the crown of championship on the brows of you two connoisseurs. You tasted both iron and leather in that liquor, and upon investigating I find that in order to keep the keg from leaking at the bung-hole, I nailed a small piece of leather around the stopper with two iron tacks."

Pokey Joe Blowed First

Several of us were gathered at Business Bill's store at the mouth of No-Business Creek last Saturday, staring glumly at the cold misty rain that was falling outside. The hot stove felt good, and most of us were gathered close to it, but Brandy Bill and Willie B. were sitting on the counter near the door.

"Wonder whut's got ol' Feverweed Sim'son so stirred up?" asked Brandy Bill, staring through the rain-splashed window. "Don't know as I ever seed him in sich a hurry."

We all peered out through the window and open door watching the old "root an' yarb" doctor as he came striding up the road. I had met Feverweed a few weeks previously, and I knew that he was well liked and respected over the Devil's Apron where he had been administering cures for the ills and ailments of both man and beast for a good many years. He brewed strange concoctions out of roots and herbs and apparently some of them achieved surprising results.

Across his shoulders was slung a haversack which I had heard contained a supply of his salves and medicines, and his long legs were carrying him along the road at a surprising pace.

"Hey, Feverweed!" called Brandy Bill as the doctor started to turn up the No-Business Creek road. "What's the matter? Somebody sick?"

"Yes, it's Leetle 'Bijie's mother-in-law — A'nt Hellfirey."

"Is she bad tuck?"

"Leetle 'Bijie sent me word that he figgered mebbe she

was a-dyin'." He wheeled and started on up the road.

"Wait a minnit!" yelled Brandy Bill. "I can git ye thar a heap quicker in my jeep."

He nodded at me, and a few minutes later he and I, with Feverweed between us, were driving up the steep and muddy road in the direction of Little 'Bijie's cabin.

"Whut do ye reckon is ailin' A'nt Hellfirey?" mused Brandy Bill.

"I ain't got no idee," replied Feverweed. "I was up thar yistiddy, an' she shore 'peered to be all right then. I was a-tryin' to do somethin' fer 'Bijie's mule — ol' Pokey Joe."

"H-m-m-m!" murmured Brandy Bill. "Looks like Leetle 'Bijie's a-havin' a streak of bad luck — with his wife's mammy an' his mule both sick at the same time. Is Pokey Joe purty bad off?"

"He's ailin' with somethin'. I give him a dose of med'cine, an' I left some more fer him to take ef'n he got any wu'ss."

It didn't take us long to drive to Little 'Bijie's home, and we found him and his wife — Snowdy Jane — running in circles. Aunt Hell-firey was tossing and moaning on a

bed and Little 'Bijie led us into the room.

"Whut 'peers to be wrong with her?" asked Feverweed of Snowdy Jane.

"It was that med'cine ye left fer Pokey Joe," spoke up Little 'Bijie. "She got a dose of it."

"But — but that was fer the mule — not fer people," stammered Feverweed, and to my surprise he did not seem to be unduely disturbed. In fact there was the hint of a grin at the corners of his mouth. He turned and patted the crying Snowdy Jane on the shoulder.

"Don't worry none, Snowdy Jane," he comforted. "It ain't a-goin' to kill yore mammy. Fact is, it'll be a good spring tonic fer her. Jest give her a dose of salts an' she'll be fit as a fiddle in a couple of days."

He turned and walked out of the room with me and Brandy Bill at his heels. Lettle 'Bijie came out on the porch and joined us.

"Jest whut happened, 'Bijie?" queried Feverweed. "Did she take that stuff that I left by mistake — er whut?"

"No," replied Lettle 'Bijie, trying hard to suppress a giggle. "It was like this. Ye left that sul-fur an' assy-fitty-dy an' them t'other powders, an' I mixed 'em all up like ye tol' me to do in case Pokey Joe got to heavin' ag'in.

"This mornin' when I got up he was wu'ss, so I made a paper funnel like ye tol' me to do, an' I filled it up full with that stuff, an' got ready to give it to Pokey Joe. Now, I'm hyer to state that gittin' them powders down Pokey Joe's throat is a two-man job, one to hold the blamed mule's head an' t'other'n to blow 'em down his throat.

"Elvirey she come out to help me, an' she figgered as how she was skeered to try to hold Pokey Joe's head, a-feared he'd bite her, an' that she'd do the blowin' instid. I got ever'thing ready an' then I pulled Pokey Joe's mouth open.

"Elvirey she tuck a deep breath an' started to blow, an' that was when it happened. Ye see, boys, ol' Pokey Joe he blowed fu'st."

Pointers and Setters

I drove over on the Devil's Apron last Saturday afternoon and parked at Brandy Bill's grist-mill. Quite a gathering of Aproners were there getting their "turns" of corn ground, and I bought a peck of meal from Brandy Bill. Fried cornmeal mush for breakfast, made from water-ground meal, is a dish that is out of this world as far as I'm concerned.

Bad 'Lige and Little 'Bijie were sitting by the glowing stove engaged in a desultory argument over the merits and sagacity of their favorite hounds. Little 'Bijie was firmly convinced that his dog, Mary Lou, was the smartest dog on the Apron, and Bad 'Lige was equally convinced that his hound, Blue Thunder, took the blue ribbon in the canine world. As the argument waxed warmer, everyone gathered closer about them.

"Why not have a contest between them?" I suggested, eyeing the two dogs, both of whom were asleep beside the stove. And to my suggestion Little 'Bijie and Bad 'Lige both agreed quickly. Brandy Bill turned the grinding over to his son, Toddy, and came over to join us.

"Ye try yore dawg's tricks fu'st," said Bad 'Lige, and Little 'Bijie nodded and snapped his fingers, calling sharply to Mary Lou. She came to him, rearing up and placing her paws on his knee, and looking at her master adoringly.

"Whut do ye do when it comes bedtime, Mary Lou?" demanded Little 'Bijie, and Mary Lou dropped to the floor, curled up at his feet, yawned a couple of times, and then closed her eyes.

"Now, whut do ye do when the revenooers show up?"

Immediately Mary Lou sprang to her feet, and her hair stood straight up along her back. She began to growl and bark so viciously that old Blue Thunder bristled and started to take a part in the proceedings.

"Now, whut do ye do when the game warden comes, an' ye ain't got no dawg license?"

Mary Lou dropped her tail between her legs and furtively crawled back under a bench in the darkest corner she could find.

"Thar!" crowed Little 'Bijie triumphantly. "Le's see ef'n Blue Thunder can match that?"

Bad 'Lige thrust his hand down in his pants pockets, and pulled out a bright new fifty-cent piece. He held it out to Blue Thunder and the dog opened his mouth and clamped his teeth on the money. Then he stood motionless, wagging his tail expectantly.

"Ye go down to Dutton's store," ordered Bad 'Lige, pronouncing each word distinctly, "an' fetch me a plug of Red Bull chawin' terbacker, an' a can of sardines. Onnerstand?"

Blue Thunder wagged his tail again, and then turned and vanished down the road in a long lope in the direction of Dutton's store half a mile or more distant.

"For the love of Mike!" I gasped. "That dog can't talk — even if he did understand what you told him. How do you expect him to tell Dutton what he wants?"

"He picks it out hisself, an' he knows whar ever'thing is kept thar better'n Dutton hisself knows."

Nearly half an hour passed before Blue Thunder returned from his mission, and in his mouth was a small paper bag. Bad 'Lige took it from him, and removed from it a can of sardines and a plug of chewing tobacco, and also a couple of dimes in change.

As far as I could see it was just about a draw between the two hounds, and I said so, but there were others there who thought that one or the other of the dogs had won.

The argument grew in warmth and intensity, and a general melee seemed to be imminent.

Then Brandy Bill suggested that we take the problem to Good 'Lige, the pastor of the Hard-Rock Firm-Foundation Church, for a final decision since practically all controversial matters on the Devil's Apron were left up to him anyway. So we all marched in a body to his home and walked into his living room.

Good 'Lige was seated beside a table before a roaring fire, and in another chair on the opposite side of that table sat a droopy hound. I knew instinctively that he was Brandy Bill's dog, the fabulous Big Howdy, one of the greatest foxhounds in the history of the hill country. And believe it or not, Good 'Lige and Big Howdy were deeply engrossed in a game of checkers. Brandy Bill choked back a belly-laugh.

"Bad 'Lige an' Leetle 'Bijie was a-argy'in' a-bout whose dawg was the smartest," he explained, "but it shore looks to me like Big Howdy thar wins the prize — him a-playin' checkers with ye thataway."

"Now shucks!" murmured Good 'Lige. "He ain't so smart atter all. I've done beat him three games outta five."

She Ain't Got No Mule

A few Sundays ago I attended services over at the Hard-Rock Firm-Foundation Church on the Devil's Apron. I hadn't heard Good 'Lige preach in several months, and I wondered how he was getting along with his rather volatile congregation.

I arrived a bit early and, since it was a rather cold morning, some of the boys had built a fire out near the old "Jockey Street' where the hillmen once traded horses on Saturdays and Sundays. There were no horses on hand that day, and "hoss swappin' " was almost a forgotten art.

As I expected, I found Brandy Bill, Bad 'Lige, Little 'Bijie Birdsong, and Business Bill seated around the fire. They were always the first to arrive although it was not because of any religious fervor on their part, but rather their inherent urge to foregather and talk of the happenings in the neighborhood.

The congregation was slow in arriving that morning, but from time to time small family groups began to put in an appearance and, for the most part, go on into the church. Smoke was pouring from the chimney, promising a warm building when the services were started.

From the point where we were gathered we could see all the way down the hill from the meeting-house to the highway, almost half a mile distant. We saw a man turn from the highway and start the climb up to the church, and he was riding a large black mule. A few yards behind him a woman came trudging along on foot.

"That's ol' Greenberry Green an' his wife," declared 'Little 'Bijie, squinting his eyes.

"Shore is," grunted Brandy Bill. "Ye'd think he'd let his wife ride that mule onct in a while."

"They pass my place nigh a-bout ever' day," declared Bad 'Lige. "He's allus a-ridin' in front an' her a-walkin' behindst him."

"Who in the world is Greenberry Green?" I queried. "Is it a real name?"

"He's reel all right," agreed Brandy Bill. "Nobody knows much a-bout him. He ain't never been whut ye might call a good mixer with his neighbors. Fer years he's been a-livin' over thar on Whisperin' Crick, an' I reckon he never did have nobody that he could egg-zackly call a frien'. He's stayed by hisself an' made a sort of a livin' huntin' an' diggin' 'sang an' sich.

"But a couple of years ago he moved up hyer on the head of No-Bizz'ness jest a-bove the Lost Meetin'-House, an' fixed up a ol' shack up thar. He patched up a couple of rooms an' fenced in a leetle gyarden fer his wife to 'tend.

"He's got a couple of purty good houn's, an' he hunts a heap, an' digs 'sang an' yaller-root an' may-apple an' sells it endurin' the summer, an' in the winter he traps an' sells furs. He sold some prime mink an' coon skins down thar to Dutton's store fer meal an' flour an' cawfee an' sugar an' stuff he needed, so I reckon him an' his ol' woman ain't a-sufferin' none.

"Seems as though his wife goes with him ever-whar he goes an' is allus a-walkin'. I don't know whar all they go, but they air allus on the road. It shore does look funny — him a-ridin' an' her a-walkin' thataway, but I reckon it's their bizz'ness. Ef'n I was in her place I'd bounce me a good-sized rock off'n his head, an' ride a spell."

The old couple had drawn close to us by this time, and then Greenberry rode on past us and hitched his black mule to one of the paw-paw bushes that lined the riding path. His wife came to a halt near where we were standing and waited for him.

Little 'Bijie arose to his feet and stood defiantly in front of Greenberry.

"Hey, Greenberry!" he called.

The old fellow halted in his tracks and stared at 'Bijie.

"We're jest sorty curious," said 'Bijie, "but some of us have been wonderin' why ye air allus a-ridin' yore mule whilst yore wife has to walk a-long behindst ye. Why don't she ride some of the time?"

Greenberry looked his interrogator over for a full minute, and then replied sourly.

"She ain't got no mule."

Fiesty Britches and Dirty-Butt

September has always been my favorite month, particularly when the leaves take on their vivid hues against a bright blue sky, but when I drove over to the Devil's Apron the other day I saw few indications of Autumn. The intense heat was more oppressive than it had been all summer.

I found complete solace and comfort, however, when I reached Brandy Bill's home, and found the boys all gathered at the springhouse under the shade of the big spreading maple.

As Brandy Bill was mixing my julep, I noticed that there was a newcomer in the ranks, and Little 'Bijie introduced him.

"Shake hands with Pokey Poley Potter," he said, nodding at the stranger. "He bought the ol' Anderson place over ferninst Good 'Lige's."

Pokey Poley was a slow-moving giant with an infectious grin, and for some reason or other I found myself taking an instant liking for him. But I winced with pain when he gripped my hand with fingers of steel.

"Pokey Poley has been a-livin' down at Tom Bottom," explained Little 'Bijie, "but when they started to build that big dam down thar, he had to move out. He come up hyer an' some of us boys kinda pitched in an' helped him in gittin' things fixed up. The house was purty bad run down, but we had us a workin' an' put on a new roof, an' laid up some fencin', an' he moved his fambly in last week. He's still got plenty to do ef'n he's a-goin' to have things ready fer his spring plantin'. I reckon we'll have to have us a-nuther workin' to help him git that cove fiel' cl'ared fer corn. That fiel' allus has been mighty good fer corn."

The crowd became silent, and slowly with deep relish sipped their juleps. After a long pause I broke the silence.

"The squirrel season opens in a couple of weeks. Are there many up this way?"

"I've seed a leetle sign hyer an' thar, but I reckon they're purty sca'ce ag'in," replied Brandy Bill. "Ain't much hick'ry mast, an' whut thar is has already started fallin' off. Plenty of beech an' acorns though."

The others nodded in confirmation of the statement, and once more silence settled about us. Then I saw a quirk at the corners of Brandy Bill's mouth, and I knew that a tall tale was forthcoming.

"Ye'd ort to a-been hyer fer the openin' day of school last Monday," he declared with a sidelong glance at Pokey Poley, but speaking to me.

"Why, what happened?"

"Wall, like ye know, us fellers hyer on the Apern allus go up to the school on the fu'st day ever' year to see that things git started off right — kinda to look a-bout the stove, an' clean out the spring, an' ever'thing like that.

"An' I'm hyer to say that the schoolhouse was a bu'stin' at the seams when we got up thar last Monday mornin'. I never seed so many young'uns in the same place in all my life. Miss Samanthy shore did have her han's full a-tryin' to git 'em all straightened out an' started on their lessons.

"Ever' seat was full an' some of the kids was a-settin' on the floor. Thar was at least a dozen leetle fellers that was jest a-startin' in school fer the fu'st time, an' thar was some sev'ral new scholars — amongst them a boy an' a gal of Pokey Poley's.

"The gal she was the oldest, an' Miss Samanthy she called her up to her desk.

" 'Whut's yore name?' she asts.

" 'Fiesty Britches' says the leetle gal without battin' her eye.

"Her name's Mary Ann," interrupted Pokey Poley with a grin, "but we allus call her Fiesty Britches."

"Wall," resumed Brandy Bill, "Miss Samanthy she didn't like that a bit. She got red in the face, an' she come clost to loosin' her breath.

" 'Now looky hyer, little lady,' says the teacher, 'we don't let sich talk as that go on in this school. Ye can take yore books an' go home an' tell yore mammy whut ye done, an' ye can come back when ye l'arn to act an' talk like a lady.'

"Leetle Fiesty-Britches never said a word. She jest turned a-roun' an' picked up her books, an' headed towarge the door. Then she stopped an' looked back at her leetle brother.

" 'Come on, Dirty Butt!' she hollers. "Teacher ain't a-goin' to be-lieve ye n'uther.' "

Toddy and the Pot

When my family is out of town, life gets a little monotonous, and I have a yen for a home-cooked meal. So I stuck it out until Thursday last week, and then I hied me over to Brandy Bill's house on the Devil's Apron.

I timed it just right. Brandy Bill and his family were just sitting down at the table in the kitchen when I arrived, and Brandy Bill with his characteristic hospitality urged me to join them.

His wife, Sindusty, was apologetic — needlessly so — saying that she had not expected any company, but that I was more than welcome to eat it "sich as it is." And it was perfect. There was a big platter of fried country ham and red-eye gravy, hot biscuits, new potatoes smothered in white sauce, and even a bowl of warmed-over mutton — one of Brandy Bill's favorite dishes.

I did stout justice to that meal, and when I could hold no more, I leaned back with a sigh of satisfaction. A little later we went into the living room and found comfortable chairs.

Little Toddy, Brandy Bill's youngest son, brought his home-work into the living room and sat down at a table in the corner. He opened one of the books with palpable distaste, and started to reading.

"How is Toddy getting along in school?" I asked.

"I reckon he's a-doin' purty good," replied Brandy Bill with a glance of pride and affection at the boy. "He fetched in his re-port cyard t'other day. I'll show it to ye."

He found it on the mantel above the fireplace, and

handed it to me. A glance told me that he had made straight "A's" in his classes and I proceeded to congratulate him.

A little after that I glanced at my watch, and then got to my feet.

"It's time I should be starting," I said. "But I certainly want to tell you how much I enjoyed that wonderful supper —."

"Ye might as well spend the night," suggested Brandy Bill. "Ye said as how yore folks air gone, so ye jest stay with us, an' go on back home in the mornin'."

"But—."

"He can sleep with me," urged Toddy eagerly. "I've been a-figgerin' on astin him to do that fer a long time. I want him to tell me some of them big windies he allus a-tellin' an' a-puttin' in his paper."

"Toddy!" reproved his mother sharply.

" "Wall, he does tell 'em, maw," insisted Toddy, "an' I want him to tell me some of 'em." He said it so wistfully that I couldn't deny him, so I relaxed in my rocker.

Brandy Bill mixed a mint julep for a night-cap, using some of his incomparable applejack, and all was peaceful and comfortable for a while. Then it was bedtime for Toddy and I accompanied him up the stairs to his room.

We undressed and crawled beneath the old-fashioned pieced quilt that covered the bed. At Toddy's suggestion I launched into a wild adventure story of the African jungle, a brief resume of a yarn that I had sold to one of the pulp magazines a few months earlier.

It had to do with an elephant hunter who was searching for the "death-tryst" of the elephant world. I told Toddy that hunters of jungle elephants had never been able to find the skeleton of an elephant that had died a natural death, and that there was believed to be a hidden volcanic crater in those jungles somewhere to which all elephants went when they felt that death was near.

Little Toddy listened with wide-eyed interest and breathless suspense until I had finished the story and then he turned over on his side and closed his eyes. I started to extinguish the oil lamp when Toddy suddenly sat straight up in bed.

"Uh-oh!" he exclaimed. "I purty nigh fergot."

He knelt down beside the bed and leaned forward, placing his face on the quilt. I was a little surprised by his actions. Of course I knew that Brandy Bill and his wife were in regular attendance at the church, and were inherently religious, but I simply had not expected them to have taught Toddy to say his nightly prayers.

Then I realized that the least that I could do would be to follow his example, so I got out of the bed and knelt down on my side of it. Just as I bowed my head I caught little Toddy's eye, and I saw that they had grown big with surprise.

"Maw'll shore beat the tar outta ye in the mornin', he whispered. "I got the pot over hyer."

Taking A Drink At Gunpoint

The boys were in a gay and festive mood when I got over on the Devil's Apron last Saturday afternoon, and the reason was immediately visible because each of them had been supplied with a glass of Brandy Bill's famous julep. And I had an idea that they had been imbibing rather freely.

"How's ever' leetle thing over a-bout town?" asked Little 'Bijie as I sampled my julep.

"Just so-so!" I replied. "Business seems to be rather slow."

"Wall, things shore air pickin' up over hyer," announced Business Bill with an air of importance. "I jest picked up four dollars this mornin' as slick as a whissle."

"Mind tellin' us how?" queried Brandy Bill.

"I guess ye know that ol' woman's got a flock of geese up at our place an' she sets a heap of store on 'em," he explained. "She saves all the feathers fer pillers an' featherbeds an' sichlike, an' never lets us kill one to eat. I like baked goose onct in a while.

"Wall, this mornin' one of them geese was out thar in the middle of the big road in front of the house, a-paddlin' in a mud-puddle, an' one of them fellers whut's a-workin' on that big dam thar on the river, come past my place a-drivin' a jeep.

"He must a-been in a big hurry bekaze he hit that mud puddle at full speed, an' killed that goose deader'n a doornail. But he was a polite sort of a feller, an' he jumped outta his jeep an' come back to whar I was a-standin' at the gate.

" 'I'm sorry I kilt yore goose,' he says. 'Will two dollars pay fer it?'

"I sorty stopped to think things over bekaze I never did like to be pooshed in a trade thataway. Then I got me a idee that I shore did cash in on.

"Wall, I'll tell ye whut," says I, "two dollars is a fair price fer the goose, but I've got a ol' gander whut thinks a heap of that goose, an' I'm skeered that the shock an' grief that he'll suffer frum his great loss'll jest a-bout kill him.

"An' I wish I may die ef'n he didn't dig down in his pocketbook an' pay me two more dollars fer that grievin' gander."

The tale brought a roar of laughter from the others who were in the mood for it, and when it had grown quiet again Good 'Lige cleared his throat.

"To tell the truth things air a-lookin' a leetle brighter hyer this year," he said, stroking his long beard thoughtfully. "The craps air all a-lookin' fine and we've had plenty of rain. It seems like ever'body is plum bizzy a-tryin' to look ahead an' lay up somethin' fer hard times. An' I don't think I ever seed as many apples an' berries as we air a-goin' to have this year."

"That ort to mean we'll have plenty of applejack come Chris'mus," suggested Little 'Bijie with a glance at Brandy Bill.

"I reckon," replied the latter, "that it ain't a-goin' to be as bad as it was a few years ago when we had that turrible dry season an' ever'thing got parched an' scorched. Ef'n ye re-colleck, thar was b'arely e-nough stuff raised to eat — corn, beans, fodder an' ever'thing. I'm hyer to say that it was one time when we shore did run short on drinkin' likker.

"Of cou'se 'taters done purty well that year. They made theirselves afore the dry weather set in, but 'taters was a-bout all thar was. Willie B. Fuller he got plum bizzy a-makin' up a big batch of 'tater-peelin' brandy, an' it sorty kept the boys a-goin', but that stuff was purty hard to swaller with most of us.

"I mind the time when I started to the mill purty early one mornin', an' on the road I met up with Bad 'Lige thar. He was a-totin' a jug of that 'tater-peelin' brandy, an' he also had a ol' single-bar'l shotgun a-long with him. When he got up clost I could see that he was a-lookin' purty bad an' mean like he had him a awful hangover.

"When we met on the road he sot his jug down, an' leveled that shotgun right plum at my belt-buckle.

" 'Take a drink outta that jug!' he orders, grim-like, an' I figgered he'd kinda gone off his rocker. Anyhow I knowed that most gin'rilly Bad 'Lige meant egg-zackly whut he said when he looked like that, an' I lost no time in takin' a purty good sized snort. I thought I'd choke shore.

"Bad 'Lige he watched me fer a couple of secon's, I reckon to see whar I lived through it er not, an' then he reached fer jug, an' handed the shotgun to me.

" 'Now ye pint that gun at me,' he says, 'an' make me take a drink of the dam' stuff, too.' "

Little Ike Picks Chickens

Last Saturday, for a change, Brandy Bill had a big bowl of eggnog ready for us at the grist-mill when I drove over for my weekly visit with the boys on the Devil's Apron. And it was this bowl that was the center of attraction for the crowd.

"Backed an' doubled applejack," pronounced Bad 'Lige with an appreciative smack of his lips. "It makes the best aignog that I ever tasted. Mebbe the stuff is a leetle like pap fer babies, but it shore goes down slick as grease."

Little 'Bijie, Business Bill, Good 'Lige and the others grunted in solemn agreement.

"Anything new over this way?" I asked, coming up for breath. That eggnog was heavily laced.

" 'Bout the same as allus," replied Business Bill. "Frum all signs it shore looks like a hard winter a-comin' up, an' most of us has been kinda bizzy a-gittin' ready fer it."

"How's the hunting over here?" I asked. "The game warden tells me that there are several deer —."

"An' sev'ral durn fools atter 'em," interrupted Bad 'Lige. "The way they've been a-bangin' a-way with them high-powered rifles, I've been afeard to git outta the house."

Little 'Bijie refilled his cup and came over and sat down beside me. The others gathered in close because they, too, sensed a tall tale. Little 'Bijie didn't disappoint them.

"Speakin' of huntin'," he began in a tone that all could hear, "puts me in mind of the time that Big Howdy an' Bizz'ness Bill went chicken-huntin'. Big Howdy is a-gittin' too old now to do much huntin', but Bizz'ness Bill thar he takes keer of him an' pets him like a baby er somethin'.

"My son Bobby-link—yes, that kee-reck—Bobby-link! We named him Robert E. Lee Birdsong, but the young'uns at school started to callin' him Bobby-link, an' we sorty tuck it up, too.

"Anyhow, as I was a-sayin', Bobby-link, he come home t'other night, an' he was a-tellin' a tale that shore hit me in the funny spot. It seems as though all of the young'uns had come to school on time 'ceptin' Bizz'ness Bill's youngest boy, Leetle Ike — an' he come in a-bout two hours late.

"Like most of ye already know, all of Bizz'ness Bill's boys, ceptin' Leetle Ike an' Harry Byrd, air gone a-way frum home to find jobs since thar wasn't much of a livin' to be got outta that rocky leetle farm. An' thar was seventeen of them boys as I re-colleck.

"Wall, leetle Ike he came in late, long atter books had done tuck up, an' Miss Samanthy she jumped on Leetle Ike, a-wantin' to know how come he was so late in gittin' thar.

" 'I can't tell ye,' says Leetle Ike, sorty shame-faced.

" 'Ef'n ye don't have a good ex-cuse,' says the teacher, 'I'm a-goin' to have to whup ye an' send ye back home.'

Leetle Ike he stood fu'st on one foot an' then on t'other, an' then he knuckled onder.

" 'Wall, it's kinda like this, Teacher. Last night atter we'uns had done gone to bed, the chickens out at the henhouse started to squawkin' an' a-hollerin'. Fer the last week er so thar has been pole-cat er a fox atter 'em, an' they's been all a-roostin' in that per-simmon tree jest behind'st the hen-house.

"Pap he jumped outta bed in his onderwear, an' grabbed his ol' double-barl'ed shotgun, an' headed outta the house. I seed when he went through the door that the flap on his onderwear had come onbuttoned, an' was sorty a-hangin' down.

" 'But Pap was in a hurry, an' I don't reckon he noticed that the flap was unbuttoned. I follered him out thar as quick as I could git my britches on. Pap was a-standin' thar onder that tree, a-lookin' up to see ef'n he could locate the varmint that was atter the chickens, but it was too dark to see much.

" 'A-bout that time Big Howdy, our ol' houn'-dawg, he come out to see whut all the ruckus was a-bout. He come up behindst Pap, an' then stuck his cold nose ag'inst Pap's bar' behindst.

" 'Pap he let out a yell, an' jumped a-bout six foot straight up in the air, an' he let off both bar'ls of that shotgun at the same time. It rained chickens fer a few minnits, an' me an' maw have been a-pickin' chickens up ontel jest a few minnits ago.' "

Whut Did Paul Say?

Last weekend Good 'Lige was in trouble with his church flock again. This much I gathered from talking with a few of the boys from over on the Devil's Apron. As far as I could ascertain no definite action had been taken against him, but a number of the good sisters were reported to be up in arms about it.

According to Brandy Bill, the trouble had started on the previous Sunday morning during the services, and the events that led up to the tragical climax took place in the following manner:

Good 'Lige is as devout a churchman and preacher as can be found anywhere in the hill country, but he does like a "leetle dram" once in a while. Apparently he had recently become accustomed to imbibing just a small nip before starting out for his Hard-Rock Firm-Foundation Church of which he has so long been the pastor.

"He said it sorty onloosens his tongue an' lifts his sperrits," explained Brandy Bill in relating the story to me.

Anyway, on that Sunday morning Good 'Lige saddled up his mule, and was riding over to the meeting-house just a short time before the services were to begin. In a bush-lined secluded bend in the path he stopped his mule and reached into his saddle-bags where he always kept his morning nip. The saddlepockets were empty. He had forgotten the flask before he left home. Meanwhile in Brandy Bill's words, one "Piddlin' Paul" Venters had started to "shake the beech-tree" down close to the mouth of No-Business Creek. Anyone placing money there in a certain hollow beech-tree could return to it later and find his moonshine liquor where the money had been deposited. For years off and on Piddling Paul had been doing this and thus far had succeeded in eluding the revenue officers.

Now, Brandy Bill's son—Little Todhunter, but called Toddy by everyone — happened to appear on the scene. Knowing that he could trust "Toddy", Good 'Lige called to him.

"Toddy, I want ye do me a favor. I want ye to go down thar to Piddlin' Paul's place an' tell Paul I said to send me a pint of his best apple brandy. Don't fool a-roun' with that beech-tree — jest go straight to Paul. Tell him I'll pay him next time I drap by. I'll be waitin' fer ye right hyer."

Little Toddy obediently trotted off down the path toward the mouth of the creek. It was just a short distance to Paul's home, but Toddy naturally found a few things to interest him on the way, particularly a pair of squirrels chasing each other up and down a tall hickory tree.

Good 'Lige waited patiently, glancing every few seconds at his watch, and when he could not wait any longer, he sighed with disappointment. At long last he tightened the bridle reins, and slowly climbed the hill, leading his mule behind him.

His congregation, somewhat larger than usual, was gathered in groups in the church-yard, and as soon as they saw him coming, they all trooped inside the building and found seats. Good 'Lige lingered for another minute or so, hoping that Toddy would show up, and finally, in resignation, he entered the meeting-house briskly and strode down the aisle. He climbed upon the rostrum, and sat down behind his pulpit, thumbing his old Bible, while the choir sang the first song. Then he offered up a long and perfervid prayer.

He took his text from a verse in the Acts of the Apostles that promised everlasting life in the world to come, and then he began to paint a vivid and beautiful picture of the golden streets of the New Jerusalem as well as the other joys that awaited the faithful. He left little to the imagination of his listeners after he had described the gates of pearl and the walls of alabaster, and the everlasting happiness that was in store for all of those who repented of their sins and joined the Hard-Rock Firm-Foundation Church.

"Whut did Saint Luke say?" he thundered, and then answered his own question.

"Luke says, 'Whomsoever shall lose his life fer me the same shall be saved.'

"An' whut does the gospel of John say?

"He says, 'Whutsoever ye ast in my name, that I shall do.'

"An' whut did Paul say?" he shouted.

There was a dead silence as the congregation awaited the words of the Apostle Paul. At that instant little Toddy appeared in the front door where he paused uncertainly.

"An' whut did Paul say?" repeated Good 'Lige in a stentorian voice.

"Paul said," piped up little Toddy, "that ef'n ye didn't pay him fer them seven pints ye already owe him fer, ye'll not git a-nuther drap frum him as long as ye live."

Dog Breaks Neck From Admiration

Bad 'Lige came into my office one morning last week and took his customary seat, leaning back against the radiator. Old Jeter, a gigantic Chinese Chow dog, who sleeps most of the day under a table next to the linotype machine, came in from the shop, yawning mightily.

With a startled exclamation, Bad 'Lige leaped to his feet and started toward the door. Then he stopped.

"Great day in the mornin'!" he ejaculated. "Fer a minnit I thought he was a b'ar. Whut kind is he?"

"Chinese Chow," I explained. "They use them for hunting snow tigers in Tibet and western China."

"Wall, I'd shore hate to be one of them tigers," said Bad 'Lige, gingerly patting Jeter's head. "Is he good fer huntin' — I mean in this country?"

"I don't know," I replied with a shrug. "He's never been out for any game here as far as I know."

"Wall, fetch him over to the Devil's Apern sometime, an' we'll try him out on one of them b'ars up thar. A few has done come in frum some'rs. Looks like he shore could chaw one up an' spit him out."

The old moonshiner sat looking at the dog admiringly, and then there came a twinkle in his eyes and, I knew it presaged a tale.

"Ye know," he ruminated, "we ain't got no b'ar dawgs up thar since ol' Lyin' Jim Bartley killed ol' Tough Tom, er leastwise was the cause of ol' Tough Tom a-killin' of hisself. I reckon ye knowed Lyin' Jim. Leastwise I know ye've heerd the boys a-talkin' a-bout Tough Tom."

"I may have, but go ahead with the story," I suggested.

"Wall ol' Tough Tom was one of the biggest an' best huntin' dawgs as was ever seed on the Apern. He was good fer nigh a-bout any kind of huntin' — b'ar, 'coon, wildcats, an' ever'thing. He could stay right with Big Howdy an' Mary Lou in a fox-race any day, an' Lyin' Jim was plenty proud of him. Now, over in Kaintucky last fall they had 'em a big fox-race with houn's fetched in frum all over the country to run in it. Thar was dawgs frum Missoury an' Indy-yanny, an' Lyin' Jim tuck Tough Tom down thar an' he shore done hisself proud.

"Ol' Tough Tom was a blue-ticked dawg, a-bout one-third Walker strain, an' when it comes to runnin' foxes he was most of the time at the head of the pack. He could stick on the trail the fastest of any houn' I ever knowed, an' he knowed foxes so good he could gin'rilly figger out whut they was a-goin' to do afore the foxes theirselves knowed. He'd take the nigh-cuts thataway an' head the fox off — sorty had nat'ral ab-stinks like that.

"Wall, atter the last of the races was run over thar on Beefhide Crick, ol' Tough Tom he tuck fu'st prize an' they tied a blue ribbon a-roun' his neck with a gold medal on it, an' Lyin' Jim got two honnerd dollars in cash to boot. An' they got their pictoors in the papers, too.

"Fer a while atter that nothin' was too good fer ol' Tough Tom. He even slept on Lyin' Jim's bed, an' he got fu'st crack at the vittels that Jim's wife cooked up. An' all that pettin' an' pamperin' jest plain ruint ol' Tough Tom. It wasn't long ontel he got jest downright wu'thless — wouldn't even run the pigs outta the gyarden. All he wanted to do was to strut a-roun' a-wearin' that ribbon an' medal, an' ad-mirin' of hisself in the lookin'-glass.

"An' he was shore proud of hisself too. In par-ticklar he liked to hear hisself bay, an' ever' night he'd set out thar on the porch an' bark at the moon an' howl long an' mournful ontel the sun come up. In a few months he got to be sich a pest an' all that Lyin' Jim de-cided that he'd jest have to git rid of him.

"But atter all was said an' done, Lyin' Jim still sorty loved ol' Tough Tom, an' to save his life he couldn't jest go out thar in the yard an' shoot him, er put p'izen in his vittels, er nothin' like that. He tried to give the dawg a-way, but it looked like nobody wanted him, an' he knowed he couldn't take him out an' lose him in the woods bekaze Tough Tom'd beat him back home.

"So Lyin' Jim he got to thinkin' an' he skum him a scheme that shore done the job. He tied a peacock's feather onto ol' Tough Tom's tail, an' that durn fool dawg broke his own neck a-tryin' to ad-mire his own behindst."

The Thawed Out Foxrace

Last Saturday afternoon was one of those rare times when Willie B. Fuller apparently was completely sober. I use the word "apparently" advisedly, because I was later to have serious doubts about the state of his sobriety. Anyway, on that afternoon several of us were gathered in Brandy Bill's mill, staying close to the stove because of the bitter cold outside, while Willie B. seemed to be dozing in his accustomed corner. Then suddenly he sat up.

"You fellows," he said, swaying almost imperceptably, "have been entertaining the erudite Editor for a long time with your Tales of the Tall Timbers where the woodbine twineth and the whangdoodle mourneth for its first-born. It's my turn now."

When he had finished his cup of ginger stew he caught his breath, and told me the following yarn:

There are many deep and inexplicable mysteries here on the Devil's Apron he said, and only a few daring souls have had the courage to penetrate some of the dark recesses in which sunshine is rarely seen. I had been hearing of some of the occult happenings and incidents from time to time, but it was not until a few weeks ago that I became an eye-witness. As those here may remember, several of us recently met at Brandy Bill's home on a Saturday night, including Brandy Bill, Bad 'Lige, Little 'Bijie, and Business Bill. As they will recall, we had planned to go hunting for raccoon that night. We had had some rather warm weather in the first week of February, and this was the first time that hunting had been possible because of the snow and ice.

"Thar's a big he-coon up on the head of the crick,"

Little 'Bijie had told us when we first arrived. "I reckon the game warden won't be hyer to ketch us. They say as how he's gone to school some'rs to l'arn more about the game laws, so we can slip up thar an' ketch that coon without nobody ever knowin' about it."

All of us, you remember, seemed agreeable to that suggestion, and in a little while we started up No-Business Creek. The trail was mostly mud because the sunshine had melted the ice and snow, and we had difficulty in making any progress. It was not long though until Big Howdy hit the trail of that raccoon, and then the race was on. The other hounds joined in the chorus, and in a short time the sound of their baying died away in the distance. We followed as fast as possible, and reached the point where the road turns off toward Little 'Bijie's farm when suddenly Big Howdy came back to us, bringing the remainder of the pack with him.

Big Howdy came straight to you, Brandy Bill, and every hair on his back was standing straight up. He was growling deep in his throat, and the other dogs were whining in abject fear.

"Whut do ye reckon's the matter of 'em?" demanded Little 'Bijie in a hoarse whisper.

"Danged ef'n I know," replied Brandy Bill, staring into the darkness in the direction from which the dogs had come. "Somethin's shore skeered hell outta 'em."

Just at that moment from deep back in the blanket of darkness came the sounds of a hunting pack in full cry.

"It's a-nuther fox-race," declared Little 'Bijie. "Wonder who else is out tonight?"

As you will recall, we stood in utter silence for a few minutes, trying to pierce the curtain of night with the aid of the fitful light of a lantern.

"Why—why—that's Big Howdy's voice a-leadin' that race," gasped Brandy Bill unbelievingly, his hair standing as straight up as that of Big Howdy. He glanced down with an expression of bewilderment at Big Howdy who was lying at his feet.

"An' jest lissen thar!" said Bad 'Lige in a tone of awe and unbelief. "That's leetle Mary Lou an' ol' Blue Smoke, I'd know their voices anywhar' — an' ol' Blue Smoke's been dead fer more'n two months."

"Ever'body stand still!" ordered Brandy Bill. "They're a-comin' this way."

The baying of that pack of hounds was growing so loud that it almost deafened us, and in a couple of minutes they were upon us. To our complete mystification the barking dogs appeared to be right in our midst, even running over us, but strain our eyes as we might we could not catch a glimpse of any of them. It was uncanny — unbelievable — and we stared at each other in astonishment and even panic.

The baying gradually died down as it went on down the creek toward the river. Then suddenly the race reversed itself, and came back toward us. Evidently the phantom fox had doubled back on his trail to throw the dogs off, and once more they roared right past us. We stood there hardly daring to breathe, and then Brandy Bill expelled his breath with relief.

"Fer a minnit that thar race had me guessin'," he said with a laugh. "Ye see, that race we jest heerd was the one that we had afore Chris'mus endurin' that turrible cold spell. Ye'll re-colleck that it got so cold that we had to leave the dawgs up hyer an' git in outta the twenty-below zero weather.

"It was so blamed cold that it plum froze up all the sounds of that foxrace, an', like ye know, it's been mighty cold ever since then. That old foxrace jest stayed froze up ontel tonight when this warm wind frum the south has done thawed it out."

Paw Traipsin' in Heaven in His Shirt-Tail

Good 'Lige came into my office a few days ago. I was busy at the moment, so I waved him toward the exchange table and told him that he could browse through some of the weekly papers for a few minutes until I could finish what I was doing. Finally I got through and leaned back.

"It shore looks like some of these noospapers in this part of the state air a-hittin' at the gov-ment down thar at Richmond fer tightwaddin' on the counties," 'Lige observed, lighting the stogie that I had handed to him.

"Well," I replied, "it does seem that we ought to be getting a little more help in the matter of roads and schools."

"All of us on the Devil's Apern air shore with ye on that," he said with emphasis. "I've been a-readin' hyer," he continued, gesturing toward the papers, "whar they've got mill-yuns of dollars in the—the—."

"Surplus," I supplied.

"Yeah, that's it, an' jedgin' frum whut I've seed with my own two eyes, they shore ort to have a — surplus. They ain't spent nothin' on the Devil's Apern in I don't know how long. Take our school, now! Ye could throw a dawg by the tail through the cracks, an' the mud up the No-Bizz'ness Crick road is straddle deep to High-Pockets Hen Maggard who's all of seven foot tall. Yes sir, we shore could use a leetle of that thar surplus.

"Them a-bein' so tight-fisted down thar," he continued, thoughtfully staring at the ceiling, "puts me in mind of the time that ol' Goose-neck John Hardin' died in the a-sy-lum, an' the state sent his body back home. Le's see! That must a-been all of twenty years ago — er more."

"Tell me about it," I requested when he had grown silent.

"Like I was a-sayin' ol' Goose-neck an' his ol' woman they lived up thar on Coon Branch. His wife's name was Hanner, an' they sorty kept to theirselves most of the time. They raised a passel of young'uns, an' they sorty scattered but the ol' folks got a-long allright ontel ol' Goose-neck got it in his head to run fer Jes-tice of the Peace. He made a hard race, but he got beat so bad he never ever heard the whissle blow.

"Purty soon atter that folks got to noticin' that ol' Goose-neck was sorty actin' quar', an' it wasn't long ontel he went crazy as a bess-bug. They fetched him over hyer to town whar they egg-zamined him, an' the cou't found him to be in-sane, so they sent him off. But Goose-neck he got wu'ss an' wu'ss, shet up in that place, an' then he died whilst he was thar, an' they shipped his body back home to be buried.

"But even back in them days the state wasn't a-spendin' no more money than it had to, an' one of the ways they was tight-waddin' was on the clothes they put on them as died in state horspitals an' a-sy-lems an' the like.

"When Goose-neck died they put him in a coffin an' sent it back by train. A'nt Hanner she sent fer me to come to their place an' preach ol' Goose-neck's fun'ral. We had the preachin' in the home, an' thar was a big crowd of the neighbors thar fer it. The coffin was put in the livin'-room, an' I stood jest behindst it whilst I was a-preachin'.

"Now, that thar coffin had a lid on it — one of them that ye can lift up so that all the folks can take a look at the re-mains. When that part of the lid was raised up, ye could jest see Goose-neck's head an' shoulders, but none of the boys knowed egg-zackly how to open it up when the time come fer the people to pass by an' take their last look.

"Somebody got a screw-driver, an' they onscrewed the

whole top of that coffin, ex-posin' the corpse frum one eend to t'other. A'nt Hanner an' some of the wimminfolks was the fu'st to take a look at the de-parted, an' they sorty gasped fer breath, an' then stood a-lookin' an each other — like they was struck plum dumb.

"Fer a minnit I jest couldn't figger out whut was the matter with 'em, an' then I sorty peeped over their shoulders. I seed that the corpse was all dressed up in a b'iled shirt, an' black frock coat, but he didn't have on no britches a-tall. The state had done saved the cost of them britches.

"An't Hanner she turned to one of her gran'sons.

" 'Acy,' she says in a hoarse whisper, 'ye go take off them britches of yore gran'pap's ye're a-wearin', an' fetch 'em to me quick. I don't keer ef'n ye do have to go b'ar-nekkid. Now, wouldn't yore pore ol' gran'pappy look like hell a-traipsin' down the streets of the New Jerusalem in his shirt-tail?' "

Business Bill's Cats Head for the Dirt

Brandy Bill was coming out of his gate the other afternoon when I stopped in front of his home. It was growing a bit chilly, and Bill was wearing a heavy sweater.

"Going somewhere, Bill?" I queried.

"Sorty figgered on goin' up to Shorty Hawkins' place up in Hoot-Owl Holler back up the crick a piece an' git me a houn' pup that Shorty has been a-promisin' me. He's a whole Walker breed, an' I allus have wanted one of 'em."

"I don't think I know Shorty Hawkins," I said as I got out of the car and joined him.

"Wall, he's jest Shorty Hawkins — nobody much an' mighty leetle of that. He lives up thar a couple of miles er so. Come on an' go a-long with me. It won't take long."

The air was crisp and the walking fine, and I thoroughly enjoyed the climb up the rather steep road toward the looming, serrated Cumberlands. It was almost time for the "sarvice" trees to bloom as well as the red-bud, but it was a late spring, and there were patches of snow here and there on the higher slopes.

"Shorty Hawkins is a funny sort of a feller," explained Brandy Bill as we walked along. "He never works any, ner does he try to raise anything to eat in them rocks a-bout his place. I don't know whar he gits his money er grub, but I ain't never heerd of him an' his fambly a-starvin'. I reckon he makes a leetle moonshine, but ef'n he does he's a-makin' it some-rs else 'ceptin' hyer on the Apern.

"It's so all-fired rough up thar whar he lives that ye raise no craps ner nothin', so I reckon he hunts some to keep a leetle meat on the table. He's got a wife an' a young'un er two, an' I reckon it don't take much to keep 'em a-goin'.

"His wife's a big strappin' woman, an' frum what I've heerd she shore does wear the britches at his house." Brandy Bill chuckled to himself. "I've heerd that she keeps a houseful of cats an' pets 'em all the time, an' that Shorty an' the young'uns eat whut the cats leave. But I don't know whar that's the truth er not."

Just about then a black and yellow housecat dashed past us at a speed that made just a streak out of it. It zipped past Brandy Bill and an instant later vanished around a bend in the path just below us. Brandy Bill and I stopped and stared after it in astonishment.

"Now, whut do ye reckon ailed that thar cat?" he asked of me with a puzzled frown. I shook my head in bewilderment and then we walked ahead for a few steps.

"Shorty he lives up thar in front of us jest a few honnerd yards," he murmured, "an' I reckon that was one of his wife's pets." Then he halted in his tracks. "Hyer comes a-nuther of them dam' cats. Look out!"

We leaped to one side as another of those cats, practically the same color as the first, went past us at even a more blinding speed. At first I thought that the cat had hydrophobia, or something like that, and I gave it plenty of room as it dashed by.

"Somethin' powerful funny a-bout them cats," declared Brandy Bill. "Don't know as I ever seed one act like that afore."

We started on up the path, keeping a wary look out for more cats that might be in a terrific hurry, and we didn't have long to wait. The next time there were two of them, but they were going so fast that we didn't even get a good look at them until they were gone. In the next ten minutes or so, and before we reached Shorty's cabin, eleven of those cats had passed us heading for parts unknown, and losing no time in getting there. Finally we broke into a clearing.

There was smoke coming from Shorty's chimney, and

everything about the house looked peaceful and serene, and certainly there was nothing in sight that could have frightened any cat so badly. Shorty appeared at the front door and, when he saw us entering the gate, he came across the porch to meet us.

"Come atter that pup?" he said to Brandy Bill.

"Yeah," drawled the latter, "but fu'st I want to know what on earth's the matter with them cats of yores. They've been a-goin' down the holler like hell atter a bee-martin fer the last few minnits."

"Wall, I'll tell ye," laughed Shorty, "my ol' woman she pets an' feeds them blamed cats, an' they sleep all day long. But she's been a-havin' a purty hard time house-breakin' them cats, an' she's had to flail the tar outta 'em a few times fer mesin' up the place. So when it comes supper an' bedtime fer them they know they've got to move fast. Ye see, it's nigh a-bout a mile to the clostest dirt to kivver up with."

Maw Ate Wild Onions

There was a twinkle in Good 'Lige's eyes when he stalked into my office one day last week, and seated himself in the most comfortable chair vacant. I had an idea that he had brought another of his inimitable tall tales with him so I reached into my desk and brought out a box of cigars. He selected one and lighted it with extreme care.

"Anything new on the Devil's Apron?" I asked, tossing my feet to the top of the desk.

"No," he replied between puffs. "That is thar ain't nothin' that might be called plum onusual. We've been a-havin' a few mo-lasses stir-offs, an' thar was a shotgun weddin' — I reckon ye could call it that."

"Tell me about the wedding," I urged, reaching for a pad and pencil to make a few notes.

"Wasn't nothin' much to it. Ye see, one of Bizz'ness Bill's boys wanted to marry up with one of ol' Seven-Britches Jackson's gals. I reckon ye know both Bizz'ness Bill an' Seven-Britches, don't ye."

"Of course I know Business Bill, but I never even heard of this man — Seven-Britches. That's a rather strange name."

"An' Seven-Britches is a strange feller to go a-long with it. Ever' time he buys him a new pair of britches he jest puts 'em on over the top of them that he's a-wearin' an' sometimes he's got on six er seven pairs at the same time — dependin' some on the weather.

"Now, like ye know, Bizz'ness Bill he's got some high an' mighty ideas, an' is allus a-figgerin' on some way to git rich. Anyhow he ob-jected to his son, Herbert Hoover, a-marryin' Seven-Britches' gal, but Bizz'ness Bill's wife, Nervy, she had other idees bekaze she liked the gal.

"Nervy!" I ejaculated. "That's a peculiar name, too."

"Short fer Minervy, but ever'body jest calls her Nervy, er Nerve. Anyhow, she tuck a shotgun atter Bizz'ness Bill, an' the weddin' come off on schedule."

Good 'Lige laughed silently and then squinted through the smoke at me.

"Did I ever tell ye a-bout the time that Nervy had sich a time of it a-tryin' to wean leetle Ike — her youngest son?"

"No, I haven't heard that one."

"Wall, like ye know, Bizz'ness Bill an' Nervy have done had 'em a whole passel of young'uns—I fergit how many—an' he named 'em all atter Re-publican Pres-i-dents, be-ginnin' with Abe Lincoln an' a-comin' all the way down through Grant an' Garfiel', an' McKinley, an' Taft, an' Hardin', an' Coolidge, an' Herbert Hoover, an' of cou'se they called the baby Leetle Ike.

"It happened that Leetle Ike was a puny young'un an' jest didn't grow up like all of his brothers. Nervy she sorty petted an' pampered him, an' he got to be six or seven years old. An' she had been a-tryin' to wean him fer sev'ral years, but it jest seemed like she couldn't do it. He wouldn't eat no Bartley-sop er nothin' that she fixed fer him an' like whut she raised t'other boys on.

"Purty soon it got noised a-roun' over the Apern that A'nt Nervy couldn't wean Leetle Ike, an' a few weeks ago, up thar at the Hard-Rock Firm-Foundashun meetin'-house a bunch of the wimmin gethered a-roun' Nervy whar she was a-nussin' Leetle Ike out thar onder a tree.

" 'Why don't ye wean that young'un?' said one of them wimmin. 'He must be a-gittin' nigh onto seven years ol', ain't he?'

" 'Eight, come December the tenth,' replied Nervy with a sigh. 'I've done ever'thing I can think of an' I ain't been able to break him yit. It seems like he's so leetle an' puny-like, that I jest can't make up my mind to make him quit.

" 'I'll tell ye how I allus weaned 'em when they got contrary thataway,' said a-nuther of them wimmin. 'Jest take a leetle assy-fitte-dy, an' put it on yore boosum, an' that's shore to wean him onct he gits a taste. Jest try it next time."

"That was an a Satte'day, an' A'nt Nervy follered them in-struck-shuns to the letter the next mornin' afore they started out to meetin'. It was a big 'Socia-shun meetin' an' thar was half a dozen preachers thar to take a part in it. Atter a-bout half of them had done preached fer mebbe three hours, Leetle Ike he started to figit.

" 'Maw,' he says plum out loud so's ever'body heerd him, 'I'm hongry.'

"A'nt Nervy she lifted him up an' started to nu'ss him, an' he tuck a couple of pulls an' then he turned an' spit out in the aisle. He twisted an' looked at Bizz'ness Bill.

" 'Paw,' he says, 'have ye got airy a chaw of terbacker. I'm dammed ef'n Maw ain't been a-eatin' wild onions.' "

Rosella and the Parsnips

Back several years ago, when my daughter, Rosella, was just a little girl, she finally persuaded me to take her with me on my next trip to the Devil's Apron. And so, on a warm and beautiful summer morning we headed over that way.

"Now listen, Honey," I cautioned as we drove down to Pound River, "there may be a few things happen over there today that you won't exactly understand. They do things differently in many ways, but you mustn't say anything that will hurt their feelings."

"I'll just watch you, Daddy," she said confidently, "and I'll do just as you do."

"Well, that might be all right," I agreed uncertainly, "at least most of the time. I expect we'll manage."

Good 'Lige was holding his regular services at the Hard-Rock Firm-Foundation Church, and we got there just as they were starting to sing the first song. We found seats close to the door, and sat there for the next two long hours. Good 'Lige was at the peak of his form that day, and I was worn to a frazzle on that hard bench. Rosella, to my complete surprise, sat quiet and still as a mouse throughout the interminable sermon.

"Were you interested, Honey?" I asked when we got outside again.

"In a way," she replied. "I kept watching that old preacher's whiskers bob every time he said 'ah!' Why did he say that at the end of each sentence?"

"Sh-h-h-h!" I whispered.

Good 'Lige was approaching us, and he very cordially invited us to have dinner at his home, and his wife, Aunt Marthy, echoed the invitation warmly. I accepted with haste because I was ravenously hungry, and I knew that Aunt Marthy's cooking was unexcelled anywhere. And three or four of their neighbors also had been asked to dinner, and when we got to the house, Aunt Marthy told us that she had almost all of the dinner already cooked, but that she would have to warm it up, and bake a few biscuits.

The odors that came out of that kitchen were so enticing that it was all that I could do to keep Rosella from investigating in the hope that she would get a drumstick anyway. But at last Aunt Marthy called to us and we lost no time in finding seats at that groaning table.

And what a table! The first thing to greet my eye was a huge platter of chicken fried a golden brown, and beside it a large dish of country ham and gravy to go with those fluffy biscuits. Flanking these were bowls of corn on the cob, green beans, creamed potatoes and also a large bowl of parsnips.

There were also stacks of pies and two huge cakes, jellies, preserves, jams and honey, but it was one of the cakes that caught my eye. It was an unusually large "stack-cake" made of gingerbread with applebutter filling. Aunt Marthy knew that this was my favorite of all desserts, and my mouth drooled just looking at it.

Good 'Lige asked the blessing, and he made quite a ceremony out of it. It was really a ten minute prayer, and for the first time I noticed that Rosella was squirming. I was so hungry that I could understand how she felt, and I was relieved when he expressed a stentorian "A-Men!"

Rosella had her eye on that fried chicken. On top of the platter was a large piece of breast, and I could tell by the gleam in her eye that she was determined to get it if at all possible. She looked at me a couple of times, and I shook my head and told her that we must wait until the platter was passed around.

Aunt Marthy picked up the bowl of parsnips, and walked around the table with it. On each person's plate she dabbed down a big spoonful. Rosella looked at her helping, and then whispered to me.

"Daddy, I never could eat these things."

"I don't like them either," I told her, "but we'll have to eat them. It wouldn't be polite to leave them on our plates, besides we have to make room for the chicken and all of those other good things."

She shut both of her eyes, and, after a terrific struggle, she managed to swallow the last of her parsnips. Then she looked up at me hopefully, and I was just reaching for the chicken when Aunt Marthy came past us again with that bowl of parsnips. She looked down at Rosella's plate and saw that it had been cleaned.

"Fore Gawd!" she gurgled happily. "Don't that chile love pas'nips!"

And she proceeded to fill Rosella's plate full of parsnips. With a sigh of martyrdom I swapped plates with her.

Framing Grandma's Picture

The boys were having a shooting match over on the Devil's Apron last Saturday afternoon, and I joined Good 'Lige who was standing close to a smouldering heap of logs at which, from time to time, the marksmen were warming their "trigger fingers".

"Why aren't you shooting in some of the matches?" I asked when we had shaken hands.

"Splatter matches!" exploded the old preacher in disgust. "Shootin' a shotgun at thirty steps! Do ye call that shootin'?"

"I'll admit that it's largely a matter of luck," I replied. "It's not like the old turkey-shoots, eh?"

"Not by a long sight! Ef'n ye tie a turkey down behindst a log with jest his head a-stickin' above it, an' then step off a honnerd yards, an' shoot at the turkey's head with a muzzle-loadin' gun, then ye've got a reel shootin' match. But then I reckon thar ain't no more of them ol' hawg-rifles, ner shooters neither."

Good 'Lige kicked a couple of log-ends deeper into the fire and fanned the coals with his old felt hat. I paid for a shot in the next match, and, while the officials were listing the contestants, I returned to the fire.

"I was told that you are going to move over to town," I ventured. "You bought the old Williams place, didn't you?"

"Uh-huh!" he grunted. "Marthy an' my gal, Allaphair, they kept a-pesterin' me ontel I bought the place a couple of weeks ago. I reckon they'll be movin' over thar next week — leastwise that's whut they air a-plannin'."

"Aren't you coming, too?"

"No, I reckon not. I'm too ol' a dawg to be a-tryin' to l'arn new tricks. Wouldn't feel to home anywhar 'ception' hyer on the Apern. I've lived hyer all my life, an' I figger it's too late to make sich a change now. I'll jest sorty stay hyer at the ol' place an' look atter things. I shore wouldn't be satisfied in town.

"But, now, y take Marthy an' Allaphair! They air plum ex-cited a-bout movin' into their new house an' all, an' they've been a-spendin' most of their time over thar. I've gone with 'em a couple of times, an' they tuck me all over the house, a-showin' me ever'thing they air a-puttin' in it. Marthy she had a couple thousan' dollars that she'd saved frum her share of whut they got when they sold the coal on her pappy's land, an' now she's a-buyin' new fixin's fer the house — beds an' cyarpets an' furn-i-ture an' sich.

"They ain't a-takin' none of the stuff frum over hyer. They jest turned up their noses when I ast them how much of the househol' plunder they wanted hauled over thar. No sir! They done bought 'em a new 'lectrick stove, an' washin' machine an' con-trap-tions like that, an' they've got water a-runnin' in the house. An' the floors was so slick I was afeard to walk acrost 'em fer thinkin' I'd fall an' break a leg.

"But betwixt 'em, I reckon they've got ever'thing all figgered out. Fu'st thar is a pianny room, with a pianny in it, an' Allaphair has done started to takin' lessons so's she can play on it, an' thar ain't nothin' else in the room but some cheers an' a table an' a long sofy. Then they've got a-nuther room which they air a-callin' a 'settin'-room in which ye can't do nothin but jest set.

"An' Marthy's plum ex-cited a-bout the three rooms that air jest fer sleepin', an' she's a-plannin' to take over e-nough feather beds fer all them beds. That's all she's a-takin' frum our house hyer, an' it looks like I'll have to make me a shuck-mattress. She's done set a-side one of them rooms fer the preacher when he comes a-visitin'.

"Thar's a-nuther room jest fer eatin' an' nothin' else with a table an' six fine cheers, an' a thing to put the purty dishes in. An' the kitchen ain't got no table whar a man can pull off his shoes an' eat in comfort. It's that kitchen that's got me plum bluffed — all bright an' shiney an' no place to spit er nothin'.

"An' they've got still a-nuther room that's got all of us plum flabbergasted. We ain't figgered out yit egg-zackly whut to do with it. It's got a thing with water a-runin' in it whar ye can wash yore hands, an' it's got a big pink tub whar ye can wash all over. Then it's got somethin' else that's got us puzzled a heap. It's a sort of a big funny shaped bowl with two lids on it. Marthy says as how she aims to make a dough-board outta the top lid, an' mebbe frame grandma's pictoor with t'other'n."

Sin-Sockin' Sam's Coatail

"Ye shore did play hell with that thar piece ye put in yore noospaper," greeted Brandy Bill when I climbed out of my car at the grist-mill the other day. Brandy Bill, Little 'Bijie, Willie B. Fuller, and Bad 'Lige all gathered around me, and it was easy to see that something unusual had taken place.

"Why, what did I do?" I asked. "What piece was that?"

"It was that tale ye told a-bout ol' Sin-Sockin' Sam Tolliver a-losin' his leetle yaller mule when the officers raised that still," explained Little 'Bijie.

"But I didn't print anything but the truth," I protested.

"Sometimes it's the truth whut hurts most," declared Brandy Bill with a chuckle.

"Somebody tell me what happened?"

"Wall, I reckon this has been a-comin' on fer quite a spell," related Brandy Bill. "Ye see, Brother Sin-Sockin' Sam he has been a-preachin' a leetle too much hellfire an' dam-nashun to suit some of the folks, an' they've been sorty huntin' fer somethin' to fetch ag'inst him an' mebbe git 'em a new preacher.

"When they read in yore paper a-bout him a losin' that mule — an' whar at — they upped an' called a meetin' of the deecons an' officers of the church, an' they demanded that Brother Sam re-sign as their pastor. That's a-bout the size of it."

" 'Ceptin' that he's a-goin' to preach his fare-thee-well sermon over at his church on Whisperin' Crick tomorrer morin'."

"I'll be there," I promised because I certainly was not going to miss that performance.

I was on the grounds early the following morning, and it appeared that everyone from the Devil's Apron had come over to hear that sermon. I heard that Good 'Lige had bruited it about to the effect that he would not be holding his regular services at that hour, and his entire congregation was there to augment the Whispering Creek brethern.

Brandy Bill and I squeezed into seats on a bench near the wall, and before the services opened there was not a vacant seat in the house, and very little standing room against the walls. The old Sin-Socker was seated on a chair on the platform, thumbing through his Bible, and occasionally peering over his glasses at the whispering crowd.

Then he arose and opened the program just as though nothing out of the ordinary was in the offing. He read the Scriptures that told of the Nativity, and he particularly stressed those passages referring to the bringing of gifts by the three Wise Men. When he had finished, the choir sang that beautiful old hymn — "Amazing Grace, How Sweet The Sound".

"Brethern an' Sistern," he began, letting his gaze sweep slowly over the tensed and breathless crowd, "I was intendin' to preach this hyer Chris'mus sermon at Chris'mus time, but I have been called to a new church over in Kaintucky. So I'm a-preachin' it today, an' it is goin' to be my fare-thee-well sermon to all of ye."

He then launched into his discourse on the birth in Bethlehem some two thousand years ago, and he held his audience spellbound with his words. He preached for more than an hour, and he was at the peak of form. In a rugged but impressive manner he painted a vivid picture of the first Christmas, and all that it has meant for us down through the ages.

"Now, of cou'se," he shouted, "us sinners have added a lot of things that don't reely be-long to Chris'mus, an' didn't come outta the Bible. This hyer bizz'ness a-bout Sandy Claws a-comin' down the chimbley ain't in the scriptoors, but I reckon that part of it ain't sich a awful sin fer them as wants to believe it.

"I ain't never seed no reel sin in this hyer feastin' an' a-fixin' up Chris'mus trees an' a-deck-o-ratin' with holly an' missletoe of cou'se is a sign of everlastin' life an' the promise of a new life in the worl' to come.

"Now, thar ain't no needcessity of me a-tellin' ye young boys an' gals whut missletoe means when it's hung up over the door er some'rs, an' somebody gits onder it. An' that, brethern an' sistern, fetches me to the p'int I want to make in my fare-thee-well sermon.

"In jest a minnit I'm a-goin' to step down frum this hyer pulpit, an' I'm a-goin' to march straight down that aisle amongst ye towarge the door. An' dear brethern an' sistern, I want all of ye to take particklar notice of this big bunch of missletoe that I've got pinned on my coat-tail."

Hungry Jim Sets Up In His Coffin

"Did I ever tell ye a-bout the time that Brandy Bill set in the wake when ol' Hongry Jim Maggard died over thar on Middle Fork?" asked Little 'Bijie Birdsong as we sat on the river-bank waiting for the bass to strike one afternoon last week.

"Yeah," hurriedly spoke up Brandy Bill, "some sev'ral times." Apparently he didn't want it repeated.

"I don't recall that one," I said with a wink at 'Bijie. "How about telling it again?"

Brandy Bill busied himself with his cane-pole and line, and found a seat on a rock out of hearing distance. Willie B. Fuller, who was dozing under a bush near us, opened his eyes and leaned forward to hear the tale.

"Ol' Hongry Jim at one time," recounted Little 'Bijie, "was a purty up-standin' citizen, but when he got ol' he was all crippled up with rheumatiz. It was the kind that drawns a man up in a knot, an' it pulled him over so fur that he had to walk with a cane to keep frum pitchin' on his face. Endurin' his last years he wasn't able to git outta the house.

"But he got to be nigh onto ninety afore he tuck powerful sick. Us fellers hyer on the Apern we sorty tuck turns a-settin' up with him at nights, seein' as how thar wasn't nobody thar 'ception Hongry Jim's wife, an' she was mighty feeble. Anyhow me an' Good 'Lige an' Brandy Bill sorty looked atter him.

"But atter a couple of weeks er so Hongry Jim he passed on to his reward. Now, ye might not think it, but Brandy Bill's a purty good carpenter. They didn't have none of them thar ondertakers a-roun' hyer then, so we found some seasoned boards an' we set in an' made the coffin, an' painted it an' lined it up plum nice.

"But like I told ye, Hongry Jim had been almost drawed up double thataway with his rheumatiz, an' when we started to put him in that coffin, we found out that he jest wouldn't lay down. Ever' time we pooshed his head down, his feet'd fly up, an' t'other way a-roun'. Fer a while we was plum stumped on how to git him laid out proper.

"It was Good 'Lige thar who figgered out whut to do a-bout it, an' we got a board to lay him on an' two leather strops. We stropped his feet to one eend an' his head to t'other'n, an' then we put his coat back on to kivver up them strops an' then put him down in the coffin.

"That night a passel of the neighbors gethered in to set up with the corpse, an' endurin' the fu'st part of the night ever'thing went off smooth and easylike. But as the night passed, the folks fer the most part sorty ambled outside — one er two at a time —an' didn't come back.

"Two er three of the wimmin they stayed all night with Hongry Jim's widder, but, by a leetle past midnight, thar wasn't nobody left to set up with the body but me an' Brandy Bill an' Good 'Lige.

"Good 'Lige he kept a-noddin' in a rockin' cheer over by the fireplace, an' Brandy Bill was a settin' in a-nuther cheer an' a-leanin' back ag'inst the wall. We jest had one lamp in the room, an' the chimbley to it was all smoked up an' the wick was turned down low. Ever' onct in a while the wind would blow through the open winder an' make that light flicker sorty ghosty-like. Out in the woods a couple of hoot-owls was a hootin' to one a-nuther, an' thar was a houn' dawg in the yard some'rs which was a-howlin' in a way that's make a feller's ha'r stand up. Ye know, houn's allus seem to know when somebody's dead a-roun' the place, an' they howl ontel the cold shivvers run plum down yore back.

"It must a-been a-gittin' 'long a-bout two o'clock in the mornin' when ever'thing got sorty quieted down 'ception' that howlin' hound, that a big black cat come a-slinkin through the open door.' Me an' Brandy Bill we watched that cat to see whut it was a-figgerin' on doin', an' it stopped an' looked towarge that coffin, an' the ha'r riz up on its back. Atter a couple of seconds it turned loose the most Gawd-awful howl ye ever heerd, an' I seed Good 'Lige go over backards in his cheer. Me an' Brandy Bill we jest set thar, us not a-bein' able to move bekaze we was too bad skeered.

"Jest a-bout then thar was a noise of some sort over thar at the coffin an' we looked a-roun' to see whut it was. That strop that helt down Hongry Jim must a-broke bekaze the corpse riz right up in that coffin, an' Brandy Bill jumped like somebody'd stuck him with a pitch-fork.

"He grabbed that cat by the nap of the neck, an, on his way to the door, he stopped fer a secon' er two at the coffin.

" 'Now—now—Hongry Jim, lay back down," he says in a hoarse whisper. 'Don't ye worry a-bout nothin'. I'll put the cat out.'

"Then he went through that door like he was shot outta a gun, an' he never thought to drap that cat ontel he got plum home ag'in."

Thar Ain't No Hell

There had come news out of the Devil's Apron that my old friend, Good 'Lige, was in trouble with his church members again, and was having difficulty in keeping the flock together so I hastened over there last Saturday to learn more about it.

Several of the usual crowd were gathered at Brandy Bill's grist-mill, and I saw Brandy Bill standing down near the dam that held the waters used to turn the mill-stones. He was watching his son, Toddy, and another youngster fishing for suckers.

I joined with Bill and Bad 'Lige came down and stood beside us. We watched the boys for quite a little while, and they were having nice luck and had landed several fish more than a foot long.

"Feller can allus ketch fish," observed Bad 'Lige philosophically, "ef'n he uses the right kind of bait, 'specially suckers."

"What's this I hear about Good 'Lige having trouble with his Hard-Rock Firm-Foundation Church members?" I asked after a silence of a full minute.

"Seems as though it's this hyer No-Heller doc-trine he's been a-preachin'," replied Brandy Bill. "Looks sorty like he's done run up ag'inst a snag with ol' Sin-Sockin' Sam Tolliver an' his Heller doc-trine."

"Tell me all about it," I begged, passing out a couple of stogies.

"Wall, like ye already know," began Bill, "the ol' church was done split plum wide open on the question of whar's thar a hell er not. I reckon as how both sides be-lieved that thar was some sort of a hell some'rs fer the on-repented sinners, but they shore differed on whut kind of a place it was.

"In most places through these hills the fight got so hot that the church members busted up an' some went to hear the Heller preachers, an' some to hear the No-Hellers. An' it was like that on the Devil's Apern, an' has been fer some time.

"Of cou'se ye know that Good 'Lige has allus clung to the No-Heller side, an' to tell ye the truth most of us fellers hyer on the Apern sorty helt a-long that line, too. It was sorty comfortin to be-lieve — an' to hear a preacher say — that thar wasn't no lake of fire an' brimstone waitin' fer us when we died. Most of us kinda figgered our wimminfolks had done give us all the hell we needed hyer on earth.

"Now, like ye also know, ol' Sin-Sockin' Sam Tolliver he's the head of the Hellers in these parts, an' he's been a-preachin' about hell like they ust to preach — only more so. He's got his church over thar on Whisperin' Crick, an' some of the folks hyer on the Apern has been a-goin' over thar to hear him.

"More an' more of Good 'Lige's flock has been a-goin' over thar bekaze they be-lieved that mebbe atter all the Bible meant jest egg-zackly whut it said a-bout the Hell. They was mostly the older folks sich as air too old to be in-terested in sin no more.

"Wall, to make a long story short, ol' Sin-Sockin' Sam he put it up to some of the Devil's Aperners to fix him up a meetin'-house hyer on No-Bizz'-ness Crick, an' he'd come over an' preach no matter whut Good 'Lige thought a-bout it.

"So they got bizzy on that ol' meetin'-house that Good 'Lige ust to preach in afore they put up that new buildin' whar he is now, an' they fixed it up fer the ol' Sin-Socker. Purty soon we had two meetin's a-goin' on at the same time in them two churches jest acrost the road frum each other.

"Fer the last few months them two ol' preachers have

been a-havin' a time of it, each one a-preachin' an' a-doin' ever'thing he could to take the members a-way from t'other. It sorty looked like it was a draw battle betwixt them two parsons with fu'st one an' then t'other a-gittin' the biggest crowds.

"Good 'Lige he started things off a few weeks ago by puttin' a two-booshel sack of apples at the front door so's ever'body could help theirselves when the meetin' was over, an' then the ol' Sin-Socker he come right back with a big out door dinner on the groun's on the follerin' Sunday. Then Good 'Lige he got a couple of men to make him seats with backs to 'em an' put 'em in his meetin'-house so's to rest the backs of the good brethern an' sistern, an' Sin-Sockin' Sam he bought some of the ol' the-ater seats frum that movin' pitchoor place over thar in town, an' had plush seats fer his crowd.

"About then Good 'Lige got him a big idee. He painted his meetin'-house a purty white color, an' then he got him some black paint an' he put up a big sign acrost the front of the buildin' with letters two foot high. That sign said:

" 'THAR AIN'T NO HELL.'

"An ol' Sin-Sockin' Sam he got him some black paint an' put up a sign the same size. It said:

" 'THE HELL THAR AIN'T!' "

The Watch-Dog Rattlesnake

Brandy Bill, Bad 'Lige, Little 'Bijie and several of the boys were loafing down at Business Bill's store on the river last Sunday afternoon when I drove over to the Devil's Apron for my weekly visit. It was a hot, lazy afternoon, and for the most part all of them were interested in finding the coolest spot.

I joined Brandy Bill under a big maple that grew beside the road, and in a little while all of the others had gathered around us in a semi-circle. It was apparent that they expected a tall tale out of Brandy Bill, and he didn't lose much time in producing one.

"I reckon I fergot to tell ye," he began, nodding at me, "of ol' Seven-Britches Maggard an' his rattlesnake that he l'arnt to gyard his house fer him, didn't I?"

"Let's have it," I begged.

"Wall, it's sorty thisaway. Ol' Seven-Britches—."

"Just a minute!" I interrupted. "How did this man ever happen to get such a name as Seven-Britches?"

"Jest pyore laziness, I reckon. Allus when he got him a new pa'r of britches er over'alls he jest put 'em on over the top of them that he was a-wearin' — as many as seven p'ar at a time.

"But like I was a-tellin' ye, Seven-Britches he ketched him the kingbee of all the rattlesnakes in this hyer county. This tuck place back en-durin' the last Worl' War, an' Seven-Britches he named that snake Hitler bekaze he was meaner than p'izen.

"He tuck Hitler back home with him, an' he kept a-prankin' an' a-foolin' with him ontel he'd done l'arnt him a lot of tricks like a-keepin' a watch over the house ever' night when Seven-Britches went away frum home fer a few days, an' a-runnin' the chickens outta the gyarden endurin' the daytime.

"He shore did give that snake the right name bekaze he was one rattler that'd strike fu'st an' shake his rattles atterwards. Not only did he gyard the house an' the corncrib an' the chicken-roost, but he was plum handy a-bout a lot of other things a-roun' the place. Fer instance, ever' year when Seven-Britches de-cided to make his wife wash all seven of his britches, Hitler'd stretch hisself betwixt two poles an' make hisself a clothes-line.

"One day Seven-Britches was a-lookin' a-roun' in his smokehouse, an' he seed that he was a-losin' some of his winter-meat — side meat an' shoulders mostly — an' purty soon he diskivvered that thar was a loose board on the back side of the house. He nailed it back, an' kept a watch on the smokehouse fer a couple of nights, but nothin' happened.

"Then a leetle later he went out thar to git him some ham fer breakfus', an' he foun' whar somebody'd done tuck his last ham. Right thar was whar Seven-Britches de-cided that it was time fer him to do somethin' to put a stop to it.

"He had him a idee that the feller who was a-gittin' that meat was ol' Roguin' Rant Hartsock who at that time lived up the crick jest a whoop an' a holler away, an' who allus seemed to have plenty to eat, but never had done a honest day's work in his life as fur as anybody knowed.

"Anyhow, Seven-Britches he put Hitler out thar in that smokehouse, an' fixed him a bed clost to whar that loose board was. It looked like it'd been prized loose with a axe, an' was the onliest place whar a man could git inside.

"The way Seven-Britches allus tol' it, fer a couple of nights, nobody even tried to git in that smokehouse ag'in, but on the next night, a-bout two o'clock in the mornin', he said as how he heerd the most ongodley yell out thar some'rs that he had ever heerd in all his life. It was e-nough to make a man's ha'r stand on eend.

"He said as how he could hear a awful thumpin' an' a-threshin' an' a-bangin' a-goin' on out thar at the smokehouse, an' a-bove all that racket he could hear Hitler a-rattlin' his tail fer who laid the chunk.

"He jumped outta bed an' jerked on one of them seven pa'rs of britches, an' run out thar. He lit a match, an' then his eyes nigh a-bout popped outta his head. He seed that Hitler had done wropped hisself a-roun' Roguin' Rant's neck so tight that he was plum blue in the face, an' as soon as he had got Rant plum foul, he had stuck his tail out through a crack, an' was a-rattlin' fer help fer all he was wu'th."

Too Poor To Keep A Cow

Spring had come to the Devil's Apron, and the boys were all in a happy mood when I got over there last Saturday afternoon. The ground evidently was too wet to plow, so they were all down on the river at Dutton's store learning the latest news.

"What happened to Willie B. Fuller?" I asked, searching the crowd for him. "I haven't seen him for several weeks."

"Nobody else has," declared Little 'Bijie. "I heard that somebody let him have a five gallon kag of likker, an' I reckon he's a-keepin' it comp'ny."

"That hadn't orty take more'n a week," calculated Bad 'Lige with an air of authority.

"Ye'd be the one to know," agreed Brandy Bill. "Do ye re-colleck that ten-gallon kag of red likker that feller down in Kaintucky give ye that time?"

Bad 'Lige shrugged and spat.

"Yeah," chuckled Little 'Bijie, "I helped him drink it. It shore was prime stuff."

"Never did tell ye that'n, did I?" queried Brandy Bill, turning to me.

"I shook my head in negation, and the other boys all gathered in close about us.

"Must a-been ten er twelve years ago," recalled Brandy Bill, "that a feller frum down thar at Lexin'ton come up hyer on the Apern a-huntin' fer b'ar. His name was— le's see—Martinson, wasn't it?" He looked at Bad 'Lige.

"Ye're a-tellin' it," growled the latter.

"Anyhow this feller Martinson he shore was a rich

man. He owned one of the biggest likker-makin' fac'tries in the state of Kaintucky, an' made jest a-bout the best drinkin' likker. He called his best bran' Bluegrass Dew, aged in charred wood, an' more'n seven years ol' afore he'd sell a drap of it.

"Now this hyer Kunnel Martinson was also a great b'ar hunter, an' he kept a passel of b'ar houn's that must a-cost him a bar'l of money. At that time thar was still a few b'ars back thar on the head of the Apern, an' Bad 'Lige was jest a-bout the best b'ar hunter in all these parts.

"So the Kunnel he come up hyer fer a hunt, an' he hired Bad 'Lige to go a-long with him, an' sorty show whar to go. He give Bad 'Lige ten dollars a day fer his time an' he furnished all the drinkin' likker which at that time was purty good wages. They hunted up thar a-long the Kaintucky line fer more'n a week, an' the Kunnel he got two big b'ars.

"He was so pleased an' proud of killin' them b'ars that he promised to send Bad 'Lige a present, an', shore e-nough, in a-bout two weeks Bad 'Lige got a notice from the railroad people at Elkhorn City that he had some freight over thar. We went over an' got it, an' it was a ten gallon kag of that Bluegrass Dew.

"Some sev'ral of us hung a-roun' an' helped Bad 'Lige drink up that thar present, an' I don't reckon it lasted much more'n two weeks. He was purty free with it whilst it lasted, but the fu'st thing we knowed that kag was plum empty.

"A few days atter that Bad 'Lige come past my place, an' he was a-totin' that empty ten-gallon kag on his shoulder. He stopped at my gate, a' set his kag down, an' studied the markin's burnt on the side an' at both eends.

" 'Le's go down thar to Lexin'ton,' he says to me outta a blue sky, 'an' see ef'n the Kunnel will fill her up ag'in fer us. Frum whut he said, he's got a-plenty.'

"I didn't have much to do right then, so I agreed to go with him. We tuck the train at Elkhorn City, an' got to Lexin'ton a lettle atter dinnertime. We hunted a-roun' an' at last we located that big stillin' fact'ry, an' it kivvered five er six acres.

"We marched into the Kunnel's office, an' it 'peared like he was glad to see us. Then Bad 'Lige p'inted towarge his empty kag an' says as how he'd be plum o-bleeged ef'n he'd fill it ag'in. The Kunnel sorty squinted his eye an' grinned.

"'Wall, now, 'Lige,' says he, 'I don't mind givin' ye the likker, but ain't ye sorty a-crowdin' the mourners' bench a leetle? I sent you that kag full of Bluegrass Dew jest ten days ago.'

"'Yeah, I know that,' says Bad 'Lige, 'but ten gallons don't go very fur in a fambly that can't afford to keep a cow.' He got a refill.

Scratching the Bull's Stomach

I was just about ready to close my office last Friday afternoon when Good 'Lige came in for a short visit. He was dressed in a new suit, a "boiled" shirt and flaming red tie and his shoes were smartly polished. Futhermore, he had a cane hooked jauntily over his arm.

My surprise must have been plainly visible because he smothed the wrinkles out of his trouser legs, and leaned back in his chair, trying vainly to straighten out that red tie.

"I was jest on my way to the Laurel Branch Associashun—a two-day meetin'," he explained. "Me an' Sin-Sockin' Sam air a-goin' to preach both on tomorrer an' Sunday."

"Have you two smoked the pipe of peace?" I asked.

"I ain't seed him since he left the Apern, but I reckon, ever-thing considered, him an' me air a-bout even, an' thar ain't likely to be no more trubbel betwixt us."

"Anything new over on the Devil's Apron?" I queried when the conversation lagged.

Fine wrinkles converged about the corners of Good 'Lige's eyes, and his flowing white beard bobbed with a chuckle.

"Wall, thar's a tale a-goin' the rounds over thar that tickles me as much as anything I've heerd fer a long time. I was down at Brandy Bill's mill a few days ago, an' I heerd it then, an' Brandy Bill ad-mitted that ever' word of it was true.

"Like mebbe ye already know we've got us a new teacher over thar now. The one we had last fall, she upped an' got married to a soljer boy who'd come home fer a couple of weeks last Chris'mus. When his time was up she went with him out west some'rs, an' we didn't have us no school fer a couple of months.

"They didn't git nobody to take her place ontel a few weeks ago, an' then they sent us a-nuther'un—a leetle furriner frum up north some place. I've done fergot her name, but she's jest a mite of a thing that don't know nothin' a-bout straight up 'ceptin' book l'arnin'. At fu'st none of us could onnerstand nothin' she said, an' it seems like she had a purty hard time a-figgerin' out whut we was a-sayin'.

"But the young'uns all thought a heap of her, an' thar was some of 'em onder her feet ever'whar she went. I was up thar at the school a time er two, an' she shore has got them youngsters a-hustlin'—big'uns an' leetle'uns a-like. She wasn't no bigger'n yore fist, but she pyorely made them kids toe the mark.

"An' some of 'em was allus atter her to go home with 'em an' spend the night an' tell 'em stories an' sichlike. She was plum frien'ly thataway, an' most ever' night she stayed with one of 'em. She's been a-boardin' at my place, but she ain't thar more'n a couple of days in the week.

"Well, it seems that last Thursday evenin' leetle Toddy, Brandy Bill's youngest boy, got her to go home with him. A leetle afore suppertime he tuck her up the barn to show her his new calf, an' a couple of lambs that he'd made pets of.

"Now, Brandy Bill had a leetle two year-ol' scrub bull in a lot out thar behindst the barn with a eight-rail fence a-roun' it. Toddy had been a-pesterin' an' a prankin' with that bull, an' he got plum tame an' would eat outta Toddy's hands. He allus come to the fence when anybody come clost, a-hopin' they'd give him a apple er somethin'.

"Toddy was proud of that bull, an' he was the fu'st thing he tuck the teacher to see. Brandy Bill was back at the house a-cuttin' some stovewood at the time. Anyhow, when the teacher an' Toddy got to the barn-lot fence the teacher started to pet him. She poked her hand through a crack in the fence an' rubbed that leetle bull in the flank. An' that bull he let out a beller, an' he tuck one jump an' cl'ared that eight-rail fence an' never tetched a ha'r. Then he hightailed it fer the tall an' oncut timbers.

"Brandy Bill drapped his axe an' come a-runnin' to see whut was a-goin' on. He got thar jest in time to see that leetle bull go t'arin' an' snortin' an' bellerin' through the low gap towarge the Kaintucky line.

" 'Whut's the matter with him?' Brandy Bill wants to know.

" 'I reely don't know,' says that leetle teacher, her eyes a-lookin' like a couple of eggs fried on one side. 'I jest scratched his stummick, an' he jumped over the fence an' run a-way.'

"Well, Brandy Bill he kivvered his mouth with his hand, an' it was all he could do to keep from bu'stin' out a-laffin'. Then he says to the teacher:

" 'I reckon as how ye'd better sorty scratch my stummick, too. I've got to ketch the leetle fool'."

Business Bill Gives Lesson To the Bull at the Fair

It had been a sizzler all week, and it was with real relief that I got out the next Saturday and drove over to the Devil's Apron. I got no relief, however, because it was just as hot over there. I found some of the boys in the deepest shade that they could find, down on the banks of the millpond, and I joined them.

It was too hot to do any talking, and about all we could do was to fan with our hats and fight off the gnats and mosquitoes. Except for the sharp cry of a hawk up in the woods on the opposite side of the creek there was no sound to break the silence.

After an hour Brandy Bill finished the day's grinding, and came down to the shade in which we had huddled. He looked extremely hot, and was caked with dust from the meal from head to foot. Almost immediately, as if he had brought it with him, there sprang up a cooling breeze, and we relaxed with deep enjoyment.

Little 'Bijie Birdsong was the first to recover from the lethargy, and he sat up and looked over at me.

"Air they a-plannin' to hold the Farmers' Fair over thar ag'in this year?"

"They certainly are," I replied, "It's to be the biggest and best we ever had. It will be held the last week in August, and is being staged in connection with the Diamond Jubilee that the county is celebrating this year. Yes sir, it will be quite an affair, according to the reports."

"That so?" murmured 'Bijie without particular enthusiasm. "I ain't never had no luck in the things I've tuck over thar an' put in fer prizes, an' some of the boys over hyer have been a-wonderin' whar they was goin' to have a fair er not."

Brandy Bill chuckled.

"Do ye reckon ol' Greenberry Green'll enter that thar prize whiteface bull of his'n ag'in this year—the one that tuck the blue ribbon last year?"

"I imagine he will," I replied. "Why?"

"Bekaze I figgered Bizz'ness Bill might want to know," explained Brandy Bill enigmatically.

"By the way, what's happened to Business Bill?" I queried. "I haven't seen him here at the mill for several weeks."

"He's done run outta corn," said Brandy Bill succinctly.

"What about him and that prize bull?" I asked in the hope of getting another good tall tale.

"Mebbe I hadn't ort to tell it on him," Brandy Bill chuckled, "but it's too good to keep. This tuck place last year, endurin' the Fair. Like ye alreddy know, Bizz'ness Bill's the daddy of a-bout eighteen boys, an' most of 'em was with him that day a-takin' in the Fair.

"Now I reckon Bizz'ness Bill's jest a-bout the stingiest man that ever lived hyer on the Apern. They ust to tell it on him that he'd give all his sons a penny a-piece at night ef'n they wouldn't eat no supper. Then he'd git 'em to hide their money onder their pillers when they went to bed, an' he'd steal it all back whilst they was a-sleep.

"I wouldn't sw'ar to that, but I do know that he's plum tight with cash-money. When him an' his boys got thar they found a hole in the fence, an' they crawled through it so's not to have to pay that fifty cents to git inside the groun's.

"They'd fetched somethin' to eat with 'em, an' they stood a-roun' all day a-lookin' at the things that didn't cost nothin'. They had a purty good livestock show on, an' the fu'st prize of 'em all was that thar bull of ol'

Greenberry Green's, an' he shore was a-packin' 'em in to look at him.

"He was a squat-legged critter a-bout as wide as he was long, an' thar never been none like him in these parts afore him. But it was a-costin' a lot to take keer of them bulls an' cows an' hawgs an' sheep an' everything an' they was a-chargin' a quarter fer anybody to git in an' see 'em.

"Bizz'ness Bill an' all them boys they started inside, but the County Agent who was a-takin' up the tickets, stopped 'em. Bizz'ness Bill raised a racket a-bout havin' to pay to git in, an' jest then the County Agent he happened to take a look at that long line of boys strung out behindst Bizz'ness Bill.

" 'Air all these boys yores?' he asts, his eyes a-poppin'.

" 'They shore air,' says Bizz'ness Bill plum proud of hisself.

" 'Then all of ye go on in,' says he. 'I figger ye can give lessons to that thar bull'."

That Makes Onct

Some of the boys were pitching horseshoes last Saturday when I got over to the grist-mill, and I took a part in that game with Bad 'Lige as a partner. We were soundly defeated by Brandy Bill and Little 'Bijie Birdsong who were experts.

The sun had grown a little too hot, and some of us gathered in the shade of a big scycamore beside the millpond where we found a place to sit down. Brandy Bill turned the job of running the mill over to little Toddy, and came down to sit with us.

"Bizz'ness Bill has been havin' him a leetle wife trubble, ain't he?" he asked of no one in particular. "Did he tell any of ye fellows a-bout it?"

"Not a word," replied Good 'Lige. "Whut happened?"

"Nothin' much," Brandy Bill shrugged. "He was sorty com-plainin' to me a few days ago that his wife was on a t'ar a-bout him a-takin' up so much of the time poli-tickin' an' not doin' the work on the farm—ef'n ye could call it that. Anyhow, it seems like he had been more inter-ested in the comin' 'lection than he was with his craps, an' she got kinda tired of it."

Brandy Bill paused, and squinted thoughtfully at the looming mountains above him.

"I reckon he ort to do like ol' Hosshead Bill Maggard done that time he got married up with that widder-woman, Juneybell Cantrell. "Ye re-colleck ol' Hosshead, don't ye?" He was looking at me.

"I've heard of him. Dead, isn't he?"

"He shore is. He's the feller that Good 'Lige was

a-preachin' a-bout when they buried him, an' said as how the only thing the matter with Hosshead was that he was named atter the wrong eend of the hoss. Wall, be that as it may, ol' Hosshead was a purty good citizen in his day, an' he shore did make Juneybell toe the mark.

"Ye see, Hosshead had him a wife an' a young'un er two when he shot an' killed him a man over in Kaintucky on 'lection day a long time ago. They ketched him an' tried him, an' the jury give him ten years in the pen. Whilst he was a-servin' his sentence, his wife got her a de-vorce, an' married somebody over on Elkhorn Crick.

"Hosshead he got some time off fer be-havin' himself whilst he was in the pen, an' purty soon atter they turned him loose, he got to sparkin' Juneybell, a widder with two er three chillun of her own.

"Now, Juneybell she had a plum sharp tongue—jest a-bout as bad as Leetle 'Bijie's mother-in-law—an' they said as how she'd run off both of her husbands that she had married afore Hosshead come a-courtin'. Anyway, when she got good an' mad she jest a-bout tuck the hide off'n whoever was clostest to her at the time.

"Hosshead he figgered that he was a needin' of a wife to help him take keer of his young'uns which his wife had run off an' left, an' mebbe do most of the farmin' be-sides whilst he give his time to makin' moonshine. An' Juneybell she agreed.

"They come up thar to Good 'Lige's place one day, an' both of 'em was a-ridin' a big white mule, her on behindst him. That was the tallest, biggest hard-tail that I ever seed—must a-been sixteen hands—an' jest a-bout the stubbornest. He was a-gittin' sorty ol' but he was still a purty good ridin' mule. After the weddin' they got on that mule an' rid back towarge the head of No-Bizz'ness Crick whar Hosshead was a-livin' then.

"I reckon Hosshead an' Juneybell made a purty good load fer that ol' mule to tote. Juneybell in them days was plump an' sassy, an' Hosshead weighed nigh onto two hunnerd pounds. Anyhow the mule he stumped his toe ag'inst a rock an' come mighty night a-throwin' Hosshead an' Juneybell off.

" 'That makes onct,' growled ol' Hosshead.

"That ol' mule was a-takin' his time, an' sorty a-pickin' his way amongst all them rocks an' roots—thar wasn't no road to speak of—an' in a leetle while he stumbled ag'in an' come in a ha'r of fallin' down. Hosshead jerked the bridle, an' cussed.

" 'That makes twict,' he told that mule.

"They was a-gittin' purty nigh home when that ol' mule stumbled ag'in an' went down on one knee. Hosshead he clum' outta that saddle an' pulled out his pistol. Takin' a dead aim he shot that mule right plum betwixt the eyes, an' that was the last of ol' Whitey.

"Juneybell she stood thar with her mouth open fer a minnit er two, an' then she cut loose on Hosshead, an' whut she didn't tell him a-bout whut she thought of him wasn't wu'th sayin'. She called him a few names that sorty got onder his skin, but he didn't say nothin'.

"When Juneybell was all through with blessin' him out Hosshead looked her straight in the eye.

" 'That makes onct,' he said, an' they never had a cross-word atter that."

Little 'Bijie Gets the Rabies

Last Saturday there was great excitement on the Devil's Apron when I arrived over there. It looked as if war had been declared. Everyone I saw was carrying a shotgun or rifle and walking warily and watchfully. All doors were closed, and furtive faces were peering through the windows as I passed the homes.

More than a little disturbed and mystified, I parked at Brandy Bill's gate. The latter came out of the porch, and I saw that he, too, was carrying a shotgun.

"What's the matter, Bill?" I queried guardedly. "Are the revenuers out on another raid?"

"No," replied Brandy Bill, first taking a look at the road over which I had come, and then making a keen scrutiny of the highway on up on the Devil's Apron. "Thar was a mad-dawg up hyer a few days ago, an' he bit a lot of other dawgs an' cattle, an' we air all a-watchin' things keerful-like."

"Are you certain the dog was mad?"

"Shore! Come in an' set a while an' I'll tell ye a-bout it.

"That blamed dawg come from some'rs over in Kaintucky," he explained when we were seated before the blazing fire. "He was a leetle-bitsy dawg, an' none of us paid him no mind ontel he got to bitin' our dawgs an' stock, an' ever'thing he run into. The game warden shot him, an' sent the head a-way to be egg-zamined. The re-port come back that he was shore e-nough mad.

"Some of the young'uns was purty nigh skeered to death, but I reckon that nobody got bit. We air all a-watchin' our dawgs an' cattle to see ef'n they air a-goin' mad, too. Anyhow, we ain't a-takin' no chances."

Just then heavy footsteps sounded on the porch, and in stalked Bad 'Lige. He nodded at us, and then came over to the fire.

"I heerd a few minnits ago," he announced, "that Leetle 'Bijie Birdsong had got bit by that mad dawg."

"The hell ye say!" ejaculated Brandy Bill in alarm. "Has anybody told him the critter was mad?"

"Don't know a-bout that." Bad 'Lige shook his head, and there was deep concern in his eyes. "Mebbe we'd better go up thar an' see whut we can do to help him."

"Come on—le's go!" Brandy Bill was instantly on his feet, and he led the way outside, hurrying toward his parked jeep. "Pile in! It'll git us thar the quickest."

On the way up No-Business Creek Bad 'Lige and Brandy Bill plied me with questions relative to the treatment that might be had for rabies, an' whether or not Little 'Bijie was really in danger.

"They call it the Pasteur treatment," I explained, although I knew very little about it. "Anyway it's an anti-rabies serum they have discovered, and I'm sure that some of it can be found in town."

"Is it a shore cyore?" demanded Bad 'Lige anxiously.

"It's said to be effective—if given in time—but I understand that it cannot be delayed very long."

Brandy Bill rammed the gas-feed to the floorboard, and I practically held my breath for the remainder of that trip up that rough, crooked, rocky road. Little 'Bijie was standing at the door of his home when we came to a halt at the gate.

"Bijie," called Brandy Bill, "did that leetle dawg that was through hyer t'other day bite ye?"

"He shore did. Why?"

"Ain't nobody told ye yit that the blamed thing was mad?"

"No." Little 'Bijie's face turned a shade whiter.

"Wall, we've come to take ye to town fer some of

that mad-dawg med'cine. Hurry up! We ain't got no time to waste."

"Whut kind of med'cine?" demanded Little 'Bijie suspiciously.

Brandy Bill turned to me for the explanation.

"Anti-rabies serum," I said. "You should have it as quickly as possible, an' you may be getting shots for several days, even weeks."

"Wall, come on in," invited Little 'Bijie coolly. "I'll be ready in a few minnits."

We followed him through the door, and waited for him to change his clothing. Instead he rummaged in a dresser drawer and came out with a sheet of paper.

"Gimme yore pencil," he said to me, and I handed him my fountain pen.

He sat down and began to write on that sheet of paper while we shifted from one foot to the other impatiently. But he calmly went on writing.

"Git a move on, 'Bijie!" ordered Brandy Bill. "Whut air ye a-doin'? Writin' yore last will an' testy-ment?"

"Hell no!" growled 'Bijie. "I'm a -makin' me a list of all of the people I'm a-goin' to bite afore I take that thar anti-rabbit med'cine."

Good 'Lige Rescues Drowning Girl

The rains of the following week made impassable the roads on the Devil's Apron, so when the next Saturday came I decided that I would forego my weekly trip over there. There was one incident, however, that had taken place last fall, which I had not written, so before the details were forgotten, I typed it for the next issue of the paper.

It was along last September that I was over there on a Sunday, and when I got there I found several of the boys getting ready to attend the big baptising service that was slated to take place that afternoon on Pound River near the mouth of Whispering Creek.

They told me that old Sin-Sockin' Sam Tolliver had been holding a series of revival services at his church, and that some twenty-five or thirty of the sinners had repented, and were coming into his church. It was to be one of the biggest events of that kind in recent local history.

Of course I knew of the bitter rivalry between Good 'Lige and Sin-Sockin' Sam, and that each of them was doing everything possible to increase his membership. Good 'Lige was in the crowd that was getting into cars at Dutton's store, and I motioned to him to get in with me.

"It looks like the old Sin-Socker has got the jump on you, Good 'Lige," I said as we drove along the highway that paralleled the river. "They tell me that he got twenty-five at one grab."

"Wall, they won't stick long," replied the old preacher

complacently. "Ye see, he's got 'em full of this hell-skeered re-ligion, but it never lasts long. He's been a-preachin' a-bout that lake of fire an' brimstones, an' the turrible punishment that is waitin' fer 'em ef'n they don't turn frum their ways, an' he jest skeered 'em into j'inin' his church. No, it ain't a-goin' to last," he added hopefully.

When we got to the scene of the baptising, we found a huge crowd on hand to witness that performance. The people practically covered all available space on the bridge over the river, and on both sides of the stream at the place where the services would be staged.

Old Sin-Sockin' Sam and some of his deacons, and the brothers and sisters of the church, were all gathered at the edge of the stream, just below the mouth of the creek, and were tuning up for a hymn or two. The candidates for baptism were sitting in chairs that had been brought from nearby homes.

It happened that there had been some unusually heavy rains for the season just a few days previously, and the river was still almost at flood stage. There was an eddy, however, just below the mouth of the creek where a huge pile of driftwood had been lodged on some rocks.

In this comparatively still and safe water the Sin-Socker was planning to do his baptising. The spot was some forty or fifty yards upstream from the bridge, and we pushed through the crowd to find a location from which we could best witness the proceedings.

We managed to get places on the bridge itself, at a point about midway across it. As we were waiting for the services to start, I heard a woman scream somewhere on the bank of the river just above us. I saw her pointing toward the swirling waters in front of her and heard her shouting something that I could not understand.

Then I saw a small child, apparently a girl, break from the surface of the water about ten feet from the bank, and everyone seemed rooted to the ground, too paralyzed to move. Just then I saw someone leap from the bridge close to where I was standing. He landed in the water near where the little girl had now vanished, an' when he came to the surface I gasped when I saw that it was Good 'Lige himseslf.

I was utterly astonished, and my first thought was that he had lost his footing and fallen from the bridge. I looked to see if he were hurt or stunned by the twenty foot fall, but he was swimming strongly. And when the little girl broke into view again he caught one of her arms and headed for the bank.

I simply couldn't believe that a man, eighty years of age, would be able to accomplish such an heroic deed. I hurried to the spot where Good 'Lige was crawling out on a sandbar. The water was streaming from his long white heard, and his teeth were chattering like castinets when I reached him and grabbed his hand.

"I just want to say," I declared when I had raised him to his feet, "that that was the most wonderfully brave thing I ever saw in my life. You have made all of us fellows many years younger than you utterly ashamed of ourselves."

With an effort he stopped shaking and glared at me.

"Whut I want to know is who the Devil pooshed me in?"

Aunt Poll and the Sweet Potatoes

I went up to Little 'Bijie Birdsong's home the other night to a molasses "stir-off," and while the molasses was boiling under the watchful eye of Little 'Bijie, Brandy Bill and the remainder of the gang sat near the open end of the furnace on which the evaporator rested. The night was a bit chilly and there was a hint of frost in the air.

"Pity the blight got the chestnuts," remarked Good 'Lige. "I allus did like to roast 'em in the ashes a-long a-bout this time of the year."

"Er some of Leetle 'Bijie's sweet-'taters that he ust to raise in that sandy meddar up at his place," chuckled Brandy Bill. "I reckon Bad 'Lige thar re-collecks them."

"Shore do," admitted the latter, kicking the end of a burning log deeper into the fire.

We were silent for several minutes, idly watching Little 'Bijie skim the green foam from the top of the pan of cane juice, and pour these skimmings into the convenient "skum-hole". At last Good 'Lige cleared his throat.

"That puts me in mind of A'nt Polly Sizemore," he said, staring thoughtfully into the fire. "I reckon I ain't thunk of her in night a-bout twenty years. Ye never knowed A'nt Poll, did ye?" he said to me.

"I seem to have vague recollections of her," I replied. "Crazy, wasn't she?"

"As a bess-bug, but plum harmless. She ust to live up hyer on the Apern—her an' Hawg-Dave who mostly made a livin' outta ketchin' wild hawgs. A tree fell on him one day, and killed him. Seemed like A'nt Poll was never right in her head atter that.

"Even though she did act funny an' all, people never did pay her no mind ontel one day up thar at the meetin'-house. I was a-preachin' that day an' when I got through I ast the brethern an' sistern to start up a song. They was a-singin' that thar song, 'On Jordan's Stormy Banks I Stand', an' purty soon I noticed that somethin' was wrong. I wasn't long in findin' out whut it was.

"Pore ol' A'nt Poll she had jest leaned back in her seat, an' was a-comin' down of a ol' Civil War song." And Good 'Lige raised his quavering but melodious voice in song:
" 'This is number one, an' the war has jest begun,
'Drink her down, boys, down, drink her down.
'This is number two, an' the Yankees in a stew,
'Drink her down, boys, down, drink her down.'

Good 'Lige paused and stroked his long beard thoughtfully.

"I dis-remember most of that song," he said, "but I do re-colleck the last two verses.

" 'This is number 'leven, an' the Rebels all in Heaven,
'Drink her down, boys, down, drink her down.
'This is number twelve, an' the Yankees all in hell,
'Drink her down, boys, down, drink her down.'

"Anyhow," continued Good 'Lige, "A'nt Poll was a-hittin' the high spots, an' she was blamed nigh to drownin' out everybody else. In fact, she was a-singin' all by herself atter a few lines, an' it broke up the meetin'.

"Her kinfolks seed as how they'd have to do somethin' a-bout her, so they built her a leetle house next door to her gal, who got married up with that Whorter boy. They put a high board fence a-roun' it so's A'nt Poll couldn't git out an' git lost er somethin'. An' some of 'em seed to it that she didn't want fer nothin'.

"But A'nt Poll she didn't like that bizz'ness of bein' cut off frum ever'thing thataway. She sorta wanted to see whut was a-goin' on, so she got a bench an' some boxes, an' piled 'em up so's she could git on the roof an' see over that fence, an' pass the time of day with the neighbors when they passed by.

"It was a-bout that time that Leetle 'Bijie was a-raisin' him a nice patch of sweet-'taters down thar in that sandy fiel', er at least he was a-gittin' ready fer it. One day he was a-haulin' a load of manure down thar to put on that fiel' afore he turned it onder fer the plantin' of the slips. He driv' past A'nt Poll's shack, an' A'nt Poll was a-settin' on the roof, a-smokin' her pipe.

" 'Whut air ye a-doin', 'Bijie?' she hollored when he got in front of her.

" 'Jest a-haulin' a load of manure, A'nt Poll,' he says, bringin' his team to a stop.

" 'Whut do ye aim to do with it?'

" 'Put it on my sweet-'taters.'

" 'Now ain't that somethin'?' cackles A'nt Poll. 'Mebbe I am crazy, but I allus liked mine better with butter on 'em'."

Little Toddy and George Washington

I drove over the Devil's Apron last Thursday to see if any of the boys wanted to go with me to the Congressional Convention that was to be held in Bristol on Saturday, but I didn't see anyone until I parked my car in front of Brandy Bill's home. He was out in the barnyard looking over a couple of calves.

Upon drawing closer I saw that he was also trimming a long willow switch. I eyed it questioningly, and Brandy Bill's rather grim face softened a bit.

"Looks as if someone was in trouble," I ventured.

"I'm waitin' fer Toddy to show up." Some of the grimness returned to Brandy Bill's face.

Little Toddy was the apple of his daddy's eye, particularly since his two older brothers—Rock and Rye— were in the armed forces. And for the most part Brandy Bill gave Toddy a free rein, and such a thing as punishment was rare indeed. I could not help but wonder what offense the youngster had committed to arouse his father's ire.

"What has Toddy done now?" I could not help but ask.

"Wall," replied Brandy Bill, testing his switch with a few cuts at a weed nearby, "Bizz'ness Bill drapped by hyer a couple of hours ago, a-lookin' fer two of his boys— Herbert Hoover an' Harry Byrd. It seems as though them two boys an' leetle Toddy got theirselves in a mess up at school today, an' air a-layin' out in the red-bresh some'rs, a-feared to come home."

To me, Business Bill's brood were a never ceasing source of amusement. Being a rabid Republican partisan. he had named each of his boys—and they were legion—after a Republican President, starting with Abraham Lincoln and ending with Little Ike with a Harry Byrd thrown in when Bill ran out of Presidents.

As the shadows began to gather along in the late afternoon, I saw a small form appear a couple of hundred yards up the road in the general direction of the schoolhouse. Slowly the little fellow made his way toward us. I immediately recognized Toddy, and his slow steps indicated his fear of the reception he was about to get. Brandy Bill held the switch behind him and stood motionless as the boy opened the gate and stepped into the barnyard.

Brandy Bill grabbed for the lad, but Toddy with an agile leap dodged past him and started running around the barn with his father in hot pursuit. They made a complete circuit of the barn, and as they came past me again Brandy Bill collared him. Toddy twisted and squirmed, but Brandy Bill held on tightly.

"Toddy," and there was sternness in his voice, "I heerd somethin' today that I reckon must be the truth, but I want to hear ye ad-mit it afore I larrup ye. Yore teacher, Miss Ta-by-thy, she told Bizz'ness Bill that ye an' Herbert Hoover an' Harry Byrd turned over that leetle back-house up thar behindst the school-house. Is that right?"

Toddy stared silently at the ground at his feet.

"Tell me the truth, son," ordered Brandy Bill. "Ye've never told me a lie yit, to the best of my knowledge."

Toddy looked up fearfully at his father's face, and then straightened his little shoulders.

"It's the truth, Paw," he confessed, looking Brandy Bill straight in the eye. "We turned it over with a fence-rail."

"Then I reckon ye'll jest have to take yore med'cine," decided Brandy Bill and began to wield that switch in a businesslike manner, while for a full minute Little Toddy stood still, making no effort to avert the blows. Then he grabbed Brandy Bill's arm.

"Hold on a minnit, Paw," he ventured, and Brandy Bill dropped his hand and the switch but did not loosen his grip on Toddy's overalls.

"Say whut ye've got so say," he ordered quietly.

"Our teacher told us jest a few weeks ago a-bout George Washin'ton a-cuttin' down a cherry tree. The way she told it was that leetle George got him a bran'-new hatchet, an' he started out a-choppin' with it. An' a-bout the fu'st thing he chopped was his Paw's best cherry tree. An' when his pappy ast him a-bout it he says:

"'Paw, I can't tell ye a lie—I done it with my leetle hatchet.'"

"His Paw turned him loose an' didn't whup him bekaze he wouldn't tell a lie a-bout it," concluded Toddy hopefully, and then he added: "Ye ast me ef'n I turned over the back-house, an' I told ye the truth. I couldn't tell ye a lie neither. Don't ye think that mebbe—things a-bein' like that—ye ort to let me go, too?"

Brandy Bill stood motionless for a full minute thinking Toddy's proposition and argument over, and then he shook his head sadly.

"Thar's jest a leetle mite of diff'rence betwixt them two cases," reasoned Brandy Bill, gripping his switch a little tighter. "I mis-doubt that Mister Washin'ton would a-throwed away his switch ef'n leetle George's teacher had jest a happened to be a-settin' up thar in that cherry-tree"

Persimmon Beer

Bad 'Lige sent word by one of his neighbors last Saturday asking me to come over to his place on the Devil's Apron as soon as I could conveniently make it, and that he had a surprise in store for me. And when I reached his cabin I found him digging a can of fishing worms.

We sat on an old sled in the shade of an apple tree and talked of various things. I hinted a couple of times that I was in a receptive mood to hear about that surprise, but each time the suggestion failed to accomplish its purpose.

At last he rose to his feet, and led me into the barn. It apparently was empty except for some hay in the loft, but it was cool and comfortable, and I found an old milking stool upon which I relaxed, leaning back against the wall.

"Last fall," he began, "jest atter them revenooers made them raids up hyer on the Apern, drinkin' likker got powerful sca'ce in these parts. Me an' Brandy Bill we de-cided that we ort to do somethin' to help out a leetle, so we went up thar in them ol' fiel's ferninst the Hard-Rock meetin'-house an' gethered up a few booshels of persimmins.

"We got us some mo-lasses to sweeten it, an' we bought us some yeast an' cinny-mon ex-track, an' we made us a couple of bar'ls of the best persimmin beer ye ever let run down yore gullet. We drunk some of it, an' bottled up the rest.

"But a-long a-bout then a feller frum down in Kaintucky come up hyer with a couple of mule-loads of good backed an' doubled corn likker, an' me an' Brandy Bill fergot all a-bout our persimmin beer. We hid some of them bottles onder that hay up thar in the loft, an' it wasn't ontel a few days ago that I happened to recolleck a-bout it.

"I dug up a few bottles an' sampled one. Now us a-lettin' it set thataway had done somethin' to it that made it the best drink I've tasted in many's the year. When I opened a bottle that beer sorty fizzed an' spouted up an' made a leetle puddle on the floor.

"Whilst I was a-finishin' that bottle a leetle banty rooster he came in hyer an' he tuck him a few draps of that beer on the floor. He sorty straightened up an' headed outside whar two of my houn's was a-sleepin' in the sun. He lit on 'em all spraddled out an' he run 'em both clean off'n the place."

Bad 'Lige reached into the manger back of him and pulled out a couple of bottles of dark brown liquid. I tasted the contents of one of them, and it wasn't too bad. We drank two or three bottles before I got up and started down to Brandy Bill's place for one of his juleps—as a chaser.

"Hyer!" said Bad 'Lige. "Take one of these bottles over thar to town an' give it to that County Agent—whut's his name?"

"Dinwiddie," I replied.

"That's him! He's a blamed nice feller, an' he knows whut he's a-doin'. He's been over hyer a couple of times a-dock-terin' my cow that was sick, an' he wouldn't charge me a dime."

I placed the bottle in the glove compartment of my car, and that afternoon I happened to run into the County Agent, and gave the bottle to him without any explanation other than that Bad 'Lige had sent it.

On the following Sunday I drove over to the Devil's Apron again in order to attend the services at Good 'Lige's church. A number of us were gathered in the churchyard near the front door, among them Bad 'Lige, when the County Agent came up and joined us.

"Mister Cantwell," he said, "I got that bottle you sent to me yesterday, and I thought that I should come over and tell you that your mule has got what they call azutoria—sometimes known as 'Blackwater Fever'. It's a kidney disease, and as far as I have been able to learn, there isn't much that can be done for it."

"Mule?" Bad 'Lige looked puzzled, and I snickered.

"Yes—or a horse or whatever you have," said Dinwiddie.

"Ain't nothin' the matter with my mule," declared Bad 'Lige, shaking his head.

"But—but that specimen—that bottle you sent to me yesterday?" queried the County Agent.

"Why, that was per-simmon beer," said Bad 'Lige, and then he turned on me. "An' ef'n ye put that in yore paper I'm a-goin' to shoot ye on sight."

Nine Forks and a Hand

Four of us were playing "Set-Back" up at Brandy Bill's grist-mill on the Devil's Apron a few Saturdays ago. In the game were Bad 'Lige, Little 'Bijie Birdsong, Brandy Bill an I with a few of the others standing behind us watching the game.

We played out a hand, and Brandy Bill, who was keeping the score on the back of an old envelope, busied himself with a pencil.

"We got high, low, an' game, an' ye got the jack," he intoned. "That puts us all even."

It was Little 'Bijie's deal, and, with hands more accustomed to the plow, he was not an expert. For the first time I noticed a number of tiny scars on the back of his right hand, and they aroused my curiosity.

"How did you get all of those scars?" I queried, pointing at them.

"It was sorty a accident that tuck place ten er twelve years ago," he replied with a grin. Brandy Bill exploded in laughter.

"Tell me about it," I begged.

"Wasn't much to it," depreciated Little 'Bijie. "I was jest stabbed by nine Presidents of the United States."

"Oh, come now!" I protested. "I mean what really happened?"

"Leastwise, that's whut they called 'em," insisted 'Bijie. "It happened thisaway: I was up thar in the head of the Apern one day a-huntin' fer a couple of shoats of mine that had got outta the pen. I bought 'em from Bizz'ness Bill, an' I sorty figgered they might a-gone back to his place.

"I found their tracks, an' follored 'em down the hill. When I got to Bizz'ness Bill's yard, I seed that all of them boys of his was gethered in the shade of a tree right next to the kitchen. Thar was eight er nine of 'em thar that day. Le's see! Thar was James Blaine, William McKinley, Howard Taft, Warren Hardin', Harry Byrd, Cal Coolige, Herbert Hoover an' mebbe a-nuther'n er two. An' they shore had their eyes glued on that kitchen door.

"I passed the time of day with Bizz'ness Bill, an' he said as how them shoats hadn't showed up at his place yit, an' that he'd help me hunt 'em atter dinner. He ast me to set down an' wait, an' thar was the finest smell a-comin' outta that kitchen. I sniffed a couple of times an' then I looked at Bizz'ness Bill.

" 'Coon?' I ast.

" 'Yeah, that's whut ye smell. Cal Coolige ketched him last night, an' he was the gran'-pappy of all of the coons I ever seed—fat as a butter-ball. But I reckon he'd orty be fat bekaze he's been a livin' on my roastin'-ears fer the last three weeks.

" 'That was shore a smart coon. Cal Coolige he had him a time a-ketchin' him. Been a-settin' traps all summer fer him, an' fin'ly he got him. Maw's a-bakin it, an' I reckon it'll soon be time to eat.'

"A few minnits later Bizz'ness Bill's wife come to the kitchen door an' rung the dinner bell, an' them boys all lit a shuck fer the kitchen so fast they left me an' Bizz'ness Bill a-standin' flat-footed. But Bill he turned an' looked at me.

" 'Don't fret,' says he. 'Them boys dassent take a bite ontel I ast the blessin'.'

"Wall, we got to the table, an' I seed that all of them boys was a-lookin' at that coon with their forks in their hands. Now Bizz'ness Bill hadn't told a lie a-bout that coon. He was a whopper, an' Bizz'ness Bill's wife had cyarved it an' piled it on a dish ontel it stood a foot high.

"We sot down an' Bizz'ness Bill started to ast the

blessin'. It seemed to me that he tuck a-bout twict as long to say it as it orta tuck. An' all that time them boys was a-settin' on the edge of their chairs with their eyes glued on that coon. I looked over the table sorty slaunchwise, an' I seed that the coon was jest a-bout all they had fer dinner—that an' gravy an' corn-pone.

"Bizz'ness Bill he ast the Lawd to bless ever'body, an' I mean ever body. I reckon it was fer pyore devilment that he started in to namin' all of the folks on the Devil's Apern to be blessed, an' he shore didn't miss anybody. Them boys was all a-figitin' an' a-squirmin', an' I ex-peck that by that time I was a-doin' the same thing. Anyhow I had my eyes on a hunk of that coonham on top of that pile of meat, an' I grabbed my fork an' got set bekaze I figgered I'd better lose no time.

"Jest then Bizz'ness Bill said 'A-men!', an' ever-body made a dive fer the coon. Now I allus was purty quick thataway, an' I got my fork in that piece of coon alright, but I got nine forks in the back of my hand afore I could jerk it out."

Same Thing For Supper Last Night

Brandy Bill visited me one day last week, and he sat down to talk a while and tell me the happenings on the Devil's Apron. It developed that he had been summoned for jury service in the term of court which had been in session, but the first two trials had been moonshining cases, and his name had been stricken by the prosecution.

"Fu'st time I've been fetched over hyer fer jury duty in many a year," he declared, leaning back in his chair and gravely looking at the tendrils of smoke that arose from his cigar. "I reckon the last time they had me hyer was endurin' them Pro-hy-bishun days, an' mostly they struck me off'n the jury that time, too."

He was in a mood for talking, and I encouraged him by saying nothing, but giving him my undivided attention.

"Likker was a-fetchin' better prices then than they ever have," he continued after a brief pause. "A man could git seven-eight dollars a quart, an' that was plenty of boys in the bizz'ness then. But Bad 'Lige he de-cided that we would make us a couple of runs of good malted corn—jest fer our own use, ye onnerstand.

"We sprouted our corn an' I groun' it at the mill, an' we made us some of the best likker ye ever tasted. It was so pyore that it never made a man feel bad—jest put him to sleep an' made him have the finest dreams that a feller could dream.

"Wall, one day a deppity sheriff he come to my house, an' Bad 'Lige he happened to be thar at the time.

That deppity give us a couple of summonses to set on the jury at the next term of cou't. Me an' Bad 'Lige we got us a early start so's be be on hand when the cou't opened that Monday mornin'.

"At that time thar was a hotel down thar jest below the cou't-house on Main Street, an' we put up thar. Bad 'Lige had fetched a-long his saddle-bags an' they was a-bout full of that malted corn. We figgered we'd need a leetle endurin' the week.

"Bad 'Lige he got out one of them fruit jars an' he filled a flat bottle with the likker, an' stuck it in his pocket afore we went up to the cou't-house. We was all swore in, an' the jedge he give us our in-structions a-bout whut we had to do.

"The lawyer fer the county he must a-figgered that me an' Bad 'Lige was too frien'ly with the boys that was a-bein' tried bekaze he kept a-strikin' our names off as fast as a new trial come up. This lasted all endurin' the day, an' two er three times me an' Bad 'Lige we'd slip out an' git us a snort er two outta his bottle, sorty to keep us a-goin'.

"Anyhow, come time fer the cou't to ad-journ fer the day, I reckon me an' Bad 'Lige wasn't a-feelin' of no pains. We went down to the hotel, an' the both of us was powerful hongry. We sot down by a big stove an' waited fer a while an' then they opened the door to the dinin' room.

"Me an' Bad 'Lige we was a-bout the fu'st to set down at the long table. Thar was a-bout fifteen er twenty people eatin' at that table, an' thar was plenty of good grub on it. An' all of us shore did do ourselves proud in doin' it jestice.

"When Bad 'Lige had done filled himself to the p'int whar he couldn't eat no more, him an' me went out thar in the lobby whar they had that big red-hot stove. It was a-long in March, I re-colleck, an' the nights was still purty cold. Anyhow Bad 'Lige he got himself a cheer an' put it behindst that stove an' r'ared back ag'inst the the wall.

"Like I told ye that malted corn was a fine sleepin' likker, an' it wasn't but a few minnits ontel Bad 'Lige was sound a-sleep, an' a-snorin' to beat the band. I sot a-roun' an' talked with some t'other fellers fer nigh a-bout a hour.

"Some of the late comers was still eatin' in the dinin' room when Bad 'Lige woke up plum sudden-like, an' looked a-roun' kinda wild-eyed fer a minnit. Then he seed that the door to the dinin' room was still open an' he jumped up an' headed fer the table ag'in. I trailed a-long behindst him to see whut he was aimin' to do.

"He found a place to set down, an' then he stopped an' looked that table over frum one eend to 'tother. Then he turned an' looked at me.

" 'Hell!' he growls. 'Same thing they had fer supper last night'."

Forgot To Hitch Mules To Plow

"I seed that piece ye put in yore paper a-bout Willie B. Fuller's 'tater-peelin' brandy," said Bad 'Lige as we loafed on the porch of Dutton's store down at the mouth of No-Business Creek. The whole gang was gathered there for their weekly get-together.

"It isn't half as bad as you pretended that it was," protested Willie B. vehemently.

"But I'll have to ad-mit that it's plum powerful," interposed Bad 'Lige. "I helped Willie B. to git things ready to make thar run. Atter them revenooers was hyer the last time Willie B. hid out his b'iler, an' it was a mess to clean up ag'in. 'Long in the shank of the evenin' we got ever'thing ready, but we de-cided to wait ontel the next day to fire her up.

"Somethin' happened up to my place that mornin'—I fergit now whut—an' I didn't git back to his still ontel a-bout two-three o'clock. William B. had her all fired up an' a-goin' full blast, an' he'd done scorched the fu'st run some, but it was drinkable an' we sot a-roun' an' had a few snorts.

"He didn't have nothin' in that mash 'ceptin' the 'tater-peelin's an' sugar, but he did pour in jest a leetle lye an' he put in some red-stemmed ivy to kick it off. An' them singlin's was so strong they'd knock ye down an' throw rocks at ye fer the rest of the day.

"We doubled an' twisted them singlin's, an' even then we had to water it so a man could take a swaller without plum losin' his breath. Like I said, we downed a few drinks of it an' was a-settin' in the shade of a beech tree, sorty keepin' a eye out fer revenooers, an' a-talkin' a-bout one thing an' a-nuther.

"Now we had set that still up purty clost to the fence a-roun' a ol' fiel', an' jest inside that thar fence was a couple of hay-stacks that the feller who sold the land to Willie B. had put up last year. Willie B. he didn't have no cow, him a drinkin' nothin' but hard likker that-away, an' that hay was a-startin' to rot down."

Bad 'Lige winked at some of the other boys, and I realized that he was stretching the truth a little for my benefit. After a moment of silence he resumed his tale.

"We dumped the still-slop outta that fu'st run into that ol' field an' it run down to them hay-stacks. The fust thing I noticed was a pair of jay-birds which had lit in that field an' was eatin' that slop. I didn't think nothin' of that ontel a big red-tailed chicken hawk flew over an' swooped down on them jaybirds. But they was full of that 'tater-peelin' slop, an' they riz up an' tuck atter that hawk an' sent him a-hightailin' it outta thar.

"A leetle later I seed a couple of tumble-bugs come a-wanderin' up, an' they tuck on a load of that still-slop. They looked like they was plum peaceful fer a minnit er two—sorty stunned, I guess—then they staggered off down the hill. They come up to them hay-stacks an' kinda looked 'em over, an' ye can be-lieve it er not, them two tumble-bugs backed up to them two hay-stacks an' tried to roll 'em down the hill, samelike they do in the barn-yard. Yes sir! I'd say that Willie B's brandy is a mite powerful."

When the boys had quieted down a bit, Little 'Bijie Birdsong came edging through the ring and the boys made room for him and then waited for him to have his say.

"I shore agree with Bad 'Lige," he said with his tongue in his cheek. "I know how powerful that stuff is bekaze I tried me two er three shots, an' danged ef'n I've been able to git over it since then.

"I run plum outta drinkin' likker a few days ago,

an' I went up thar to Willie B's place, an' borrowed a quart off'n him sorty to tide me over ontel I could git a chance to find somethin' better.

"I reckon most of ye know that my boys got bizzy this spring an' cl'ared a piece of newgroun' of a-bout five acres in that south cove. That land is plum full of sassefack, an' red-bud, an' I knowed that I was a-goin' to have a tough job a-gittin' the roots out so's I could plant it in corn.

"But I was a-bettin' on them two leetle yaller mules of mine. Eff'n that newgroun' could be plowed without grubbin', I knowed they could do it. They air the best plow-mules on the Apern, an' I'll match 'em ag'inst all comers any day in the week. But still an' all I had been kinda a-holdin' back bekaze I was reely a-dreadin' that job.

"Then a couple of mornin's ago, I got up an' et me a big breakfus', an' tuck me two big swigs of 'tater-peelin' brandy. An' boys, I'm a-tellin' ye the blessed truth when I say that I plowed up nigh onto three acres of that newgroun' afore I diskivvered that I'd plum fergot to hitch them two leetle mules to the plow."

Good 'Lige Gets Religion

Between showers last Saturday I drove over to the Devil's Apron and parked at Brandy Bill's mill. Instead of the usual crowd of Aproners gathered there I found only Little 'Bijie Birdsong, and he had already loaded his turn of meal on the back of his mule, and was getting ready to leave for his home.

"Where are Brandy Bill, Bad 'Lige, Business Bill and all the boys?" I asked in surprise.

"Gone to meetin'—been gone since dinnertime," replied 'Bijie with an expressive shrug.

"Where are they holding services today—this is Saturday?" I was frankly non-plussed.

"Up to the Hard-Rock Firm-Founday-shun meetin'-house," he explained. "This is the big July two-day meetin' an' it jest got started to goin' good atter dinner today. I was up thar fer a while, but I had to come back hyer an' git on home with my meal fer supper."

"I didn't know that Brandy Bill and Bad 'Lige were very keen on going to church," I ventured after a pause.

"Bad 'Lige he's done changed a heap," 'Bijie informed me with a widening grin. "He's done had him a vision."

"A what?"

"A vision—a dream. Set down an' I'll tell ye all about it." We found a couple of up-turned boxes on the floor of the mill-porch.

"It seems that it sorty happened thisaway," began 'Bijie. "Bad 'Lige was up thar in his corn-fiel' whar he'd been a-plowin' t'other mornin', an' it got mighty hot.

He laid down in the fence corner whar thar was some shade, an' went to sleep. An' he had him a dream. He drempt that he was a-climbin' up a steep trail, an' the higher he clum' the more that trail petered out.

"It kept a-gittin' darker in that dream, so Bad 'Lige says, an' the trail got to be nothin' but red-bresh an' thorny thickets, an' whilst he was a-tryin' to git through 'em, a rattlessnake started to buzzin' in the bushes clost by, an' a big storm was a comin' up with the lightnin' a-flashin' an' the thunder a-roarin', an' all told it must a-been a skeery sort of a time.

"When he woke up he found the sun a-shinin,' an' the leetle birds a-singin', an' he was so s'prized that he didn't know whut to think. He said as how he got to figgerin' on whut that dream meant, an' that he come to the idee that mebbe it was a warnin' to him to break up outta the path that he'd been a-follerin' all his life, an' sorty change his ways some.

"Ye know, Bad 'Lige he's a-gittin' a-long in years now, an' he's a-goin' to have to go to a lot of meetin's an' sichlike afore he gits fergiveness fer all that he's done. Anyhow he's been a tryin' to make all of us fellers go to meetin', to, an', ef'n we don't, he raises hell an' puts a chunk onder the corner."

Little 'Bijie looked at his watch, and then arose to his feet.

"Looks like we might have time to mosey by thar this evenin' fer a few minnits afore they quit," he suggested. "Ol' Sin-Sockin' Sam is a-preachin' right now, sorty helpin' Good 'Lige out."

We walked up the hill with Little 'Bijie leading his mule. When we reached the church, 'Bijie carefully placed the sack of meal across the limb of a tree out of reach of the mule, and then tied the reins to a bush. We went into the church and found seats.

Sin-Socking Sam was hitting on all eight cylinders, and his listeners were silent and motionless, drinking in his every word. His text was on the Atonement of Sin, and he was building a strong case against the boys on the Devil's Apron. Most of the good brethern and sisters were nodding their heads in agreement although the preacher's statements about the dire punishment that awaited the sinners were not in complete accord with Good 'Lige's "No-Hell" doctrine.

I looked over on the mourners' bench and sitting on the front row was Bad 'Lige. He was leaning forward working rhythmically on a quid of tobacco, and shouting "A-men" every few minutes. I sat staring at him unbelievingly. It was hard to realize that this was the same Bad 'Lige I had known for the last several years.

At last the old preacher closed his Bible and ended his sermon with a single quotation.

"The Lawd giveth an' the Lawd taketh away," he intoned.

"A-men!" bellowed Bad 'Lige, coming to his feet and glaring at the crowd about him. "An' ef'n that ain't a squar' deal, I'd like to know whut the hell is?"

Couldn't Hold His Water

Brandy Bill sent word by one of the boys that he had a treat for us, and that I was specially invited to come over at any time on Saturday afternoon. Naturally I made a point of being on hand, and I found that he had included several of the others in his invitation to share that treat. They were gathered at the grist-mill, and I found a convenient seat and waited for further developments.

Brandy Bill looked ghostly as he stood beside the hopper and watched the corn being fed in between the grinding stones. A thin stream of meal was pouring from a spout into the open-mouth sack that was just beneath it. He nodded at me, and then spat a stream of tobacco juice into a sandbox at least twenty feet distant with marvelous accuracy.

"What's Brandy Bill's surprise?" I asked of Little 'Bijie as I glanced over the crowd. All of the old gang was on hand and waiting, and I knew that they, too, were more than a little curious.

"He ain't said yit," replied 'Bijie.

Brandy Bill finished the grinding job, and tied up the mouth of the last sack of meal with a bit of string.

"That finish the job fer today, Bill?" demanded Bad 'Lige.

"That's her," announced the miller, slapping the powdered meal off his clothing and coming over to join us. "I reckon ye fellers air sorty a-wonderin' a-bout that s'prize I promised ye. Wall, le's go down to my house afore somebody else comes an' wants a turn groun'."

We strung out behind him and then followed him into his yard and around the house to the kitchen door. We sat down on the rear porch, and Brandy Bill vanished inside the house. He returned a moment or so later with a stone jug, holding something like a gallon. This he placed carefully on the floor.

"Boys," he explained, "a-bout three years ago I hid five of these hyer stone jugs onder a false bottom in my 'tater bin in the cellar, an' fer some reason er t'other I plum fergot a-bout a couple of 'em. Ye could a-knocked me over with a feather t'other day when I happened to run acrost 'em. They was filled with some applejack I made that year, an' them three years has shore made it the best I be-lieve I ever tasted. So, I sorty figgered all of us'd have a reel treat today."

Little 'Bijie helped him build a fire in the cookstove, and in a few minutes a kettle of water was boiling merilly. Then Brandy Bill got some sugar, cinnamon bark, and some large mugs—one for each of us. Very carefully he worked the cork out of the jug and then we all got a whiff of the contents. It smelled out of this world.

"Help yoreselves, boys!" he invited cordially. "Pour out whut ye think ye want, an' then mix the water an' sugar to yore taste. Then jest stir it a leetle with a stick of that cinny-mon."

Bad 'Lige picked up that jug and poured out one of the biggest drinks that I ever saw any man attempt to take at one time. My eyes bugged out, but the other boys gave no hint of surprise.

"Have ye got a eye-drapper, Bill?" demanded Bad 'Lige, peering into his mug.

"Eye-drapper?" Brand Bill looked at him surprise. "Seems like I seed one a-roun' some'rs. I'll see ef'n I can locate it."

Everyone paused in mixing his toddy and watched Brandy Bill and Bad 'Lige with interest. The former brought the eye-dropper from a wall cabinet and handed it to Bad 'Lige. He took it and then poured a little hot water from the kettle into a glass tumbler. With the dropper he put exactly three drops of water in his mugful of applejack.

"Wall, I'll be dammed!" murmured Brandy Bill, his jaw dropping wide in astonishment and unbelief. "Will ye tell us why ye put jest three draps of water in it, 'Lige?"

Bad 'Lige stirred the contents of the mug slowly for an instant before replying while we waited with baited breath.

"Wall, boys, I'll tell how 'tis," he explained. "I reckon as how I've made an' drunk as much likker as any man on the Devil's Apern. I figger that right now I can drink more an' hold it better'n any of ye. That's one thing I've allus been plum proud of an' that's my ability to hold my likker.

"I can still do that as good as I ever could, but to tell ye the plain truth, boys, I reckon I can't hold my water like I ust to could."

Lying Luke's Reputation

With my family down on one of the South Carolina beaches, it had been a lonely week for me. To escape the oppressive heat I was doubly anxious to get over on the Devil's Apron for a little cool relaxation and enjoyment with Brandy Bill and the gang.

I found that he had started operating his grist-mill at daybreak in order to finish the day's work before it got too hot in the afternoon, and when I arrived the boys were already gathered in the shade of the big maple down in the backyard near the springhouse at Brandy Bill's home.

One of his superb mint juleps certainly did hit the spot, and I almost immediately forgot the discomforts and worries that I had been undergoing for the past week.

"I was a-readin' t'other night," Brandy Bill was saying, "whar some feller had done figgered out that we was three honnerd an' ninety-two millyun miles frum the sun. Whut I want to know is how the hell does he know how fur it is."

"These scientists have discovered methods of measuring space," I explained airily. "I am told they do it rather accurately."

"I ain't so blamed shore a-bout that," chimed in Little 'Bijie. "The way I figger it, them fellers jests up an' say that it's so many miles to the sun an' the moon, an' the stars, an' we have to take their word fer it bekaze we ain't got no way of provin' that they air liars."

"I sorty feel that way, too," said Business Bill, nodding his head. "I ain't a-sayin' that they're straight out a-lyin', but I kinda claim that they air mebbe a-stretchin' the truth some when they say they know whut's a-goin' on up thar in the heavens."

"A-men!" seconded Good 'Lige. "That's the Good Lawd's bizz'ness, an' I reckon He's plenty able to handle it without us a-tryin' to stick our noses in it. We've done made a awful mess of whut He give us hyer in this worl'—let a-lone them other worl's."

I didn't want to get mixed up in that controversy so I kept my mouth shut, giving all my attention to my julep.

"Talk a-bout tellin' the truth," remarked Brandy Bill after a pause, "things shore ain't like they ust to be. I can re-colleck the time when a man's world was his bond—'ceptin' a few fellers who jest couldn't tell the truth onder no sar-cumstance.

"Take ol' Lyin' Luke Jackson, fer instance, who ust to live over thar on Whisperin' Crick. Seems like Lyin' Luke couldn't tell the true facts ef'n he could think of a lie fu'st. But he told one lie too many one time when he had ol' Hook-Nose Bud Potter indicted on a hawg-stealin' charge.

"Lyin' Luke an' Hook-Nose was both a-gittin' a-long in years, an' I reckon they didn't feel up to tryin' to settle the matter with their fists, so Hook-Nose he sues Lyin' Luke fer slander, an' de-manded five honnerd dollars to sorty squar' up his rep-petashun thataway.

"This hyer tuck place many years ago, an' in them times sich cases was tried afore a Jes-tice of the Peace. Good 'Lige thar was a-servin' this deestrick as Jes-tice at that time, an' the case was fetched up afore him. That trial brung out a big crowd bekaze that was the fu'st case of that kind that was ever tried in these parts.

"Lyin' Luke, he got Willie B. Fuller thar to de-fend him, an' Willie B. was reasonably sober that day, but he shore did start out in a funny way to de-fend the case that time. In a leetle speech to Good 'Lige when the trial started, he says as how Lyin' Luke was sich a big liar that nobody ever believed him, an' onless somebody be-lieved that tale a-bout him a-stealin' the hawg, thar was no slander.

"Good 'Lige says as how he'll take that onder consideration, an' the case got onder way. Ol' Hook-Nose he proved whar he got the hawg that Lyin' Luke said he stole, an' that sorty put Willie B. out on a lim'. But Willie B. he called Bad 'Lige to the witness stand as whut they call a char-ack-ter witness.

"Seems as though Bad 'Lige knowed Lyin' Luke better'n anybody else bekaze they'd made moonshine together, an' had lived clost to each other. So Willie B. he jest asts Bad 'Lige one question.

"'Whut's Lyin' Luke's reppy-tay-shun fer truth an' ve-rassity-'

"Bad 'Lige frowns an' scratches his head fer a minnit, an' looked over at Lyin' Luke.

"'Wall,' says he, 'since I swore to tell the whole truth an' nothin' but the truth, all I can say is that Lyin' Luke's own hawgs don't be-lieve him, an' when he wants to call 'em outta the woods to feed 'em, he has to git his wife to do the callin'.'"

Uncle Hezzykiah
and the Shotgun Wedding

For some time Brandy Bill had been promising me that he would take me over on Whispering Creek for a visit with the folks over there. At that time I had never been up there although it was only three miles above No-Business Creek on the Devil's Apron. Last Saturday afternoon he made his promise good, and on the way he told me about the people in that community. I gathered from his descriptions that they were a clannish folk, mixing rarely with other people, and attending strictly to their own business.

"Good people though," complimented Brandy Bill. "Thar ust to be a lot of moonshinin' on the crick, an' a leetle fightin' an' shootin', but I reckon ol' Sin-Sockin' Sam has done put a stop to most of that. It's plum quiet an' peaceful-like now frum all I hyer."

I was busy for a minute or so dodging a couple of calves that refused to give me the right-of-way.

"We air almost thar," announced Brandy Bill a little later. "Ye turn right at the next crick we come to."

I followed his directions and a moment later we were starting to climb a steep road that appeared to be winding back toward the crest of the Cumberlands. We came to a clearing with a small cabin nestling in a grove of walnut trees. In a field beside the house an old, grizzled hillman was hoeing the young corn with unusual energy and enthusiasm.

"That's Oncle Zeke Hoback," explained Brandy Bill, so I parked my car alongside the fence. The old man looked up and came walking briskly toward us.

"Howdy, Oncle Zeke!" greeted Brandy Bill affably. "When I fu'st seed ye I figgered ye was a-killin' snakes. Whut air ye in sich a hurry a-bout?"

"Howdy, Bill!" Uncle Zeke leaned on the topmost rail, and spat into the road. "I reckon I was jest a mite in a hurry to git this hyer job done afore it rains. Besides I gotta git finished by three o'clock be-kaze I promised to meet Pappy then."

"Wall, ye ort to git it done in ten fer fifteen minnits," surmised Brandy Bill. "We'll wait fer ye an' take ye up thar."

Uncle Zeke returned to his work, and when he was out of earshot I turned on Brandy Bill.

"What did he say?"

"Ye heerd him right," chuckled Brandy Bill. "He said he was a-goin' to meet his Pappy at three o'clock."

"But—but—how old is he?" I simply couldn't believe it.

"Hey, Zeke!" boomed Bill. "How ol' air ye?"

"Seventy-two—come October," replied the old man without looking up from his work.

"How ol' is yore Pappy?"

"Ninety-one last May."

We sat for a few minutes in silence. Brandy Bill was buried in thought, and then he stroked his drooping mustache.

"Zeke's Pappy is mighty spry fer his age. Still does his farm work, an' cuts a fancy buck an' wing at a hoedown dance."

I marveled at his longevity, and watched with a hint of admiration as Uncle Zeke cut the weeds and hilled the corn with effortless ease. He reached the end of the last row, and then hurried into the cabin. Some ten minutes later he reappeared dressed in his "store clothes," and wearing a big wide-brimmed hat.

"Much obleeged to ye fer waitin'," he said as he

climbed into the car. "I'm sorty tuckered out. That corn was weedier than I figgered."

A couple of miles further up the creek we came to another house, and Brandy Bill told me to stop.

"This is whar Oncle Hezzy lives," he explained. "I think they called him Hezzy-kier er somethin' like that. An' thar he is."

I couldn't see much difference between Uncle Zeke and his father, Uncle Hezzy. Their hair was black, and they were not wearing glasses. And their step was as light and springy as that of a young man. It was hard to believe that the older man was ninety-one years of age.

"Ye an' Zeke shore air a-steppin' out," declared Brandy Bill with a grin.

"We air at that," admitted Zeke. "I reckon ye know that my gran'-pappy is a-gettin' married today."

"Your what?" I almost fell out of my car.

"My gran'-pappy," he repeated. "The weddin's at six o'clock."

"Well, for Pete's sake," I gasped. "How old is he?"

"One honnerd an' 'leven his next birthday."

"Holy Smoke!" I ejaculated. "At his age I wouldn't think that he'd want to get married."

"He don't," said Uncle Zeke.

"It's a shotgun weddin'," said Uncle Hezzy.

Willie B.'s News

A few days ago, I was sadly in need of a tall tale for next week's issue, so I drove over to the Devil's Apron, and foregathered with the boys at Brandy Bill's grist-mill. It was a cold day, but it was quite apparent that they all had enough 'anti-freeze' to keep from suffering any hardships.

Brandy Bill jerked his head in the direction of the stove where the familiar pot of ginger stew was simmering. A little later I placed my empty cup on the window sill and sat down on the bench, gratefully thrusting my feet to the warmth of the fire.

Practically all of the boys were present, but a closer look told me that Willie B. Fuller was not among them.

"Where is Willie B.?" I asked.

My question was greeted with a roar of laughter, and I looked up in surprise.

"Hadn't ye heerd?" sputtered Little 'Bijie. "Tell him a-bout it, Brandy Bill. Ye had a part in it."

Brandy Bill refilled his cup with the stew, and then sat down on an upturned box, sipping his drink with apparent relish.

"I reckon ye know that it's been sorty hit an' miss betwixt Willie B. an' his wife ever' since they got married. Ever' onct in a while she's been a-packin' up an' leavin' him an' goin' back to her folks in Kaintucky. But fer the last five-six months she's been a-stayin' at home —a-tryin' to keep Willie B. sober—an' not a-havin' too much luck.

"Now, afore I fergit it, Willie B., when he gits purty

high, most gin'rilly calls his wife 'Toosy-Wootsy' an' she shore don't like that a leetle bit, but she put up with it as best she could.

"But to git back to the tale I was a-tellin', Willie B. he'd done been be-havin' fer a while an' had been a keepin' half-way sober, an' we figgered him an' his wife was sorty settled at last so to speak.

"Yistiddy mornin' she come to my house bright an' early, an' she wanted to know ef'n I didn't have a half-blind ol' mule that I'd sell to her purty cheap. I couldn't figger out whut on earth she wanted with it, but I told her I did have sich a animal, but that it was a-gittin' ol' an' wasn't good fer nothin' much.

"I told her the truth when I said that ol' Betsy was still able to plow a leetle, an' haul in stovewood an' leetle things like that. I made a p'int of tellin' her that the mule couldn't see, an' that she had to be driv keerful er she'd bat her brains against a tree.

"'But she's good fer two-three more years,' I says, 'an' I couldn't sell her fer less'n thu'tty dollars.'

"She didn't even bat a eye when I give her that figger, but she dug down in her pocketbook an' handed me a twenty dollar bill an' a ten. Then she looked me squar' in the eye.

"'I'll take her,' she says plum de-termined-like, 'ef'n ye'll do jest egg-zackly like I tell ye. The fu'st thing is to take her up to my house, an' I'll tell ye the rest of it on the way.'

"As we walked up the road with me a-leadin' ol' Betsy on a halter, she told me she was a-gittin' sick an' tired of the way Willie B. was a doin', an' that with the mule she was a-goin' to l'arn him a lesson he'd never fergit.

"I ast her whar Willie B. was, an' she says as how him an' Bad 'Lige has been a-makin' moonshine most of the time, an' that Willie B. he jest come home when he was hongry an' wanted some decent vittels. The way she told it, Willie B. he'd git him a few snorts too many an' then he'd come in the house a-whoopin' things up. Most of the time she'd be a-workin' in the kitchen, an' he'd come a-bustin' in an' holler:

"'Hi-ya, Toosy-Wootsy! Whut's the news?' An' he'd slap her on her r'ar eend an' laff fit to die.

"She said that it didn't matter ef'n she'd been hard at work all day, an' didn't have no chanct to git out an' l'arn the news, he'd allus ast her that. So she says as how she's a-goin' to break him of that habit onct an' fer all.

"We got up to her house an' she made me take ol' Betsy right plum into the livin' room. I couldn't figger out whut she had in mind, par-tick-larly when she told me to take the mule on into Willie B's bedroom. Then she went into a-nuther room an' fetched out a single-bar'l shotgun, an' handed it to me.

"'Shoot her!' she orders as ca'm as ye please.

"I couldn't be-lieve my ears, an' I reckon I jest stood thar with my mouth open.

"'It's my mule. I done bought an' paid fer her,' she says with her jaws tight. 'I said, shoot her!'

"Thar wasn't nothin' left fer me to do, so I upped with the gun an' downed ol' Betsy.

"'Now,' says she, 'when Willie B. comes in tonight, an' wants to know whut's the news, I shore as hell have got some fer him.'"

Brandy Bill and the Yeller Corn

Having slowly and painfully recovered from an attack of the flu, tonsilitis, and a few other complications, I was debating whether or not I should attempt to drive over on the Devil's Apron and see how the boys had come through with the record-breaking weather we had been having. So I was both relieved and pleased when I saw Brandy Bill bring his jeep to a halt before my office. Out of it climbed Little 'Bijie, Bad 'Lige, Willie B. Fuller, and Business Bill. They all stamped the snow off their boots and crowded into my sanctorium.

Evidently they had heard about my illness, and they brought with them an ample supply of medicine that I needed for what had been ailing me, and we adjourned to the back shop where we would not be interrupted. I found glasses and they found seats.

"Well, I'm glad that you fellows came through the Eskimo weather in good shape," I told them when we were comfortably situated.

"We jest bar'ly did," replied Little 'Bijie. "I've lived thar on the Apern fer forty-six years an' it's been the coldest I ever seed it."

"Anything new been going on over there?" I asked.

"Nothin' much could happen," complained Brandy Bill. "Ever'thing's done froze up tight—even No-Bizz'ness Crick is plum solid ice, an' I reckon my mill is done shet down fer the rest of the winter. But I guess we'll all make out some way er t'other."

"We allus have," added Little 'Bijie, "includin' Bizz'ness Bill the time he got foundered on sweet-corn."

"That's one you never told me," I interrupted.

"Shucks! I figgered ever'body heerd a-bout that," Little 'Bijie got his stogie to burning evenly before continuing.

"I know ye've heerd talk of the Stuart-Slemp political race back that somethin' like forty years ago. That was a-bout the hottest fight—I mean knock-down an' drag-out—that was ever seed in this dee-strick fer Con-gress. Slemp won, but 'twas awful clost.

"Bizz'ness Bill he was a-votin' fer the fu'st time in that 'lection, an' he shore did ride the ridges a-tryin' to git folks to vote fer Slemp—he was the Re-publican. He worked night an' day, an' when the votes was counted on the Apern they was blamed nigh all fer his man.

"Now when Congress-man Slemp got up thar to Washin'ton, he sent Bizz'ness Bill a package of seeds of all kinds—gyarden sass an' truck like that. An' in that package was some sweet-corn of a kind that hadn't never been raised in these parts.

"Bizz'ness Bill had him a leetle level land down on the crick an' that's whar he planted that sweet-corn. He worked it an' tended it, an' even watered it when thar come a dry spell. Ever' time anybody happened to go up thar to his place fer somethin' he'd show 'em that patch of sweet-corn, an' it was right purty corn.

"Come roastin'-ear time, he went up thar an' pulled him off a armful of it an' shucked it out. Then he tuck it down to the kitchen an' put it on the kitchen table an' told his wife to git the big pot an' the leetle'n on. It was strange lookin' corn at that, the grains not a-runnin' in rows like we'd allus been ust to.

"'Cook 'em all fer my dinner,' he ordered.

"'But Bill, ye can't eat no twelve ears at a time,' she told him.

"'That's the finest corn any man ever raised,' says he. 'Cook ever ear of it.'

"She done like he told her, an' put 'em on the table

with plenty of butter an' salt. He sot down an' et, an' thar was twelve cobs a-layin' beside his plate when he got up.

"He went out an' sot down on the porch, an' purty soon he got to feelin' a leetle sick. He kept a-gittin' wu'ss an' wu'ss, an' in a little while he hollored to his ol' woman to come out thar an' do somethin' fer him afore he plum died.

"She fixed him up a sheepskin pallet to lay down on in the shade of the porch, an' told him that ef'n he'd stay still fer a leetle he'd feel better. But he was a yellin' an' a-carryin' on so much that his wife she got plum worried a-bout him.

"'I don't know of nothin' else I can do,' she tells him. 'Mebbe ye'd better pray a leetle ef'n ye're that sick.'

Bizz'ness Bill he figgered that she might be right, so he shet his eyes an' folded his hands.

"'Oh, Lawd!' he says. 'I ain't never been a prayin' man, an' I ain't never ast Ye to do nothin' fer me afore this, but I shore do need Yore help right now. Now Lawd, I've allus been a reasonable man, an' all I ast is that Ye take keer of a-bout six ears of that corn. I be-lieve that I can handle the rest of 'em my-own-self. A-men!'"

Fresh Goose

It was Sunday afternoon last week before I managed to break away and go over on the Devil's Apron to see the boys. I found Brandy Bill sitting on his front porch talking with Bad 'Lige, Little 'Bijie, and Willie B. Fuller. He rose to his feet as I was finding a place to park, and halted me with a gesture when I stepped out of the car.

"Le's go back up to the mill," he said. "The house is full of some of the wimminfolks, an' Good 'Lige is in thar a-drinkin' tea with 'em." He jerked his hand toward the other boys and we all followed him up the road toward the grist-mill.

"I've got a jar of applejack up thar, an' some mint an' some ice an' sweetenin', an' we was waitin' on ye afore we drunk it. We was a-figgerin' that a cold mint julep'd hit the spot on a day as hot as this."

None of us appeared to be adverse to that idea, and when Brandy Bill had gathered up the ingredients, we left the mill and went down to a little spring near the mill-pond. For some time there was no sound to break the stillness except the tinkling of the ice in the glasses as Bill filled them.

"Willie B. thar was jest a-tellin' us that he was havin' some more wife trubbel," said Brandy Bill, glancing at the glum and taciturn Willie B. The latter drained his glass and held it out for a refill.

"She's gone back to her people in Pike County, I suppose," he said. Brandy Bill mixed another julep for him out of sympathy.

I had met Willie B.'s wife. Her name had been Carrie

Potts, and she was reported to have been a chambermaid in a hotel at Pikeville at the time he married her, and as a result her name became Carrie Potts Fuller.

After a long, gurgling drink Willie B. came up for air. "I don't know what's the matter with her this time," he mourned. "Bad 'Lige and I had been making a run of malt corn, and when I came home last Saturday night she was gone. She didn't leave a note or message of any kind for me, but I imagine she has gone back to her folks."

Willie B. was more sober than I had seen him in months, but he was rapidly making up for that deficiency.

Bad 'Lige was staring intently at a flock of geese that was lazily swimming on the small millpond. There were seven or eight geese and one gander in the haggle and they appeared to be catching tadpoles in the shallow water on the opposite side of the pond from where we were sitting. Occasionally they would turn with one accord and paddle back up the pond and around a bend out of sight, but in a little while they would reappear and come back to their old feeding grounds. Leading the flock was the big gander, and beside him swam a goose with a few brown feathers in her tail.

"People air funny things," observed Bad 'Lige philosophically after a long silence. "Seems as though a man an' a woman jest natch'elly got to have some fu'sses an' rackets ever' onct in a while—mebbe more often. Now, take Willie B. thar! Him an' Carrie they've been a-quarrelin' most all of the time. How many times has she left ye this fur?"

"I haven't kept an account," replied the latter sadly.

"Wall," continued Bad 'Lige, "us humans shore could take lessons frum that thar gander an' them geese out thar. They've all been a-swimmin' a-long plum happy an' contented in that pond. They ain't allus a-fu'ssin' an' a-fightin' like most of us air."

We sat motionless, watching those geese as they swam back up the pond and once again vanished around the bend.

"Yes sir!" resumed Bad 'Lige, nodding sagely at Willie

B. "Ye can shore take a lesson frum things in nature any time. Jest keep yore eyes on the leetle birds an' the cats an' the chickens an' the geese a-roun' the house. They ain't allus a-fu'ssin' an' a-feudin' thataway.

"An' ye take Leetle 'Bijie thar! Him an' his wife's mammy, A'nt Hellfirey, air allus in a racket a-bout somethin'. They could shore foller the egg-zample of them geese an' not be havin' a fight ever' time they got onder the same roof. An' then mebbe him an' Snowdy Jane'd git a-long better."

At that moment the geese came swimming past us in a stately procession, exceedingly sedate and dignified.

"I reckon we might at that," chuckled Little 'Bijie. "In fact, I know we could ef'n things with us was like it is with them geese. Ef'n ye'll look plum clost ye'll see that that thar gander has got him a fresh goose ever' time he comes by us."

Good 'Lige Hides From the Lawd

Brandy Bill and I were squirrel hunting last Friday afternoon, and, after climbing to the top of the dividing ridge between No-Business and Whispering Creeks, we decided to hunt in opposite directions, and meet in a low gap at sundown. I was the first to reach that rendezvous, and when Brandy Bill arrived we sat down to rest a bit after our strenuous exertions.

I had killed a couple of squirrels and Brandy Bill had five in his belt. He glanced at my kill, and then leaned back against the bole of a tree with a tired grunt.

"Found 'em sorty wild, didn't ye?" he asked, leaning back and scratching among some leaves and dead brush beside an old log. To my surprise and, I must say, delight, he pulled out a fruit jar filled with some of his famed applejack.

"I was up hyer a-huntin' some two er three days ago, an' I hid this, sorty figgerin' that we might need it today. In fact, I keep some hid hyer most of the time in the huntin' season."

"I'll remember that," I promised.

"I sorty looked fer ye last Sunday," he said a little later, "an' ye shore missed somethin' by not a-bein' at ol' Sin-Sockin' Sam Tolliver's meetin'-house then."

"Why, what happened?" I asked, grinding out my cigarette in the dry ground.

"Wall, mebbe I'd better ex-plain a leetle fu'st. Ye see, Good 'Lige an' Sin-Sockin' Sam they've been a-fightin' amongst theirselves so much that their churches air jest a-bout to peter out. It's got so folks jest don't go to meetin' no more no matter who's a-preachin'. Ever'bdy's sorty a-hellin' a-roun' an' things have been sorty a-gittin' outta hand.

"So Good 'Lige an' the Sin-Socker they kinda got their heads together, an' de-cided that they'd better fergit their racket over whar thar's a hell er not, an' do whut they could to clean up these parts. They agreed that they wouldn't preach on the same Sunday, an' that the folks frum both churches could go to all the meetin's.

"They also agreed that Good 'Lige'd preach on the fu'st an' third Sundays, an' Sam'd take the t'other two. Both of 'em promised to be on hand to hear t'other'n preach, an' last Sunday was the Sin-Socker's time, an' Good 'Lige was in the 'A-men' corner.

"An' Sam he opened that meetin' up, an' thar was a purty good crowd thar outta both churches, but mostly they was the ol' an' stove-up folks that wasn't able to do nothin' else. Anyhow Sam was a-hittin' the high spots, an' I reckon none of us ever heerd him preach a more powerful sermon.

"He started off by sayin':

" 'I don't know whut I'm a-goin' to say to ye today. I don't be-lieve in this hyer studdyin' an' gittin' up a sermon beforehan'. I never have done that, an' I don't aim to. I've allus made a prac-tice of jest gittin' up hyer in the pulpit an' openin' my mouth an' let the Good Lawd put the words into it.'

"I reckon mebbe he was a tellin' the truth," continued Brandy Bill, "but all I've got to say is that ef'n it worked out thataway he shore kept the Lawd a-workin' overtime fer the next two hours. I guess that he tetched on most ever'-thing thar is in the Bible an' some things that wasn't.

"Anyhow he told the crowd that they was all a-headin' fer hell in high gear with the brakes bu'sted, an' that they'd be a sizzlin' an' a-fryin' in that lake of fire ferever-more.

"Afore he got through he had the men all a shoutin' an' the wimmin a-cryin', an' I could see that all this wasn't settin' too good with Good 'Lige 'specially when Sam started to pokin' fun at the No-Hellers an' even Good 'Lige hisself.

"Atter mebbe two hours Sin-Sockin' Sam he sorty got run down an' outta breath, an' his voice was so hoarse ye couldn't onnerstand him. He closed his Bible, an' then sorty looked over the crowd in a stern-like way ontel he located Good 'Lige.

" 'Now,' says he, 'I see amongst us Brother 'Lige Cantwell frum No-Bizz'-ness Crick. I'm shore glad to have him with us today, an' I'm a-goin' to ast him to close this wunnerful meetin' with a pra'r.'

"Good 'Lige riz up in his seat, an' I could see his whiskers a-quiverin' like he was mad e-nough to bite somebody.

" 'Brother Sam,' says he, 'it was agreed that we'd go to each other's meetin's. That I have done today, an' right thar I stop. We didn't agree to help each other out, so I reckon, Brother Sam, ye'll jest have to do yore own prayin' like I ex-peck to do in my own church.'

"He looked a-roun' an' sorty grinned at some of t'other Aperners on the benches clost to him.

" 'Be-sides,' says he, 'I was sorty anx-shus that the Good Lawd didn't see me hyer today.' "

Heavenly Music from the Hounds

Brandy Bill and Little 'Bijie came to town one day last week and dropped by my office. They told me that they were planning to have another big foxrace on the following Saturday night, and that I had a special invitation to go along. Since the weather was getting comparatively warm again, I reasoned that it wouldn't be too chilly to spend most of the night in the deep woods back on the head of the Devil's Apron, so I accepted. Accordingly I drove over there at the appointed time.

All of the boys—and their hounds—were gathered in Brandy Bill's yard. There must have been a dozen of the hunters, and so many dogs that I lost count of them. I recognized three of the hounds—Big Howdy, Mary Lou, and Blue Thunder—and I knew that they were the three best "cold trailers" to be found in the hill country.

"We've been a-waitin' on ye," said Brandy Bill when I came through the gate. "Vic Vanover an' Corb Hamilton over thar said they might j'ine us. See anything of 'em?"

"Not for the last day or two," I replied.

"Wall, they'll know whar to come. Time to head out, boys. Le's go!"

I walked along with Little 'Bijie and Business Bill, with Brandy Bill and Bad 'Lige just in front of us. Brandy Bill had Big Howdy on a leash, and the giant dog was straining to get loose and into the woods along the side of the road.

"He's a-r'arin' to go," said Little 'Bijie admiringly. "I'll lay ye a bet that he'll be the fu'st to give voice when they jump that fox tonight."

Business Bill dug out his wallet, and produced two grimy one dollar bills.

"I'm still a-backin' Mary Lou," he declared, handing the bills to me. "Ye hold the stakes." Little 'Bijie contributed his two dollars, and I put them in my billfold.

A little further along we came to the clearing in which Willie B. Fuller had his home, and he was standing on the porch staring at us. As we came near he walked uncertainly down the path to the gate.

"Come on, Willie B., an' j'ine us," invited Brandy Bill.

"Thank you! I believe I will." Judging by the gravity of his tone, and his exaggerated politeness, I knew that he had been finding a little solace with his notorious potato-peeling brandy. He turned and hurried back to the house.

"He's gone atter a bottle of that brandy of his," declared Little 'Bijie. "I watched him make a run of that 'tater-peelin' stuff t'other day, an' my ad-vice to all of ye is to jest per-tend to be a-drinkin' it ef'n he passes his bottle a-roun'. Ef'n ye reely need a drink, me an' Brandy Bill we've got a leetle applejack with us that's fitten."

"Does he really make it out of potato-peelings?" I asked. "I thought you boys were just kidding about that."

"He shore does," replied Little 'Bijie emphatically. "An' whut's more he's been a foolin' a-roun' with it an' a-mixin' this an' that into it, an' he claims he's got him somethin' now which he called the 'Lixir of the Gawds er somethin', but I ain't anx-shus to try it out.

"I watched him mix his mash a couple of weeks ago, an' as best I could tell, he tuck a-bout a booshel of cut-up 'taters, a couple of boxes of prunes, somethin' like ten pounds of sugar, an' a cupful of carbide to trigger it off. Then to give it a taste, he put in a few bottles of peppermint ex-track, an' when he run that stuff off it had the kick of a bay mule."

As we slowly climbed to the top of the dividing ridge, I noticed that Willie B. and a few of the boys had dropped behind, and that his bottle was being passed around, but I took Bijie's advice, and refrained from joining them.

At last we reached the crest of the ridge, and there they turned the dogs loose. The entire pack vanished back down that ridge toward the river, and it was only a few minutes later that I heard the resounding bay of one of the dogs. Brandy Bill grunted with satisfaction, echoed by Little 'Bijie.

"Ye can pay me," said the latter, reaching out his hand.

Everyone was in agreement that it was Big Howdy who had first found the trail of the fox, so I gave the four dollars to Little 'Bijie. Some of the boys had gathered firewood and started a big blaze, and we all gathered about it.

Willie B., evidently warmed by an inner fire, sat down on a bed of moss some distance away and leaned back against a gnarled old oak. An instant later he was sound asleep.

The pack of hounds by this time was in full cry, making the night echo with their medley. All of the hunters sat in rapt and mute enjoyment as the sounds of the chase reverberated through the darkness.

"Wake up, Willie B.!" shouted Brandy Bill, slapping the latter on the shoulder with a heavy hand. "Wake up an' lissen to that heavenly music."

Willie B. opened his eyes and gazed about owlishly, and then he shook his head as if to clear it of the fogs.

"Hell!" he growled. "I can't—hic—hear nothing for those infernal hounds."

And he went peacefully back to sleep.

Didamey Jane Lights on Pile of Manure

I happened to meet Good 'Lige and his wife, Aunt Marthy, in town the other day, and both of them had their arms filled with packages and paper sacks loaded with groceries. I stopped to talk with them for a minute or two.

"You must be planning to have a feast over at your house," I said, and Good 'Lige nodded but said nothing.

"Nothin' much to speak of," said Aunt Marthy with a smile. "I'm jest invitin' some of the neighborin' wimmin to come to my house Satte'day an' have a quiltin'. I've pieced a few quilts an' I kinda wanted to git 'em finished afore winter set in. Ain't no men in-vited," she added apologetically.

Good 'Lige winked broadly at me and Aunt Marthy leaned forward and half-whispered:

"But ef'n ye happen to be over thar on Satte'day, I'm a-goin' to have a passel of pies an' cakes baked up, an' I guess we can spare ye a few pieces of 'em."

So when I arrived at Good 'Lige's place, and parked my car beside the barn, I found Brandy Bill, Bad 'Lige, Little 'Bijie and Business Bill all gathered in the shade, whittling and idly talking.

I walked on up to the house to talk with Good 'Lige, and I saw that there were some fifteen or twenty women gathered in the large living room. Two large frames were suspended from the joists overhead, and in each of those frames was a quilt of patchwork, showing many vivid colors. They were sewing the cotton "batting" so that it would be held securely in place in the finished quilt.

Among those helping Aunt Marthy supervise the work was Didamey Jane, Bad 'Lige's wife, and Sindusty, Brandy Bill's better-half. Also I saw among the workers the twin old-maid sisters, Icy and Snowdy Morehead. And gone was every vestige of their usual retiring and self-effacing characteristics, and they were chattering and laughing and evidently enjoying themselves to the fullest.

It was the first quilting-bee that I had seen in many a year, and I stood and watched the activities for several minutes Good 'Lige came and stood beside me. Then we went back to the barn where the other men were lounging. Four of them were pitching horseshoes with a sort of lackidaisical effort, and by the time that the noon hour arrived we were furtively watching the kitchen.

We saw the women quit their work and go into the kitchen, and they certainly took their time eating. When finally they had finished we were famished, and we lost no time in getting at the piles of food left on the table. There were platters of fried chicken, home-baked light-bread, pickled eggs, pies, cakes, jams and jellies, and for the next fifteen minutes we simply gorged ourselves. Then once more we gathered outside in the shade of the apple tree, and took things easy while we digested that dinner. A sudden burst of laughter came from the house, and we all glanced at the open window.

"Wonder whut tickled 'em all of a sudden like that?" said Little 'Bijie.

"My guess'd be that one of them twins—Icy er Snowdy —has told one of them funny tales of theirs," replied Good 'Lige.

Bad 'Lige and Brandy Bill looked at each other and then rose to their feet.

"Le's slip a-roun' thar back of the house an' lissen to 'em," suggested Brandy Bill with a grin. "Might be we could hear somethin'."

That idea caught on quickly, and a minute or so later all of us were tiptoeing around the building toward another window in which white curtains were rippling in the breezes. We crouched down and kept as quiet as we could, and the women kept on talking and laughing, evidently unaware of the fact that they had listeners.

After a little while the talking and laughing in the room died down, and there was a complete silence as the workers gave all of their attention to the sewing. Then a voice near the window said: " 'I was jest re-collectin' a-bout when I was young, an' a-goin' to parties an' corn-shuckin's an' stir-offs, an' a-courtin' this'n an' that'n, an' not payin' much mind to none of the boys'."

"That's Bad 'Lige's wife," whispered Brandy Bill, nudging me in the ribs with his elbow. "That's Didamey Jane."

"As I was a-sayin'," continued Didamey Jane with a giggle, "I couldn't get my mind set on none of 'em. I was jest like one of these purty, yaller-winged butterflies. Ye know how they do on a hot summer day. They fly all a-roun', an' a-roun' over the purty flowers an' never seem to even look at 'em. They fly on past the apple trees an' the honeysuckle, an' they jest won't light down a-tall.

"Wall, I was jest like one of them leetle butterflies. Whilst I was a-sparkin' the boys, I flew all over them purty flowers an' things, an' fine'ly when I did de-cide to come down, I lit right plum spang on a pile of manure."

And that broke up the quilting party, both inside and out.

The Teacher's Experiment

I ran into Brandy Bill on the street early one day last week, and we dropped into a restaurant for a cup of coffee.

"I was a-comin' down to yore office," he told me as he poured some of the contents of his cup into the saucer and blew upon it to cool it. "I figgered ye'd ort to be over on the Apern next Friday a-bout three o'clock," he added mysteriously.

"Why, what's going to take place then?" I asked.

"I don't rightly know," he replied doubtfully, "but thar's somethin' in the wind. I'll be lookin' fer ye, an' I'll tell ye a-bout it Friday."

All during the rest of the week I kept wondering about Brandy Bill's mystery, and why he had stressed the point that I should be there at three o'clock, but by dint of hard work I managed to clear my desk by noon on the appointed day, and two o'clock found me parking my car at Brandy Bill's gate. He came out on the porch and greeted me jovially.

"Ye got hyer early," he said glancing at his old silver watch. "I wasn't expectin' ye fer a while yit. Come on in to the fire. It's a mite chilly out hyer."

We sat in front of the blazing logs for several minutes, and Brandy Bill at last came to the mystery for which I had been impatiently waiting.

"I ast ye to come over so's we could go up thar to the school-house an' see jest egg-zackly whut is a-goin' on. My son, Toddy, tells me that the teacher is a-goin' to do somethin' up thar jest a-fore school lets out that's shore got me a-guessin'."

"But I thought your school was closed—that you lost your teacher."

"We didn't have no school endurin' most of the winter. The fu'st teacher she got homesick I reckon be-kaze she jest didn't come back atter Chris-mus, but we've got us a new teacher now—Miss Tabythy Higgenbottom. She's mebbe fifty years old an' frum whut I hear she shore is all fire an' tow.

"She's a-stayin' up to Good 'Lige's place, an' I reckon as how her an' him has a fine time a-talkin' a-bout the bad an' e-vil things which air a-goin' on hyer on the Apern. Ye see, I gether she's plum sot on re-formin' us, an' she ain't got no use a-tall fer anybody that takes a nip of brandy now an' then.

"But the thing that's got me hawg-tied an' runnin' in circles is that yistiddy she sent word by leetle Toddy that she wanted a half-pint of my applejack, an' that Toddy was to be shore an' fetch it to her on Friday. Toddy says as how she's a-goin' to l'arn 'em a lesson a-bout the e-vils of drinkin' likker, an' that she's a-goin' to use that half-pint in that thar lesson."

I must admit that my interest and curiosity were keyed to a high pitch, and I could hardly wait for the appointed hour. It was getting close to three when Brandy Bill and I tiptoed through the school-house door, and unobtrusively sank into seats in the back row.

Miss Higginbottom came down the aisle, and spoke to us in a warm and sprightly manner.

"I'm glad you men came," she declared, "but I must ask you to wait for a few minutes until I can complete this class. Then we will have the experiment which I am sure you came to see."

Brandy Bill looked at me, his eyes round with apprehension, and for a moment I thought that he was going to take to his heels.

"Do ye reckon she aims to ex-peerement on us?" he whispered anxiously.

"I wouldn't know," I told him, and we sat silent and

uneasy until that class ended. Then Miss Tabythy walked up to her desk on the raised platform at the end of the room.

"Children," she said with a smile, "I am going to perform a little experiment here, and I believe it will be one that will teach you a lesson that you will never forget. I have been talking to you about the evils and terrible effects that the drinking of alcoholic beverages causes. I have told you how it destroys not only your mind, but your body as well. Today I am going to show you how terrible and deadly the vile stuff is."

From the drawer of her desk she brought out two ordinary glass tumblers and a small bottle that evidently contained Brandy Bill's applejack. Then from a pitcher on her desk she poured out a full glass of water, and she filled the other glass with an equal amount of brandy.

"Too much water!" chuckled Brandy Bill under his breath. "Thar won't be no taste to the brandy."

Very gingerly she opened a small cardboard box, a little

larger than a match-box, and pulled out an earthworm about three inches long. It was wriggling frantically as she held it up for all to see.

"Children, I have here a worm with which you are all familiar. Now into one of these glasses I have poured some water such as God intended for us to drink. In this other glass I have poured some liquor—moonshine, I believe it is called. Now watch me closely!"

She dropped that worm into the glass of water and it swam around and around, apparently quite happy and contented. Then she dipped it out of that tumbler and dropped it into the applejack. The worm turned a sickly white color and dropped to the bottom of the glass—lifeless.

"Now what does that teach you, children?" she asked triumphantly.

Little Toddy quickly held up his hand.

"All right, Todhunter," nodded Miss Tabythy, "tell us what lesson you got from that experiment."

"It means that ef'n ye drink good applejack ye won't never have no worms."

Snowdy Jane and the Skin Graft

Brandy Bill was in an expansive and talkative mood when I ran into him at Dutton's store at the mouth of No-Business Creek last Saturday. After the corn was ground at his mill, he and several other Devil's Aproners had come down on the river to replenish their supply of eating tobacco and other necessities.

Brandy Bill moved over on the bench to give me a seat on the shaded porch where the boys were lounging in indolent ease.

"I was jest a-fixin' to tell the boys," he said, "a-bout the time that Leetle 'Bijie's wife—Snowdy Jane—fell in a burnin' bresh-pile when 'Bijie was a-cl'arin' his newgroun' some sev'ral years ago." He eyed me questioningly. "Did I ever tell ye that'n?"

I shook my head without speaking, fearful of breaking his thread of memory.

"Wall, it was somethin' like this: Ye see, Leetle 'Bijie he upped an' got married to ol' Adam Potter's gal, Snowdy Jane, an' he built him a house up thar on the head of the Apern. I reckon ye never knowed ol' Adam, an' his wife, Hellfirey, did ye?"

"What?" I ejaculated, sitting straight up. "Say that again!"

"Her name's Elvirey," he explained with a chuckle, "but Leetle 'Bijie an' most ever'body as knowed her called her Hellfirey, an' it shore fitted her to a tee-wighty. Anyhow, A'nt Hellfirey had only the one gal, an' atter she married Leetle 'Bijie, Hellfirey spent a-bout half the time a-livin' at 'Bijie's place.

"An' betwixt A'nt Hellfirey an' Snowdy Jane, they shore did lead Leetle 'Bijie a tomcat's life. Ef'n he so much as tuck a leetle drap of applejack he shore had to sleep out with the dry-cattle. But Snowdy Jane was as purty as a red heifer in a strawberry patch, an' Leetle 'Bijie he put up with her an' tried to make the best of things.

"Wall, one spring eight er ten years ago, Leetle 'Bijie he c'lared him a piece of newgroun' to tend in corn, an' late one evenin' he started in to burnin' the bresh-piles. Snowdy Jane she went a-long with him, an' she got to settin' fire to the bresh, too, a-takin' a torch an' goin' frum pile to pile.

"Her torch went out, an' she went back to a burnin' pile to light it up ag'in. She ketched her foot in a root er somethin' an' pitched right plum ker-spang into that burnin' bresh-heap. Leetle 'Bijie run to her as quick as he could, an' pulled her out, but not ontel she had got bad burnt. She must a-hit her head ag'inst a rock er somethin' bekaze she never moved ontel 'Bijie got her out an' rolled her over a few times to put out her burnin' clothes.

"He toted her to the house, an' they doctred on her fer a week, but it looked like they couldn't git them burns to heal up. The wu'st place was on the right side of her face, an' atter a couple of weeks Leetle 'Bijie he tuck her over thar to Doc Burton's horspital to see what could be done fer her.

"The Doc he kept her thar fer a couple of days, but it didn't look like he was a-goin' to be able to make that burnt place heal neither. An' even ef'n it did, he said thar would be a bad scar. Leetle 'Bijie was plum proud of his wife's looks, an' didn't want that to happen. Anyhow Doc he called Leetle 'Bijie over to the horspital.

" 'Bijie,' says he, 'it don't look like I'm a-goin' to be able to cyore that place up. Seems as though we air a-goin' to have to do a leetle skin-graftin', an' I reckon as how we'll have to take that skin off'n ye. Whar a-bouts do ye want me to take it frum?'

Leetle 'Bijie he thunk that over fer a couple of minnits.

" 'I reckon,' says he, 'ye'd better take it off my backside, sorty low down thar behindst. With all the work on the farm, an' the cookin' an' tendin' to the young'uns like I'm a-doin', I ain't a-goin' to have no time to set down nohow.'

"So Doc he tuck a-bout two squar' inches of hide off'n Leetle 'Bijie's r'ar eend, an' dawg my cats ef'n it didn't cyore up plum quick. In less'n a week Snowdy Jane was outta thar as fit as a fiddle. She an' Leetle 'Bijie they went down to the bank, an' Leetle 'Bijie drawed out a five honnerd dollar bill, an' tuck it back to the horspital.

"He handed it to Doc, an' he reached fer his pocketbook to make the change.

" 'Hol' on thar, Doc!' says 'Bijie. 'That's all yores.'

" 'But 'Bijie, my bill is fer jest three honnerd an' forty dollars.'

" 'It don't make no diff'rence, Doc. I'm a-goin' to git back my money ever' time that Hellfirey comes a visitin' to my house an' kisses Snowdy Jane on that thar cheek.' "

The Fastest Hogs on the Apron

"Le's go up to Leetle 'Bijie's an' see them shoats that he's jest bought," suggested Brandy Bill after the cool shadows of evening had closed in and had tempered the sweltering heat. It had been a sultry afternoon on the Devil's Apron and we had been sprawling in the shade in Brandy Bill's backyard for the past two hours.

"Whar at did he git 'em?" asked Bad 'Lige without particular interest.

"Frum Bizz'ness Bill," replied Brandy Bill, reaching down and helping me to my feet. I really didn't want to make that stiff climb back up the mountain to Little 'Bijie's home, but I decided that I'd go along anyway.

On the way we talked little because it was still uncomfortably warm, and the road was rough, making walking difficult. Good 'Lige and I walked side by side, but he was limiting his conversation to monosyllables.

When we came to Little 'Bijie's cabin, we found him busily engaged in building a pig-pen for the shoats.

"Whar's them hawgs ye bought off'n Bizz'ness Bill?" demanded Bad 'Lige glancing about the barn-lot.

"I put 'em onder the house ontel I can git this pen built," replied 'Bijie. So we all walked over and peered under the latticed porch. I soon located the two pigs fast asleep.

"Whut kind air they, 'Bijie?" asked Brandy Bill.

"Wall, I reckon they air half ridge-runner, an' half jug-sucker," chuckled 'Bijie. "They're jest plain razorbacks."

After the boys had looked them over for a few minutes, we went back to Little 'Bijie's springhouse where he produced a jug of malted corn. Then we sat down to talk a while.

"Did I ever tell ye a-bout the time that the revenooer come mighty nigh a-ketchin' Bad 'Lige makin' a run of likker?" queried Brandy Bill of me.

My disclaimer was quick because I wanted to hear the story. In fact I needed it for the next issue of the paper.

"Wall, it was mebbe ten er twelve years ago." Brandy Bill accepted the stogie that I dug up, and took his time in lighting it to his taste. "Bad 'Lige was a-makin' a run of brandy outta them winesaps he raises, an' he had his still on some coal comp'ny land right next to his prope'tty line. He had a new copper outfit, an' he shore did make some good drinkin' likker in them days.

"He fixed up a few bar'ls of sweet-mash an' let it set fer a-bout a week to let it come to a proper head. In the meantime he toted his b'iler an' worm up thar an' set her up. That was afore they got to makin' this blamed thumpin'-kag stuff. Anyhow Bad 'Lige was shore set up nice with water handy an' some good dry white-oak that don't give off no smoke.

"One mornin' bright an' early he got out an' headed fer his still, aimin' to start his fu'st run. When he got in sight of the still he stopped an' sorty looked over ever-thing keerful-like, a-figgerin' that somebody could be a-watchin' the still-site.

"He drapped down quick behindst a bush when he seed somebody raise his head up frum behindst one of them bar'ls of mash. Then he kinda scrooched out back'ards, an' lit a shuck outta thar, a-goin' plum over in Kaintucky to spend a few days.

"A-bout a week later he come back an' went up thar to whar he could see his outfit, an' shore as shootin' he seed that revenooer pop his head up ag'in at that same bar'l. He watched it fer a long time an' it bobbed up sorty reglar-like so at last he got a leetle suspi-shus. He crawled a-roun' the hillside a piece, an' then peeped outta the bushes ag'in. He could see behindst that bar'l an' thar wasn't no revenooer thar. Then he seed him poke his head up right outta the bar'l itself.

"Bad 'Lige knowed that the bar'l wasn't big e-nough to hold a man, an' atter a long time he crawled up reel clost, an' it was not ontel then that he seed that his revenooer was a dead pig that had clum' up an' fell in the bar'l an' got drownded. That sweet-mash was a-workin' reel good, an' it was a-makin' that dead pig bob up an' down thataway. An' Bad 'Lige he made that run—dead pig re-gyardless—an' never said nothin' a-bout it."

"An' that's the truth," admitted Bad 'Lige with a grin. "That pig shore did look like a revenooer to me."

"Them blamed razorbacks can shore look atter their-selves that away," opined Little 'Bijie after the laugh sub-sided. "I'll bet none of ye ever seed one starve to death, no matter how sca'ce food is. That's why I bought them leetle fellers onder the porch. In partick-ler I wanted one of them kind that Bizz'ness Bill has been a-raisin'.

"Them hawgs," he continued, "air the fastest things on their feet that I ever seed. Ye wouldn't be-lieve this ef'n ye'd a-seed it with yore own eyes. I was over thar to Bizz'-ness Bill's last fall, an' the mammy of them two shoats I bought was a-layin' thar in the yard.

"Thar was a big chesnut-oak tree up thar next to the woods a-bove the house, an' we later measured the distance frum the house to that tree. It was three honnerd an' sixty-seven yards. Now, ye might think I'm a-stretchin' the truth a leetle, but I'll take oath that the sow heerd a acorn fall outta that tree, an' she got up thar so quick she ketched it on the fu'st bounce."

Mixed Medicines

"Set down," ordered Brandy Bill, "an' I'll tell ye the tale a-bout the time ol' King David Combs got his wife an' dawg med'cine all mixed up by accident."

We were all standing around in Brandy Bill's backyard, nursing our tall, cold juleps, and Bad 'Lige, Little 'Bijie, and several of the other boys all drew closer to hear the story.

While collecting his thoughts, Brandy Bill chewed reflectively, and then knocked a bug off a weed ten feet away with á blob of tobacco juice.

"I reckon some of ye'll re-colleck ol' King David an' his houn', Rowdy Joe. That must a-been ten years ago when this e-vent which I am relatin' tuck place. King David an' A'nt Hanner they lived up hyer on the Apern, but they later moved back to Kaintucky.

"I figger thar ain't no use in me a-talkin' a-bout Rowdy Joe bekaze all of ye knowed him, er ye've done heerd a-bout him. He was one of the best coonhoun's that was ever hunted in these hills, an', like ye know, he was the daddy of Big Howdy thar."

He pointed toward the gaunt dog sleeping near us, and the hound, upon hearing his name called, opened his eyes and thumped his tail lazily on the ground. Then he went back to sleep again.

"Wall, it seems as though ol' Rowdy Joe he got to ailin' a leetle an' jest seemed to want to lay a-roun' the house all day an' do nothin. No matter how hard he tried King David jest couldn't git him out to treein' coons no more, an' he got so's he wouldn't eat nothin' much an' when he walked acrost the floor ye could hear his toe-nails a-scratchin'—he was that dooless.

"About that time A'nt Hanner got somethin' wrong with her. I expect some of ye re-colleck her. She was a big woman, an' a hearty eater, but it seemed as though she jest lost all interest in her vittels, an' she fell off ontel she was jest a shadder of her ol' self.

"Now, King David was plum worried a-bout Rowdy Joe, an' A'nt Hanner, too, an' atter a week er so in which they didn't git no better, he figgered that he'd better see a-bout gittin' some med'cine fer 'em.

"So he saddled up his mule an' rid over thar to town, an' hunted up the drug-store. He told the feller as was a-runnin' it, a-bout ol' Rowdy Joe an' A'nt Hanner, an' he wanted to know ef'n somethin' couldn't be fixed up to cyore 'em.

"The store-feller he reckoned as how he had the very things they needed, an' he sold King David a bottle of Liddy Pinkham's Veg-e-tubble Compoun' for A'nt Hanner, an' some sort of a dawg tonick fer ol' Rowdy Joe, an' he told him how to dose 'em.

"As King David was a-comin' back frum town, he run into Bad 'Lige an' Willie B. Fuller down at the mouth of No-Bizz'ness Crick. I got with 'em a leetle later, an' we all went down the river a piece an' started to fishin'. We had us a couple of jugs of applejack that was prime stuff, an' King David he figgers as how he'll stay with us a while to see ef'n we ketched any fish. Then he said as how he reckoned he'd jest spend the night.

" 'One more day without these hyer med'cines,' he explains sorty to excuse hisself, 'Ain't a-goin' to hurt Rowdy Joe an' Hanner too much, so I reckon I'll jest bed down on this sand-bar.'

"Next mornin' King David wasn't a-fellin' any too good bekaze we'd done drunk up all of that applejack. When he got ready to head fer home, he got out them two bottles of med'cine, an' showed 'em to me. Like mebbe ye know, King

David couldn't read ner write, so he helt 'em in front of me an' told me to tell him ag'in which was fer Rowdy Joe an' which was fer Hanner.

"Thar was a picture of dawg on one bottle an' a woman on t'other'n an' I figger any fool ort to be able to keep 'em straight even ef'n he couldn't read whut was on 'em. I knowed that A'nt Hanner couldn't see nothin' without her specks, an' it turned out that she had bu'sted 'em at the time this hyer tuck place. Anyhow King David put them bottles in his pocket an' headed fer home.

"It was jest a couple of mornin's later, jest a-bout the crack of big day, that somebody woke me up a-hollerin' at the gate. It was King David an' he was nigh a-bout skeered to death. A-bout all he could do was stutter, an' try to git his breath back. I jerked on my britches, an' we headed back up the crick in a long trot.

"We stopped at his gate to blow a leetle, an' it was then that King David told me as how he'd done got them med'cins mixed in spite of them pictures on 'em.

" 'I shore don't see how I could a-done it,' he groans, 'but I can't figger it out no t'other way. Come on! I'll show ye whut I mean.'

"We went in the house, an' when we got in the kitchen, I'm seven diff-rent kinds of a liar ef'n Rowdy Joe wasn't a-settin' on a stool a-washin' the dishes, an' A'nt Hanner was out thar in the pasture fiel' a-runnin' down a rabbit."

The Original Lazy Man

Quite a gathering of the boys from up on the Devil's Apron were lounging about the store at the mouth of No-Business Creek last Saturday afternoon, and a general air of laziness and somnolence pervaded the entire scene. Some of them nodded to me when I drove up, but none of them had the energly to get up and offer the customary handshake.

I saw that Brandy Bill, Good 'Lige and Little 'Bijie were holding the center of the stage at the moment, and I walked over and joined them.

"Go ahead with your discussion, boys," I urged. "Don't let me interrupt you."

"Wall," said Good 'Lige, gently stroking his long, white beard, "we was jest a-talkin' a-bout how lazy some folks can git, speshully in weather like this. It allus seemed to me like, when the corn was laid by, an' it gits too hot to go fishin', thar comes a time when a man ain't wu'th much of nothin'.

"Take Hen Hardy, now, who ust to live up thar on the head of Wolf-Pen Crick," he mused as the boys all gathered closer about him. "I reckon he was jest a-bout the laziest white man I ever seed. He was married up with Polly Hill an' she was a hard worker. They had a whole passel of young'uns, an' it wasn't long ontel Hen had done turned all the work over to her an' the kids.

"Jest to give ye a idee how lazy that critter was, I stopped at his place one time, an' I seed him a-settin' on the porch a-rockin'. It was powerful hot, an' I figgered I'd set with him a leetle ontel I sorty cooled off. I noticed that he'd rock fer a while with his back turned towarge the east, an' then he'd hitch his cheer a-roun' an' rock frum north to south. I ast him why he was a-doin' that an' he tol' me that he'd been a-tryin' all summer to figger somethin' out.

'Ive been a-tryin',' says he, 'to see ef'n I could find out whar it's easier on a feller to rock with the wind at his back an' him a-facin' east, er to rock with the grain of the wood frum north to south.'

"Anyhow, thar come a bad year with the craps—frost got all the fruit, an' dry weather ruint the corn, an' it shore looked things was a-goin' to be mighty bad. Polly an' Hen an' their chillun was jest a-bout to starve to death, but that didn't make no diff'rence to ol' Hen. He jest sot thar on his porch an' rocked an' com-plained a-bout the weather an' the hard times, but it seemed like he wasn't a-figgerin' on doin' anything a-bout it.

"Some of the boys was a-talkin' a-bout Hen, an' they figgered that he wasn't no help to his fambly er to hisself either, an' that he reely didn't have no reason fer stayin' a-live nohow. A bunch of 'em got together an' made him a coffin, an' they put it on a sled an' hauled it up to Hen's place.

"They foun' him a-layin' on a sheepskin pallet on the shady eend of the porch, an' the boys driv up an' onloaded the coffin' in the yard. They tol' Hen that it was up to him to git out thar in his fiel's an' go to work er they was a'goin' to bury him—that he wasn't no good fer nothin' an' that his fambly'd be better off without him. Hen he lissened to 'em, an' then he shook his head slow-like bekaze it was too hot to talk.

"The boys sorty argy-ed with him fer a leetle while, but Hen wasn't in no notion of goin' to work, so they picked him up an' laid him in that coffin, a-thinkin' they'd shore bluff him into doin' somthin'. They headed down towarge the graveyard thar at the ol' Lost Meetin'-house, an' on the way they met up with one of them Jackson boys that lived up thar on Coon Branch.

"He stopped an' ast whut was a-goin' on, an' they tol' him how it was, an' whut they was a-fixin' to do.

" 'Wall boys,' says the Jackson boy, 'that ain't whut I'd call doin' per-zackly right, a-buryin' a man an' him still a-live thataway. Ef'n it'll do any good, I've got a booshel of corn that I'd be glad to give him to tide him over fer a few days.'

"When he heerd that ol' Hen he riz up in his coffin an' looked at this Jackson.

" 'Is that thar corn shelled?' he ast.

" 'No, ye'll have to shell it.'

" 'Then drive on, boys,' says Hen, a-layin' back down."

Bad 'Lige and the First Automobile

All was quiet and serene over on the Devil's Apron last Saturday when I foregathered with the boys at Brandy Bill's grist-mill. On every hand were the visible evidences of a very hard winter—deep snows, freezes, rains, high winds and other violent acts of nature—but the gang was out in full force, exuberant in having thrown off the frozen shackles.

The corn grinding for the day was over, and the boys were sitting in the sun on the porch, swapping the latest news and gossip before returning to their respective homes.

"Whut's this hyer Jubilee bizz'ness we've been a-hearin' so much a-bout lately?" queried Little 'Bijie of me when I had found a seat among them.

"Why, I thought everyone knew about that. It's the celebration of the seventy-fifth anniversary of the county. Ours was the last county in the state to be organized just seventy-five years ago."

"Yeah," drawled Brandy Bill, "we got that much frum readin' yore paper, but whut's all this hullybaloo a-bout huntin' up ol'-time things like weavin' looms an' hawg-rifle guns, an' sich?"

"It's for comparison between the old ways and the new," I explained. "For instance, there is a big difference in the means of transportation. Only a few years ago all of the people here on the Apron had to ride mules or horses when they wanted to go anywhere. Now they hop in a car, and almost before you know it they are where they wanted to go."

"Not through this Devil's Apern mud, they ain't," spoke up Business Bill.

"I see." Brandy Bill was giving the matter deep thought. 'It's like the ol' backin' an' doublin' way of makin' likker, an' this hyer new-fangled thumpkin'-kag sugar-top moonshine. Wall, as fer me I'll take the ol's ways ever' time. These new ways don't give us nothin' but belly-wash that'd kill a mule."

"A-men!" murmured Good 'Lige reverently.

"Ef'n it's the ol' things they air a-huntin' fer," continued Brandy Bill, "why ain't nobody been a'roun' to look over that thar ol' cyar that's been a-settin' in that shed behindst Bad 'Lige's barn fer the last forty years er more?"

"Whut ol' cyar?" demanded Little 'Bijie.

"I don't rightly re-colleck it's name, but it's shore a old-timer frum a-way back. I don't think that they air a makin' 'em no longer bekaze I ain't seed one fer years."

"It's a M-A-X-W-E-L-L," replied Bad 'Lige, spelling it out slowly. "It was made back in nineteen honnerd an' ten er 'leven."

"You don't say!" I exclaimed. "That should be a real relic, and I'm sure the committee will want it in the parade. Where did you get it, 'Lige?"

"That's a tale I was jest a-figgerin' on tellin' ye," spoke up Brandy Bill. "It tuck place purty soon after I fu'st come up hyer on the Apern to live, more'n forty years ago. Bad 'Lige had jest got hisself married, an' built his house whar he lives now.

"Thar wasn't no roads to speak of hyer on the Apern then, an' nobody'd ever heerd tell of these auty-mobiles, let a-lone a-seein' one. But we all got our heads together an' we 'lected Good 'Lige fer Super-viser, an' he got us a purty good road fer them days—waggin-road, that is.

"It run right past Bad 'Lige's house, an' him an' his wife they ust to set on their front porch in the evenin's when the work was done an' pass the time of day with the folks as went by—mostly on mules.

"They was a-settin' thar one evenin'—long in the shank of daylight—when all to onct thar come a bangin' an' a roarin' sound a-roun' the bend in the big road that they'd never heerd afore. It was a-comin' up the crick frum the river, an' in a minnit er two it come in sight.

"It was that thar cyar we was a-talkin' a-bout, an' it was the fu'st cyar that was ever seed on the Apern. Fer a few secon's Bad 'Lige an' his wife they jest froze in their seats, an' couldn't move a muscle. Then his wife screamed:

" 'Gawddlemighty, 'Lige! Whut is it?'

"Bad 'Lige didn't take time to talk to her. He jest made a dive fer his hawg-rifle inside the house. His wife follered him an' crawled onder the bed, an' in a-nuther secon' he cut loose with his gun.

" 'Did ye kill it, 'Lige?' she yells.

" 'I don't know yit,' says Bad 'Lige, peepin' through the crack of the door, 'but I shore as hell shot it loose frum the feller it was a-runnin' off with.' "

Good 'Lige Suggests A Second Marriage

Having been a bit under the weather for several days, I missed my weekly visit to the Devil's Apron, but I felt better on Sunday, and, the afternoon being perfect although a little chilly, I drove over to Brandy Bill's home. A number of the boys were also visiting Brandy Bill.

"We heerd ye was sorty puny," said Little 'Bijie as I entered the select circle.

"And you heard right," I replied, forcing a cough to indicate how ill I had been.

"We kinda figgered ye'd be over today, so me an' Brandy Bill we fixed ye some hot ginger-stew. It's a-steamin' on the stove in the kitchen, an' it ort to be good fer whut ails ye."

"Gittin' purty clost to 'lection," observed Good 'Lige, stroking his patriarchal beard thoughtfully. "Is it gittin' hot over in town?"

"I've seen them hotter," I declared, "but not in recent years."

"Same way over here," asserted Business Bill. "We figger to git out the biggest vote we ever had, an' it's goin' to be mighty clost."

"An' we shore aim to have us a clean 'lection this year," put in Little 'Bijie. "We've got Good 'Lige named as a 'lection jedge, an' we air a-goin' to vote in the meetin'-house. Ef'n they have one of them con-tests ag'in this year we figger we won't be in it."

We were all silent for several minutes, and then someone called attention to a car that was being parked on the road in front of Brandy Bill's house.

"Wonder who that is?" queried Brandy Bill. "I don't know as I've ever seed that cyar afore."

A tall, broad-shouldered young man, wearing overalls and a denim jacket, got out of the dilapidated vehicle, followed by a young woman. The man didn't offer to assist her, but stalked through the open gate toward us with the girl at his heels. We stood motionless awaiting them.

The visitors halted a few steps away, and the young giant eyed us questioningly.

"I'm Big Jim Potter frum over on Skin Fork," he announced, "an' I'm a-lookin' fer a preacher named Good 'Lige Cantwell."

Good 'Lige came slowly to his feet.

"I guess I'm the man ye're a-lookin' fer," he said quietly. "Whut can I do fer ye?"

"Me an' Melissy Maggard hyer, we was kinda a-figgerin' on gittin' hitched up, an', seein' as how ye married Melissy's maw an' paw some thu'tty years ago, she is shorely sot on the idee of gittin' ye to marry us."

"That so?" murmured Good 'Lige. "Wall, I reckon that can be fixed up. Have ye got yore license?"

'Shore have, an' the blood-test papers, too. They told me at that store on the river that I might find ye hyer."

"I never thought to fetch my Bible a-long with me today," said Good 'Lige apologetically, "but I reckon I know e-nough of it to make it stick good an' tight."

"That's good e-nough fer us," said Big Jim with a wide grin. "Go ahead an' shoot the works."

The couple stood before Good 'Lige at the foot of the kitchen steps, and the old preacher intoned the marriage ceremony in a manner that bespoke long practice. All of us stood around in a semi-circle and when the wedding was over we all passed by them in a line, wishing them much happiness.

Big Jim kissed his blushing bride, and then strode off in the direction of his car.

Good 'Lige stood motionless for a minute, and then he took a couple of steps toward the newlyweds.

"Hold on, Potter!" he called. "Ain't ye a-fergittin' somethin'?"

"Whut?" demanded Big Jim non-plussed.

"Wall, folks gin'rilly pay me somethin' fer hitchin' 'em up thataway."

"That's the way of ye blamed preachers, allus a-tryin' to git somethin' fer nothin'," snarled Big Jim. "The law don't say as how I've got to pay ye fer marryin' us, an' I ain't goin' to give ye a single copper-cent."

"Wall, that's all right, brother," said Good 'Lige softly, but I could see from the glint in his eyes, and the manner in which his beard stiffened, that he was as mad as a hornet.

"Would ye do me a favor?" he asked in a deceptively mild tone.

"De-pends," replied Big Jim surily.

"I want ye to tell yore mammy an' pappy to come up to my church next Sunday."

"I'll tell 'em, but whut do ye want 'em to come all the way up hyer fer?"

"I sorty figgered that they ort to git married, too."

And I don't believe that Big Jim has figured that one out yet.

Good 'Lige Holds A Royal Flush

Brandy Bill, Little 'Bijie, Bad 'Lige and Business Bill were enjoying a little game of penny-ante poker at the grist-mill on No-Business Creek when I went over last Saturday afternoon. I found a moss-covered rock and sat down to watch the game.

It was a lazy spring day, and the boys soon grew tired of playing. Brandy Bill gathered up the cards and thrust the deck in his pocket. Then we all adjourned to the pot of ginger-stew on the stove inside the mill. Brandy Bill got the deck of cards out of his pocket and placed it in a box on a shelf behind the stove.

"A-totin' them cyards a-roun' like that puts me in mind of the time we dammed up No-Bizz'ness Crick down thar below my place, so's Good 'Lige could hold that big bab-tizin' that time." Brandy Bill turned to Bad 'Lige. "Ye re-colleck that don't ye?"

"Shore do!" declared Bad 'Lige with a grin. "That was the time Good 'Lige helt the highest poker hand in the deck."

"I never heard that one—tell me about it," I suggested.

"Wall, last year a-bout this time, Good 'Lige he lined him up some five er six of the brethern an' sistern, an' he was a-fixin' to bab-tize 'em into his Hard-Rock Firm-Founda-shun Church. Now, I reckon ye know that Good 'Lige be-lieves in puttin' 'em deep onder the water so's to wash a-way their sins. Anyhow we had to dam up a lot of water down thar in the crick so's it'd be plenty deep.

"Thar was me an' Bad 'Lige an' Leetle 'Bijie who pitched in an' helped Good 'Lige git ever-thing ready. The word had gone out over the Apern, an' we knowed that a whoppin' big crowd'd be thar bekaze thar's nothin' that'll fetch out a crowd like a bab-tizin'.

"Come the mornin' of the bab-tizin' Good 'Lige he come past my place kinda early, sorty a-figgerin' on seein' ef'n the dam was all right, an' thar was e-nough water. He was all dressed up in his best suit of clothes, but he was a'totin' a-long a dry suit of onderwear, an' a ol' pair of britches which he aimed to use endurin' the bab-tizin'.

"It was sorty a chilly day, an' it had been a-rainin' some, an' I knowed the water was plenty cold. Good 'Lige was a-goin' to freeze when he got all wet that-away, so I went in the house an' hunted up a ol' coat of mine an' give it to him to wear, an' save his new coat.

"Wall, ever'thing went off plum slick an' smooth right up ontel Good 'Lige waded out in the pond with Sister Jerushy Hardy. She was kinda hefty, weighin' night onto two honnerd pounds, an' Good 'Lige tuck her out whar the water was the deepest. It come up jest a-bout to his armpits an' he had a purty hard time a-keepin' his footin'.

"Me an' Bad 'Lige an' some of us was a-standin' at the edge of the water a-watchin', an' Good 'Lige's ol' woman, Marthy, was crowded in clost beside us. Whilst Good 'Lige was a-gittin' Sister Jerushy all fixed an' ready to souse her onder, I seed the ace of spades come a-floatin' outta Good 'Lige's pocket. It come down the pool right past whar we was a-standin' an' I heerd A'nt Marthy ketch her breath.

"Me an' Bad 'Lige we jest stood thar, an' hoped that nobody'd se ewhut we seed. But I'll be e-tarnally dang-bu'sted ef'n the king of spades didn't float up outta the pocket an' come on down past whar we was. Me an' Bad 'Lige jest froze up, an' we couldn't be-lieve our eyes when we seed the queen an' then the jack, an' fine'ly the ten-spot all float by, a-makin' it a royal flush— a-bout the fu'st'n I ever seed.

"A'nt Marthy was fit to be tied. She was a-twistin' an' a-wringin' her hands, an' a-lookin' plum pop-eyed at that thar royal flush. Then she grabbed Bad 'Lige by the arm.

" 'Git in thar an' do somethin',' she says hoarse-like. 'Do somethin' to halp him.'

" 'Lissen, Marthy,' say Bad 'Lige, a-watchin' that ten of spades sink outta sight, 'ary man that holds a pat royal flush in spades, shore don't need no help frum nobody.' "

A Really Hot Summer

"Looks like a-nuther long dry spell's a-comin' on," observed Good 'Lige, gazing thoughtfully at the unbroken expanse of blue sky overhead. It was a sultry day, and the leaves on the big maple in Brandy Bill's backyard hung limp and dejected.

"Shore does," agreed Little 'Bijie. "All the signs air a-p'intin' that way. I've been a-noticin' that the snakes an' toad-frawgs air all a-headin' down grade towarge the river, an' when they do that it's allus meant that the water was a-goin' to dry up."

"In a way the Devil's Apern is plum onlucky," continued Good 'Lige thoughtfully. "I've been a-watchin' things up hyer fer many a year, an' it seems that thar can be plenty of rain in other places a-roun', but nary a drap on the Apern."

"How do you account for that?" I asked, my curiosity aroused.

"Wall, it seems as though them black rain-clouds allus come up acrost the mountains an' when they pass ol' Baldy, that highest p'int up thar, they sorty split up," he pointed toward the serrated crest of the Cumberlands above us. "It'll rain cats an' dawgs over on Whisperin' Crick, an' they'll have a flood on B'ar Waller Branch on t'other side of us whilst we git nothin' but a leetle wind."

All of the boys nodded in agreement with the old preacher's statement, but none of them had any further suggestions about this phenomenon. I sighed and found solace in my julep.

"I re-colleck the time a-bout ten years ago when we shore did dry plum up hyer on the Apern," declared Bad 'Lige, biting off a liberal chew from his plug of tobacco. "In my o-pinyun that was the wu'st we ever had up hyer. It got so dry ye had to prime yore mouth to spit.

"Frum a-bout the middle of July ontel well up in September, as best I re-member, we didn't have a drap of rain—more'n sixty days anyhow. An' the cricks had all done run plum dry, an' the wells got so low that we had to drive all our stock down to Pound River fer waterin', an' by the time we got 'em back home it was time to start out with 'em ag'in. Couldn't hardly take time out fer the milkin'.

"No-Bizz'ness Crick hyer run plum dry purty early in the season. Thar wasn't nothin' but a few leetle pot-holes left hyer an' thar, an' mighty leetle water in 'em. The deepest of them pot-holes was up thar ferninst the ol' Lost Meetin'-house, an' the wimminfolks they was a-usin' it fer to wash clothes in. An' they used the same water over an' over ag'in.

"It was a-bout that time Oncle Hen an' A'nt Abby-gil Hatfiel' j'ined Good 'Lige's church. They ast to be babtized into that faith, an' that put Good 'Lige in a sort of a pickelment bekaze he shore didn't believe in that sprinklin' bizz'ness. He allus soused 'em plum onder so's to wash a-way their sins fer good.

"Wall, Good 'Lige he prayed fer rain, but that didn't do no good, an' then he went down thar to that pot-hole whar the wimmin had been a-washin'. It wasn't no use in dammin' up the crack bekaze no water was a-runnin', an', like I said, that hole was full of soap-suds. But Good 'Lige he waded out in it an' found that it was a-bout three foot deep. Since that was all thar was he figgered it'd have to do.

"Now, A'nt Abby-gil, ef'n any of ye re-colleck her, was a big woman, broad acrost the beam, an' it was doubtful ef'n thar was e-nough water even to kivver her flatwise. Oncle Hen he needed a long hole, but it didn't matter how shaller it was. They could a-bab-tized him in a heavy dew he was that skinny.

"When the day come fer the bab-tizin' Good Lige tuck Oncle Hen out, an' thar wasn't no trubble a-bout gittin' him fixed up proper. But me an' Brandy Bill an' a few of us crowded up clost to see how he managed with Abby-gil. They waded out to the deepest place, an' Good 'Lige got him a good grip on the back of her neck, an' pooshed her down. Her head went onder alright, but her feet flew out. He turned loose his holt, an' tried to put her feet onder, but her head popped up.

"Then Good 'Lige grabbed her an' tried to lift her up, but them soap-suds had done made her as slick as grease, an' in a minnit he yelled fer help. Some of us jumped in thar an' snaked her out afore she was plum drownded, but they say as how she blowed soap blubbers whilst she was a-sleep fer the next three nights hand-runnin'."

When the laughter had died down, Little 'Bijie cleared his throat.

"It shore was dry that year," he attested. "After A'nt Abby-gill's bab-tizin' it 'peared like things got still wu'ss an' wu'ss. Ever'thing I had planted got dried up an' blowed outta the groun' by the wind. But the thing that had me stumped was the way the trees got to actin'.

"Ef'n ye'll all re-colleck thar was a lot of hot wind endurin' them dry days, and when it blowed through the trees it made a sort of a funny soun'. At fu'st I didn't pay it no mind, but one evenin' late I got to lissenin', an' purty soon I ketched on. It was them trees a-makin' that noise, an' they was so dry that they was a-whisslin' fer the dawgs."

Aunt Serrepthy Gets Baptised

There were glints of humor in Brandy Bill's eyes when he greeted me at the grist-mill last Saturday. It was the first time that the mill had been in operation for several weeks because of the drought, but the recent rains had given a "full head of water," and the boys were all on hand for their corn-meal.

"Set an' talk with the boys a spell," he said, indicating a bench near the stove. "I've got ye a peck of the best meal I ever groun', an' I'll hunt a sack fer it atter a while."

I nodded my thanks and joined Little 'Bijie, Good 'Lige and Business Bill who were awaiting their turn. After a few minutes Brandy Bill cut off the flow of water and brought the mill to a stop.

"Ef'n I a-had a-nuther turn to grind, I couldn't a-made it," he declared, slapping the fine coating of white dust from his overalls. "The water's all gone outta the dam, an' we'll have to wait ontel it rains ag'in." He sat down beside us and began whittling tobacco from a home-spun twist to fill his pipe.

"Wall, I see they've done got A'nt Serrepthy Maggard back frum the ocean," he said to no one in particular.

I looked at him in surprise unable to believe that I had heard him aright.

"Will you kindly repeat that statement in words of one syllable?" I asked.

"Ye'd better tell him a-bout it, Good 'Lige," suggested Brandy Bill, nodding at the latter. "Ye was a-long an' seed it all happen."

Good 'Lige gave expression to a low laugh, and accepted the cigar I offered him. He lighted it carefully and then leaned back against the wall.

"I reckon ye've heerd tell of A'nt Serrepthy, ain't ye?" he asked of me.

"Wasn't she the bootlegger who was so big they couldn't get her out of the house when the revenue officers arrested her?" I vainly searched my memory for the details of that story.

"The same," was his succinct reply. "Ye see, they knowed she was guilty, but thar wasn't no law that'd let 'em t'ar down her house so's they could git her out an' take her to jail. So they jest had to leave her thar. An' I reckon she'd done sold more moonshine in her day than anybody else in these parts anywhar.

"But it so happened that purty soon after her trubble with the revenooers, she got to thinkin' that mebbe she hadn't been a-doin' egg-zackly like she'd ort to, 'speshully a-handlin' that sugar-top likker which ain't fitten to drink, an' she sorty figgered it was time to mend her ways. Anyhow she give up bootleggin' an' started to readin' of her Bible.

"She sent fer me to come up to talk to her a-bout her soul's salvay-shun, an' mebbe pray fer her a leetle. So one day I went up thar to her place, a-takin' my wife with me so's nobody wouldn't start a-doin' no talkin'. She told me she had done re-pented of her sins, an' that she was aimin' to j'ine the church, an' git bap-tized as quick as it could be done.

"She had been sorty ailin' fer the last month er so an' she was off'n her feed so's she didn't weigh much more'n three honnerd pounds. She said as how she'd been a sinner all her life, an' that she had been guilty of so many sins, an' was so big that it wasn't a-goin' to be possible to wash her sins away in none of these leetle cricks er rivers that we've got back hyer, an' that nothin' short of the big, wide ocean would be big enough to do the job.

"She'd been a-pesterin' her kinfolks a-bout that trip down thar to the ocean, an' astin' 'em to take her down thar an' be bab-tized whar the water was deep e-nough to drownd out her sins. So, last week they rigged up her bed in a truck, an' headed east. She told 'em as how she wouldn't have nobody but me to bab-tize her, so they tuck me a-long with 'em.

"We driv down thar to Virginny Beach, an' thar must a-been a thousan' people thar a-swimmin' at the time we arriv. I led A'nt Serrepthy out thar in the ocean, an' I was jest a-gittin' ready to put her onder the water when them people which was a-swimmin' an' funnin' a-roun', they started to yellin' an' hollerin', an' a-gittin' outta the water as fast as they could.

"I looked out thar whar some of 'em was a-p'intin', an' I seed a big fish a-bout thu'tty foot long—they called it a shark—an' it was headed right plum towarge me an' A'nt Serrepthy. Me an' her we tuck a-bout one jump a piece afore we hit dry land, but that thar shark must a-got skeered of A'nt Serrepthy bekaze he headed back into the deep water.

"Atter a leetle while them swimmin' people started to go back in the water, an' I figgered it'd be safe, so I says:

"'Come on, Serrepthy! Le's git on with the bab-tizin'.'

"'Not by a dam' sight!' says she. 'I'm a-gittin' right back in that truck, an' when I git back home I'm a-goin' to j'ine the sprinklin' Methy-dists whar thar won't be none of them blamed sharks.'"

The Alcoholic Cure

When I got over on the Devil's Apron last Saturday the day's grinding at Brandy Bill's mill was finished, and the boys were gathered out in the yard in the warm sunshine. The subject of conversation seemed to be an Easter-egg hunt that Good 'Lige was planning for the children of the church on the following day.

They were practically all there—Good 'Lige, Brandy Bill, Bad 'Lige, Business Bill, and Little 'Bijie—and peacefully sleeping with his back against the porch post was Willie B. From the expressions on their faces I saw that they were deeply interested in the discussion.

"Mebbe ye can help us out," suggested Brandy Bill when I found a seat among them. "We was a-tryin' to figger out why they have these hyar Easter eggs all colored like they do."

"You've got me there," I replied, shaking my head. "I haven't the slightest idea. Of course we all know what Easter means, and why it is observed, but the colored eggs, I imagine, were merely to amuse the children."

"Anyhow," said Brandy Bill, "I reckon ye ort to come over tomorrer when Good 'Lige puts on his reg'lar Easter egg hunt up thar at the meetin'-house. He's been a-doin' that ever' year fer a long time, an' at fu'st it was jest fer the young'uns, but more an' more the growed-up folks got into it, an' last year the chillun didn't have a chanct."

"An' I reckon this hyer rabbit bizz'ness at Eastertime is sorty like the eggs, ain't they?" asked Business Bill after a pause. "Some of my boys got 'em a couple of these hyer white rabbits, an' afore they knowed it, they had a pen full of the danged things. Still they figgered they' have 'em a big s'prize fer my baby boy—Leetle Ike.

"They got 'em some Easter-egg colorin' some'rs an' they ketched 'em six er eight of them leetle rabbits, an' they made 'em ever' color ye could think of. They was the funniest lookin' leetle things ye ever seed, but the trubbel was that colorin' killed ever' blamed one of them rabbits afore Leetle Iike got a chanct to play with 'em."

"Speakin' of colored eggs," spoke up Brandy Bill, "my son, Toddy, last year shore did fool me an' Willie B. thar. Ye'd a-figgered it was one of these Aprile fool jokes. I reckon I never did tell ye fellers a-bout that."

Without waiting for a reply, he plunged into his story.

"Ye see, sometime afore Easter, Toddy he was a-readin' in my Farmers Frien' Weekly, an' he seed in it whar, by feedin' the hens some kind of colorin' stuff, ye could make them hens lay eggs with the yallers most any color ye wanted. So he set down an' ordered him a box of them colors to see ef'n they'd work.

"I knowed he was up to somethin' bekaze I seed that he was a-keepin' some of his hens in one pen an' some in a-nuther'n, an' he was powerful keerful a-bout doin' all the feedin' hisself. I didn't pester him none a-bout whut he was doin' bekaze I've allus sorty let him have his own way.

"It was the night afore Easter that leetle Toddy sprung his big s'prize on me an' his mammy. He fetched in a hatful of eggs an' tol' his mammy to fry him a few fer his supper. Wall, Sindusty she broke one of them eggs an' the yaller was as red as blood. She throwed it in the slop-bucket, an' broke a-nuther'n. It was as green as grass.

"She night a-bout had a fit fer the next few minnits ontel leetle Toddy tol' her a-bout whut he was a-doin'. He had them eggs marked so's he could tell which was whut color, an' Sindusty fried him some, but me an' her jest couldn't tetch the things.

"A leetle atter suppertime Willie B. he come by my house, an' drapped in to set a while. He was sorty cellybratin' somethin' er t'other—I fergit whut—an' I kinda j'ined in with him. An' then one thing led to a-nuther'n, an' it wasn't very long ontel he jest a-bout passed out on me. I had to put him to bed bekaze he never would a-been able to git home.

"We woke up the next mornin' a-feelin' plum fuzzy an' mean, but I fixed things up a leetle an' then I tuck Willie B. down to breakfus'. Now, Willie B. likes his eggs b'iled—jest two minnits—with the whites cooked some an' the yallers runny. I picked up a couple of Toddy's eggs an' b'iled 'em egg-zackly two minnits.

"He broke his fu'st egg in a cup an' it was purple. Then he broke the next'n an' it was green. He looked at me, his eyes a-poppin', an' then he got up frum the table an' headed towarge his home."

"Did he stop drinkin' atter that?" asked Little 'Bijie.

"No, he jest quit eatin' eggs."

Mule Eggs

Although there were several hints of spring in the air, a bitterly cold wind was sweeping down off the Cumberlands when I got over to the grist-mill on the Devil's Apron last Saturday. The boys, however, had an antidote for that chill, and it was simmering on the back of the heating stove.

They found a cup for me, and filled it brimful with ginger-stew for which I was duly grateful. Then Brandy Bill turned the grinding chore over to little Toddy, and came over to us.

"You have any snow over here last week?" I asked by way of opening the conversation.

"In spots mostly," replied Little 'Bijie. "It drifted in piles over my head in some places."

"That wasn't too deep," chuckled Brandy Bill, measuring the little man from head to foot.

"It ketched me plum outta feed fer my cows," volunteered Business Bill, "but I had me a few pun'kins in the barn, an' they pulled 'em through ontel I could buy a leetle chop."

"Speakin' of pun-kins," said Brandy Bill, "did I ever tell ye fellers a-bout the time ol' Zeb Hartsock sold a mule-egg to that city slicker?" And the Liars' Club was automatically in session.

"A mule-egg!" I exploded. "That's one I want to hear."

"This hyer tale is the truth ef'n I ever told it, so help me. It happened back more'n twenty years ago. Fer some time we had been hearin' of a furriner of some kind a-campin' back up thar on the head of No-Bizz'ness Crick. He was a funny lookin' feller, a-wearin' ridin' britches an' boots an' a bright red shirt, but we later found out that thar was no harm in him.

"At fu'st we figgered him as a revenooer, an' we kept a purty clost watch on him, a-follerin' him ever-whar he went. But we soon dis-kivvered that he wasn't a-lookin' fer no stills er likker. He said as how he was a-huntin' fer that ol' Swift Silver mine—."

"I've heard of that mine," I interrupted. "Did he think it was located up here?"

"I reckon so. Anyhow, he had him a map, but it was so ol' an' tore up ye couldn't make heads ner tails of it. Still he figgered that the mine was in these hills somewhar. He found a leetle black stuff that run in streaks in the rocks, an' he tried to melt a leetle of it, but it wasn't silver.

"He had him a tent up thar, an' he was a-tryin' to do his own cookin', but he nigh a-bout starved hisself to death. Some of the wimminfolks tuck pity on him an' ast him to come an' eat with them, an' some of 'em cooked vittels an' had the young'uns take 'em up thar.

"One day he happened to pass by a fiel' whar ol' Zeb Hartsock was a-workin' up thar nigh to whar he had his tent. Ol' Zeb was a-shuckin' out his corn, an' the whole fiel' was kivvered up with big yaller pun-kins.

"This hyer furriner—I never did know his name—was a strange sort of a feller—simple-like ye might call him. He'd be-lieve ever'thing that anybody told him, an' some of the boys got a lotta fun outta him a-joshin' him.

"He leaned acrost the fence an' hollered at ol' Zeb.

" 'Whut air these yaller things in yore fiel'?' he asts.

" 'Them air mule-eggs,' replies ol' Zeb without blinkin' a eye.

" 'I'd shore like to have me a leetle mule,' says this furriner. 'I'll give twenty dollars fer one.'

"Fer a minnit that knocked ol' Zeb off'n his feet,

an' then he sorty grinned, an' picked out the biggest pun'kin thar was in a whole fiel'. Then this furriner he grabs it an' heads out fer his leetle camp back up towarge the forks of the crick.

" 'Better keep it in the sun endurin' the day an' wrop it up with a quilt ever' night,' ad-vised ol' Zeb, a-doin' his best to keep from bu'stin' out a-laffin'. 'It's jest a-bout ready to hatch now.'

"Wall, this furriner started up the road an' it was purty steep down below the path towarge the crick. Purty soon he stumped his toe an' fell down, a-drappin' his mule-egg. It started to roll down the hill, an' he tuck atter it as hard as he could go. But afore he ketched up with it, it rolled into a rock an' busted all to pieces.

"Jest then a rabbit jumped outta some sage-grass clost to that rock, an' headed fer the red-bresh.

"The furriner he lit out atter it a'yellin': 'Kwup, colty! Hyer's yore mammy! Kwup, colty! Hyer's yore mammy'

"A leetle later this furriner, he come back to the fiel' whar ol' Zeb was still a-workin,' an' told Zeb whut had happened.

"'I'd like to buy me a-nuther of them eggs,' he says, 'but make this'n one that'll start in low gear when it's fu'st hatched out of its shell.'"

The Prize Was A Groundhog

I saw Willie B. Fuller and Bad 'Lige attending the Republican County convention at the courthouse the other afternoon, and when that meeting was adjourned they walked down to my office with me, and sat around for a while discussing the political situation.

Willie B. was painfully sober, and I had no immediate way of elleviating that condition, but Bad 'Lige produced a flask, and pretty soon we had the situation well in hand.

"I'll say one thing," declared Willie B., with a soft hiccough, "and that is that politics are certainly getting hot here in the county. Looks like some real races are in the offing."

"An' that's a fact," added Bad 'Lige. "I never seed the Devil's Apern so stirred up this fur in ad-vance."

Willie B. took another short one from the flask, and then handed it back to Bad 'Lige.

"Yes, even the children over there are getting rather excited," stated Willie B. in the precise English he used when he was reasonably sober. "I was rather amused last Saturday afternoon when we held the Republican precinct mass meeting to elect delegates to this convention today.

"Practically all of the Republicans on the Apron gathered at the school along about two o'clock in the afternoon. School was still in session, but the teacher invited us all to come into the building and sit until she could complete a class she was holding.

"The youngsters were all anxiously watching the

clock on the teacher's desk, and they were twisting and figiting and staring at us because I suppose they were not accustomed to having so many visitors at the same time. When that class was over, Miss Samantha walked back to her desk.

" 'Now, children,' she said, we are going to have a special program for the benefit of our visitors. I am sure that they will enjoy it, and it won't take but a few minutes. You children all know that the time has come for candidates for the county offices to be nominated, and that is what these visitors are doing here today.

" 'You have been showing a great deal of interest in these political affairs, and all of you know that we have only two political parties here—the Republican and Democratic parties. Some of you are Republicans and some of you are Democrats, and I am going to call upon any of you who may want to tell which party you favor and why you are a Republican or a Democrat.

" 'Now I want you simply to get up and tell us in your own words why you believe in the party of your choice, and I am quite sure that these men will listen with interest. And now the surprise! I am going to give a prize to the boy or girl who makes the best speech. It is a tiny little groundhog that has grown tame, and will drink milk from a baby bottle. Now who will be the first one to come up here and tell us what you are and why?'

"The first hand to go up was that of Calvin Coolige, Business Bill's son.

" 'All right, Calvin, you are first.'

"The boy marched up on the platform and proudly declaimed:

" 'I am a Republican because George Washington and Alexander Hamilton were Republicans and they founded our nation and a government of the people, by the people, and for the people.

" 'I am a Republican because Abraham Lincoln was

a Republican, and he freed the slaves and saved the United States when there was a war with the South. I am a Republican because my pappy and my grandpappy are Republicans, and they would whale the tar out of me if I was a Democrat.'

"We Republicans thought that was a fine speech, and we applauded it loudly while the teacher beamed at her young protege. Then little Toddy, Brandy Bill's pride and joy, held up his hand.

" 'All right, Todhunter!' said the teacher. 'Let's hear your side.'

"Toddy proved himself to be a chip off the old block, and his speech, as best I recall it, was this:

" 'I am a Democrat because the greatest Presidents this country ever had were Democrats. I am a Democrat because Thomas Jefferson was a Democrat, and he wrote the constitution on which all of our laws were founded. I am a Democrat because Andrew Jackson and Woodrow Wilson were Democrats, and they did more for all the people than any of the other Presidents. I am a Democrat because Franklin D. Roosevelt was a Democrat, and he was the greatest man that ever lived in this country.'

"Now, we Republicans didn't think so much of that speech, and we didn't cheer him very loudly. Then another boy raised his hand, but I had never seen previously—."

"That was Big Son Combs' boy," interrupted Bad 'Lige. "They call him Leetle Son."

"Well, Little Son made his bow and looked us over.

" 'I am an Independent,' he said, and then looked at the teacher to see how she reacted.

" 'Go ahead, Sonny,' she said. 'Tell us why you are an Independent.'

" 'I am an Independent,' he repeated, 'because I want that groundhog.' "

A Ten Dollar Mule

Spring had come again, and the Devil's Apron was abloom with "sarvice" trees and red-bud, and I could sense the season's awakening in the bubbling goodwill and excessive energies of the boys who were gathered at Brandy Bill's grist-mill last Saturday.

They were naturally concerned with their spring planting, and plowing mules appeared to be the chief topic of conversation when I joined the circle. Little 'Bijie Birdsong had the floor.

"Yes sir, I bought me the finest mule that ye ever seed a couple of weeks ago," he was saying. "He goes by the name of Brownie, him a-bein' a dun with a black streak down his back. Got him frum a feller over on Indian Crick in Kaintucky, an' paid a honnerd an' ten dollars fer him.

"But when I fu'st come home with him he was shore the most con-trary critter that I ever tried to hitch to a plow. I couldn't make him go 'Gee' ner 'Haw', an' most of the time I couldn't git him to even move. He'd jest plant all four feet on the groun' an' stand thar come hell an' high water. He jest wouldn't move no matter whut I done.

"I was out thar at my newgroun' last—le's see—last Toosday mornin' when Bad 'Lige come by to borrer a leetle seed corn. He watched me an' that mule fer a while, an' he seed that I wasn't a-gittin' no-wh'ar with him.

"'Thar ain't but one way to handle a mule like that,' says he. 'Hyer, let me show ye.'

"He got him a piece of two-by-four scantlin', an' he hit leetle Brownie over the head so hard he knocked him cold as kraut.

"'Whut do ye think ye're a-doin'?' I yells at him. 'Air ye a tryin' to kill him?'

"'I see ye don't know nothin' a-bout mules,' says he. 'Fu'st thing ye've got to do is to make 'em notice ye.' An' Brownie ain't balked since."

"Speakin' of mules," said Brandy Bill, "I'm afeard my ol' mule that died on me a few weeks ago is a-goin' to git me in trubbel yit. Ye all re-colleck that ol' white mule—Maudie—that I've had fer the last ten years."

There were several affirmative grunts from his listeners.

"Wall, I never could figger out whut got wrong with ol' Maudie this past winter. She ust to be a hard workin' gentle mule, an' Toddy rid her her all over the place. But last fall she got to be the most ca'tankerous brute I ever owned, an' I'm skeered she's got me in trubbel with my income tax."

"Your income tax!" I exclaimed. "How on earth could that happen?"

"It was like this. Ye see, I was a-tryin' to make out my income tax report a few days ago, an' I was a-doin' my blamedist to do whut they tol' me to do on that paper. I was a-puttin' down all the things I'd done an' got money outta 'em, an' them things I put money in an' got nothin' back, an' that's whar Maudie come in.

"Now, I fu'st bought Maudie when she was jest a puny leetle thing, an' the feller I got her frum figgered she'd die in a week er two, so he let me have her fer ten dollars.

"Anyhow, I put down that she cost me ten dollars. Then last fall she got mean, like I was a'tellin' ye, an' kicked out two stalls in my barn. It cost me ten dollars to fix 'em up ag'in—lumber an' all—an' I put that down.

"A leetle later when the mud got reel bad a feller got stuck with his cyar down thar below my house, an'

I got ol' Maudie an' we pulled him out an' helped him git on down to the mouth of the crick. Fer that job he paid me ten dollars, an' I put that down on the profit side.

"I got tired of foolin' a-roun' with her, an' I sold her to Long Tom Mullins fer ten dollars, but he wouldn't keep her bekaze she wouldn't plow fer him neither, so I had to take his money back, an' I put all that down on that paper.

"Last fall a bunch of young'uns frum over thar in town was down on the river a-swimmin'. I was a fetchin' Maudie back frum Long Tom's, an' I let them kids ride her at two-bits a ride. That fetched me in a-nuther ten dollars, an' I put that down.

"Afore I could git her home that evenin' she balked on me right plum in the middle of the road, an' a feller a-drivin' a truck hit her an' bu-sted her up some. He

paid me ten dollars to squar' things, an' I put that down on that piece of paper.

"A few days atter that Maudie she upped an' died on me, an' I had to pay one of Bizz'ness Bill's boys ten dollars to haul her off an' bury her. Atter figgerin' fer a long time I couldn't tell whar Maudie owed me ten dollars er I owed her ten dollars er we both owed the gov'ment ten dollars.

"So I jest got a new re-port an' filled her out. I jest writ on it:

" 'One mule—ten dollars', an' the gov-ment'll jest have to take it frum thar."

A Seated Horse Upon A Rock

On last Sunday I drove over to the Hard-Rock Firm-Foundation Church on the Devil's Apron, and, finding the church crowded to capacity and three preachers scheduled to deliver long sermons, Brandy Bill, Bad 'Lige and I decided to drive on around the mountain and find a cool shady loafing place.

After going a short distance we stopped at the old "Jockey Street", and sat staring at the wilderness that was growing up in that once thriving spot. No longer were the hillmen riding their horses up and down that straight stretch of road, and gathering in knots to discuss the merits of this and that horse or mule, and perhaps to take a round of drinks from someone's fruit-jar.

In truth, it was a far cry from the old days when Jockey Street was one of the most colorful and interesting institutions in the entire mountain area. With regrets I realized that, with the passing of that era, the Appalachian Highlands had suffered an irreparable loss. It required no effort on my part to visualize a couple of hundred men and even more horses crowding the scene, busily engaged in the business of horse trading.

Strangely enough all of those horses and mules were "sound as a dollar an' ain't shed their colt teeth yit." Everyone showed the gaits of his animal before a critical crowd, and the man who got the best of any trade won a high place in the public's regard, and he never lost an opportunity of boasting about his achievement.

We three got out of the car and walked over and sat down on an old moss-covered log. Bad 'Lige filled his pipe with shavings from a plug of chewing tobacco, and gestured toward the empty road.

"I can re-colleck the time when that thar road was crowded with two er three hondred hosses, an' more was tied up in them bushes back thar as fur as a man could see. Hoss traders come in hyer frum all-a-roun' the county an' frum a way down in Kaintucky, a-fetchin' with 'em two er three hosses er mules fer tradin'.

"In them days they had three full days of preachin' a-bout one time a month—Friday, Satte'day, an' Sunday —an' thar was plenty of hoss-swappin' ever' day frum mornin' ontel night." Bad 'Lige turned to me, a faraway expression in his eyes. "I reckon ye've seed a reel Jockey Street in yore time, ain't ye?"

I nodded affirmatively, but offered no comment.

"I reckon a-bout the biggest Jockey Street that we ever had up hyer on the Apern," he continued, "was a-bout thu'tty years ago—give er take a year er two— an' I re-colleck it was endurin' the month July. It was at this meetin' that two of the best hoss-traders in the whole country got hooked up in a deal. They was Brandy Bill an' Bizz'ness Bill.

"That was long afore Bizz'ness Bill moved up hyer on the Apern. At that time was a livin' on Stinkin' Crick down thar in Kaintucky, an' he was allus to be found on Jockey Street, no matter whar it was a-bein' helt, with a hoss er two that gin'rilly had somethin' wrong with 'em.

"Now, Bizz'ness Bill had him a big roan hoss that was blind as a bat, but it seemed like he had some way of pickin' his way a-long without stumblin' er buttin' into somethin'. An' Brandy Bill had a leetle brown mare with a white star a-bove her eyes, an' she had one bad habit.

"I reckon them twin boys of Brandy Bill's—Rock an' Rye—had pranked an' played with her when she was leetle, an' anyhow, when she got tired she had the habit of backin' up an' settin' down on a rock in the shade to cool off. That's the ack-chual truth ef'n I ever told it, an' I've seed her do it, many's the time.

"Wall, Brandy Bill an' Bizz'ness Bill they talked an' they argy-fied, an' they hemmed an' they hawed, an' then on Satte'day evenin' late they fine'ly traded even-steven, an' rid their hosses home. But on Sunday mornin' bright an' early both of' em was back on Jockey Street a-pawin' the earth, they was that mad. Brandy Bill jumped all over Bizz'ness Bill a-claimin' that the roan hoss he got in the trade was so blind that he walked right through the fence without even knowin' it was thar, but Bizz'ness Bill he said as how that hoss was jest a mite stubborn, an' didn't give a dam'.

"An' Bizz'ness Bill he lit on Brandy Bill all spraddled out. He was a-cussin' a blue streak bekaze he said that leetle mare he got set right plum down in the middle of Pound River as he was a-ridin' acrost the ford, an' that he had to git a rope to drag her out on dry land.

"'But I warned ye that she'd be li'ble to back up an' set down on a rock ef'n she gits tired,' says Brandy Bill with a grin.

"'I know that,' yells Bizz'ness Bill, 'but ye didn't tell me that she'd set down in the middle of the river with the water a-runnin' outta banks.'

"Brandy Bill sorty shook his head, an' then says sad-like:

"'To tell ye the truth, Bizz'ness Bill, I plum fergot to tell ye she'd ruther set on a fish than a rock any day in the week.'"

Bad 'Lige Shoots A Ghost

It was raining when I got over on the Devil's Aporn last Saturday afternoon, and I found the boys gathered on the back porch at Brandy Bill's home. Despite the gloomy atmosphere they were in a gay mood, and I suspected that Brandy Bill had put a little more applejack in the juleps than had been his custom.

"I reckon this hyer rain'll let up in a-bout a week," he said, handing a tall glass to me. "It allus rains fer forty days when it rains on the fu'st day of dawg-days."

"Shore been a fine year fer weeds an' frawgs," observed Little 'Bijie in a disgruntled tone.

"Thar'll be the thickest fog tonight ye ever seed," predicted Brandy Bill. "It allus come atter days like this'n."

"Yeah," drawled Business Bill skeptically. "That's how Eb Reed over thar in town figgers out how many snows we air a-goin' to have endurin' the winter, ain't it?

"He shore did misfigger last winter," recalled Brandy Bill. "He said as how we'd have a snow fer each foggy night—er mornin'—in August. Now, August's got jest thu'tty-one days, an' we had sixty-two snow."

"Speakin' of foggy nights," said Little 'Bijie with a grin, "puts me in mind of the time that I seed that ghost up thar at the ol' Lost Meetin'-House. Onliest time I ever seed a ghost.

"Like most of ye know, the graveyard is out thar back of the meetin'-house an' I was a-takin' a short cut through thar to git to my place. It was a-gittin' clost to midnight, an' I allus sorty dreaded to pass a graveyard atter dark nohow, so I sorty slowed down an' looked a-roun' to see whut I could see.

"Right then an' thar is whar I plum lost my breath. Whut I seed was a woman all-dressed up in white with flashes of fire a-shootin' outta her head. It was a black night, whut with the thick fog an' all, an' I couldn't see nothin' much, an' I shore couldn't figger out whut that thing was.

"The longer I looked the skeerier it got, an' the ha'r riz up on the back of my neck. I frez right thar in my tracks, an' fer a long time I jest couldn't move. But I never did be-lieve in ghos-tes thataway, an' fine'ly I de-cided that I was a-goin' up thar clost an' git me a look-see. I was a-totin' some sugar an' cawfee home, so I set my sack down an' clum' up that hill towarge the thing, but the closter I got the more awful it looked, an' the slower I walked.

"But I kept on a-goin', an' when I got up in a few foot of it, I seed whut it was." He paused and looked around the hushed and breathless circle. "Ye could a-knocked me down with a feather when I seed that it was six or eight geese a-roostin' beside the fence—sorty in the shape of a woman—an' thar was some lightnin'-bugs that had settled on some weeds jest behindst them geese."

The boys got a good laugh out of that story, and then Brandy Bill drained his glass.

"I can tell ye a ghost tale that was shore e-nough a ghost," he said. "Bad 'Lige thar shot it. Of cou'se all of ye have noticed that he allus walks with a leetle limp in his left foot. He don't like to talk a-bout it much, but I reckon he won't mind a-tellin' us how it happened."

Bad 'Lige refused to cooperate at first, but at last agreed to their pleading.

"Wall, back a good many years ago thar was a house on the head of Whisperin' Crick that they said had ghos-tes in it," he began. "Nobody'd live in it bekaze they could hear chains a-rattlin' an' lost souls a-mournin' all through the night that was e-nough to skeer a man outta his mind.

"Wall, one evenin' down hyer at the mouth of the crick a bunch of us got to talkin' a-bout that ha'nted house, an' Brandy Bill an' some of the boys bet me that I wuoldn't sleep in it all by myself. The last feller that lived thar tuck off so fast he left his beds an' house-plunder thar.

"The upshot of it was that I agreed to try it, an' some of us moseyed a-long up thar. The other boys all stopped an' spent the night at Bud Tolliver's place, an' let me go on alone. To tell the truth, I figger they was too skeered to go any further.

"Wall, I went on up to that house, an' I found me a lamp with a leetle 'ile in it, an' purty soon I tuck off my clothes an' went to bed. I wasn't long in gittin' to sleep, it a-bein' plum peaceful-like thar, an' I was plum shore no ghos-tes ner sperrits was a-goin' to pester me. Then a-long a-bout midnight I come awake with my eyes bugged out an' me a-holdin' my breath.

"I looked down at the foot of the bed whar the moon was a-shinin' bright through the winder, an' I seed a hand a-reachin' in the bed atter me. I grabbed fer my ol' pistol which I had stuck onder my piller, an' I yelled at whoever it was to speak up—an' mighty quick.

"Thar was no answer, an' I tuck dead aim at that hand an' cut loose, an' I'm dammed ef'n I didn't shoot off two of my toes."

Kissing the North End of a Mule

This thing of going to Brandy Bill's spring-house every Saturday afternoon had grown to be quite an institution, so I went over early last week to make Brandy Bill think that my only purpose in making the visits was not the applejack juleps. I'll have to admit, however, that they were still lurking in the back of my thoughts.

The work was about over for the day at the mill when I arrived, and a little later we gravitated once again to that springhouse. I felt all along that the boys had something up their sleeves. They kept grinning and chuckling and acting mysteriously, but they managed to keep their secret until Brandy Bill had gone through the ritual of lightly bruising the fresh mint, and adding the exact amount of each of the other ingredients.

Then we settled back in the shade, and for a few minutes a blissful and uninterrupted silence obtained.

"Wall," said Little 'Bijie at long last, "ye left jest a leetle early last Satte'day. Ye'd ort to gone back up the crick with me an' Bad 'Lige."

"Why, what did you fellows do?" I demanded.

"It was mostly Bad 'Lige's doin's. Let him tell it."

Nothing loth, and with apparent relish, Bad 'Lige launched into the details with a wide grin.

"Wall, me an' Leetle 'Bijie we was a-headin' fer home atter we left ye fellers down hyer. We was a-walkin' an' leadin' of our mules, an', it a-bein' powerful hot, we was sorty a-takin' our time. I figgered that my leetle mule couldn't tote me an' that sack of meal, too.

"Afore we got very fur a-bove the mill, we heerd somebody a-shootin' up the road a piece, but we didn't pay much mind to it right then.

"When we got up thar jest this side of Turkey Branch we seed somebody a-comin' down the road to-warge us. He looked like he was done loaded fer b'ar—a-swaggerin' an' a-singin', an' a-takin' both sides of the road all at the same time.

"He had him a big pistol in his hand, but he was so bizzy a-tryin' to stay in the road that he wasn't doin' no more shootin'. Leetle 'Bijie knowed him right off.

"'It's that Bart Gobel frum over on Elkhorn Crick in Kaintucky,' he says, sorty whisperin' so's this feller couldn't hear him. We stopped an' waited to see ef'n anything was a-goin' to happen.

"Now I'd done heerd tell of this Bart Gobel an' frum all re-ports he was as mean as a striped snake—born that way an' havin' had a back-set. Seems as though he had done got into so much trubbel over thar he had to skip out an' stay out fer a spell.

"They said as how he'd j'ined the army, but that made him meaner than ever. The army kicked him out purty soon, an' he come back home even meaner than when he left. He was said to be wu's when he was drinkin' which was most of the time, so I figgered mebbe we was in a fer a leetle ruckus.

"Anyhow he staggered up to us, an' stopped, a-wobblin' on his feet.

"'Ol' man, can ye dance?' he hollers, a-p'intin' his gun towarge my feet.

"I told him I reckoned I could—ef'n I had to.

"'Wall, ye shore have to,' says he, a-bu'stin' out in a laugh. 'Give us a buck an' wing!'

"Then he shot onct right under my feet, an' I done him a leetle jig, but when I stopped he shot ag'in. Atter that I give him a few fancy steps that I hadn't tried in years with him a yellin' an' a-laughin' fit to bu'st.

"Fer the next few minnits I put up some of the best dancin' that was ever seed on the Devil's Apern, an' whilst I was a-doin' it, he shot four more times a-roun' my feet. Then he stopped shootin' an' started to feelin' a-roun' in his pockets. I stopped dancin'.

" 'Whut's the matter?' says I. 'Don't ye like that dancin'?'

" 'I done run outta bullets,' says he.

" 'That's jest whut I figgered it was,' I told him, an' I stuck my hand inside my shirt 'an come out with my ol' snub-nosed forty-four. I stuck her ag'inst his belt-buckle, an' I says:

" 'Son, did ye ever kiss the south eend of a mule a-headin' north?'

"He looked into the bar'l of that gun fer a minnit, an' then he shore did wilt down.'

" 'No—no sir,' he stammers, 'but I allus wanted to.' "

Little Toddy and the Constitution

Little 'Bijie and Business Bill were having quite an argument when I got over to Brandy Bill's grist-mill last week, and several of the boys were occasionally getting into the conversation. Little 'Bijie was insisting that the best time to plant potatoes was in the dark of the moon, and Business Bill contended that the planting should be done during the full moon.

"I planted two rows of my patch when the moon was full," declared Little 'Bijie in a tone of finality, "an' them 'taters was all tops an' no 'taters. I'm admittin' that them two rows was the purtiest to look at that I ever raised, but I didn't hardly git my seed back when I dug 'em."

"Same way with killin' hawgs," interposed Bad 'Lige. "Ef'n ye want all grease an' no meat, jest kill 'em on a full moon."

I listened with interest to their arguments because I realized that these "signs and portents" were the result of many years of patient observation. I did not get into the discussion but I did make a mental note or two that I planned to consider when planting my own garden. After that, gradually the crowd scattered to their respective homes, leaving me, Brandy Bill and Little 'Bijie all alone. Brandy Bill closed and locked the mill, and we walked back down to his home where I had parked my car. On the way Little 'Bijie told me that he and his son, "Buddy," were planning to spend the night with Brandy Bill since the remainder of his family was away on a visit.

Brandy Bill invited me to stay for supper, too, and of course I accepted. We went around to the springhouse where he mixed a toddy for us, sweetened with molasses, and it wasn't half bad. All this time Toddy, Brandy Bill's youngest son, was playing with little Buddy in the barn-lot a little distance away. Buddy apparently was some two or three years younger than Toddy, but seemingly they were on good terms, and having a good time playing with a couple of pups.

"That's my Buddy a-playin' with Toddy," explained Little 'Bijie proudly. "He's jest a leetle over seven now, but he's been a-r'arin' to go to school fer the last year. The teacher 'lowed as how she'd try to find a place to put him an' we let him go fer the fu'st time last Monday.

"An' it seems as though he got hisself in trubbel the fu'st day out. Accordin' to whut some of the other young'uns was a-tellin', he had jest got to the schoolhouse an' found him a seat when the teacher come a-roun'.

" 'So ye're Buddy, ain't ye?' she asts. 'Ye look like a bright boy. Do ye know yore A-B-C's yit?'

" 'Hell's fire, Teacher!' says Buddy. 'I jist got hyer.'

Brandy Bill and I rocked with laughter, and Little 'Bijie echoed us, but we all grew grave and silent as we saw the school teacher, Miss Samanthy Throgmorton, coming across the yard toward us. We hid our glasses, and came to our feet.

"I came to talk to you about your son, Todhunter," she said to Brandy Bill.

"Whut's he been into this time?" he asked, glancing toward the two boys playing near the barn.

"Well, I'll tell you, and you can judge for yourself what should be done about it. I was teaching a class yesterday afternoon, and your son, Todhunter, was in that class. I was explaining to the children about the Declaration of Independence, and I asked Todhunter who signed that immortal document. His reply was 'damned if I know!'

"You probably know that I never resort to corporal punishment for the children unless I think that it is absolutely necessary, so I thought I should talk the matter over with you."

Brandy Bill looked back at the barnyard again, and then raised his voice.

"Toddy, come hyer!"

Little Toddy, followed by Buddy, came slowly through the gate and drew fearfully near us.

"Whut did ye tell the teacher when she ast ye that thar question yistiddy?" he demanded sternly.

"I jest said I didn't know who signed the blamed thing," replied Toddy a bit defiantly.

"Wall, Miss Throgmorton," said Brandy Bill after a few seconds of silence, "ye jest go in the house an' visit a while, an' I'll take keer of this young sprout."

We stood motionless until she had vanished in the house, and then Brandy Bill turned to Toddy.

"Now lissen, son," he said, "we air honest an' truthful folks, an' we allus stand squar'ly behindst ever'thing we do. Ef'n ye signed that thar thing she was a-talkin' a-bout, go straight in thar an' tell the teacher that ye done it, an' I'll stand squar' behindst ye."

Polly Ann Gets A Divorce

Last year, during the sweltering heat of mid-summer, my doctor told me to take a rest from work for a while. I knew exactly where I could do that best of all, so I drove over to the Devil's Apron and hunted for some of the boys.

I was informed that most of them were down on Pound River fishing, and I soon located them on the sandy bank beside a long pool with their cane fishing poles thrust into the sand at the edge of the water.

It was almost dark when I joined them, and they had started a couple of big bonfires so that they could watch their fishing lines and see whether or not the fish were biting. I sprawled in the sand between Good 'Lige and Brandy Bill.

"We heerd ye was sorty on the sick list," said Good 'Lige solicitously.

"The doctor told me that I was a bit run down from overwork—."

"Haw! Haw!" exploded Brandy Bill. "I reckon I've got jest the proper med'cine fer whut ails ye right hyer in my jacket—jest whut the doctor ordered."

He unrolled a jar of his finest applejack, and it quickly went the rounds. Then all became quiet as the boys gave their attention to their fishing lines.

Little 'Bijie Birdsong with a deep sigh of content stretched out on his back.

"I was over on Beefhide Crick in Kanitucky last week," he announced, "an' I run into Big Ike Maggard over thar."

"Ye don't say!" ejaculated Good 'Lige. "Has he got married ag'in?"

"I reckon so. I didn't stop at his place, but he's shore got a nice farm, an' a-makin' a good livin'—looks like."

"Wall, I'm shore glad to hear it," declared Good 'Lige with feeling. "He had a hard time of it with his fu'st wife." He turned his attention to me. "Ye see, he ust to live up hyer on the Apern. He bought him a leetle bound'ry of land an' built his house, an' then he got to lookin' a-roun' fer a wife. His eye got sorty set on Milt Combs' gal, Polly Ann.

"Now Polly Ann was a funny sort of a gal. She was allus a-talkin' in po'try—a-makin' ever'thing she said rhyme with somethin'. She started it when she was a leetle gal, an' never did git herself broke frum the habit.

"I re-colleck one time when we got us a new teacher up hyer by the name of Mary Duncan. We had a leetle party fer her hyer at the school-house, an' Polly Ann was thar. She shuck hands with the teacher, and made her some po'try:

" 'Wall—wall, Miz Duncan, ye take the cooshaw an' I'll take the pun'kin.'

"Now when Big Ike was a-sparkin' her he thought that her a-makin' up that po'try thataway was cute an' funny, an' one day they come up to my house an' said as how they wanted to git married. I lined 'em up an', whilst I was a-goin' through the cerry-mony I ast Polly Ann ef'n she tuck Big Iike to be her lawful, wedded husban', an' she come right back at me with some more po'try.

" 'I take Big Ike to be my man, an' I'm a-goin' to hold him as long as I can.'

"Atter the weddin' Big Ike an' Polly Ann lived up thar on the head of the crick fer a-bout three years, an' had 'em a young'un ever' year. I never paid much mind to Polly Ann, but I did hear some of the wimmin a talkin' an' a-whisperin' that Polly Ann was a-steppin' on Big Ike ever onct in a while.

'One day I met her a-goin' down the road, an' I stopped her.

" 'Whar at air ye a-traipsin' off to, Polly Ann?' I asts.

" 'Now Good 'Lige, don't git in a tizz, whar I'm a-goin' ain't none of yore bizz.' An' she kept on goin' down the road.

"At fu'st Polly Ann, when she left home, jest stayed away fer a day er two, but purty soon she got to bein' out fer a week er more. Big Ike wasn't much of a feller to do a lot of talkin', an' he didn't say nothin'. He'd git his sister, Louviny, to come in an' look atter the young'uns.

"But atter so long, Big Ike he got plum tired of Polly Ann's runnin' a-roun', so he fetched him a suit fer dee-vorce over in the cou't. But Polly Ann she didn't 'pear to keer much, an' she didn't even have a lawyer to look atter her side. They was a-holdin' the hearin' over thar in town, an' a purty good crowd was on hand to hear the proceedin's. When they heerd all the evy-dence, the Jedge he asts Polly Ann ef'n she had anything to say.

" 'Go on Jedge an' give him his de-vorce 'kaze I'd ruther live with a spavined hoss,' she tells him.

"The Jedge he give Big Ike his dee-vorce an' also give him the chillun to take keer of. When we all walked outta the cou't-room, Polly Ann stopped on the steps an' winked at some of the folks a-roun' her. Then she cuts loose with some more po'try.

" 'I love that Jedge an' I love his dee-cision, 'kaze he give Big Ike the young'uns an' they wasn't even his'n.' "

To Smell Like A Man

Not so long ago back I happened to glance out of my office window, and I saw Brandy Bill park his jeep across the street. Then he and Willie B. Fuller got out with their arms full of packages. I surmise that they had been to the liquor store, and did not want to take a chance on leaving their purchases unguarded.

They came in and, after carefully depositing their burdens on a chair, sat down to talk a while.

"Anything new on the Apron?" I queried to start things off.

"Nothin' much," replied Brandy Bill, "'ceptin' the census-taker he's been over thar a-countin' heads, but he ain't had much luck. Ever'body's been a-takin' him fer a revenooer, er one of them A-B-C men that the state sends out to ketch us moonshiners. Seems as though Virginny, since she's gone into the likker bizz'ness, is shore set on not lettin' nobody else cut in on the trade."

"You have a point there," I replied. "How many people do you have over on the Apron anyway?"

"Shore is a passel of 'em ef'n ye count the wimmin' an' young'uns. Some of the boys'd be a leetle hard put to tell ye how many chillen they had."

"The census taker?" I was a bit puzzled. "I didn't know they had started the actual work of counting yet. You say he's already been at work over there?"

"He shore has. He started out last Monday, an' he's done kivvered a big part of the Apern. He headed up Coon Branch an' then crossed over on the head of No-Bizz'ness Crick, an' back down towarge the river, an' I reckon he's done got nigh a-bout ever'body down in his leetle black book. I was a-talkin' with some of the boys, an' Lance Calloway was a-tellin' me a-bout it.

"Frum whut he told me his maw, A'nt Sib Calloway, was a-settin' on her porch t'other day a-rockin' in the sunshine. She seed this hyer stranger a-comin' up the road -walkin', an' a-tryin' to keep his shiney shoes outta the mud-holes. He was all dressed up in some funny lookin' britches an' a bright green shirt.

"Anyhow he didn't look like nothin' A'nt Sib had ever seed afore, so she got up an' hobbled down to the gate to see ef'n she could find out who he was, an' what he was a-doin' on the Apern.

" 'Howdy, young feller!' she says, a-puffin' on her corn-cob pipe, an' a-lookin' him over frum head to foot. 'Whar do ye reckon ye're a-goin'?'

"He told her as how he was a-countin' all the people hyer fer the gov'ment like it does ever' ten years. That sorty made A'nt Sib a leetle suspishus, an' she figgered mebbe she'd ort to ast him a few more questions. In fact, he sounded like a revenooer to her, an' she wanted to be shore.

" 'Wall,' she says as he starts on up the crick, 'ye go on an' do yore work, son, but ye drap back by hyer come dinnertime, an' I'll see ef'n I can have a few vittels cooked up. A man gits powerful hongry a-climbin' these hills.'

"The census-taker he thanks her, an' when he got back in that neighborhood, a leetle atter twelve o'clock he was a-gittin' powerful hongry. So he showed up at A'nt Sib's house, an' she p'inted towarge a bench on the back porch an' told him he could wash up, an' then come on in the kitchen fer his dinner.

" 'Been kinda a-lookin' fer ye,' she tells him plum friendly-like. 'Whut might yore name be?'

"He told her, but I've done fergot whut it was— some sorty furrin' name of some kind.

"'Wall,' says A'nt Sib, 'set down an' take a smoke whilst I git it dished up.'

"'Thank ye, but I don't smoke,' says the censustaker.

"'Lawsy me!' says A'nt Sib. 'I figgered ever'body smoked er chawed. Thar's a plug of store terbacker on the fireboard in the front room. Help yoreself. It might whet yore appetite fer dinner.'

"'But I don't chew neither,' says he.

"'Humph!' snorts A'nt Sib, a-lookin' him over like she didn't know whut to make of him. She went in the kitchen an' was bizzy fer a few minnits, an' then she come out on the porch ag'in.

"'At fu'st,' she tells him, 'I figgered ye to be a revenooer, but I reckon ye ain't. Ye don't look an' ack like they do, an' I'm a-goin' to trust ye. Ef'n ye'd like a leetle dram of good moonshine, thar's a jug onder the bed in thar.'

"'I thank ye ag'in,' says this feller, 'but I never tuck a drink of likker in my life.'

"'Wall, Gawdelmighty, Mister,' gasps A'nt Sib, 'whut do ye do to smell like a man?'"

The Tornado

Up at the Farmers' Fair a few days ago I got with Brandy Bill, Bad 'Lige and Little 'Bijie, and they were a bedraggled looking lot. It had been raining all day, and they were wet and muddy, and apparently they did not have anything with them to put them in a more cheerful frame of mind.

"You fellows having lots of fun?" I asked.

" 'Wall, we ain't egg-zackly a-bu'stin' out with it," growled Brandy Bill. "We've been a-tryin' to make out on this hyer stuff they air a-sellin' an' callin' it beer. It shore is puny stuff—this hyer near-beer is."

"We'll drive over to the state liquor store at Pound after a while," I suggested. "In the meanwhile have you seen everything here yet?"

We had been making our way into the grandstand where it at least was dry, and we could find out whether or not there would be any races that afternoon. The track was a veritable sea of mud.

"I reckon we've seed a-bout all thar is," replied Brandy Bill. "We went into that monkey-house, an' ever' one of them leetle critters let out a squeal an' clum' plum to the top of their cages. I reckon they seed Bad 'Lige's whiskers an' figgered he was one of them go-rillas er somethin'."

"Heck!" grunted Bad 'Lige. "They jest smelt Willie B. Fuller's breath atter he'd drunk all his 'tater-peelin' brandy."

"Is Willie B. here?" I queried.

"He was a while ago," spoke up Little 'Bijie, "a-watchin' one of them gals wiggle. Ef'n his wife—." He lapsed into silence as if appalled by that possibility.

We sat in complete silence for a few minutes, staring through the drizzle at the ferris wheel and the other dizzy rides and attractions that were partly visible through the murk and mist.

The weather apparently had failed to dampen the ardor of the crowd, however, and hundreds of hillmen were milling around and plainly having a grand time. They were ignoring the thickening clouds overhead that presaged a real storm. Brandy Bill glanced toward the looming Cumberlands to the west.

"Looks like we've got a-nuther storm like that'n we had last week," he declared, and, as if in echo to his words there came a flash of lightening and a heavy clap of thunder.

"That shore was a humdinger of a storm," agreed Little 'Bijie. "I sorty begun to think we had us one of them hurry-canes."

"Did it do much damage?" I enquired.

"Wall, it shore done some funny things," declared Bad 'Lige, with a surreptitious wink at Little 'Bijie, and I instinctively realized that I had invited a few "whoppers". "It blowed so hard it rammed rye-straws half-way into my bee-gums, so all I gotta do now is suck the honey out."

The Devil's Apron Liars Club was off to a good start, and I wisely held my tongue.

"Leetle 'Bijie was a-tellin' me a-bout whut happened up to his place," chuckled Brandy Bill, lighting one of the biggest cigars I ever saw. "He said as how that thar windstorm an' big wind come right through his chicken-lot an' blowed the feathers off'n all his hens, an' he sw'ars that them hens air now a-layin' bal-loons."

"Uh-huh!" grunted Bad 'Lige. "Storms like that'n somctimes do onusual things that away. I re-colleck one time we had us a wind that was reely somethin'. It was back a-bout the time I got married the fu'st time. Poor Mandy! I reckon she never did git plum over that storm bekaze she passed on to her reward soon atter that—lived mebbe a year.

"Anyhow, when that storm hit, she was out thar at the barn a-milkin'. The wind blowed her up ag'inst the face of a clift acrost the road an' then it jest flattened her out so blamed thin we had to sorty scrape her off bekaze she wasn't no more'n two inches through at the thickest place. An' she couldn't eat nothin' but corn-flitters an' skimmed milk fer a week."

Little 'Bijie shrugged his disdain for that effort.

"Yeah," he drawled, "ye fellers might think ye know somethin' a-bout storms, but all of ye live down hyer a-long the crick whilst I live up thar on top of the mountain ferninst the Kaintucky line. Thar ain't nothin' up thar to keep them winds off'n me, an' when I tell ye that it blowed up thar, I mean it blowed with both bar'ls.

"Now ye take that storm last Satte'day that ye was jest a-talkin' a-bout. I've seed an' lived through many a storm but I never seed nothin' like that'n. Ye know, my place is jest a-bout half a mile this side of Kaintucky. An' boys, I'm nineteen kinds of a liar ef'n it didn't blow the state line plum back past my house as clean as a whissle, an' it looks like I'm a-goin' to have to go plum down to Pikeville to pay my taxes this year ef'n they don't put it back ag'in."

Brandy Bill Goes A'courtin

At Brandy Bill's urging I had supper with him the other night, and in my honor he cut a ham, hickory-smoked and still further cured with a covering of ashes from white-oak wood. And even Brandy Bill's cooking couldn't take the wonderful flavor out of it.

We were alone that evening, Brandy Bill's wife and son, Toddy, having been away visiting relatives over the week-end, and we sat before the fire and reminisced of the olden days. The pot of ginger-stew remained at exactly the right temperature, simmering on a bed of coals on the hearthstone to which he added a fresh supply from the fire from time to time.

After a long silence he gave expression to a low laugh.

"Don't know whut put me in mind of it, but I was jest a-thinkin' of the fu'st time I ever went a-sparkin' of a gal."

I stirred my cup of ginger-stew and waited.

"I was jest a young'un," he continued, the corners of his eyes wrinkling humorously, "an' ol' Clem Hartsock had a gal a-bout my age—Bessie May. She was as purty as a red-heifer in a strawberry patch, an' I had sorty been a-makin' sheep's-eyes at her at the meetin'house a couple of times afore I screwed up my nerve to go over an' see her.

"Wall, I put on my best tow-shirt an' clean pa'r of over-alls, an' I saddled up my mule an' rid over to her house. It was on a Satte'day, an' I got thar a-long in the shank of the evenin'. Me an' Bessie May ye set a-roun' on the porch fer a while, but we didn't have nothin' much to say, both of us a-bein' kinda bashful thataway. I felt plum tongue-tied when the ol' folks come out to talk with us.

"Atter supper some of the boys an' gals frum a-roun' an' a-bout come in an' one of 'em had a banjer. I could pick a few toons, an' we danced a few sets of doe-see-doe, an' the fu'st thing we knowed it was atter midnight. The other boys an' gals went home, an' me an' Bessie May kept a-settin' afore the fire ontel ol' Clem stuck his head through the door.

" 'Bessie May, it's time to wash yore feet an' clim the ladder," says he.

"Wall, Bessie May she clum' the ladder to the loft whar t'other young'uns was a-sleepin', an' left me a-settin' thar. I had a notion of gittin' out an' saddlin' my mule an' headin' fer home, a-bein' sorty ashamed to sleep thar. Ye see, I voted afore I ever wore onderwear 'ception' atter the fu'st snow-fall.

"Now, thar wasn't but two rooms an' the loft in the house, an' ol' Clem an' his wife was a-sleepin' in t'other room downstairs. Whar we had been a-dancin' was the livin' room, an' they cooked an' et in it, too. Thar was a bed in one corner, an' Besie May's mammy come in an' turned down the kivvers a-tellin' me I could sleep in it.

"Atter she was gone I got up an' blowed out the lamp, an' crawled in the bed. It wasn't but a minnit er two ontel I was sound a-sleep. In them days I was shore hard to wake up, an' I must a-slept a leetle overtime the next mornin'.

"An' when I did git awake the whole house was up an' stirrin'. Bessie May an' her mammy was a-gittin' breakfas' over on the fur side of the room, an' the table was all set an' ready. Ol' Clem was a-settin' afore the fire a-smokin' his pipe, an' one er two of the young'uns was a-playin' with the cat in the middle of the floor.

"I laid thar as still as a mouse a-wonderin' whut on earth I was a-goin' to do. I'd done hung my overalls on a chair at least ten foot frum my bed, an' thar I was, jest in my tow-shirt a-layin' onder the kivvers. I measured the distance a-tryin' to figger out whar I could make it in one jump er not.

"I was a-watchin' the wimminfolks plum clost an' when I ketched 'em both with their backs towarge me, I throwed the kivvers off, an' made my jump fer that chair—an' my britches. They had one of them punch'on floors which was laid down an' not nailed fast to the sills, an' they was a-bout ten inches wide. I lit right squar' on the eend of one, an' then things shore did happen fast.

"That board riz up an' smacked me right plum in the face, an' I slid through the hole, an' got my legs wedged so blamed tight I couldn't even move 'em. Thar I was stuck fast, an' couldn't git out to save me. It didn't seem like my tow-shirt come down to my waist. I reached out an' grabbed them britches, but I couldn't put 'em on bekaze I couldn't git my legs outta that hole.

"I sorty helt them britches afore me an' stood thar, an' ol' Clem an' his wife was a laffin' fit to bu'st. Atter whut seemed to me like half a day, ol' Clem he come over an' wropped that quilt a-roun' me, an' pulled me outta the hole. The next jump I made was through the door whar I drapped the quilt an' got into my britches. An' I didn't stop runnin' ontel I hit the tall an' oncut timbers whar the hootowls hoot in the daytime."

King Solomon's Diet

"That shorely was a powerful sermon ye preached up at the meetin'-house last Sunday," complimented Brandy Bill to Good 'Lige as the latter joined our circle around the stove at the grist-mill last Saturday afternoon. There was a chorus of affirmative grunts from the others, but Good 'Lige merely nodded his thanks.

"Ye know," continued Brandy Bill after a brief silence, "ol' King Solomon must a-been much of a man—a-doin' all of them things that the Good Book says he done."

"An' that's the gos-pel truth!" ejaculated Little 'Bijie with enthusiasm. "He shore must a-been a plum on-usual sort of a feller that could build him a temple, an' run his army, an' hold cou't to try folks fer evil-doin', an' still make ever'body happy. It's no wonder they called him the wisest man that ever lived."

"Wall now, I don't know a-bout that," spoke up Business Bill, shaking his head. "Him a-marryin' up with a thousan' wimmin thataway don't look to me like he had much sense. He'd ort to a-knowed that one was a Gawd's plenty."

"Say, Good 'Lige!" called Little 'Bijie. "Do ye think he reely had a thousan' wives at the same time er was he jest braggin' a leetle er somethin'?"

"It's writ down thar in the Book in black an' white," replied the old preacher emphatically. "All of ye heerd me read it last Sunday word fer word an' line fer line.'

There was a silence for a full minute, and then Business Bill cleared his throat.

"King Solomon must a-been a rich man, too, er he

couldn't a-kept that many wimmin. I'd shore hate to turn a thousan' wimmin' loose in one of these big dee-part-ment stores an' then have to foot the bill. Come wintertime, it'd bu'st a millun-air jest to buy a pair of shoes fer each one of 'em."

"Whar at did he git all his money nohow?" demanded Little 'Bijie a bit suspiciously.

"He had a few gold mines in Africa," I explained, proud of Biblical knowledge. "They were located in Ethiopia, I believe."

"Wall, he shore did need 'em," growled Bad 'Lige. "I bet he had to work 'em double-shif'."

"Like I was a-sayin'," persisted Little 'Bijie, "he shore must a-been a-bu'stin' out with wisdom ef'n he knowed how to keep the peace betwixt a thousan' wimmin. Ol' Tucker Floyd he had him jest two wives, an' they fit an' pulled ha'r all over the place."

"I've jest been a-wonderin'," said Business Bill, again pushing his views into the conversation, "how he managed to feed 'em. Take a thousan' people thataway an' they can eat a powerful lot of vittels ef'n he fed 'em three squar' meals a day. Must a-had him a whale of a big cookstove in that thar palace."

"Whut did they eat mostly back in King Solomon's time?" queried Little 'Bijie. "I mean did they raise corn an' 'taters an' beans an' sich? I know they had sheep, but a feller can't eat mutton all the time."

"I think I've read somewhere that they ate locusts and wild honey," I ventured uncertainly.

"Ye mean them seventeen-year locusts like we've got?" Little 'Bijie's brows were deeply creased. "Must a-ben a hell of a long time betwixt meals."

"Ye've got yore Bible mixed up a leetle," Good 'Lige corrected me softly. "It was John the Babtis' that et the locusts an' wild honey. That's in the New Testy-ment, an' not in King Solomon's time."

Undaunted, I continued to diseminate my store of information.

"I have heard that one of the favorite foods that the old Sheiks of Arabia were accustomed to serving in their harems was a baby camel boiled in milk. It was said that this diet kept the complexions of the women as pink and beautiful as the clouds at the first blush of dawn."

"Ye don't say!" murmured Little 'Bijie wonderingly.

"Wall, I'm afeard that'd be jest a leetle too rich fer Snowdy Jane's blood."

"Comin' back to them locusts," interrupted Business Bill, "how do ye reckon they cooked 'em? Fried or b'iled er roasted?"

"I imagine they fried them," I explained. "They consider fried bees quite a delicacy in those countries over there."

"Fried bees an' baby camels b'iled in milk!" exploded Business Bill with a shrug. "King Solomon must a-been bad in need of them thousan' wimmin ef'n he'd put up with sich as that."

"All that don't make me no never-mind," said Little 'Bijie. "I don't keer whut them thousan' wimmin' had fer breakfas'. Whut I want to know is whut they fed to King Solomon?"

Was I Thar?

It was rather a glum looking bunch that was gathered on Brandy Bill's porch when I got over on the Devil's Apron last Sunday afternoon. Evidently Brandy Bill had asked a few boys in for dinner, following the services at Good 'Lige's church, and they were lounging in various attitudes of ease when I joined them.

"What's the matter, boys?" I wanted to know. "You look a bit the worse for wear. What's happened? Have I been missing something?"

"I'll say ye have!" growled Bad 'Lige from his rocking chair.

I glanced around the crowd and saw that Bad 'Lige, Business Bill, Willie B. Fuller, Good 'Lige and Little 'Bijie were there, but not one of them seemed to be in his customary good spirits.

"Well, tell me what took place," I persisted, finding a seat.

"I reckon it's jest a hangover," admitted Brandy Bill, stroking his melancholy mustache. "Ye see, the boys all sorty celebrated last night up at Leetle 'Bijie's place."

"Any particular reason for that celebration?" I asked facetiously.

"Wall, yes, ye might say so. Ye see, Willie B's wife she upped an' left him ag'in, an' he's been sorty down in the dumps since then. Anyhow, the boys all went up thar last Satte'day night sorty to cheer him up a leetle bit.

"We all tuck a leetle somethin' a-long with us kinda to help him drown his sorrows. I had a couple of half-gallon fruit-jars of good applejack, an' Bad 'Lige tuck some good corn. An' of cou'se Willie B. had plenty of his 'tater-peelin' brandy on hand. Whut with one thing an' a-nuther thar wasn't no reel ska'city of pain-killer—that is ef'n Willie B. was ack-chully in pain to begin with.

"We all got to Willie B's place, an' we found that he didn't have nothin' to eat, him not a-bein' much inter-ested in eatin' thataway no time. Leetle 'Bijie he told us that Snowdy Jane had tuck all the young'uns an' had gone a-visitin' some of her kinfolks an' wouldn't be back fer a week. So we got out an' made it to his house.

"We had us a few more drinks, an' we made a pot of ginger-stew, an' Leetle 'Bijie fried us up a mess of ham an' eggs, an' we was a-havin' a fine big evenin', but the more that Willie B. drunk the sadder an' more mournful he got ontel he bu'sted out a-cryin' an' a-carryin' on a-bout pore Carrie an' how he had been a-treatin' her.

"Now, Willie B. he knows the Bible, an' he got to quotin' the Scriptoors a-bout this an' that, an' the fu'st thing we knowed he was a-standin' up thar behindst the kitchen table an' a-preachin' jest a-bout the most powerful sermon I ever heerd in my born days.

"He had the boys all a-singin' an' a-shoutin', an' havin' a reg'lar ol'-time ree-vival. An' atter a leetle while Bizz'ness Bill, Bad 'Lige an' Leetle 'Bijie all per-fessed re-ligion' an' re-pented of all of their sins which was a plenty. Yes sir, that leetle celebra-shun turned out to be the best camp-meetin' I ever seed.

"Wall, right in the middle of it all, Willie B. he stopped preachin' an' told the boys that he was a-goin' to babtize 'em afore they sobered up an' fergot all a-bout it. They was all willin', so we lined up two an' two an' atter wanderin' a-roun' a leetle we found the crick, an' a pool big e-nough fer the pu'pose.

"I stuck my hand in the water, an' it was ice-cold, but that didn't faze Willie B. an' the boys. He led 'em all out thar in the middle of that pond, an' he soused 'em onder. They come out a-shiverin' an' a-shakin' an' jest a-bout freezin' to death.

'I got 'em started out, an' I had to poosh 'em a-long an' git 'em in some dry clothes afore all of 'em got pew-mony. But atter they got dried out, they all went to sleep, an' I reckon thar ain't no danger now."

I suppressed a yelp of laughter, and then I glanced across at Good 'Lige. He was getting to his feet, and there was a stern look on his benign old face.

"Ye boys ort to be a-shamed of yoreselves," he said, shaking his head sadly. "Ever' last one of ye ort to git down on yore knees an' ax the Lawd to fergive ye. Ye'd ort to be a-shamed to face yore fam'lies an' yore feller man."

Then he lowered his voice, and looked at Brandy Bill anxiously.

"Thar's jest one question I want to ask ye? Was I thar?"

The Incense Pot

Bad 'Lige was sitting on the fence near his home on the Devil's Apron when I came down out of the woods last Monday afternoon. I walked around the edge of the field to him, and leaned my gun in the fence corner before I sprawled in the shade for I was both hot and tired.

"Looks like ye had purty good luck," he observed, nodding toward the bulge in the back of my hunting coat which I had tossed down beside me.

"Fair," I reported, exhibiting my kill of five squirrels. Then I dug into a pocket of the coat and brought out a nice ripe paw-paw which I started to consume.

"Ever taste any paw-paw brandy?" queried the old moonshiner with a twinkle in his eyes. "It ain't half bad ef'n ye're keerful, but it scorches plum easy an' ye have to watch it clost as a hawk." He paused and a low laugh rumbled in his grizzled beard.

"Puts me in mind of that tale a-bout Good 'Lige an' his incense pot. Did I ever tell ye that'n?"

"Incense pot?" I wasn't certain that I had heard him aright. "Tell me about it."

"Wall, like ye know, Good 'Lige has been a-havin' hisself a lot of trubbel a-tryin' to hold the members of his Hard-Rock Church in line, an' keep 'em frum j'inin' up with ol' Sin-Sockin' Sam Tolliver's bunch. He done ever'-thing he knowed to git 'em to come to his meetin's, but it seemed as though he jest couldn't git 'em to come out no more.

"Atter givin' it much thought an' a few prar's, he decided that he was a-goin' all the way down thar to Cincynatty an' see whut they done in them big fine churches to git the brethern an' sistern inter-ested, an' then keep 'em that way.

"Anyhow he tuck the train an' went down thar, an' he went to the biggest an' finest church in that city. It was one of them whar they have leetle boys all dressed up in white robes an' things like that, an' all kinds of fol-de-rol.

"I reckon as how it was awful fine an' purty to look at, an' Good 'Lige was plum pop-eyed when he was a-tellin' a-bout it atter he got home. An' the bizz'ness that got his eye the most was whut he called a in-cense pot. He said as how a leettle boy fetched into the church a big gold pot that was a-smokin' an' a-givin' off a smell like Good 'Lige said he never had smelt in all his life.

"Wall, Good 'Lige he thunk over all of them things he'd done seed down thar an' he begun to plan on doin' some of 'em in his church an' see ef'n he could git a crowd out. Of cou'se that thar singin' by the leetle boys was plum outta the question bekaze the boys that size on the Devil's Apern didn't know no songs fitten at meetin'-time.

"Anyhow he got the idee that he could shore fix him up one of them in-cense pots, so he got him a middle-sized cookin' pot, like ye cook with on open fires, an' he put some paw-paw brandy in it bekaze it shore did have a fine smell. Then he got him some mint frum down thar on the crick, an' he got some vanilly ex-track, an' some of his wife's per-foom, an' a lotta stuff like that to mix up somethin' that'd smell like that in-cense pot.

"He went down to see Brandy Bill that Satte'day, an' ast him ef'n he might have leetle Toddy to stay up to his house fer a couple of days to help him out with that in-cense pot idee. An' he told Brandy Bill to spread the news that he was a-goin' to show the folks somethin' that they shore wouldn't want to miss at 'leven o'clock on Sunday mornin'.

"An' it 'peared like ever'body heerd a-bout it allright, but that's a-gittin' a-head of my tale. Good 'Lige he tuck leetle Toddy up thar to the meetin'-house an' they built 'em a fire, an' cooked all that stuff up together. An' when they let it b'ile fer a while Good 'Lige said as how it smelt like nothin' in this worl', an' a heap-sight better'n that down in Cincy-natty.

"It tuck him an' Toddy most of Satte'day to git ever'thing ready fer the big e-vent. Him an' Toddy made it up for Toddy to keep the pot a-b'ilin' out thar in the bushes on Sunday mornin' whilst Good 'Lige got the meetin' onder way. When he had read the Bible an' said a pra'r, the choir was to start a-singin' the fu'st song.

"That song was a-bout the saints an' sinners a-comin' marchin' in, an' when they come to that part leetle Toddy was to come a-marchin' into the meetin'-house, too. So Good 'Lige, like he allus does, read off the fu'st verse of that song, an' the choir come down on it. At the right place Good 'Lige he looked towarge the door to see ef'n leetle Toddy was on time.

"He shore was. He come a-marchin' through that door an' down towarge the front—only he didn't have no incense pot. Good 'Lige was a-singin' an' without changin' the toon he sung:

" 'Oh whut did ye do with that in-cense pot?'

"Leetle Toddy come right back at him an' never missed a note:

" 'I throwed it in the bushes, it was too dammed hot.' "

A Far Piece From Home

It was good to get away from the worries and cares of a hard week, and on Sunday I headed fer the Devil's Apron where I could find complete rest and relaxation. As I had anticipated I found some of the boys gathered in Brandy Bill's yard waiting for the time to walk up the hill to Good 'Lige's Firm-Foundation Church.

And we found the patriarchal old preacher restful, even soporific, in his sermon through which I and several others slept. Afterwards I thoroughly enjoyed dinner at Brandy Bill's home, and then we all gathered out in the warm sunshine and whiled away the afternoon.

"Wall," said Brandy Bill, leaning his chair back against the wall, "now that the big political con-venshuns air over whut do ye think about it all? Our side got a chance?"

"To tell you the truth," I replied, "I hardly know what to think. Both parties are so mixed up and split up these days that I don't know who is which, or why a man is what he is. As best I can gather both parties are against sin and Castro, and in favor of mother and home and additional government handouts. Beyond that I'm completely lost."

"An' that's the pyore truth ef'n I ever heerd it," declared Business Bill nodding his head vigorously. "Thar's times when I think a Re-publican is a blamed Demy-crat, an' t'other way a-roun'. I don't know whar me an' my ol' woman, an' the boys air a-goin' to vote this year er not."

"To my mind," declared Little 'Bijie feelingly, "thar's somthin' wrong with a Demy-crat that gits Re-publican votes like whut's been a-happenin' hyer in Virginny fer a good many years."

"The way I see it," growled Bad 'Lige, "thar ain't been no tellin' whut was a-goin' to happen ever' since the wimmin started to votin'. Most of 'em don't pay no 'ten-shun to polly-ticks an' jest vote fer the candy-date that's got the smoothest tongue an' the purtiest face, er somethin' like that. Ain't that so, Brandy Bill?"

"Ye might be right at that," replied Brandy Bill guardedly. "Take my wife fer instance! She upped an' voted fer Ike in his secon' race in spite of ever'thing I could do. Our twin boys—Rock an' Rye—was over thar in Korea a-fightin' them heathern Chinese at the time, an' she figgered that all Ike had to do was go over thar an' step on the groun' an' them Chinese'd hightail it fer parts onknown. An' thar wasn't no manner of use in tryin' to argy with her.

"When Rock come home atter the war he said that them 'Gooks', as he called 'em, did start to run when Ike landed on the shore, but they run towarge our side instid of a-way frum it. Seems like they didn't have a lick of sense that-away."

"Wall," interposed Good 'Lige after a silence, "the wimminfolks don't seem to be much interested this year. I've heerd that a lot of 'em air a-goin' to stay to home on 'lection day. My wife, Marthy, thinks it ain't fitten fer woman to git mixed up in it. She says as how no matter which feller we e-leck, we wish to heaven we'd e-leckted the t'other'n, an' I think mebbe she's got somethin' thar."

"We ort to be plum thankful that we've all got good wimmin like we've got," observed Business Bill piously. "I don't know how I would a-got a-long without my wife."

"Ye wouldn't," Little 'Bijie told him bluntly.

"Anyhow, Bizz'ness Bill's plum right," agreed Good 'Lige. "Now you take Willie B. thar. He's a fine eggzample of whut a good woman can do fer a man. Since she come back home atter leavin' him the last time, she's done kept him sober fer three days at a time. An' that's somethin' I never ex-pected to see."

That last round of mint juleps was fast mellowing the entire crowd, and the boys were growing quite jovial—even a little maudlin. This was particularly true with Willie B. "A woman is truly the greatest blessing—hic—a man can have," he burped softly. "No matter how far one transgresses from the paths of rectitude and righteousness—hic—he can still return to his domicile—hic—and be assured of complete forgiveness. More than once, and with good reason, Carrie has left me—hic—and gone back to her people, but when she thought that I needed her—hic—she has always come back to help me.

"I have stated previously, and I will repeat it now. My wife is an angel—hic—coming down from Heaven to administer to this sordid old world. She's just an angel straight from the golden gates of Heaven—."

"Humph!" interrupted Little 'Bijie. "She's a hell of a fur piece frum home, ain't she?"

The Egg Beatin' Cyclone

I ran into a heavy rainstorm on my way over to the Devil's Apron last Saturday, and was forced to walk the last half a mile to the grist-mill because of the slick dirt-road. The day's grinding was completed when I got there and the boys were waiting for me on Brandy Bill's porch.

He brought out a chair for me, and handed me the mint julep that he had been saving for me.

"Wall," said Little 'Bijie, "how do ye like this streaked an' striped weather?"

"I ran into a streak of something coming over, and had to walk up from the river—if that's what you mean?" I replied.

"That's it! It comes in streaks an' stripes thataway, I've seed it a-rainin' cats an' dawgs on one side of the big road an' dry as a chip on t'other side."

And the Liars' Club of the Devil's Apron was off to a fine start on one of its favorite topics.

"It's pyore fact," vouchsafed Business Bill. "I was up thar on the ridge back of my place a couple of days ago, an' it was a-rainin' in the holler on my right, an' the sun a-shinin' in the holler to my left, an' dang my picture ef'n it wasn't hailin' on the ridge whar I was—all at the same time."

"It must be be-kaze of them blamed Rooshians a-shootin' off them big bombs," declared Bad 'Lige with conviction. "They done ruint the weather ontel a feller don't know whut to ex-pect next."

"I reckon I don't go a-long with that," said Good 'Lige

thoughtfully. "We had wu'sser weather back in the ol' days, didn't we, Brandy Bill?"

"We shore did," replied the latter. "I reckon some of us still re-colleck that big harri-cane we had up hyer a good many years ago."

"Was that the one that blew the Kentucky line half a mile back into Virginia?" I asked with a giggle.

"No," Brandy Bill squinted at the ceiling of the porch. "I reckon this'n I'm a-talkin' a-bout was back twelve er fifteen years ago. We called it the 'Big Blow', an' it was a diff'rent kind of a storm frum any others we ever had. It was one of these twistin', turnin' wind-storms that jest knocked ever' thing flat that got in its way. They call 'em——." He hesitated, searching for the word.

"Cyclones," I supplied hopefully, and Brandy Bill nodded his head.

"Yeah, an' it shore was a dandy! At the time it struck us, I had jest built this hyer house, but my springhouse was up thar jest this side of the mill whar a bold spring come out frum onder a cliff. My wife was allus a-complainin' a-bout it a-bein' too fur frum the house, an' that thar storm shore tuck keer of that in short order.

"It was a-long in the shank of the evenin', as I recall, when thar come up outta the south the blackest clouds that I ever seed. An' purty soon I seed that it had one of them long funnels a-stickin' down outta it, an' I knowed whut it was.

"My twin boys—Rock an' Rye—was jest young'uns then, an' they had 'em a pet pig which they was a-tryin' to ketch an' put up afore the storm hit. But I hollered to them to come a-runnin', an' I got my wife, an' we all lit a shuck outta hyer, an' run over to them cliffs acrost the crick, an' sorty scrooched back in the shelter.

"Endurin' the next few minnits it was the most Gawd-awful sight I ever seed. That thar twister picked up my barn an' corn-crib, an' the air was full of shingles an' chickens an' logs, an' corn, an' cows an' things a-flyin' in all di-reck-shuns at the same time.

"It sucked up my springhouse an' whirled it straight up outta sight. Now my wife she kept her eggs an' butter an' milk an' sich in that springhouse, an' I had a couple of kags of fine applejack in thar. Also thar was four er five empty gallon jugs in thar on a shelf.

"Like I was a-sayin', that storm picked up the springhouse, jest a-leavin, the b'ar floor. But I was so tickled that the storm had done missed my house by a-bout fifty yards, an' my wife an' young'uns was safe, that I figgered I'd got off plum lucky.

"I went up thar to look over the damage that it'd done, an' it shore had flattened the mill, an' had toted off the springhouse an' all that was in it. Now, I figger ye won't ever be-lieve me when I tell ye whut it done to that springhouse an' whut was stored in it, but it's a fact.

"In whirlin' a-roun' like that, it tuck that milk an' eggs an' brandy an' mo-lasses, an' mixed 'em all up together an' shook 'em good. Then it filled them empty jugs with the best egg-nog ye ever tasted, an' corked 'em up tight with corn-cobs off'n which it had blowed the grains of corn. A leetle later it set them jugs down gentle-like in a straight row on Good 'Lige's back porch—."

"Jest like manna frum Heaven!" murmured Good 'Lige softly.

Sophygene and Her Half-Brothers

I had started fishing down on Pound River the other afternoon when I happened to run into the boys from the Devil's Apron gathered at Dutton's store. They were engaged in an animated discussion on some subject, and I walked over and joined them to hear the news.

"Well, what brought all of you fellows out today?" I queried, when they halted their conversation.

"Ye got hyer jest a leetle late," declared Little 'Bijie with a grin. "We was all at the weddin' at the Hard-Rock meetin'-house a leetle while ago, an' we jest drapped by hyer to git a leetle eatin' terbacker an' a few things like that."

"A wedding!" I ejaculated. "Who got married?"

"That youngest gal of Dooless Dave Farmer's—the one they call Sofygene," explained Brandy Bill. "She got married up with ol' Hop Hill's son, Oval."

"A church wedding?"

"Shore, an' they done it up in style," Brandy Bill assured me. "Good 'Lige he married 'em, an' they're a-havin' a big in-fare dinner at Dooless Dave's this evenin'. They didn't in-vite none of us fellers.

"Some of the boys was a tellin' of a tale up thar at the meetin'-house that kinda tickled me," continued Brandy Bill with a twinkle in his eyes. "Ye know, ol' Dooless Dave he has allus been a-doin' ever'thing he could to keep that gal frum gittin' married. Him an' his ol' woman had done raised a passel of young'uns, but all of 'em had got married an' left home but Sofygene.

"Now, I don't have to tell ye fellers hyer on the Apern that Sofygene was mighty purty—jest a-bout the purtiest that was ever seed in all these parts. She wasn't more'n fifteen when she had all the boys a-buzzin' a-roun' like flies a-roun' the mo-lasses jug. Fer a year mebbe it looked like she couldn't make up her mind, an' then she slowed down an' started to goin' steddy with Oval.

"But Dooless Dave's ol' woman was ailin' most of the time an' wasn't able to do much of the work a-bout the place. An' Dooless Dave was too lazy to work so he figgered he'd be in a bad shape ef'n he lost Sofygene. He'd either have to go to work hisself an' mebbe do all the cookin' an' all, er hire somebody to do it.

"Frum whut I'd allus heerd, Sofygene was a mighty good cook, an' Dooless Dave he aimed to keep her to home re-gvardless. When he seed that she was a-gittin' plum thick with Oval, he de-cided that it was time that he was a-doin' somethin' a-bout it. So he tuck Sofygene to one side an' says to her:

" 'Honey, air ye an' Oval a-fixin' to git married?'

" 'I reckon we air," says she with a giggle.

" 'Ye can't do that, Honey," he tells her in a whisper. 'It's ag'inst the teachin's of the Bible. Ye see, Oval's yore half-brother.'

"Wall, that put the skids onder Oval right plum quick, an' a leetle later she started courtin' up a storm with Cal Coolige, one of Bizz'ness Bill's boys. Dooless Dave he seed how that was progressin', an' he was plum pleased with hisself on how he got rid of Oval so he figgered on tryin' the same trick ag'in. An' it shore e-nough worked a secon' time when he told her that Cal Coolige was her half-brother, too.

"Sofygene she looked a-roun' an' purty soon her an' a boy frum over thar a-bout town was a-sparkin' to beat the band. An' Dooless Dave he kept a clost watch on her an' this boy by the name of Higgins, an' when it looked like they was a-goin' to git hitched, he tells her that this Higgins boy was a-nuther of her half-brothers.

"Right thar was whar Sofygene blowed up. She told Dooless Dave that ef'n he was the pappy of all of the boys in the state, she was a-goin' over in Kaintucky, an' git her a man. Dooless Dave he didn't say nothin', but he shore wasn't aimin' to let her git a-way ef'n he could help it. He still figgered he'd pulled a mighty smart trick.

"But Sofygene she went straight to her mammy an' told her a-bout her pappy a-claimin' to be daddy of all of the boys she went with. Dooless Dave's wife she set thar in her rockin' chair an' lissened to the story without sayin' a word. Then she sorty smiled an' patted Sofygene's hand.

" 'Sofygene,' she says soft-like, 'Ye go a-head an' git married to the boy ye like the best. It wouldn't be no sin even ef'n he was the pappy of all of them boys bekaze, Honey, ye ain't no kin to yore pappy.' "

Old Hide and Taller

Brandy Bill told me that Bad 'Lige was "down with his rheumatiz" and not able to get out of his home, so on Sunday afternoon of last week I decided to pay him a visit. At my knock on the door he called to me to come on in, and I found him sitting before the fire reading his copy of my weekly newspaper.

He was alone in the house, and he explained that his wife was visiting one of the neighbors and that the boys had gone ground-hog hunting. He had a pot of ginger-stew on the hearth, close to the fire to keep it warm, and he gestured toward it.

"Set an' help yoreself," he invited hospitably.

As we carried on a bit of small talk, I glanced around the room, and saw that the walls were gaudy with old magazine cover girls, tending toward the curvaceous, and a number of calendars of past years that had caught his fancy. Over the fireplace, resting on a pair of deer antlers, was a gun that caught my attention. It appeared to be a muzzle-loading double-barreled weapon with one barrel directly over the other. I arose and took it down to examine it a little more closely.

"That's ol' 'Hide an' Taller'," he explained, "the best gun that I ever owned. I got her thu'tty er more years ago frum one of them Hatfiel's when he was a-scoutin' frum the officers down thar in Kaintucky."

"Hide and tallow?" I queried, groping for an explanation.

"Yeah, we ust to have shootin' matches fer beef cattle an' sheep an' hawgs, but mostly beef-critters.

Cattle wasn't wu'th much in them days, an the fu'st choice at them matches was the hide an' taller be-kaze they was wu'th the most in cash-money. I allus won with that thar rifle-gun.

"She's a double-bar'l, an' the onliest'n I ever seed with one bar'l on top of t'other." He took the gun from me and caressed it fondly. "Ye see, the top bar'l is fer a single ball, an' the bottom'n fer shot. An' she shore has been a meat-gun. Ef'n it wasn't Sunday I'd take ye out thar an' show ye how she shoots."

Bad 'Lige was silent for a minute or two, and a crinkle appeared at the corners of his eyes. I had an idea of what was coming, and prepared myself accordingly with another cup of his ginger-stew.

"I allus used a double charge of the Frenchman's powder in them days, an' greased my patchin's with melted sheep-taller, an' the bullet shore did go true fer a long distance. Of cou'se the boys was a-stretchin' it a leetle, but they ust to say as how I put salt on them bullets to keep the meat frum sp'ilin' afore I could git to it an' skin it out.

"At one time I had me a leetle feist dawg that was purty good at treein' wild turkeys. Back in them days thar was plenty of turkeys hyer, an' it wasn't plum onusual fer that dawg to tree five er six turkeys up one tree, an' sometimes they'd be all a-settin' on one limb.

"All I had to do was to take dead aim an' split that limb with my bullet, an' them turkeys'd all git their toes ketched in the crack, an' then I'd climb up thar an' wring their necks.

"An' she was allus the best b'ar-gun that was ever seed on the Apern. I never had to pull the trigger but onct, an' I had b'ar meat fer dinner. I don't know how many b'ars I kilt with ol' Hide an' Taller, but I ust to sell b'ar-meat to all the neighbors, an' it got so I was plum wore out a-skinnin' them b'ars. They air mighty hard to skin thataway, 'specially when the critter weighs nigh onto four honnerd pounds.

"One day I got to thinkin' a-bout all that skinnin' bizz'ness an' I sorty got to figgerin' on how I might git outta it, an' save myself a powerful lot of hard work. I got ol' Hide an' Taller down, an' I loaded both bar'ls plum keerful-like with a double charge of powder. I rammed home a bullet in the top bar'l, an' in the bottom bar'l, instid of pourin' in a han'ful of shot like I allus done, I drapped in the blade of a ol'skinnin' knife, an' a han'ful of nails, an' pooshed the waddin' down on 'em.

"I clum up on the head of Wolf Crick, an' my dawgs they jumped a b'ar outta a huckleberry patch an' he headed up the hill towarge a row of cliffs that was full of holes whar he knowed he'd be safe. I tuck a fine bead on him, an' pulled both triggers at the same time.

"The bullet frum the top bar'l tuck him right spang in the back of the head, an' afore he could fall that knife-blade an' them nails ketched up frum the bottom bar'l. The blade split his hide right down the belly, an' he run plum outta his skin, an' then them nails toted his hide to the closest tree an' hung it up to dry better'n I ever could."

The Reluctant Son-In-Law

The High Sheriff called to me in front of the courthouse the other day, and motioned for me to join him. He was sitting in his car and I got in the front seat beside him.

"How about going along with me?" he asked.

"Where?" I countered before committing myself.

"Over on the Devil's Apron. I've got a warrant for the arrest of old Frank Baker."

"Old Feudin' Frank?" I interrupted. "Why, what has he done?"

"The way I heard it, he shot his son-in-law, Arlie Barton. I think that Arlie will recover, but his mother came to my office and swore out the warrant, and I'll have to serve it."

Chiefly out of curiosity I agreed to accompany him, and we drove over there and parked in front of Brandy Bill's home. He came out to the gate and eyed us questioningly.

"No, we aren't raiding moonshine stills today," laughed the Sheriff. "I'm over here looking for old Frank Baker. Do you suppose he's at home?"

"I reckon so," grunted Brandy Bill with a shrug. "I heerd they had some sort of a ruckus up thar yistiddy, but I guess Frank's thar—he ain't much fer runnin'."

"How's the best way to get to his place?" queried the Sheriff a little uncertainly.

"Drive on up the road to the head of the crick ontel it peters out on ye, an' then take the secon' right-han' holler. "Ye'll have to hoof it fer the last mile."

"Want to go along with us?" I suggested.

"Nope!" There was something in Brandy Bill's tone that made me wonder about the wisdom of my going.

"Dave jest might take it a leetle onfriendly, so to speak," he added as he turned and walked back into the house.

The Sheriff drove on up the road, and I sat silently beside him. At the spot designated by Brandy Bill we parked the car, and then began our long climb toward the towering crest of the Cumberlands.

"Think you'll have any trouble arresting old Frank?" I asked uneasily.

"I don't think so," replied the officer confidently. "Now if I were a Catron or related to any of that clan he'd probably shoot me on sight, but I don't expect him to offer any resistance."

"I've heard that the old Baker-Catron feud was rather bloody," I remarked thoughtfully.

"I'll say it was," agreed the Sheriff. "Old Frank an' a couple of his nephews, and some of the women were all that were left of the entire Baker generation. The Catrons got the best of it—there were more of them. I've always heard that old Frank was one of the leaders, and he is one of the best rifle-shots that I ever saw. He must be seventy-five or more years old now."

We were silent as the climb grew stiffer, and both of us were blowing hard by the time we reached the Baker farm. It was a well-kept place with a neat white house and an apple orchard just behind it, and there was every evidence of comfortable living.

We halted at the gate, and a tall old hillman arose from a rocking chair on the porch and came down the path toward us. He was six feet tall and as straight as an Indian with hair as black as night. I was surprised when the Sheriff addressed him, calling him "Uncle Frank", because he did not look anything like his age.

We went up on the porch and sat down. The talk for a few minutes was about the weather and other generalities, and then the Sheriff reached into his coat

pocket and pulled out a slip of paper.

"I'm sorry, Mister Baker," he said diffidently, "but I have a paper here that I have to serve on you. I expect you know what it is."

"A war'nt I reckon," he grunted, reaching for it.

"I guess you'll have to go back to town with me," said the Sheriff. "I don't imagine you will have any trouble making bond. From what I've heard this Barton boy isn't seriously hurt. Anyone who knows you will put up bail for you."

"Shore!" Feudin' Frank did not appear to be disturbed in the least. "I'll be ready any time."

The Sheriff eyed Feudin' Frank with an humorous expression.

"I was just thinking as I came up here," he ventured, "that it was a bit strange that you shot your own son-in-law. You have enough enemies without picking a member of your family."

"Wall, it was like this," explained Fuedin' Frank with the hint of a grin. "Arlie wasn't my son-in-law ontel atter I shot him. I jest shot him in the left heel when he started to run."

The Hounds and the Fiddle

There was a wintry chill in the air when I got up on the Devil's Apron last Saturday afternoon, and I parked in front of Bad 'Lige cabin, having noted that a column of smoke was rising from the chimney. I had promised to bring him a history of the Hatfield-McCoy, the French-Eversole, and the Bloody Breathitt County feuds, and I carried it inside with me.

He was sitting before a roaring open fire, and in a semi-circle about the fireplace lay half a dozen hounds. They stirred a bit when I entered, but they failed to show any of the hospitality or friendliness of their master.

"Come in an' set," Bad 'Lige called, and seeing that the dogs had all of the space about the fire occupied, he reached for the poker.

"Git the hell outta hyeh!" he yelled at the hounds, raising his poker. Two of the dogs dashed madly through the door into the kitchen, and the other four found a haven of refuge under the old four-poster bed.

"Or onder the bed, one er t'other," he amended with a grin. "See how I've got them houn's trained?"

"Looks like you and the dogs are taking things easy today," I said drawing up my chair. "This fire feels good."

"Them dawgs air a-bout the laziest critters that I ever seed," said the old moonshiner, sending a stream of tobacco juice into the fire. "I reckon I'm a-gittin' too ol' to hunt 'em like I ort, an' they jest lay a-roun' the fire hyer, or in the shade some'rs on a hot day."

While we were talking I saw out of the corner of my eye that the hounds were cautiously emerging from under the bed, eyeing Bad 'Lige closely, and it was not but a few minutes until all of them were back again, close to the warmth of the blazing logs. Bad 'Lige, if he was aware of their presence, gave no indication of it.

"I've heerd folks talk a-bout somebody a-leadin' of a dawg's life," said Bad 'Lige after a long silence. "Take these houn's of mine now—I jest wish I could take things as easy as they do."

He scowled balefully at them for several seconds, and then he got up from his chair and reached for his old fiddle that was resting on the mantle above the huge fire-place. With an instinctive reaction all of those dogs leaped to their feet, and I thought that they would break all their necks trying to get through the door. Bad 'Lige replaced his fiddle, and resumed his seat without offering any explanation of the strange behavior of the hounds.

"Like I was a-sayin'," he continued as if nothing had taken place, "take them dawgs of mine. They don't have to worry none a-bout gittin the vittels fer the next meal, er a-bout laying' up an' cannin' an' dryin' an' storin' stuff fer winter use. An' they don't have to pay no taxes er docter bills, an' when they git sick all they's got to do is swaller a few blades of grass an' they git rid of whut ail's 'em.

"Yeah, they know that when I eat they eat, an' when I sleep they sleep, an' sleep al day ef'n they want to. When they want to go huntin' they ups an' off they go a-huntin', an' thar ain't nobody to tell 'em to hoe 'taters an' corn, an' patch the roof, an' feed the hawgs.

"An' when it comes time fer them to die, they die an' that's all thar is to that, but when I die, I've got to go to hell—yit. A dawg's life? Why, shucks! I'll trade for dawg's life any day in the week an' twict on Sunday."

By that time all of the hounds had furtively reappeared in the room, and again they fearfully kept an eye on Bad 'Lige. Then one by one they edged forward and lay down noiselessly beside us. Their master glanced down at them, and then with a wink at me, he once more reached for that fiddle.

Again those dogs went into whirlwind action, and in a fraction of a second they had vanished to parts unknown.

I couldn't contain my curiosity any longer.

"Would you mind telling me why those dogs get scared to death each time you reach for your violin?"

"Wall," replied Bad 'Lige with a grin, "ye see, them dawgs ain't a-takin' no chances. It's like this—ever' time I start to play a toon on that fiddle them houn's has jest got to howl. Thar's something' a-bout fiddle music that works on 'em thataway.

"An' ever' time they start to howlin' in the house, the ol' woman she comes in hyer with a broom an' flails hell outta ever' last one of 'em. That a-bein' the case, they head for the tall timbers ever' time they see that fiddle."

Little Sooner and the Ironing Board

It was election day and I drove over to see how the boys in the Devil's Apron Precinct were voting. There was a scattering of hillmen lounging about the grounds, but there did not appear to be any big rush of voters. In fact, everything appeared to be unusually quiet and serene.

I located Bad 'Lige, Brandy Bill, Little 'Bijie, and Business Bill gathered about a small fire near an old pile of fence-rails at the edge of the grounds. The polls were in the school building where classes had been dismissed for that purpose.

When I joined the boys, I found to my surprise that they were not discussing the election or politics.

"What's the matter, boys?" I quieried. "This doesn't seem like an election."

"It shore don't," agreed Little 'Bijie. "Time was when we'd a-had a dozen fist-fights by this time. She's a dry 'lection in more ways than one."

"I reckon I can help out a leetle on that," said Bad 'Lige, walking over to the rail-pile, and digging out a quart fruit jar.

We adjourned to a more secluded spot and found seats on a convenient log. The fruit jar went the rounds, and then Bad 'Lige tossed the empty container into a clump of bushes.

"We was jest a-talkin' a-bout dawgs," Business Bill informed me. "I was a-tellin' the boys that I knowed that Big Howdy was jest a-bout the best houn' on a foxrace er coonhunt in the whole Apern. But at that he ain't got nothin' much on my leetle Mary Lou. She's allus helt her own ever' time we've put 'em on the trail together, an' thar's been times that it was her who done the treein'.

"Take the way she's got a-barkin' on the trail. I've got so I can tell by the tone of her voice whut she's a-trackin'—a fox, er a rabbit, er a squirrel er a coon. She's got a diff'rent tone fer each one of 'em, an' she can tell me whut to ex-pect jest like she was a-talkin' to me."

He scratched his chin and eyed Bad 'Lige expectantly, but the latter shook his head. Apparently there was nothing more hidden in the rail-pile.

"Yeah," he continued, "I'm ad-mittin' that Big Howdy an' Mary Lou air both mighty smart, but we've got a pup up to my place—outta Mary Lou by Big Howdy—that's got 'em both skinned to a frazzle. He's jest five er six months old, but I never yit seed his beat.

"We call him 'Sooner' be-kaze he'd sooner use a bed-post than a tree. He's not much bigger'n a good-sized tomcat, an' he's got a stump tail, an' the longest ears any dawg ever had. Frum the time he was ol' e-nough to crawl over the doorsill he's been a-tryin' to hunt. He's been a-follerin' his mammy an' he's as good as she is right now—an' better in some things.

"I got to prankin' with him, an' a-long last fall I got out some of the boards on which I dry an' stretch possum-hides, coon-skins, minks, foxes, an' polecats. Them boards of cou'se air diff'rent sizes a-runnin' from the two-inch size fer minks to big-'uns fer coons an' foxes.

"Leetle Sooner he watched me purty clost an' he seed whut kind of skins I put on them boards. An' it wasn't long ontel all I had to do was to git out a possum-board ef'n I want to hunt possums, an' a coon-board ef'n I was goin' atter coons.

"Now, him a-bein' jest a pup thataway, I never fetched out them big roun' boards that I stretched wildcats on. I knowed that he'd git chawed up fer fair ef'n he got tangled with one of them bob-cats. But I ain't got the least doubt that ef'n I'd a-got that board out, leetle Sooner would a-done his best to fetch one in."

Business Bill's eyes crinkled, and he gave expression to a chuckle.

"But of cou'se somethin' was boun' to happen to leetle Sooner sooner er later," he concluded with an exaggerated sigh, "an' jest a few days ago the ol' women was a-doin' some ironin,' an' it got powerful hot in the kitchen.

"She picked up her big ironin' board an' fetched it out on the back porch whar my skinnin' boards was. Pore leetle Sooner he stood thar an' he looked at that ironin' board fer a while, an' then he sorty shook his head sad-like, an' tucked his tail betwixt his legs. Then he turned a-roun' an' headed fer the big woods in a mighty slow walk, an' we ain't seed hide her ha'r of him since."

Big Foot and the Rattler

There was a carnival in town last weekend, and I ran into Bad 'Lige standing before the "Hollywood Girls" tent-show. Three girls, dressed chiefly in goose-pimples, were dancing with more energy than grace in the chilling breeze, and Bad 'Lige was watching them without much show of interest.

"Whar at can a man set down fer a few minnits," he asked when I stopped at his side. "My feet air a-killin' me."

We made our way to the grandstand of the Fairgrounds, and sat down. For a while I listened to a hillbilly band playing and singing a song called "What Will You Give In Exchange For Your Soul?"

Bad 'Lige thrust his feet out before him with a sigh of relief.

"I bought them blamed shoes over in Kaintucky a couple of weeks ago, an' they ain't built right," he complained. "They crimp my toes."

I murmured my sympathy, and Bad 'Lige remained silent as he removed the offending shoes and wriggled his toe gratefully.

"Sometimes I sorty feel like I'll do whut Big-Foot Milam ust to do up thar on the Apern—jest go b'ar-foot summer an' winter. He was pestered with corns an' sore feet a heap, but he got so his feet never hurt him no more. I reckon he never had a shoe on his foot fer nigh a-bout twenty years, an' when he died they buried him b'ar-foot.

"Big Foot was a powerful man, a-weighin' a-bout two

honnerd an' fifty pounds an' nary a ounce of fat on him. His feet was nothin' but a-bout eighteen inches of his leg turned onder an' sorty flattened out. Thar was a feller over on Elkhorn Crick that made all his shoes fer him at fu'st, but he died an' ol' Big-Foot couldn't find shoes big e-nough in none of the stores, so he jest turned off b'ar-foot fer good.

"The bottom's of a feller's feet can shore git mighty tough thataway even ef'n he jest goes b'ar-foot endurin' the summer. But take Big-Foot now, the skin on his soles got to be a full inch thick, an' snow an' ice didn't mean nothin' to him.

"No matter how cold it got, an' all of us a-freezin' to death, Big-Foot he'd come to the mill on Satte-days with no shoes on, an' the ice froze on his whiskers. An' with his toes outside thataway he could git a good grip on the groun' an' keep his footin' whar the rest of us couldn't stand up.

"Back when thar was chestnuts in this country he'd allus stomp the chestnuts outta the burrs with his heels, an' crack black walnuts like they was egg-shells, an' onct I seed him step on a ten-penny nail a-stickin' outta a board an' bend it jest like ye'd a-hit it with a hammer. An' he paid no more mind to a saw-brier patch than I would to a cyarpeted floor.

"I re-colleck one time when me an' Big-Foot we started out to a big meetin' over on Whisperin' Crick. Big-Foot looked sorty funny all dressed up in his store clothes an' no shoes on, but he didn't mind, an' I sorty felt like takin' my shoes off an' walkin' in that cool sand in the road be-kaze I knowed how good it'd a-felt.

"It was in the summertime, an' I re-colleck that the blackberries was ripe. We come to a patch of them big, long sweet kind that grows in the woods, an' me an' Big-Foot we started to pickin' a few of 'em as we went a-long an' eatin' 'em. Now like ye know, blackberry patches like that is a fine place to find rattlesnakes. The birds come to the blackberry bushes, an' the snakes ketch 'em.

"Big-Foot was a rakin' off handfuls of them berries an' a-crammin' 'em in his mouth, an' not a-payin' much 'ten-shun to nothin' else. He was standin' clost to a ol' log, an' he leaned over it an' raised one hind foot. I jest happened to look down on the groun' an' I seed a big yaller rattler that was big aroun' the middle as the calf of my leg.

"It was quiled up in them berry bushes not more'n a foot frum whar Big-Foot was a-standin'. I seed it strike Big-Foot's heel as he lifted it, an' then it sorty bounced back an' lay thar sorty like it was stunned er somethin'.

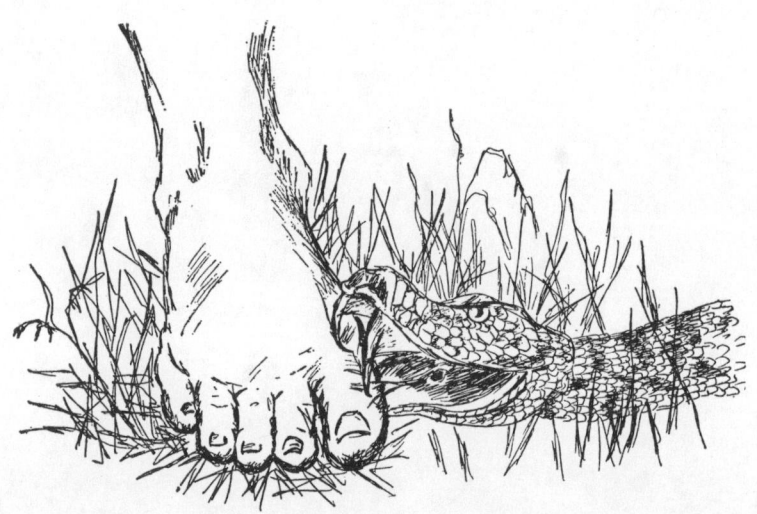

"'Lookout, Big-Foot!' I yelled. 'A big rattlesnake jest bit ye. I seed him hit yore heel.'

"Jest then that snake must a-got plum mad be-kaze he come a-chargin' out frum onder them bushes an' made fer Big-Foot. With a grin he jest stuck out that b'ar foot to let it bite him, but that snake tuck one good, long look, an' then shook its head plum sad an' sorrow-ful-like an' crawled back onder that log. He'd done had e-nough."

Uncle Iry's Transmigration

It remained for Brandy Bill to tell the tale to end all tall tales on the Devil's Apron. As best I can recall it went something like this:

"Oncle Iry an' A'nt Nicey Dutton had done spent most of their lives on their leetle twenty-acre farm up thar ferninst the Kaintucky line. They had brung up a whole passel of young'uns, but in the due cou'se of time they all got married an' moved a-way whar they could find jobs.

"So them two ol' people was left thar all a-lone, but that didn't seem to trubble' em much. All they ever knowed was hard work, an' they managed to git a-long jest a-bout like they allus had. Some of the young'uns tried to git' em to come an' live with 'em, but Oncle Iry an' A'nt Nicey jest wouldn't leave the ol' homeplace.

"As time passed Oncle Iry got to thinkin' a leetle a-bout hisself an' whut might be a-head of him. He knowed that he was a-gitten' a-long in years, an' mebbe didn't have much more time left. He never had been much of a feller to go to meetin's, an' he hadn't never give much thought to re-ligion, er whut might happen to him in the worl' to come.

"So he got down his ol' Bible, an' started to readin' it at night. He read it from kivver to kivver, an' atter that he hunted a-roun' amongst his neighbors an' got him some more books a-bout re-ligion an' sich, an' he read 'em all. Then he got aholt of a book that told a-bout some heathen country whar they be-lieved that the soul of a man would come back to this worl' atter he died an' it'd be in the body of some animal er t'other. I fergit now whut they called this hyer be-lief—."

"Transmigration of Souls," I interrupted. "The theory of the Hindoos in India."

"That's it," agreed Brandy Bill. "Anyhow Oncle Iry he read that book plum through an' one night whilst him an' A'nt Nicey was a-settin' afore the fire he finished it, an' then he turned to A'nt Nicey and says:

" 'Nicey, I've been a-readin' this hyer book an' it tells as how the soul of a man atter he dies come back ag'in in the form of some livin' critter. Now, I be-lieve this book, an' when I die I want ye should bury me up thar on that hill whar we put our two babies, an' then I want ye to watch all the leetle critters that come to this farm. I'm astin' ye to keep a eye on all the leetle pigs an' calves, an' chickens, an' pups, an' ever'thing, an', ef'n I can, I'll come back to ye, Nicey.'

"She promised him she'd do that, an' not long atter that Onle Iry got sick an' died. She had him buried in their leetle graveyard up thar on the hill, an' then fer a year she kept a close watch on the leetle pigs an' chickens, an' kittens an' sich, but she didn't see nary a sign of Oncle Iry.

"She got to worryin' a-bout that, an' she had done give up jest a-bout all hopes of ever seein' him ag'in in any form er animal. Then one day somebody told her a-bout a woman—name of Smith—that could talk with the sperrits of the de-parted. This woman lived down thar in Ohio acrost the river frum Catlettsburg, Kaintucky, so A'nt Nicey got on a train an' went down thar.

"She found somebody to show her whar at this sperrit woman lived, an' she went up an' knocked at the door. A voice told her to come in, an' she said that when she got inside the house, it was a skeery-like place, all hung with black curtains a-roun' the walls, an' thar wasn't no place to set down. By that time A'nt Nicey said she was a-gittin' purty shakey in the knees.

"A-bout this time the sperrit woman come through them curtains, an' A'nt Nicey told her as how she wanted to speak with the sperrit of her de-parted husban'. The Smith woman she p'inted towarge a table that stood in the middle of the room, an' on it was a horn a-bout six inches wide acrost the mouth an' mebbe two foot long.

" 'Go over thar an' pick up that horn,' says the sperrit woman, 'an' ef'n it gits heavy in yore han's, it means that the sperrit of the de-parted is ready to talk to ye.'

"A'nt Nicey sorty sidled over thar, an' picked up that horn. It looked like it was empty, but purty soon it started to git heavy like somebody was a-pourin' melted lead in it. A'nt Nicey she gripped that horn plum tight to keep frum drappin' it an' helt it up ag'inst her bosom.

"Then sudden-like thar come a voice outta that horn, an' it was the voice of Oncle Iry.

" 'Howdy, Nicey!'

" 'Howdy, Iry! How air ye?' gasped A'nt Nicey.

" 'Jest as fine as frawg-h'ar, Nicey. I wisht ye could be hyer with me. It's the purtiest place ye ever seed—jest wide, rollin' medders as fur as ye can see, an' the grass knee-high ever'whar. The leetle flowers air a-noddin' of their leetle heads, an' the leetle birds air a-singin' of their leetle songs, an' all of my com-pan-yuns air fe-male, an' they're jest a-standin' a-roun a-lookin' me with their big soulful eyes—.'

" 'But Iry,' gasps A'nt Nicey, plum flabbergasted, 'I didn't figger as how they let sich goin's-on be done up thar in Heaven.'

" 'Heaven!' snorted Oncle Iry. 'Who said anything a-bout heaven? I'm a penny-r'yal bull on a blue grass farm in Kaintucky. Moo-o-o-o!' "

The Hardworking Hen

It was a raw windy day in March, and when I got over on the Devil's Apron I found the boys gathered about the stove in Brandy Bill's mill. Those incessant gusts of wind had a sting in them, and I was glad to find a refuge from them.

And it was, of course, the weather they were talking about when I joined the circle.

"Wall, we've shore been a-needin' these rains we've been a-gittin' this last week," declared Good 'Lige. "Whut with ever'body outta work, an' the groun' a-bein' dry all winter, I was a-gittin' worried. But I reckon the Lawd'll per-vide. He allus has."

"Ef'n He don't blow it a-way," interrupted Little 'Bijie. "I figgered that wind was a-goin' to take off my roof last night."

Brandy Bill left the hopper and came over and joined us.

"It has been a leetle windy at that," he said, dusting the meal off his jeans, and winking at me. "An' all that wind ain't been outside thar nuther. Leetle 'Bijie was jest a-tellin' us a-bout a big wind one night that shucked a whole fiel' of corn fer him, an' piled up that corn in one big pile right ferninst his barn door."

"It's the truth," reiterated Little 'Bijie. "An' ye fellers all laffed when I told ye sometime back that a cy-clone up thar on top of the mountain blowed the Kaintucky-Virginny line back down plum past my place, nigh onto a mile frum whar it allus has been.

"Wall, I reckon ye'll be-lieve when I tell ye that that

state-line mess-up has done started the dangdest bunch of lawsuits ye ever heerd of. Them fellers who live up thar a-long the line, an' have been a-payin' taxes, air a-bringin' suit to git their money back so's they can pay 'em to the state of Kaintucky.

"An' ol' Lafe Whittaker frum up thar, who's a-servin' time in the pen fer killin' a deppity sheriff up thar in the Notches, is a-claimin' that his case was blowed outta Virginny joor-is-dick-shun, an' he a-demandin' that he git a new trial in Kaintucky."

Most of us were ready to give Little 'Bijie the prize for the day, and then Bad 'Lige took the floor.

"Since ye fellers have done turned this getherin' into a meetin' of the Liars' Club, I'm a-goin' to put in my two-bits' wu'th.

"I re-colleck a couple of years ago that thar come up one of the wu'st storms that ever hit the Devil's Apern. It was a-long a-bout this time of the year, an' a-gittin' late in the evenin'. I was a-workin' a leetle up thar at the barn-lot, a-fixin' up the chicken house. My ol' woman she was a raisin' the finest flock of chickens she ever had.

"I'd done built a good house fer them chickens to keep the foxes out at night an' the hawks in the day-time. Them chickens was all out thar in the lot, a-scratchin' an' a-runnin' a-roun' when that thar storm come up. It was a-thunderin' an' a-lightnin', an' the wind was jest a-bout to blow ever'thing off.

"Them chickens all started to runnin' fer the chicken house, an' they got a-bout halfway thar when that cy-clone met 'em an' stopped 'em dead in their tracks. Fer a minnit er so they jest managed to stan' still, an' then they started to git blowed plum a-way. The wind picked 'em up one by one an' blowed 'em up outta thar.

"I happened to look up in the sky out in front of that thar cy-clone an' I seed at least a dozen big red-tailed chicken-hawks. They was a-tryin' to fly ag'inst the wind, but they wasn't makin' no headway. A-bout all they could do was to stand still up thar in the sky. Jest then I seed somethin' that was purty hard to believe. Them blamed hawks was jest a-waitin' fer that wind to fetch the chickens to 'em up thar in the sky, an' they stayed right thar ontel I didn't have nary a chicken left."

That one stopped the boys for a few minutes, and then Little 'Bijie cleared his throat.

"Puts me in mind of whut happened up thar in my chicken-lot the day that storm moved the state line," he said, rubbing his chin thoughtfully. "I had me a ol' hen then whut allus stole her nest off some'rs, an' most gin'rilly the foxes got the leetle chickens as soon as they hatched 'em. I was out thar in the fiel' a-huntin' fer her nest when that thar storm hit.

"I seed them big black clouds a-b'ilin' up, but I didn't pay no mind to 'em much. I found the ol' hen, an' she had a nest full of eggs. She was a-settin' on the nest when I found her. Now, that ol' hen allus set on her nest a-lookin' east. Mebbe she liked to see the sun come up—I don't know.

"Anyhow she was a-layin' a egg when that blamed cy-clone hit us. I got down behindst a stump an' grabbed a-holt of a root, an' that hen she got her a toe-holt an' hung on fer all she was wu'th. An' boys, she shore done a fine job. I'm nine diff'rent kinds of a liar ef'n she didn't lay that same egg nine times ag'inst that wind."

More About Farming and Less About Preaching

I almost didn't make it up the mountain to Brandy Bill's mill on the Devil's Apron last Saturday. In truth, I would have turned back if a couple of Business Bill's boys had not happened along and pushed me through the mud that came up to the hub-caps.

But when I got to the mill I found that most of the boys had come on horseback instead of in their jeeps and pick-up trucks. There was an unusual number of mules and horses hitched beside the mill, and it was rather like old times again. The boys were all gathered closely about the stove when I entered.

The talk naturally was about the freakish weather of the past few days that had brought almost continuous rainfall.

"I'll be dad-burned ef'n it don't stop rainin' purty soon we air all a-goin' to grow gills like a fish," growled Little 'Bijie. "Then we'd have to onbutton our shirts to breathe."

Brandy Bill emptied a sack of corn in the hopper, and then came over and joined us.

"Sorty puts me in mind," said he, "of the time we got Good 'Lige thar to pray fer rain, an' we got us a cloud-bu'st. Ye fellers re-colleck that, don't ye?"

There was a chorus of grunts and chuckles, and I saw that their levity and lack of consideration for such a serious matter had the old preacher just a little disturbed and resentful.

"I don't believe you ever told me about that," I said.

"Wall, ye're the fu'st that never heerd a-bout that flood," declared Business Bill, biting a liberal chew off his plug. "I reckon it must a-been all of ten years ago when we had us the wu'st dry spell that ever hit the Devil's Apern.

"Best I re-colleck, it was a-long the last of August, an' thar hadn't been a drap of rain since early June. Ever'thing was plum shriveled up, an' a-dyin' on the vine, so to speak. It got so bad all our moonshine stills had to shet down, an' it shore looked like we was agoin' to be up agin'st it fer fair.

"Some of the good brethern an' sistern of the Hard-Rock Church," he continued with an apprehensive glance at Good 'Lige, "they sorty got together, an' de-cided to hol' 'em a big meetin' an' pray fer rain. So they went up thar to Good 'Lige's place, an' tol' him why they had come an' that they wanted him to take the matter up with the Lawd.

"Wall, Good 'Lige he agreed, an' on the next Sunday the meetin'-house was full to overflowin'. Good 'Lige he read 'em some scriptoors, an' then he got down on his knees an' started to prayin'. An' boys, I'm hyer to state that he prayed a pra'r that none of us air ever a-goin' to fergit. He shore outdone hisself frum the very start, an' when he got to goin' good, he had us all a-holdin' our breath, afeard we'd miss a single word.

"Right in the middle of that pra'r I heerd a deep roarin' sort of a soun', an' I looked outta the winder an' I seed that big black clouds was a-rollin' up, an' that lightnin' an' thunder was a-gittin' closter an' closter to us. Then it started to rain, jest a few scattered draps at fu'st, an' then it started to come down purty keen.

"Them clouds got blacker an' blacker, an' purty soon the rain was a-comin' down in buckets, an' a-makin' so much noise ye couldn't even hear Good 'Lige. The folks all begin to git off'n their knees, an' look plum pop-eyed outta the winders. I'm a tellin' ye it shore was a skeery time.

"A-bout then Good 'Lige he stopped prayin', an' tuck a look-see at whut he'd done. An' I'm hyer to say that it shore was a-plenty. Fer a while it looked like the whole worl'd was a-goin' to be washed off.

"I seed corn an' terbacker a-floatin' down No-Bizz'ness Crick, an' then I begin' to see hawg-pens an' barns an' fence rails a-bobbin' a-long, an' I figgered all of us was ruint. Whut hadn't dried up was a-gittin' washed a-way.

"Atter a while the rain let up, an' we all got outside the meetin'-house an' tuck a look at the drownded worl'. All the dirt in the fiel's was done washed off, leavin' nothin' but the b'ar rocks, an' it shore looked like we was a-facin' hard times an' mebbe starvation.

"Bad 'Lige thar he had in a purty good crap of corn an' oats, an' we could see frum the meetin'-house that he didn't have nothin' left a-tall. He stood an' looked his fiel's over, an' then he looked at Good 'Lige.

"'Next time we git somebody to pray fer rain,' he growls, 'I reckon we'd better look fer somebody who knows a leetle less a-bout prayin', an' a leetle more a-bout farmin'.'"

Willie B. and the Cookoo Clock

Some of the boys had built a fire out in the yard at Brandy Bill's mill last Saturday afternoon, but the fitful winds kept filling their eyes with smoke, so they moved inside the building and started a fire in the rickety stove.

A majority of the members of the Tall Tale Club was present, including Brandy Bill, Little 'Bijie, Business Bill, and both Good and Bad 'Lige, two of the Jacksons and some of the Maggards and Tollivers from over in Whispering Creek.

Then Willie B. Fuller came into the mill, and to my surprise and astonishment he appeared to be perfectly sober. At least he was walking as straight and steady as anyone there, and furthermore he appeared to be both alert and energetic. I drew Little 'Bijie to one side.

"Is Willie B. on the wagon?" I asked unbelievingly.

"I don't reckon he is," replied 'Bijie, shaking his head, "but he's shore actin' funny. Mebbe he's jest a-taperin' off—er sort of."

"Yeah?" Brandy Bill smothered his laugh. "He's a-taperin' off, but it's the wrong way. He begins at the leetle eend an' goes on to the big eend. His trubbel is that he's got a seventy proof stummick, an' his 'tater-peelin' brandy is a honnerd an' ten proof."

"How are Willie B. and his wife getting along now?" I asked. "She had left him the last time I was up here."

"He got her to come back afore Chris'mus," replied Brandy Bill, "an' to tell the truth, he's been kinda behavin' hisself since then. He did sorty have a leetle trubbel with her a few nights ago. Tell him a-bout that cookoo clock up at yore house t'other night, Willie B."

Willie B. laughed apologetically, and then faced us.

"As some of you know," he began in his precise English, "I recently purchased a cookoo clock. I picked it up down at Pikeville when I went down there after my wife a couple of weeks ago. She was rather delighted with that clock, and she seemed to be fascinated when she saw that little bird come out on its perch and perform.

"Everything was going on nicely and on an even keel at my house, and Carrie seemed to be happy and contented. She even agreed to let me to go down to Brandy Bill's home for a few hours one evening about a week ago when he and some of the other boys were having a little party.

"In return for her being so nice to me about that, I promised that I would get back home by eleven o'clock at the latest. We had a fine evening of it at Brandy Bill's, and he mixed a few juleps and toddies, and we tried out a few other drinks, and the time slipped up on me. The first thing I knew it was two o'clock in the morning.

"I hurried home as fast I could make it, and I was fervently hoping that Carrie would be asleep when I got there. When I got into the yard no lights were burning in the house, and all seemed to be quiet and peaceful. I crept softly up the steps and across the porch, and then I removed my shoes so that I could slip inside without making any noise whatever.

"I opened the door and listened for a short time, but I could not hear a sound anywhere in the house. I started to tip-toe across the living room floor to our room, but I had not taken more than a step or two before that cookoo clock popped open and that bird started its cookooing.

"It made that sound three times and then stopped, but by the time it stopped I had a brilliant idea. I imitated it perfectly eight more times so that Carrie would think it was eleven if she heard it. About that time I stubbed my toe against a chair and made a terrible racket, but it apparently didn't awaken her.

"I slipped into the room, and Carrie was sound asleep, or at least she seemed to be, so I undressed and eased into the bed. I went to sleep immediately, and Carrie awakened me the next morning for breakfast. I went into the kitchen and sat down at the table, congratulating myself for my quick wit that had saved me when I came in.

" 'William,' she said in a tone that brought me back to realities, "you really should get someone to fix that cookoo clock.'

" 'What's wrong with it?' I asked with pretended innocence.

" 'Why, last night, or rather it was early this morning, I heard it strike three times, and then it hiccoughed and cookooed eight more times. A minute later I heard it say damn, and then it cookooed seventeen more times.' "

Little 'Bijie Flavors the Gravy

I was completely whipped out after sitting up several nights with the T-V version of the National Republican convention, and then getting out a particularly exasperating edition of the paper, and I felt that a few hours with Brandy Bill and the gang on the Devil's Apron was just what I needed.

So on Saturday afternoon I lost no time in getting away from it all, and I found the boys all gathered at Brandy Bill's mill. They were talking politics, but with added animation.

"Wall, whut do ye think of it now?" demanded Brandy Bill. "Reckon our side might be in trubbel?"

"No, of course not." But I wasn't half as confident as I tried to sound.

"I've got ten dollars that says we air a-goin' to win," growled Bad 'Lige, reaching for his pocketbook.

"They shore had 'em a time on that thar platform," declared Little 'Bijie. "Whut does that civil rights thing mean?"

"Just another gimmick to get votes—particularly the negro vote in the northern cities. The civil rights law is already on the books."

Brandy Bill was staring intently at Little 'Bijie.

"Whut's the matter with ye, 'Bijie?" he asked. "Ye soun' funny."

"It's my store teeth." Little 'Bijie opened his mouth, and it was completely toothless. "Ye see, I bu'sted 'em t'other day, an' had to send 'em off to git 'em fixed. They ain't back yit."

"That makes it purty hard on ye right at roastin'-ear time, don't it?" asked Business Bill sympathetically.

"I'd tell a man!" Little 'Bijie's lisp was ludicrous, but no one dared to laugh. "I'm danged nigh starved to death on mush an' milk an' soup an' mashed 'taters an' sichlike. A feller never knows how much he misses his vittels ontel he has to go without 'em fer a few days. I shore wish them teeth'd git back."

We loafed an hour or so while Brandy Bill finished the corn grinding for all of the boys. Little 'Bijie's turn was the last one, and when Brandy Bill had ground it, there were only three of us remaining at the mill. After he locked the door he heaved a sigh of relief.

"Boys," he said, "my wife, Sindusty, has gone a-visitin' over on Whisperin' Crick fer a day er two, an' won't be back ontel tomorrer evenin'. She tuck leetle Toddy with her, an' I'm sorty a-keepin' house all by myself, cookin' an' ever'thing.

"Ef'n ye fellers think ye can stand it, I'm astin' ye to go down an' have supper with me. Sindusty left some bread an' vittels all cooked up, an' we can warm 'em up a mite, an' mebbe fry some ham. I've jest cut one of the best I ever cyored."

"Sounds good to me," I agreed with alacrity. I had sampled some of Brandy Bill's hams, and they were tops.

"Guess I can gum a piece of that ham," lisped 'Bijie with a grin. "Be a change frum whut I've been a-tryin' to eat."

We walked down to Brandy Bill's home, and then adjourned out to the springhouse where he mixed three tall, cold mint juleps. We took our time in enjoying it and its successors. Then Brandy Bill picked up the jar of applejack and carried it back into the house with him. We sat down at the kitchen table and he began rummaging about, hunting up the things we needed for our supper.

He went down into the cellar and came back a few

minutes later with a large platter of sliced ham, beautifully cured, and looking so delicious that I could hardly wait for it to be fried. He filled a large frying pan with it, and then opened his refrigerator.

"Ye watch that ham, 'Bijie," he ordered, "whilst I look to see whut else I can find."

Little 'Bijie stood over the sizzling pan, and a minute or so later I saw him pour a liberal amount of that applejack into the sizzling meat. Almost immediately it caught ablaze and Little 'Bijie let out a yelp. Brandy Bill went to his rescue, and soon they managed to extinguish the flames.

"Whut the heck did ye pour brandy into that meat fer?" queried Brandy Bill. "Ham don't need no applejack to flavor it."

"Dam' the meat!" lisped Little 'Bijie. "It's the gravy I'm a-thinkin' a-bout."

Brandy Bill and the Churn

After a week of tiresome and monotonous work I was anxious to get away on Saturday for a few hours with the boys on the Devil's Apron. The weather was superb, and I knew that the corn would be ground in the morning so that they could have the afternoon for tale telling and fun, regardless of how pressing the farm work might be.

I found them engaged in a horseshoe pitching contest in Brandy Bill's backyard, and the rivalry between the opposing teams was running high. I stood and watched that battle until Little 'Bijie and Business Bill won the championship. Then we all gathered in the shade of the spreading maple close beside the springhouse.

"Wall," said Bad 'Lige after the crowd had grown quiet, "it looks like ye blamed Demy-crats air a-havin' a leetle fight amongst yoreselves. Le's see, the 'lection is Toosday a week, ain't it?"

"Yes, we are holding our primary then," I replied, "but you Republicans aren't invited."

"Who's a-goin' to win?" Brandy Bill wanted to know.

"Hard to say. There doesn't seem to be a great deal of interest."

"Same over this way," spoke up Little 'Bijie. "The way some of us fellers've got it figgered out, ef'n ye vote fer airy one of 'em, ye'll wish to hell ye voted fer t'other'n."

"This hyer 'lection is jest a-bout the tamest that I ever seed. Whut we need is one of them reg'lar old-time knock-down an' drag-out fights like we ust to have."

"We'll give ye one come next November," promised Bad 'Lige grimly. "We've got us a candy-date fer Gov'ner, an' we aim to put him in office."

"With all that mess they've got us in down thar at Richmon', some of us don't give a hoot ef'n ye do," was Little 'Bijie's sour comment.

Good 'Lige chuckled deep in his snowy beard.

"I reckon I'd pyorely like to see one of them ol'-time 'lections afore I die," he declared softly. "We had some humdingers in my time, but it seems as though we've sorty tapered down some. Folks don't keer who's elected like they ust to.

"I re-colleck that jest a-bout the hottest battle we ever had hyer was that'n betwixt Brandy Bill an' Red Jeff Hill that time somethin' like fifteen years ago, wasn't it, Bill?"

Brandy Bill merely grinned.

"I was not here then," I hurriedly spoke up. "Tell us about it."

"She was a red-hot fight from the very start," obliged Good 'Lige. "Brandy Bill was named by the Demy-crats on a wet ticket, an' the Re-publicans put up Red Jeff on a dry ticket fer the Sheriff's office.

"That was purty soon atter the country went wet ag'in, followin' pro-hi-bishun, an' the likker question had a lot of folks stirred up. The moonshinin' bizz'ness hyer on the Apern, which had bene mighty prosp'rous endurin' them dry times, was dead as four o'clock, an' a lot of the boys was all fer dryin' it up ag'in.

"Brandy Bill loaded his saddle-bags with some of his best applejack, an' fer a while it was makin' purty good pro-gress. Trubbel was he run outta brandy too quick.

"Meantime, ol' Red Jeff wasn't lettin' no grass grow onder his feet, an' he got the brethern an' sistern of the church behindst him, an' then he lined up the moonshiners an' bootleggers, an' that sorty left Brandy Bill a-holdin' the sack, but he stuck to his guns.

"He rid over the county day an' night, an' he stopped at ever' voter's house, not a-missin' nobody. Come the last week of the campaign, an' Brandy Bill was jest about whipped out. It was a-gittin' late in the evenin' one day when he rid up to A'nt Becky Sizemore's place. A'nt Becky was out at her milk-gap, a-milkin' her cows, an' she had a frisky young heifer that'd jest come in fresh, an' was hard to milk.

"Brandy Bill he hopped down off'n his hoss an' grabbed A'nt Becky's milk-bucket. He finished the cow that she was a-milkin', an' then he tackled that leetle heifer. She shied an' she kicked an' she twisted, an' she slapped him in the face with her tail, but Bill he gritted his teeth an' stayed right with her.

"Then he picked up the milk bucket an' toted it to the house fer her. She opened the door an' he follered her into the kitchen. An' right that was whar Brandy knowed he was licked in the 'lection. Red Jeff was a-settin' in the middle of the floor, a-churnin' fer who laid the chunk."

Getting the Crop Before the Fencing

I was too busy to get over on the Devil's Apron last weekend, but late Saturday afternoon when I was cleaning up my desk, I was pleasantly surprised by a visit from my old friend, Good 'Lige. I think I needed the respite that he brought, and we sat down and talked for the better part of an hour while he was waiting on his bus.

"I've been up at the cou'thouse a-lissenin' to 'em hol' a trial," he explained, "but I sorty got tired of all of that palaver, an' figgered I'd drap down an' talk to ye a few minnits. I didn't have no bizz'ness in cou't, but I thought I'd jest set an' watch a spell—like ever'body ust to do in the ol' days.

"But ever'thing's shore changed frum whut they was thu'tty er more years ago." He stroked his snowy beard thoughtfully. "In them days it seemed like ever'body was thar on cou't days, speshully when they had one of them big murder trials like they ust to have.

"Of cou'se they've still got murder trials, but somehow they ain't nothin' like they was when ol' Oscar Vickers was a wavin' the dead man's bloody shirt, an' yore Oncle, Jedge Skeen, had 'em all a-cryin' fer some blamed scut that ort to a-been hung. Take the time they tried them two Bryant boys fer killin' Will Vanover. That was a trial I'll never fergit."

"That was before my day," I said when he had grown silent. "At least I was too young to remember much about the details of the trial. I can still recall 'Aunt Poll Chunk', the Bryant boys' mother, and her marching up and down the street singing an old Civil War song."

Good 'Lige nodded his head, and a smile wrinkled the corners of his eyes.

"I re-colleck one trial they had hyer one time when Jedge Skeen was on the bench," he continued with a soft chuckle. "It was a land suit that come up when them coal comp'nies was in hyer a-buyin' up all the coal lands in the county. Thar was a lot of law suits bekaze we never had good surveyors to run the lines. Most of that sur-veyin' had been done back in the ol' days by men who didn't know too much a-bout it, an' a big part of it was done jest by guess an' by Gawd.

"They was a-havin' a lot of trubbel a-gittin' some of them bound'ry lines straightened out, an' them coal comp'nies they had 'em a big lawyer by the name of Van Stotesberry, er somethin' like that, an' he was jest a-bout the slickest lawyer that ever was seed in these cou'ts hyer—er at least he figgered he was.

"They was a-havin' a suit over the prope'tty lines of ol' Counterfeit Dave Farmer who'd sold his land to the comp'ny. Dave he showed 'em whar his lines run, an' they run a new sur-vey, an' they got into a tangle with Ham Jackson. Ham he owned some land a-j'inin' Dave's, an' he claimed that the new survey fudged over on him a con-siderable a-mount.

"One of the witnesses was Ham's gal, Nick-y-tie, who got married up with Long Jim Bartley. I reckon ye've heerd tell of Nick-y-tie." He paused and looked over his spectacles at me, and I shook my head in negation for fear of breaking his thread of thought if I said anything aloud.

"Wall, she was one of the finest wimmin that ever lived on the Devil's Apern. She was as honest as the day's long, an' ever'body knowed that her word was as good as her bond. She raised a passel of young'uns, an' she made honest Gawd-fearin' citizens outta ever' last one of 'em. Jedge Skeen he knowed her, an' so did the men as was a-settin' on the jury. In fact, ever'body knowed an' re-spected her 'ceptin' that thar big lawyer I was a-speakin' of.

"Now, Nick-y-tie she swore that afore she got married, an' whilst she was still a-livin' at the ol' home place, she helped 'em when they run that line in question. She said that she cut bresh mostly, an' that the new line come over on Ham's land as much three honnerd yards in places.

"This hyer smart lawyer he lissened to whut she swore, an' then he ast the Jedge to hol' up cou't fer a few minnits. He left the cou'troom an' in a few minnits he was back ag'in. Then he started to astin' Nick-y-tie some more questions.

" 'Ye swore ye was at home an' wasn't married at the time this hyer bound'ry line was fu'st run,' he says to her. 'Wall, I see by the records in the Clerk's office that yore oldest son was born in nineteen honnerd an' seven. Is that right?'

" 'That's kee-reck,' she says.

" 'An' that thar survey line, accordin' to the records, was run in nineteen honnerd an' eight. Will ye tell the cou't how that happened?'

"Nick-y-tie she looked up at Jedge Skeen, an' never batted her eye.

" 'Wall, Jedge,' says she, 'I reckon me an' Long Jim we started to plantin' a crap afore we started fencin'.' "

Brandy Bill Tests 'Bijie's Special Brandy

After a particularly trying week, including more actual work than a man of my age and disposition should attempt, I drove over to the Devil's Apron for a bit of relaxation. I found the boys at Brandy Bill's mill, but I was anxious to get in touch with Little 'Bijie Birdsong, and he was not among those present.

My gladiolas had not been growing with their customary luxuriance because of unseasonable weather, and I had asked 'Bijie to bring me a small sack of chicken manure. Somewhere I had read that this was the finest possible fertilizer for glads, and I was anxious to try it out.

I hadn't been at the mill long until I saw Little 'Bijie coming down the road. He had told me on my last visit to the Apron that he was raising a new breed of chickens—barred rocks—and this conversation had eventuated in his promising to bring the fertilizer.

I walked out to the paw-paw bushes where he was hitching his mule, and watched him as he removed the sack of corn from the saddle, and then loosened the girth. I noticed that a smaller sack had been tied on the pommel of the saddle.

"Yes," he said, "I fetched yore chicken-manure." He reached up and removed it also. "Might as well put it in yore car now."

We walked back to the highway where I had parked, and he dumped the sack of manure on the floor in the rear. Then he untied the string around the top of that sack, and brought out a quart fruit jar of what appeared to be either brandy or corn liquor. He grinned as he thrust it into his coat pocket.

"I was a-fetchin' this a-long today," he explained, "an' I got to thinkin' a-bout them revenooers who's been a-raidin' up hyer on the Apern, an' I figgered they might stop me an' search me to see ef'n I had any moonshine. So I put this in with the manure, a-knowin' they'd never think of lookin' thar."

"What is it?" I asked.

"Huckleberry brandy. I got a leetle of it over on the head of Beefhide Crick in Kaintucky last Satte'day night. Them officers has done skeered ever'body outta makin' any likker on this side of the state line." He sniffed the jar critically.

"Mebbe we'd better wash it a leetle in the crick," he said, shaking his head doubtfully. "It smells a leetle."

He scoured the jar of brandy diligently with sand and water, and then dried it with his bandana.

"I'm aimin' to give Brandy Bill a taste of this brandy, an' see ef'n he can tell me whut it is an' whar it was made, like he says he can. Ye know, him an' Bad 'Lige think they air the best likker tasters an' can tell ye more a-bout drinkin' likker than anybody on the Apern. I'm a-goin' to see ef'n they're as good as they claim."

We waited until the last sack of meal had been ground, and most of the boys had gone on to their homes. In fact, those remaining were Brandy Bill, Bad 'Lige, and Willie B. Fuller, the latter having fallen asleep in a sunny spot on the porch.

Brandy Bill closed and locked the mill, and Little 'Bijie got ready for his test. Bad 'Lige had shouldered his sack of meal and started toward his mule, but 'Bijie halted him.

"Jest a minnit, 'Lige!" he called. "I got somethin' hyer fer ye."

Then he turned to Brandy Bill, pulling that quart jar out of his pocket.

"Bill," he said with a grin, "I've got this hyer quart of good drinkin' likker that I want ye an' Bad 'Lige to taste. Ye fellers say ye can tell whar it was made, whut it was made outta, an' how long ago an' things like that. I figger I've got ye stumped this time."

He unscrewed the cap from the jar, and handed it to Brandy Bill.

The latter sniffed the jar and its contents several times, and then took a lingering drink. Bad 'Lige followed his example, and then both of them remained silent for a full thirty seconds.

"It's blackberry brandy," pronounced Bad 'Lige without hesitation.

"No." Brandy Bill shooked his head emphatically. "It's huckleberry brandy, made outta this year's berries. Moreover it was made on the head of Beefhide Crick acrost the mountain."

"Wall, I'll be dad-blamed!" gasped Little 'Bijie. "Ef'n ye know so blamed much, whar a-bout was the still set up."

"As best I can tell," replied Brandy Bill with a faraway look in his eyes, "it must a-been clost to the chickenhouse whar they air a-raisin' them 'Barred Rock' chickens."

Little 'Bijie's jaw dropped a foot.

Bad 'Lige Falls In A Grave

Brandy Bill, braving the bitter cold, came into my office for a while last Friday. He told me that his wife was suffering with "quinsey" and that he had come for some medicine for her, but that he had time for only a short visit.

"What's new on the Devil's Apron?" I queried.

"Nuthin' much to speak of," he replied, holding his hands on the radiator. "Me an' Good 'Lige had a leetle fun outta Bad 'Lige a few nights ago, an' I figgered ye'd like to hyer it.

"This tuck place last Satte'day night, an' ef'n ye recolleck, it was a humdinger. Wu'st blizzard I've seed in many a year. A leetle atter supper-time Bad 'Lige come down to my place, an' I put on a pot of ginger-stew, an' spiked it purty heavy with applejack sorty to thaw him out.

"We kept a samplin' that stew an' a-settin' a-roun' a-gassin', an' Bad 'Lige he tol' me as how he'd bought him one of these thingimajigs whut tells ye how hot er cold it gits. He swore that that red stuff in it drapped down so fast an' hard that it bent the nail it was a-hangin' on an' fell an' broke.

"Wall, a-bout a hour later Good 'Lige he happened to drap by, an' come in outta that blizzard. Mebbe he smelt that ginger-stew plum up to his place, an' mebbe he had to go down to Bizz'ness Bill's store—he didn't say. Anyhow, he j'ined in with us an' we sot a-roun' fer anuther hour er two, an' I had to make a new pot of stew. By that time Bad 'Lige had a-bout all he could tote home—speshully in that kind of weather.

"Fact is, me an' Good 'Lige we was sorty skeered to let him try to make it all by hisself, an' he wouldn't lissen to us when we said we'd go up thar with him. So, we de-cided to foller a-long atter him, so's we could see that nothin' happened to him.

"Like I was a-tellin' ye, that blizzard was plum awful, an' in the face of that blowin' snow it was all we could do to keep him in sight without him a-seein' us. An' he was makin' mighty slow time, an' we was nigh a-bout froze to death.

"I don't know whar ye heerd a-bout it er not, but A'nt Kizzy Jackson, who lived up thar in that holler jest back of Good 'Lige's place, died last week—Thursday, it was. She was more'n ninety years ol', an' they had kinda been ex-pectin' her to die fer some time. Some of the boys had gone up thar an' dug the grave in that graveyard jest this side of Bad 'Lige's place whar the ol' Lost Meetin'-house ust to stan', an' they was a-fixin' to bury her Sunday.

"They'd left that grave open, an' I reckon that Bad 'Lige had plum fergot a-bout it bein' thar. Anyhow, he was a-weavin' an' a-wobblin' a-long the road with me an' Good 'Lige on his trail somethin' like a honnerd yards back.

"I reckon ye knowed that thar's a short-cut through that graveyard that ever'body allus takes a-goin' up that way in bad weather, an' when Bad 'Lige got to that turn-off, he headed into the graveyard. The snow had kivvered up the fresh dirt, an' I reckon Bad 'Lige never did see it, er, like I said, had fergot it.

"We heerd him let out a yell, an' then we couldn't see him no more. I knowed he'd done fell in that grave, so me an' Good 'Lige we hurried up thar as quick as we could go to see ef'n he'd hurt hisself—mebbe broke a bone er a leg er two.

"We stopped n' looked down in that grave, an' thar was Bad 'Lige a-layin' on his back in a-bout six inches of snow. An' ye can be-lieve it er not, he was soun' a-sleep, an' he shore did look peaceful an' comfortable.

"Me an' Good 'Lige we sorty backed off a leetle to figger out the best way to git him outta thar. Good 'Lige he sorty grinned at me, an' raked the snow outta his whiskers.

" 'Le's skeer him outta thar,' says Good 'Lige. 'We'll skeer him so bad he'll dodge a graveyard fer the rest of his days.'

"I agrees to that, but I didn't have no idee how he was a-goin' to do it.

"Good 'Lige crawled up to the edge of the grave, an' leaned over it.

" 'Whut air ye a-doin' in my grave?' he hollers in a deep voice like a ghost er somethin'. 'Ans'er me, 'Lige Cantwall! Whut air ye a-doin' in my grave?'

"Bad 'Lige opened his eyes an' squinted up at us.

" 'Whut in the hell air ye a-doin' outta it?' he growls, an' then goes back to sleep. We had to haul him out an' tote him home."

The Echo

Back a good many years ago, before I got so well acquainted with the boys over on the Devil's Apron, I found that I was in need of a little apple brandy for the Christmas fruit cake. And I thought that I knew the very place where I could find some.

I had visited the Devil's Apron a time or so, and had formed a slight acquaintanceship with some of the denizens of that wild area, including Brandy Bill Hopkins, Bad 'Lige Cantwell, and a few others, and I was hoping that they would trust me enough to fill my wants for the Yuletide.

This was back in the days of Prohibition, and the noble experiment had proved a boon to the boys on the Devil's Apron, most of whom were engaged in the manufacture of illicit moonshine. And they were doing well at the business despite the fact that the woods were overrun by revenue officers and other law enforcement agents.

I found Brandy Bill at his home on No-Business Creek, and told him frankly what I wanted. He took a long and careful look at me, and after a full minute the hint of a grin appeared at the corners of his mouth, and there was a distinct twinkle in his eyes.

"I've seed ye a-roun' town when ye was a leetle shaver," he declared, thrusting out his hand. "An I've knowed yore folks fer a long time so I guess some of us fellers can fix ye up."

We sat around on the porch for a while talking of this and that, and then he led the way out into the backyard and around the house. We stopped at his springhouse where his wife apparently kept the milk and butter, and he proceeded to mix a couple of mint juleps that to my way of thinking were the best tasting drinks I had ever enjoyed.

"I'd certainly like to get a little brandy like this," I suggested tentatively.

"I never sold a drap of likker in my life," he said quickly, "an' I don't never ex-pect to. I'm ad-mittin' that I make a leetle now an' then fer my own use, an' fer some of the boys when they drap in, but right thar I stop."

A little later we walked back up the creek toward the deep woods that clothed the Cumberlands above us, and on the way he told me of the difficulties that the men on the Devil's Apron were experiencing in dodging the swarms of officers.

"Thar's allus two er three of 'em up hyer a-long the Virginny-Kaintucky line, an' they air a-snoopin' an' a-watchin' fer smoke er anything that'll tell 'em whar a still might be located. Some of 'em air purty smart, an' we soon l'arnt that we couldn't take no chances.

"I know a feller a-roun' hyer who makes the best backed an' doubled corn ye ever tasted. He malts his own corn, an' dries it, an' I've been a-grindin' it fer him at my mill. Then he runs off the singlin's, an's puts 'em through a secon' b'ilin', an, strains the likker through a felt hat that's full of charcoal an' sand. An' when he git through it's as pyore as the dew on the clover at the crack of big day. I think he's got a leetle good brandy on hand, too."

He turned off on a side path, and we climbed a steep hill, and walked around to the top of a high cliff several hundred yards back from the main road. He came to a halt and I stopped beside him.

"Thar's one of the finest echoes up hyer that ye'll ever find anywhar a-roun'," he said. "Figgered ye like to hear it."

He cupped his hands around his mouth and shouted: "Hey, over thar!"

Back came the clearest and most perfect echo I ever heard.

"Hey, over thar!"

I looked across the deep ravine before us, but I could not see any cliffs or anything that could have thrown back that echo.

"This hyer's Brandy Bill," he shouted.

"This hyer's Brandy Bill," repeated the echo.

'We're frien's," yelled Brandy Bill.

"We're frien's," the echo replied, and I was growing more and more curious as to what exactly was going on.

"One jug of applejack," shouted Brandy Bill, "an' ef'n thar's any sugar in it we don't want it."

"Go to hell!" growled that echo, and a moment later Bad 'Lige came through the bushes carrying a stone jug.

A New Breed of Turkeys

Bad 'Lige was in the hospital this week with a mild case of pneumonia, and I went up there the other afternoon to see how he was getting along. He appeared to be in a cheerful frame of mind when I entered his room, and he greeted me warmly.

"They told me you were a sick man," I said, looking for a chair.

"I was, but it looks like I'm a-gittin' over it purty good," he agreed. "I reckon I got to the horspital jest in time to head it off."

"How did you catch pneumonia—falling in that grave a few nights ago? Brandy Bill was telling me about that."

"Brandy Bill talks too much." He beckoned me to draw my chair up closer to his bed. "I'll tell ye how it happened," he whispered hoarsely. "I was a-helpin' ol' Turkey-Britches Cartwright patch up the ol' Settin Hen last week an'—."

"Maybe you'd better not try to talk too much, 'Lige," I cautioned anxiously. I thought that he was delirious.

"No, I ain't outta my head," he chuckled. "Didn't ye ever see ol' Turkey-Britches' still—the one he's allus called the ol' Settin' Hen?"

"No, I never did."

"Wall, that ol' still has done been cut up by the revenooers at least a dozen times, but ever' time ol' Turkey-Britches has got him some sheet copper an' patched her up ag'in. She's jest patches on top of patches, but she's still in runnin' shape. A couple of weeks ago the revenooers chopped her up ag'in, an' I was helpin' him put on some more patches up thar in the woods behindst his house. I ketched a cold an' it got wu'sser and wu'sser, an' they fetched me over hyer.

"But that name—Turkey-Britches—surely there's a story behind that," I suggested.

"Wall, I reckon thar is," he admitted thoughtfully. "It shore is a funny name, but I heerd some of the boys a-tellin' a-bout it one time many years ago. I wasn't thar when it tuck place, but I reckon it's ever' word the truth.

"Seems as though Turkey-Britches was a-runnin' the ol's Settin' Hen at that time up a holler not fur frum his house, an' he had him a flock of turkeys that was a-rangin' the woods on all sides. Mostly he jest let 'em look atter theirselves.

"But to git back to that tale, them turkeys they got to scratchin' up beechnuts down the leetle dreen below the still an' they fed up towarge it. Purty soon they got into the sweet-mash still-slop that Turkey-Britches had dumped out atter making a run.

"They et all they could hold, an' they all got plum pie-eyed an' staggered off towarge home. Come sundown, an' whilst Turkey-Britches was a-washin' up fer supper, his ol' woman happened to look out in the yard.

" 'Lawsy mercy!' she hollers. 'Ever' last one of them turkeys is dead.'

"Ol' Turkey-Britches he run out thar, an' he seed them scattered a-roun' the yard, an' it looked like they was all as dead as doornails. He didn't know it, but they had jest passed out dead drunk.

" 'Looks like they've got limber-neck.''

"His wife she grabbed one of the young'uns.

" 'Jake,' says she, 'git out thar an' pull all them soft feathers outta them turkeys. Leave the wing an' tail feathers be. I can use the soft'uns to make pillers with.'

"Leetle Jake an' a couple of younger brothers they

pitched in an' picked 'em clean, an' then they throwed them turkeys in the crick. That cold water must a-sobered 'em up plum quick bekaze they was all back in the yard a-gobblin' an' a-cowkin' like all git-out.

"Ye never seed sich a time as they had that night. It was a cold night an' Turkey-Britches an' his ol' woman had to wrop up them turkeys in blankets to keep 'em frum freezin' to death. An' then they had to make britches an' shirts fer 'em to wear all endurin' the winter months. That's how he got the name of Turkey-Britches."

Bad 'Lige was silent for a moment and then he continued his tale.

"But ol' Turkey-Britches he come out a-head atter all in that deal. He never could wean them turkeys frum that still-slop, but they made a fine breed of turkeys. That mash was good fer 'em, an' they all got fat an' tender off'n it, an' the meat had the finest flavor that ye ever tasted in all yore life.

"Them turkeys air now knowed all over the Devil's Apern as the Hick-Cup breed bekaze ever' time they start to gobble they hick-cup."

Nailing the Roof on the Fog

I had been quail hunting back in the Ramey Flats where Bad 'Lige had told me I would find plenty of birds, and I had enjoyed a wonderful morning of shooting. But by the time I had swung around the mountain to Bad 'Lige's home I was dead tired.

I got a drink of water at the well, and then I found the old moonshiner comfortably rocking on his front porch.

"Have any luck?" he demanded as soon as I had dropped on the front step and prevented my bird-dog from going on into the house.

"I'll say so! I found five coveys in the Ramey Flats, and I think I have the limit."

"I tol' ye that they was thar." The old man grimaced when he started to get out of his rocker to see my kill which I was counting and tossing to the floor. "Must be some bad weather a-comin' up. My rheumatiz is a-beginnin' to act up ag'in."

"It's turning colder by the hour," I declared, glancing at the piling clouds in the west. "After all it's about time for the first snow."

"An' thar was a heavy fog on this mornin'," he added. "Don't know when I ever seed it git thicker than it was jest atter daybreak. A feller could almost slice it with a butcher knife.

"An' that sorty made me re-colleck the time the boys was a-puttin' a roof on ol' Thumpin-Kag Jim Barton's house up hyer on the Devil's Apern that time a good many years ago."

I made no reply while he resumed his seat with several grunts and groans, and then creased his brows in thought.

"Ye'll be re-memberin' ol' Thumpin'-Kag Jim, I reckon," he continued. "He was the fu'st feller ever' to make likker with the thumper hyer on the Apern, an' that's how he got his name. Anyhow, he'd been a-livin' in a boxed up shack hyer on the Apern fer a long time, an' his ol' woman she kept a-pesterin' him to build her a new log-house afore winter set in.

"She made him call fer a big workin' at his place, an' the boys all gathered in an' put up the walls fer him in one day. They figgered he'd be able to put the roof on an' finish her up afore winter, but Thumpin'-Kag was kinda dooless, an' it looked like he wasn't never goin' to git it finished.

"Then he sent the word out that he had done rived him a pile of shingle an' was in need of a leetle help to nail on the roof. I went up thar sorty to help out a leetle, an' thar was two er three t'other fellers thar—Tom Hawkins an' Bud Tolliver amongst 'em frum over on Whisperin' Crick.

"By the time we got them roof-boards toted in, an' ever'thing ready to start on that roof it was too dark to see, so we de-cided to spend the night thar, an' then git up early the next mornin' an' git that roof nailed on afore it got too hot in the middle of the day.

"But come daybreak the next mornin' thar was the thickest fog settled over the Apern that was ever seed in these parts. The fu'st thing I noticed was when I went out to the barn with Thumpin'-Kag to milk, an' the calf was a-bawlin' it's head off fer its mammy an' her a-standin' less'n ten foot away. The fog was so thick that calf couldn't see her.

"Atter breakfus' we set a-roun' fer a while a-thinkin' that fog'd lift so's we could git to work, but it got thicker an' thicker. 'Long a-bout ten o'clock we went out to that new house an' them two Whisperin' Crick boys—Tom

Hawkins an' Bud Tolliver—they clum' up an' started nailin' on them boards. I j'ined 'em, but I couldn't locate the nails an' bu'sted a finger the fu'st crack.

"Me an' Thumpkin'-Kag we went back to the house an' set in front of the fire ontel nigh a-bout dinner time an' we went out to see how them two boys was a-gittin' a-long on that roof. The sun was a-comin' out, an' the fu'st thing I noticed was that the roof on that new house was a-clim'in' right straight up in the air. Fer a minnit I jest stood thar not a-knowin' jest egg-zackly whut was a-happenin'.

"I yelled at Bud an' Tom an' tried to tell 'em whut was a-takin' place, but they was so bizzy a-nailin' on them boards that they paid me no mind. Them two fellers in that thick fog had been a-nailin' them boards onto the fog instid of the rafters like they ort.

"Afore I could make 'em onderstand whut was a-happenin' to 'em they was done up thar sixty er seventy foot a-bove the groun', an' a-risin' fast. As they went outta my sight they was both a-settin' thar a-wavin' their hammers an' headed towarge the top of the mountain. An' they was both a-singin' at the top of their voices that ol' toon—"When the Roll is Called Up Yander, I'll Be Thar."

The King of the Cold Trailers

There was a big argument going on over at Brandy Bill's mill on the Devil's Apron last Saturday when I arrived. The discussion was centered about the cold-trailing abilities of the two best hounds in that section—Big Howdy and Mary Lou—and the sentiment appeared to be about evenly divided.

The debate had grown so warm that a number of bets were being made by the admirers of each of the dogs. Then came the question of how to settle that argument. Business Bill, the owner of Mary Lou, could offer no suggestions, and neither could Brandy Bill, the proud possessor of Big Howdy.

Finally Little 'Bijie tossed away his whittling stick and cleared his throat sententiously.

"Of cou'se we all know how they stand on a hot trail, but, ef'n it's a cold trail ye want to put 'em on, ye can take 'em up to my place. I seed a big gray fox cross my upper pasture fiel' a leetle atter daybreak last Thursday. This makes three days since then. Ef'n either of them dawgs can pick up that trail I say they ort to win han's down."

His suggestion was greeted with delight, and in less than half an hour the entire party was headed up No-Business Creek toward Little 'Bijie's place. I trailed along to see the fun, and when we got there Brandy Bill and Business Bill loosed their dogs.

"It was up thar that I seed it," explained Little 'Bijie, pointing toward a field up above his house. "The fox went right through that low gap, an' he come up outta that leetle holler over thar on the right."

Brandy Bill and Business Bill led the dogs to the designated spot, and we all stood back to watch them. They circled about aimlessly for a short time, nosing here and there and apparently finding nothing of interest. Then little Mary Lou climbed up to the top of the field near that low gap, and an instant later she let out a sharp yelp.

"She's hit that trail," said Business Bill with a wide grin of elation, and we all stood motionless and watched her as she worked out the problem and at last vanished into that gap. At intervals we could hear additional barks, growing fainter each minute.

"She's headed straight fer them run-a-roun's back thar," declared Little 'Bijie. "No use in follerin' her— we'd never find her in them laurel thickets an' rocks. Mebbe she'll come back this way atter a while."

In the meantime Big Howdy had circled off to the left and had disappeared in a low, rhododendron-covered flat on the other side of the pasture field. Hardly had Mary Lou's voice died away in the distance when Big Howdy made the welkin ring with his baying. He headed back toward the head of No-Business Creek, and a little later we could hear him barking steadily.

"He's done treed a coon jedgin' by his tone," said Brandy Bill with a peculiar expression on his face. He listened to Big Howdy for a full minute, and then he let out a deep breath.

"Come on, boys!" he half-shouted. "I'm a-goin' to show ye some cold-trailin' that is cold trailin'."

Silently we followed Brandy Bill for nearly a mile, and at last we found Big Howdy rearin up on the bole of a large dead chestnut tree not far from Bad 'Lige's farm. The tree was full of holes such as raccoons use for dens, but there wasn't an axe in the crowd. We all stood gazing up into the top of that tree.

"There's no coon up thar," stated Brandy Bill positively. He turned and looked us over with an expression of triumph.

"Set down an' make yoreselves comfortable," he urged, "an' I'll tell ye a leetle tale ye air a-goin' to have a hard time in believin'. But it happened jest like I'm a-goin' to tell ye.

"A-bout four years ago I got a coon outta that tree," he continued. "It was treed by ol' Ginger. Like ye know Ginger was Big Howdy's mammy, an' I tuck her an' went coon-huntin' up thar ferninst Leetle 'Bijie's place. She hit the trail of a coon right per-zackly whar Big Howdy picked it up a few minnits ago.

"She trailed that thar coon over the same route that Big Howdy follered to this hyer same tree. Now, boys, thar's no two ways a-bout it. Big Howdy, havin' been borned with natural ab-stinks thataway, jest follered the trail his mammy made a year afore he was borned.

"Now, that is whut I call a nice piece of cold-trailin'."

The Peach Tree Deer

Bad 'Lige dropped into my office the other afternoon in order to escape a heavy downpour of rain, and I noticed that he was limping slightly more than usual as he walked over and drew a chair out from the wall.

"Bad weather for rheumatism," I said as he cautiously lowered himself in his chair.

"'Tain't rheumatism," he declared, brushing the raindrops out of his long chin whiskers.

"Well, I noticed you limping, and this is fine weather for it," I ventured.

"Didn't I ever tell ye how I got cripped up?" he asked with a twinkle in his eyes and without further ado he launched into his version of an old folk tale I had heard many times previously.

"It was egg-zackly twenty-six years ago, come next October the fifteenth. In them days I was young an' spry, an' I done a sight of huntin', mostly deer. Fact is, I jest a-bout kept me an' my fambly in meat thataway.

"One day a-bout three years afore I got crippled up, I was a-huntin' over thar in the South of the Mountain, an' I re-colleck it was a-long in the fall of the year. Thar was one of them October peach trees on my place, them kind that grows leetle mealy peaches, an' I allus liked 'em better than any other kind I ever tasted. When I started out huntin' that day I filled my pockets with them peaches an' was eatin' 'em as I slipped a-long a game path a-roun' the mountain.

"Atter a while I got tired out, an' I set down on a log to rest a spell. Jest out afore me a leetle piece thar was a open place in the woods whar a leetle spring trickled out from onder a cliff. As I set thar two of the biggest buck deer I ever seed stepped in sight out thar an' one of 'em started to git him a drink.

"I tuck keerful aim, an' let him have it right plum betwixt the eyes. He drapped like he'd been hit with a pole-ax, an' t'other'n jest stood thar like he was too bad skeered to move. I had a ol' muzzle-loadin' gun, an' I poured a charge of powder down the bar'l, an' grabbed fer a bullet in my pouch.

"But that pouch didn't have nary a bullet. I re-colleckted that I had moulded some bullets the night afore, an' I was minded that I'd rolled 'em over to the side of the hearthstone to let 'em cool, an' then I'd plum fergot all a-bout 'em.

"So thar I was with a empty gun, an' one of the biggest bucks I ever seed a-starin' me in the face, an' not movin' a muscle. Ef'n I was to tell ye how reely big he was ye'd never be-lieve me.

"Now I was sorty a-suckin' one of them leetle peach seeds, an' the bar'l of my gun was big e-nough to stick my fist in—one of them ol' Civil War kind—so I jest spit that peach seed down the bar'l, an' driv it home with the ramrod.

"I upped an' tuck my aim ag'in, an' let her go, an' at the crack of the gun that buck jumped a-bout ten foot straight up, an' then lit a shuck outta thar. In two jumps he was halfway to the mouth of the crick.

"Wall, time passed, an' on the day I got crippled up, I started out deer huntin' ag'in. I tuck the South of the Mountain ag'in, an' I was a-makin' my way through the onderbresh along one of them benches up thar when I seed some fresh deer sign.

"I eased back in a clump of bushes an' set down to see ef'n I could locate it. Out in front of me I seed a peach tree that had come up wild thataway, an' it was plum full of them leetle October peaches I was a-tellin' ye a-bout. That sorty fooled me a leetle bekaze I knowed that peaches had to have a leetle sunshine afore they'd git ripe, an' this'n was all kivvered in the shade. But them peaches looked awful good to me an' I slipped over thar to git me a few.

"I clum' up to whar I could reach 'em, an' jest then that thar tree come purty clost to jumpin' out frum onder me. I drapped my gun an' hung on to a limb as tight as I could, an' a couple of secon's later that tree was a-runnin' down that mountain a mile a minnit.

"We got plum down to the holler afore I figgered out whut had tuck place. It was that deer that I'd shot with that peach seed three years ago. That peach had sprouted, an' growed up in that buck to be a prime tree. Then that deer jumped clean acrost that crick and I lost my holt in the tree an' fell out an' broke my leg in three places. It never did mend up jest right, an' to this day it gives me a lot of trubbel ever' time the peach trees start to bloom."

Pearls Before Swine

It was uncomfortably chilly and wet last Saturday, and I wondered if the boys on the Devil's Apron would venture out to the gristmill, but I found several mules and a few horses hitched to the paw-paw bushes beside the mill when I dove up there.

Brandy Bill had a fire going in the heating stove, and its red glow was cheering and comforting as I pushed my way into the circle. The boys were out in full force, and Brandy Bill was doing a rushing business, but he permitted his son, Toddy, to take over the duties at the hopper, and he came over and joined me.

"Jedgin' by yore paper," he said, shaking hands with me, "they must be a-doin' a-bout this over thar in town these days. Fu'st time I ever seed poly-ticks git stirred up this hot in the spring afore."

"There seems to be some activity, yes," I agreed.

"Seems as though nigh a-bout ever' day somebody is a-startin' to organize somethin' er t'other fer his man. Some of the boys hyer on the Apern air a-tryin' to git up a club called the 'Jun-yers fer Jennings', an' Bizz'ness Bill he's a-gittin' up a-nuther'n called 'Wee Wuns fer Wampler'. That way their air a-ketchin' 'em all the way frum the cradle to the grave, ye might say."

"Trubbel is," spoke up Business Bill, "ye blamed Demy-crats don't stop at the grave. Ye jest go on a-votin' 'em frum the names on the toomstones. Leastwise that's whut they tell me."

Little 'Bijie rubbed his nose reflectively.

"Wall, I reckon it's a good thing we've got poly-ticks

to argy an' fight a-bout. Ef'n we didn't have somethin' like that to keep us sorty inter-ested, I figger we'd jest dry up an' blow a-way."

Brandy Bill turned to Good 'Lige.

"Do ye re-colleck that time 'way back when Hoover was Pres-i-dent, an' they had a passel of them Re-publican revenooers hyer on the Apern? Ye know they ust to app'int them fed-ral marshals, an' they app'int their deppities, an' their bizz'ness was to ketch an' jail all Demy-crat moonshiners, an' cut up their stills. Leastwide that's how some of us had it figgered bekaze no Re-publican was ever ketched a-makin' likker.

"Wall, in them days thar was a feller who lived up thar purty clost to Good 'Lige's place, an' his name as best I can re-colleck was Taze Maggard. He follered moonshinin' fer a livin', an' was a-doin' purty good at it frum all I could hear. He had him a couple of sons to do the work whilst he spent his time a-keepin' a eye out fer raiders.

"Now it happened one day that Good 'Lige missed a couple of his yearlin' cattle whut had done strayed outta his fiel's an' gone some'rs, an' he started out to look fer 'em. He was goin' down a sort of a leetle dreen that was mostly kivvered with ivy an' grapevines betwixt his place an' Taze Maggard's, an' he run right smack-dab into Taze's still. Him an' his boys was jest a-finishin' up a run of corn that they'd backed an' doubled, an' they was jest a gittin' ready to move the outfit out.

"Good 'Lige was a-gittin' purty tired by that time an' he sot down on a rock clost to the b'iler an' watched 'em work fer a leetle while. Seemed like they didn't have nobody on the lookout that mornin' bekaze, whilst they was bizzy finishin' up that last run, three of them thar deppity marshals jumped outta the bushes with their guns drawed.

"Taze an' his boys didn't have no guns with 'em so they put up their han's an' jest stood thar. One of them revenooers he knowed Good 'Lige, er leastwise knowed that he was a preacher.

" 'Preacher,' says he, 'I shore wasn't a-figgerin' on ketchin' ye a-makin' likker. Whut've ye got to say fer yoreself?"

" 'I was out a-huntin' fer some stray cattle, an' happened up on this outfit,' he ex-plains.

"Them revenooers they got a big laff outta that, an' Taze he speaks up.

" 'That's right, officer. He ain't mixed up in this.'

"Them revenooers all got to one side an' talked low-like so's Good 'Lige couldn't hear 'em. Then one of 'em says:

" 'I reckon ye'll have to tell it to the Jedge an' let him de-cide. Ef'n ye ain't guilty, ye'll make a blamed good witness.'

"Them officers tuck the boys out thar to whar they'd parked their cyar, an' they headed fer the clostest fed'ral cou't at Big Stone Gap. But purty soon them revenooers got hongry an' they stopped at a house an' got a woman to cook dinner fer 'em. When it was ready they went in an' set down at the table.

"One of them officers looked over at Good 'Lige.

" 'Preacher,' says he, 'don't ye want to ast the blessin'?'

"Good 'Lige forked out a big piece of meat.

" 'I never cast pearls afore swine,' he growls.

Constantinople

Brandy Bill sent word to me that his wife was having an apple-peeling at his home on last Friday night, and that several of the gang would be on hand for the festivities. I accepted that invitation with alacrity, and upon arrival I found unusual activity and bustle going on all over the place.

The front of the house was dimly lighted since the apple-peeling was taking place in the kitchen. And to my delight I discovered that they were also making apple-butter. I could see through the open door that at least a dozen women were peeling apples, and that Brandy Bill and Good 'Lige were assisting in the peeling.

A huge copper kettle of quartered apples was boiling over a fire out near the springhouse. Little 'Bijie, Bad 'Lige and Business Bill were supervising the operation and doing little else, and Toddy, Brandy Bill's youngest son, was stirring the apple-butter with a long wooden paddle.

Brandy Bill came out of the kitchen and welcomed me with his customary hospitality, and then shrugged expressively.

"When times git a leetle hard," he apologized, "it seems as though Sindusty tried to pickle, er can, er perserve, er dry ever'thing on the place. I'll bet she's got clost to a thousan' cans of stuff stored in the cellar right now, an' it looks like she's jest a-gittin' started."

He took the apple-butter stirrer from Toddy's hands and vigorously manipulated it to keep the contents from scorching.

"She's got forty gallons of apple-butter done put away, an' she's a-makin' me fetch in dang nigh ever' apple on the place to make more. Looks like thar ain't a-goin' to be many left fer makin' applejack."

I mourned silently with him, but said nothing because both of us knew the futility of attempting to change Sindusty's mind.

Suddenly Toddy came running to us, and a grin was splitting his face from ear to ear.

"The teacher an' Andy Jack air a-courtin' up a storm in the swing on the front porch," he told us, his eyes dancing with excitement.

"Who is Andy Jack?" I asked of Brandy Bill.

"He's Willie B's cousin, Andrew Jackson Fuller frum over thar in Pike County," replied Brandy Bill. "He's a-visitin' Willie B., an' they say as how he's done made a pile of money in the coal bizz'ness. Wu'th a honnerd thousan' dollars, Willie B. says, an' Miss Ta-by-thy is shore a-shinin' up to him."

"Wonder whut they find to talk a-bout?" queried Little 'Bijie. "He's as ignerant as a hoss—can't more'n jest sign his name. Le's slip a-roun' behindst them vines an' lissen a leetle."

I held back at first because I didn't particularly like the idea of eavesdropping on them, but the others began a stealthy march around the house, and I fell in step. We halted at the end of the porch, and we could hear the creaking of the swing, and make out the vague form of its occupants.

"Oh," Miss Tabitha was cooing, "isn't this the most wonderful night you ever saw? Just look at that great round moon, hanging suspended up there among the stars. Isn't it the most romantic thing you could imagine?"

"Yes'm," murmured Andy Jack in a tone of awe.

"Such a pure white! Platinum, wouldn't you say?" She paused breathlessly. "No, it's alabaster—translucent, that's the word I wanted."

"Yes'm," repeated Andy Jack meekly.

"It reminds me of that wonderful line in Gray's *Elegy in a Country Churchyard.* How does it go? 'All the air a solemn stillness holds.' Don't you just love Gray's Elegy?"

"Yes'm." It was readily apparent that Andy Jack's vocabulary was no match for Miss Tabitha's.

"You know," she purred, "a night like this is just made for poetry. I could just sit here and quote some of the really great things that the poets have said, and never stop. I have always loved William Cullen Bryant —he's one of my favorites. Do you remember his 'Lines to a Water Fowl'?

"'Whither midst falling dew, whilst glow the heavens in the last steps of day—.'" Evidently she had forgotten the remainder of that stanza, and she was silent for a few seconds. Then she broke loose in a new place.

"And his *Thanatopsis*—that's the greatest poem that I ever read.

"'To him who in the love of nature holds
'Communion with her visible forms
'She speaks a various language.'

"Don't you just love Thanatopsis?"

That apparently was all of the polysyllabic words that Andy Jack could take. He leaped to his feet and exploded:

"Constantinople, by Gawd!"

'Bijie's Path to Education

It was raining last Saturday afternoon, and my family was away, so I decided that despite the weather I would drive over to the Devil's Apron and see how the boys were getting along. I found them as usual at Brandy Bill's mill.

Four of them were sitting on the ground around an upturned box on which they were playing a desultory game of seven-up. Two or three others were standing looking on and offering advice or ribald comment.

Little 'Bijie and his partner, Bad 'Lige, won the game, and Bad 'Lige pocketed the deck. The conversation became general.

"Well, how's bizz'ness over in town?" queried Business Bill, and I shrugged.

"Dead, damned, and delivered," I replied morosely. "We are thinking of erecting a monument to its memory on the street in front of the courthouse."

"That's shore bad," commiserated Little 'Bijie, sadly shaking his head.

"Wall, bizz'ness is a-perkin' up a leetle hyer on the Apern," declared Business Bill. "Like ye know, calves air a-fetchin' a-bout half of whut they ust to, but even so things ain't too bad onder the sarcumstances."

"Is the price of calves going up?" I asked curiously.

"No, but all the cows a-havin' twin calves. That way we air jest a-bout breakin' even with whut we ust to git."

"They're Demy-crat cows," explained Little 'Bijie with a wink at me.

Brandy Bill came down from his post beside the hopper, turning the grinding job over to his son, Toddy. He shook hands with me, and the boys all came in a little closer.

"Do ye know anything a-bout them a-movin' our school thar to the Bear-Pen School this year?" he demanded of me. "I seed on yore paper whar they air a-haulin' our young'uns a-roun' an' a-bout an' a-mixin' up things gin'rilly, an' we heerd that they was a-movin' our whole school down on the river."

"I put all that I knew in the paper," I explained.

"Wall, we'd sorty like to keep our young'uns, an' in partick-lar the leetle fellers, closter to home. The school sorty give us folks a chanct to meet with our neighbors, an' see how the kids air a-doin'. An' we sorty figgered on gittin' Miss Ta-by-thy to come back to teach."

"I thought she ran off with a Holy-Roller preacher," I said in mild surprise.

"She did," replied Brandy Bill with a laugh, "but he turned a-roun' an' run off an' left her, I reckon. Anyhow she was back hyer on the Apern last week, a-lookin' a-roun' an' seein' whar she could find a place to board. I tol' her she could stay at our place, but leetle Toddy raised the roof, so I reckon she'll go back to Good 'Lige."

"Yeah," agreed Little 'Bijie, "she was up to my place, too, an' I shooed her on to Brandy Bill."

"Tell the boys a-bout whut happened whilst she was at yore house, 'Bijie," suggested Brandy Bill.

"Tell 'em yoreself," growled Little 'Bijie. "Ye seem to know more a-bout it than I do."

"Wall," began Brandy Bill, "the way my wife, Sin-dusty tells it, Miz Ta-by-thy she went up thar to 'Bijie house 'long late in the evenin', an' of cou'se 'Bijie's wife, Snowdy Jane, she ast Miz Ta-by-thy to spend the night. She done that.

"Next mornin' they was a-havin' breakfas' an' leetle 'Bijie he de-cided he'd be sorty po-lite to the teacher.

"'Jest make yoreself to home,' says he. 'I gotta go an' spread may-nure on my oat fiel'.'

"Miss Ta-by-thy she set thar an' never opened her mouth. But when Leetle 'Bijie went out she turned on Snowdy Jane.

"'Do ye let him talk like that right out afore the chillun?' she asts.

"'Talk like whut?' Snowdy Jane wants to know.

"'He called fertilize may-nure,' she whispers like she was afeard somebody'd hear her. 'Ye ort to teach him better'n that.'

"'We'd better leave Leetle 'Bijie right whar he is,' advises Snowdy Jane. 'It tuck me twenty years to git him eddicated up to may-nure.'"

It Could Have Been Worse

I almost didn't make it to the Devil's Apron last Saturday. I drove to the mouth of-Business Creek, but had to leave my car there, and walk on up to Brandy Bill's mill. What with wading the snow and deep mud, I was just about pooped when I got there.

All of the boys were there, gathered about the warm stove and discussing the weather and other pertinent questions. After I had partaken of a generous helping of the ginger-stew and found a place among them, Little 'Bijie turned to me.

"Whut's all this spe-shul 'lection a-bout they air a-figgerin' on holdin' next month? Somethin' a-bout puttin' niggers in white schools—whut's the low-down?"

"I wish I knew," I replied with uncertainty. "As best I can gather we're going to vote on changing the state constitution in such a way that the children won't be forced to go to school. It's another way of trying to keep the whites and colored separated, but whether it can dodge the Supreme Court is a question. I doubt it."

"Which leaves us jest a-bout as much in the dark as we was afore ye ex-plained it," said Brandy Bill with a heavy frown. "Do ye mean, like I seed some'rs, that this hyer Soo-preme Cou't is a-goin' to send a army down hyer to make us put 'em all together?"

"I just couldn't say," I replied frankly. "Maybe some day all of this segregation business will be settled one way or other, but how or when is utterly beyond me. Anyway, we might as well look on the bright side of things this close to Christmas."

"Ye're kinda like Oncle Hezzy Maggard over on Whisperin' Crick," said Little 'Bijie with a grin. "He's allus a-sayin' that things could be wu'ss than they air, no matter how bad they git. He shore is a cheerful cu'ss—fer his age."

I remembered Uncle Hezzy who a couple of years previously had married a young girl of twenty, and he was admittedly more than seventy-five. That certainly proved that he was nothing if not an optimist.

"Wall, dawg my cats!" ejaculated Brandy Bill. "Speakin' of Oncle Hezzy, hyer he comes now."

I glanced out through the door, and saw the old man hitching his mule to a bush. He had not grown any older, at least in appearance, since I had last seen him, and he appeared to be as spry as a man half his age. He tied the reins to a bush, and lifted the sack of corn off the saddle.

He came into the mill and shook hands all around, talking incessantly, his small goatee jabbing straight at the person to whom he was speaking.

"How's the weather up yore way?" queried Brandy Bill.

"Purty bad—wu'st I've seed in a while," replied Uncle Hezzy. "But it could a-been a heap wu'ss. I've seed the snow five foot deep on the road a-comin' down the crick many a time. It ain't much more'n three inches up thar today."

"How's the wife an' babies?" asked Brandy Bill, coming back from the hopper where he had dumped Uncle Hezzy's corn.

"Wife's fine, but the young'uns air sorty ailin'," replied the old man. "They've the chicken-pox an' measles at the same time, an' they air mighty porely, but I reckon it could a-been wu'ss. This hyer's good pew-mony weather an' I'm thankful they ain't got that, too."

Brandy Bill leaned over and whispered in my ear.

"I'm a-goin' to fix him so's he can't say it could a-been wu'ss?"

"Say, Uncle Hezzy!" he called. "Did ye hear a-bout that awful thing that tuck place up thar a-bove the mouth of Whisperin' Crick last night?"

"Whut was that?" Uncle Hezzy was instantly interested.

"I reckon ye know ol' Dave Carter that lived up thar at Beech Crick. He got married up with a young wife last year, ef'n ye re-colleck, an' it seems as though she got to steppin' out on him, an' was a-runnin' a-roun' with some of them young sprouts over thar.

"Anyhow he come home sorty onexpectedly last night, an' found one of them Whittaker boys thar. They wasn't a-figgerin' on him gittin' home ontel next week frum whar he was a-workin' over in Kaintucky. When he got in the house he ups with his pistol an' he shot the Whittaker boy to rags an' his wife, too. Then he put a bullet through his own head."

"Ye don't say!" Uncle Hezzy was horrified. "That shore is bad, but I reckon it could a-been wu'ss."

"Will ye tell me how it could a-been wu'ss? All three of 'em air dead."

"Wall, he could a-come last Toosday night when I was down thar."